ASTORIA RUMORS

by

CHERYL COLWELL

INSPIRED FICTION BOOKS

ASTORIA RUMORS

Second edition. August 10, 2021

Copyright ©2020 CHERYL COLWELL

Written by CHERYL COLWELL

Cover Design ©Damonza.com

ISBN: 978-0-9970791-9-7

PUBLISHED BY INSPIRED FICTION BOOKS

inspiredfictionbooks.com

Printed in the United States of America

Astoria Rumors is a work of fiction. Though some actual towns, cities, and locations may be mentioned, they are used in a fictitious manner and the events and occurrences were invented in the mind and imagination of the author. Except for historical figures, any similarities of characters or names used within to any person past, present, or future is coincidental.

Category: Fiction/Christian Suspense; Fiction/Women's Suspense

DEDICATION

First, I want to thank my brilliant editor, Brenda Windberg, for inspiring me to create a more courageous protagonist - in the story and in my life.

Thanks go out to my friends and family whose feedback tightened the plot and reduced many errors. To those of you who came to my aid when my home burned during my launch by pre-ordering and leaving reviews, you've warmed a place in my heart that, like Eaven, is slowly learning to trust again.

Also, my gratitude goes to Liisa Penner, archivist for the Clatsop County Historical Society in Astoria who enlightened me on Astoria's rich history during my many research visits at the Heritage Museum. Her knowledge allowed me to bring authentic details to this fictional story.

Thank you, Bruce Faling, Commodore of the Astoria Yacht Club, for graciously offering advice on the correct usage of nautical terms, saving me embarrassment from such things as referring to the boat's sheets as ropes. Also, your insight into the fun and welcoming nature of Astoria's Yacht Club gave me a glimpse of the good nature of Astoria's residents. I trust no offense will be taken from my setting a villainous family in your midst to create this suspense novel.

Damonza team, thank you for this amazing cover. You delivered beyond expectation.

Blessings on you all for your generosity.

CHAPTER 1

Lake Quinault, Washington

The wind shifted. "Coming about!" Eaven's voice all but drowned in the gusting wind but it was loud enough for Michael to duck before the sailboat's boom swung over the mesh deck of their Hobie Cat. Working as a synchronized team, they pulled hard on the nylon sheets, drawing the sails taut, launching the craft forward. She breathed in the challenge and excitement she'd felt with every race, even this local favorite.

Driven by the blustery wind, dozens of colorful catamaran sails billowed as they raced over the waves, leaving a shimmering kaleidoscope on the water's surface. She watched Gail speed toward the leading contenders on the *Siren*, husband Jerry at her side. Sweet move! Eaven grinned. She would need to up her game today to compete with her adept student.

Near them, Carl and Kim caught a favorable gust. First-timers here, the team from Florida tacked directly toward Gail's bow and cut her off. To avoid a collision, Gail fumbled, releasing the sheets. Eaven watched helplessly, unbelieving, as the *Siren* capsized, its sails fluttering flat on the water like a fish tail on dry land. "Protest!" she screamed.

High on the mast, a flag whipped furiously. Cat-claw patterns sped across the water's surface. A gust drew near. "Hold on!" she yelled, trimming her sail, ready when the wind hit. The boat heeled as one pontoon rose into the air. She and Michael hiked over the side to offset the pull of the sails. Flying the hull, they balanced precariously on one slim edge. With every sense focused, she bore down on Carl's craft, closing the distance. No way was he winning. Not like that.

The rush of adrenaline pounded strength into her limbs while she used every technique she knew to reduce Carl's lead. The wind lifted the hull higher, dangerously close to capsizing. She straightened her legs and willed their weight to hold the catamaran steady, clearly nearing their limit.

She stole a glance at her husband's wide-eyed scowl. The silent rebuke tore at her defenses, grown thin from his constant criticism. He hated losing. Her fingers hesitated on their hold, threatening to succumb.

You're the captain—her dad's words.

The message buoyed her resolve. Out here, on the water, it was her call. She studied the sails, the shifting waves. Her next move would put them at the front of the race, or off the back. She set her jaw and pulled harder.

They sped neck-and-neck with Carl, the finish markers in view. Inside the zone, he tacked hard to force her to change direction and lose speed. He played dirty but she held, repelling the intimidation. Flying true, her vessel cleared his boat with only inches to spare. "Unbelievable," she fumed.

Muscles straining, they held the line as the distance closed to the finish. Carl and Kim increased their speed, but not enough to keep Eaven and Michael from slipping between the markers in first place. "Yes!" she shouted. She eased the lines, tilted her head back and laughed at the intense pleasure of sailing—that satisfying sense of going all out, of pouring everything she had into one, clear purpose.

As they passed, Carl and Kim flung rude gestures and shouted obscenities. Eaven let her steady glare speak for her, but Michael couldn't resist. "Go back to your swamp!"

On the way back to shore, he refused to rejoice in their win, his mouth retaining a scowl. "I can't believe that move you pulled. What are you trying to prove?"

His accusation drained the victory from her heart and limbs. She wasn't trying to prove anything. More like trying to measure up, to find the way home where she'd once felt secure. She didn't doubt his love, but truly knowing her seemed beyond him. The wind ruffled the blond curls around his bright blue eyes. There was so much about him to love. What he gave would have to be enough.

As he readied the boat at the dock, his movements were jerky, deliberate. "You could have capsized us."

A new thought occurred to her, a foreign thought. Had he been afraid? She softened her reply. "But I didn't." She coiled a line and attempted to make light of his skepticism. "If you weren't so cute, I'd get a new crew member who trusts me."

"You forget, it's my boat." He wasn't smiling.

Tired and deflated, she sighed under the weight of managing his emotions. Yes, the boat was his, and they rented his father's old cabin—two things that came up more frequently these days. So what? She carried her weight, always had. Certainly, they were capable of more, but they'd chosen sun and simplicity. A good life, for the most part.

While Eaven dried the last of the dinner dishes that evening, reruns of Gail's loss still festered. For months, she'd poured herself into her friend's training, building her confidence on the water, donning wet suits in the off seasons. This would have been Gail's first win. She tossed the forks in the drawer. They'd try again next year.

Michael slipped his arms around her waist. "Pretty intense."

He'd pulled himself out of his mood. Good. She relaxed into him and folded the dish towel. "Gail should have won."

"But we did." He chuckled. "Loved the look on Carl's face."

Remembering Carl's comedic expression of, *This can't be happening after all the work I've done to cheat,* she grinned. "It was classic."

"Let's sit outside and celebrate." He scratched Duke's ear then headed for the bar. Their lab grinned after him, thrilled with any affection Michael offered.

She squatted in front of Duke and cupped his intelligent face in her hands. The dog had the heart of a lion. "Too bad you don't sail." She stood and called to Michael. "I'll get my sweatshirt."

In their bedroom, she leaned forward and pulled the thick hoodie over her head. When she stood, nausea hit, worse today. She stilled and sucked in a breath, more at the possible meaning rather than the need for air. Grabbing her phone from the nightstand, she checked the calendar, scrolling backward while she counted. It had been nine weeks since her last period. Tiny, crocheted booties marched across her mind. Not so fast, girl. She stopped the parade, tempted to forego another futile pregnancy test.

Michael's father had warned him about marrying an older woman, hinting—no saying outrightly—that it might rob him of grandchildren. She had been twenty-eight and Michael twenty-one, not exactly robbing the cradle. Yet the seeds of doubt he planted seemed to grow, undermining Michael's certainty. She felt it, saw it in his eyes, in the way he phrased his words at times.

Carefully, she counted the weeks again, her hope growing with the numbers. Though she never admitted it, every year it felt less likely they would conceive. Still, she kept buying the tests. Clinging to a sliver of hope, she used a strip and watched the time. Anticipation and despair swam neck-and-neck.

And there it was.

Her hand flew to her mouth seconds ahead of her laughter. "Yes!" She sauntered to the kitchen and kissed Michael on the back of the neck.

He grinned. "I opened some wine."

"I shouldn't really be drinking." Her heart danced as she watched his face.

Their eyes met, and his mouth sobered. "You aren't...?"

She knew he didn't want to say the word and jinx the long-awaited hope. She laughed. "You're going to be a daddy."

"Oh, babe." His hands cradled her cheeks while he kissed her. "How far along are you?"

"Nine weeks, or so." She feasted on the joy in his face.

His eyes narrowed. "Should you have been sailing today?"

"Look at you. It shouldn't be a problem. I'm fit."

"Well, you're stopping now. We've tried for so long. My father will be stoked."

The elation sank. She lifted a plate and turned her back on him, taking her time to put it away, tempted to smash it over his head. She'd taken care of her own body for thirty-seven years just fine. And why did he have to think of his father at this moment, the man who'd remained her enemy?

A sudden foreboding sucked the strength from her legs, causing her to grip the counter while Michael continued his excited chatter. Her pulse raced in her temples, mind searching for meaning. As quickly as it came, the darkness faded. She calmed her breathing. Silly, right? Just hormones.

She shut the cabinet door and relaxed her shoulders. Everything was right as rain. His father had been wrong. This baby would cement her marriage, would remove the unspoken hint of doubt she saw in Michael's eyes. After nine years, they had succeeded. She turned back and kissed him. "Guess you'll just have to call New York and let him know."

He returned her kiss and rushed from the kitchen. Soon, his excited voice filled the air.

Outside, she leaned back on her new red Adirondack chair and pulled a plaid throw around her legs. The day's blustery winds had flown away. Stars reflected off the glassy lake, marking the beauty of this perfect moment. She tilted her head back, eyes raised, and let gratitude flow upward. "Thank you."

CHAPTER 2

Lake Quinault, Washington, Nine years later

Eaven squinted into the mirror and tugged out a wiry white hair that resisted her attempts to smooth it. At forty-six, more appeared every day. Depositing the traitor in the basket, she glanced through the window and spotted Michael outside. Wavy blond hair still framed his devastatingly handsome features. A sad sigh escaped. Their seven-year age difference didn't use to be so noticeable.

She tugged on wool socks and headed down the hall that served as a gallery for her photographs. Once just a hobby, it had become an obsession, something to bring in a bit of money, to occupy her mind since the accident. Shots of rescued owls, wolves and other wildlife embodied the injustice she'd worked to expose over the last nine years. Hard emotions filled their faces—fear, distrust, withdrawal, feelings she understood. She stared at the wall, eyes running over each one. It was past time to replace them and move on.

At the back door, she pulled a green jacket off the hook and buttoned the warm wool around her neck. *Moving on* had a nice sound, and she'd been trying. In her pocket sat the check from selling one of her photographs. Though their anniversary was still a week out, she grinned about the reservations she'd made at the Quinault Lodge. Her favorite dress waited in the closet along with the heels she rarely had occasion to wear.

Careful not to spill the hot coffee, she carried two mugs out the slider and breathed deeply of the fresh pine air. Mornings on the lake were heaven. Fall mornings especially. Her eyes skimmed across the peaceful water that resonated with her soul. She'd left a lot to move here, but she'd found paradise with Michael.

He stared quietly at the glassy water, broken by fish snapping up unwary bugs from the surface. He stared into space a lot lately.

"Hey." She handed him a steaming mug.

"Morning." He offered a tight smile and took the coffee without meeting her eyes.

"Going fishing today?" Weeks had passed since he'd taken his creel bag and headed for one of the pristine creeks that fed Lake Quinault. *Their lake*, he'd called it when they first moved here. They'd felt enraptured about everything then, especially each other. But eighteen years had a way of rubbing off the shine.

He didn't answer.

Lying next to him, Duke wagged his tail as if to say *he* was in the mood for fishing. After dropping onto her Adirondack chair, its red paint faded from years of sun, she blew on the hot coffee to warm her nose and stroked Duke's golden coat. An eagle skimmed across the lake. With a swoop, it skewered a fish and rose off the water, a squirming largemouth bass caught in its powerful talons. "Did you see that!" She turned to Michael, expecting to share a millionth glorious moment.

He gave a silent nod.

Time for a mood change. "I have a surprise. We have anniversary reservations at the lodge next week—my treat this year." She grinned, waiting to see his eyes smile, to hear the delight in his laughter, things that had drawn her to him. Instead, he buried his face in his hands. Alarmed, she touched his arm. "What's wrong, hon?"

He took forever to answer. "I don't know how to say this. I...we're not working."

Her heart thumped unevenly in her chest. *No. No, no, no.* She knew what he was about to say, had felt it for months, maybe years if she was honest. She pushed out of her chair and escaped to the far side of the deck as if she could outrun the squall. Her hands grabbed hold of the rough, wooden guardrail.

He approached and put his hands on her shoulders. "I'm sorry. I can't go on like this, lying to you."

Heat flashed through her body. She whipped around, shoving his hands away, and glared into the anguished face that stood level with hers. "What lies?"

His chin quivered, eyes closed.

This wasn't easy on him either. Maybe they just needed to talk it out. More softly than she felt, she said, "What lies?"

"There's someone else. There has been for a while." He turned his face away, its handsome features twisted, tortured. "I should have handled this a long time ago."

She opened her mouth, but dry gauze seemed to fill her throat, muting her response. Beyond him stood the forest. Reflections of the trees blurred in the lake, the way her future suddenly grew unclear. Everything she'd counted on tipped on edge and slid into the deep, black waters of the unknown. She gulped air, drowning, unable to get enough. *Get a grip, girl*—her mother's words.

Remorseful eyes met hers. The dam broke and tears coated his cheeks. "I love you and I've tried for years to leave the relationship except..."

"Except what?" Her voice sounded like a stranger's, someone pragmatic, not someone whose life washed away with every new revelation.

"Crystal had a mental breakdown and...we have a daughter. She's eight."

She gasped. "A...daughter? So, *our* baby dies, and you cheat to get your *own*?"

He glanced away.

It felt as though her lungs had stopped working. She fought to breathe while her brain ticked off the bits of data. *Michael has a daughter. Michael loves someone else. Michael is leaving her.* How could she have missed it? Sure, he traveled a lot, but he was home more. Vaguely, she heard her name pierce through the thick emotional fog.

"Eaven," he said, touching her cheek.

"Don't touch me." She headed toward the cabin but felt dizzy and grabbed one of the smooth peeled logs of their timber home for support.

He followed her. "Let me help you."

Laughter bubbled out. "Help? No. You can leave. Now!" After all they'd been through, how could he do this to her? They'd made commitments...

His mouth shut like the pouting child he was. He sidestepped her, sprinted up the outdoor stairs, and turned back. "You always knew I wanted kids." He slapped his thigh. "Come, Duke." Seconds later, the Jeep flung gravel onto the street, taking away the only two guys she loved.

Her hand gripped her forehead while she fled to the haven of their cabin. Inside the porch they had enclosed, she collapsed on her chair, the one with cheerful Native American designs that did nothing to cheer her. The fireplace failed also, doing little to warm her icy hands. She pulled a throw around her and stared at the flames. Trip after trip, they had gathered the stones from local riverbeds to build it. The flat one that jutted out to hold a candle came from the Quinault River the year they met. The stones derided her. They were permanent. Apparently, she was not.

Her abdomen knotted. She cradled the area over the scar and rocked. They'd almost had a child, a baby the EMTs had to pull from her body after the accident. A son who would have been nine. It wasn't enough she'd lost the ability to have children, she'd lost Michael too. Had wasted her grief on him, never blamed him for speeding. And all the while he had another family. Her head continued to throb, warning of an oncoming migraine—another remnant from the accident.

She lifted her face and screamed at God but knew the cry would stop at the rafters. He'd stopped answering when the baby died.

She called the lodge to cancel their anniversary dinner and tried to ignore the bleak sense there would never be another.

Late the next morning, Eaven heard Michael's Jeep roar into the carport. She clutched the soft flannel of her rumpled blue pajamas. Catching sight of her disheveled bed hair and swollen eyes in the entry mirror, she cringed at the mess the night had inflicted. She had planned to look fresh and beautiful, make him realize what he was throwing away. Too late. He entered before she could escape.

Be strong. She'd always been strong. Well, not always. Recently, she'd needed more. More of him. More reassurance. It was hard to put a finger on it. Her doctor mentioned hormones. She pulled back her shoulders and turned to face him, hating how his pressed white shirt showed off the intense blue of his eyes. Her heart yearned for his arms to wrap around her, to say it was all a mistake.

He regarded her inglorious state, then averted his eyes. "We need to talk."

She flinched at his sharp tone and fought the urge to snap back. *About what? Life goes on. See ya.* That's what she'd told herself between beating her pillow and hugging it as though it were a life raft. She lifted her chin and caught his eyes, speaking calmly, hoping to bring him back to reason. She was a great wife, had molded her life to fit his, buoyed his ego until she wondered how his feet stayed on the ground. "Talk about what?"

"About the cabin." He stood in their kitchen, hiking boots planted on the rustic wooden planks, hands in his jean pockets. But where was the man she knew? "I want to bring my daughter to live here. And her mother. Face it, Eaven, we lost our passion a long time ago."

Her sight blurred, and she slapped the counter. "No. This is *my* home, our home. I'm not leaving."

He rolled his eyes. "Wrong. It's my father's house. We're only renters."

She smirked at his argument, one his father had no doubt provided, then dropped her chin to mask a swallow. His father had deep pockets. "I will not be forced from my home." She clenched her fists under her flannel cuffs.

He let out a long breath. "Look Eaven, we're grownups. We can handle things, but my daughter's just a child. I need to offer her stability."

"What about *my* stability? *Our* marriage?"

He slammed his fist on the counter. "You're forty-six. Zoe's eight. She's been through enough, watching me leave and not understanding why, feeling like she doesn't matter to me. She started seeing a counselor last month. He says I'm putting her at risk." He rubbed the back of his neck. "I want them here."

His voice carried an unfamiliar note of anguish, but her empathy jug was corked tight. She couldn't care less about his wants. "You'll have to find another house."

"Crystal likes this one."

"You brought her here?"

He glanced away.

What else didn't she know? She folded her arms to hide the trembling. "I'm not leaving"

He smirked. "Yes, you are, unless you want to live here with Crystal and Zoe."

"That won't be happening."

"I'll give you a month to find a new place. Take anything you want."

Outrage nearly strangled her. "You can't give me these things. I bought every piece with my money because you were too cheap to buy decent furniture."

His lip curled. "Your expensive tastes aren't all you inherited from your mother. I'll have divorce papers prepared." He stormed out the door and headed for his precious Jeep.

She rushed after him and launched her coffee mug at his windshield. It cracked the glass and splattered it with mocha and cream. "And you're just as self-centered as your father!"

He swore, turned on the wipers, and peeled out of the drive.

Inside, she cringed at her outburst, shocked at her theatrics, no matter how well deserved. While she washed off the coffee that had slopped onto her hand, her gaze swept the great room. Its tall ceilings and open beams held a wall of windows that framed the mountain, its mirror image dipping into the lake. She had intended to die here and have her ashes spread on the water.

A tear slid down her cheek at the irony. *Zoe.* His daughter's name meant *life.*

Swiping the tear, she stepped to the door still standing wide open as if waiting for her husband's return. She slammed it and turned the dead bolt.

Time to change the locks. No way was he bringing anyone into her home.

CHAPTER 3

It didn't take long for the small community to buzz with the news. Eaven steeled herself, forcing her chin up, and entered the local cafe. Michael betrayed her, had continued to betray her, so why did shame dog her, make her want to hide? Family expectations? Though they weren't religious, no one had ever divorced, had toughed it out, if only for pretense. Now she, the only one who had claimed any kind of faith, would be the first.

She swallowed against the lump that had lodged permanently in her throat. Gripping her old briefcase, she ordered a mocha and headed for an empty table near the back to review her options.

A child looked up from her coloring and smiled. "Do you like my drawing?" She turned the page so Eaven could see. Though young, multiple earrings pierced her ears. "I'm not that good yet, but I'm going to be a picture book artist someday. Picture books help teach children to do the right things when they get older."

Eaven smiled at the certainty in the child's clear blue eyes. If that were only the case. "I think it's very good."

While the girl colored a dog asleep on a rug, Eaven sipped her coffee and pulled out her notepad. Her attorney had provided a short list of options. Spousal support was out. Their meager contributions to the marriage were nearly equal. The amount they'd put into the remodel to enclose the porch was negligible, but Michael owed her two thousand dollars. No doubt Mr. Dalton was working on the eviction process, but if she continued to pay the rent on the cabin, it would make it harder. At least she'd give him a fight.

The child interrupted her thoughts. "This is my dog. Well, he's gonna be. Daddy wants to teach me how to sail a boat. My dog can swim so he can save me if I fall in the water."

"Are you afraid of the water?"

She sucked in her lips. "I don't swim yet." She took out another page and outlined a boat with a triangle for a sail.

Releasing a melancholy sigh, Eaven said, "You'll have a wonderful time learning to sail with your dad. Is he here with you?"

"He'll be right back. He knows Dena, the ber-ees-ter, so I'm safe here."

Eaven smiled. "Well, if Dena gets busy, I'll watch over you."

Focused on her coloring, the girl said, "He says this time he'll keep his promise to bring me to his cabin." She drew a dog on the sailboat then glanced out the front window. "My daddy's back!" She stuffed the crayons into her bag and gathered her pictures, her eyes wide with anticipation. "You can have this one," she offered.

"Thank you." Eaven accepted the sailboat picture, surprised when the girl hugged her neck.

"Thanks for watching over me." She ran toward the front door and leapt into her daddy's embrace, arms wrapped tightly around his neck. He spun her around.

Michael. Shielded from his view by racks of coffee and mugs, Eaven's hand flew to her throat. She stared, unable to comprehend this reality. Pleasure lit his face in a way she'd never seen. So, this was Zoe. She couldn't wrench her eyes away, though the agony felt it would rip open her chest.

Father and daughter, like two blond angels sent to earth, strolled off, hand in hand. Powerless to stop herself, Eaven followed them out the door. On the boardwalk, she watched a feather-light blond woman join them, her flowered skirt swaying beneath a lacy blouse. Crystal. His new love wound her arm through his and kissed him. He pulled her closer. Zoe talked excitedly and showed them one of her drawings. After a few steps, Crystal glanced over her shoulder, sun reflecting off the diamond stud in her nose. Spotting Eaven, she glared directly into her eyes.

As though struck, as though she was again seventeen, watching her sister's triumphant glare at the ruination of her life, Eaven backed inside the door. Avoiding curious stares, she walked toward her table, tucking a strand of hair behind one ear, trying to appear normal.

Dena leaned over the counter, sympathy oozing and whispered, "Sorry, hon. It's a small town."

She took her seat without comment. Maybe she could keep Michael from evicting her, but she hadn't stopped him from moving his new family to Lake Quinault. Though her shoulders were strong from swimming, this weight crushed like a twenty-foot wave. She closed her notepad, chin trembling, and turned to hide her face.

The two men she'd adored had withdrawn their love without warning, giving her no time to prepare her heart for the impact. Her father, and now Michael, had walked away without a backward glance. They'd each erected an impenetrable wall as though she'd been nothing to them.

Her jaw clenched until she thought her teeth would shatter. Her mind swept for an explanation, for protection from ever having to feel this way again. Through the muck, the answer appeared with perfect clarity.

Trust had been learned. It could be unlearned.

For several moments, she didn't move, just turned the idea over and over, assurance building with the control it placed in her hands. She was intelligent, healthy, and talented. At eighteen, she rewrote her life. She could do it again. Her power rested in that knowledge. And in money, which brought its own challenges.

Her visit yesterday to the Dalton family investment advisor, Clarence Fishburn, revealed she had just under six thousand dollars left in her IRA account. A bitter taste filled her mouth. Fishburn had seemed aware of her situation before she'd even called. How long had he and Mr. Dalton known about Crystal and Zoe? It was all she could do to stick to business and remain civil as he formally referred to her as *Mrs. Dalton*.

On her wedding day, she'd been thrilled to replace her maiden name of *Alexander*, a grand name that had never seemed to fit. Eaven Kensington Alexander. What were her parents thinking? *Eaven* had prompted school mates to taunt, *Odd or Eaven? Let's get Eaven*. And *Kensington*, the supposed place of her conception, dripped with pretension. Now, *Dalton* grated on her ears like an old boat grinding against a dock.

Last night, her friend Gail had counseled her to stop hating everything and focus on gratitude. If Michael dropped dead, she would have something to be grateful for. As it was, he had stripped her of everything she held dear, even his pleasantly normal last name, and given it to Zoe. Zoe Dalton, the cause of all her problems.

She studied the picture of the sailboat and dog, no doubt Duke. No. Zoe was the only innocent in this whole mess, depending on her father to keep his promise and bring her to live with him in his cabin. She'd learn soon enough that keeping promises was not one of his strong suits. Besides, the cabin wasn't his to give. No one was going to force Eaven from her home.

The girl's trusting blue eyes blinked into Eaven's mind, tugging at her heart. Her own words nipped at her, *I'll watch over you.* She bit back a scream of protest. Zoe was not her responsibility. Yet, she suddenly knew without question what she needed to do. She pulled out her phone and called her attorney, all the while shaking her head. "Do you have an opening tomorrow? I've changed my mind." She made an appointment and hung up. It was time to do what she'd come here for.

Her hands trembling at the decision she'd just made, she pulled a large manila envelope from her briefcase, opened it, and studied the remnants of the career she'd left behind. Her fingers traced her gold embossed name on the parchment. *University of Edinburgh, MA joint honors in Ancient History with Classical Art.* Underneath lay her postgraduate certificate. *Architectural History,* from Oxford.

Satisfaction buoyed her churning emotions. After graduating, the hard work had paid off. Her job with Christie's Auction House in London had been fascinating work. That was before her department head suspended her while he investigated a theft, all the while, casting doubt on her sanity. Her manager had pleaded with her to stay in London and challenge the injustice, but she'd left it all behind when she met Michael.

She'd gambled everything and lost, nearly losing herself along the way. For what? The look of admiration that made her feel alive? Significant? Like she had worth again? She'd sold herself short chasing those things from the people in her life, handing over her self-respect to gain theirs. Never again.

Exhaling deeply, she stowed the documents away. A lot of women returned to careers at her age. Luckily, antiques weren't subject to new technology. She was still an expert, had kept up with trends online in the evenings when Michael was occupied. Or away, seeing Crystal.

She squeezed her eyes against the tormenting images scratching at her mind. The unfolding depth of his deceit continued to taunt her gullibility.

Had she known something was off? Had she turned a blind eye, unwilling to face what the truth would mean? Moot points, now.

Using every ounce of discipline she'd developed, she lifted the pen and listed possibilities for her future. She scratched words on the paper, but her heart wasn't in it. After an hour, she stood and grabbed the handle of her briefcase. The familiar fit of the leather in her palm offered comfort that she could do this, would get through this, yet she couldn't help worrying how long it might take.

Scooting into the driver's seat of her car, her mind toyed with possibilities. If she made enough money, she could buy her own cabin on the lake, have her own boat on her own dock. But Michael and Crystal would be here. She squeezed the steering wheel. He didn't own the lake. And maybe, after a while, it wouldn't kill her to see them together.

It almost didn't matter. To make that kind of money, she'd need to be more than an employee. She'd need a successful business, an upscale store. That meant moving and adopting her former lifestyle, at least for a while. The thought of living in a tumultuous city again threatened to sink her. She ignored the ache in the pit of her stomach. It was a price she was willing to pay to get her life back from those who stole it. It was a way to get even.

CHAPTER 4

Two weeks later, Eaven cleaned the last lunch dishes she would ever wash in her cabin. She glanced at the clock and stretched out the tightness in her neck. Travel food overflowed her wildflower-print shopping bag on the counter.

Michael would be here soon. Her eyelids pressed shut as if they could block out the nightmare. She had no idea where he'd been staying, or where he'd taken Duke, the puppy she'd given him as a birthday gift, a fact he'd argued regarding custody. Her hand pressed against her heart. She didn't have a home for him anyway.

No one besides Gail had called to see how she was doing. She shrugged a few times to ease what felt like a knife between her shoulders. Apparently, hosting eighteen years of potlucks and parties hadn't made inroads below the surface of her neighbors' loyalty.

Michael pulled into the carport and shut off his engine.

Every muscle in her body tensed.

He stalked through the kitchen door, his mouth tight. "Glad you called. I want to finalize the divorce settlement."

She bit her lip. This was it. Five feet from her stood the love of her life. In his face, she saw worry, determination, but no love. She stood tall and held out the papers her attorney had created. "No need. Here. Just don't expect me to roll over. I will vacate the house without a fight if you agree to reimburse me for my investment. With interest. Due in two months." The sum was paltry, but she wanted every cent.

His jaw dropped. "My father is having the papers drawn up."

"He's behind. I don't want to drag this out."

He grabbed the papers. As he read them, his brows knit together. "Why are you letting me off so easy?"

She glanced away and swallowed. *You meant everything to me.* "I need to restart my life as soon as possible."

He caught her gaze, and for a moment she saw her husband, witnessed his compassion.

Crystal walked in, the Jeep keys in hand. Her eyes narrowed, revealing she'd picked up on their momentary tenderness. Nose flaring, her angelic face transformed slowly like a storm building on the horizon. She took a step back and turned, arms ridged at her side, and charged stiffly back to the Jeep.

Eaven caught the fear in Michael's expression. Crystal, the beneficiary of his wandering eye, had him on a short leash. He swore under his breath. "I'll sign these and have them notarized ASAP." He hesitated. "It just got too hard. You always had to outshine me."

She opened the door for him to leave. "Take your complaints with you." He glared and stomped back to face his keeper.

Outshine? Unbelievable. What about standing on her head to please him? Zoe might have great experiences on the lake, but she'd have to learn to hold her own with her dad. Crystal would be a strong, if not neurotic, example. Poor kid.

She's not your child.

Right. She laid her hands on the cold granite counter and slowly panned the great room, committing every corner to memory. The log walls seemed to reach for her, but they weren't hers anymore. She turned away and hefted the grocery sack. Outside hung their brass sign. "*Welcome to the Daltons - Michael and Eaven.*" Her finger traced their names. She swallowed against the pressure. I can't do this.

Gail pulled into the driveway and hobbled over. "All packed?"

Eaven nodded without speaking and shoved the food next to her sleeping bag in her Suburban. At least this was hers—and paid for. She rubbed at a scratch on the door she hadn't noticed and turned, forcing a smile for her friend. "Thanks for bearing with me while I got my head on straight."

Placing her hands on Eaven's shoulders, Gail peered into her eyes. "If you don't mind me saying so, you've always seemed too vibrant for such a remote community as this."

The hair on the back of Eaven's neck prickled. "This is where I want to be, not in some chaotic city with a view of concrete buildings."

Gail nodded. "I'll give you the same advice you gave me when Jerry died. We have a good Father who loves His girls. He has a plan for you, sweetheart, a good one."

"My plan was to live the rest of my life here." She bucked up her mood. "It still might work. I've been playing with the idea of opening an antique store. If it were in Seattle, I could buy my own cabin and come home on weekends."

"I would love to have you back, but with Michael here?"

Eaven's daydream vanished like the shore in a fog. Time to deal with that later. First, she had to earn the money. A lot of money.

"Have you decided where you're going?" Gail asked.

Her mind had been running in circles with that question for weeks. "Maybe back to South Carolina. It would be fun to see if my childhood friend, Paisley Benson, still lives in Charleston. My family has been wanting me to visit."

Liar. Like she had any family who would want her. Despite the disfunction, and with no other options, she'd written weeks ago to ask if she could come for a visit. Her mother had ignored the message. Apparently, too many years of neglect had dammed the flow of goodwill.

Gail smiled and hugged her. "That's good news." A thick pile of envelopes slipped from her hand onto the gravel drive. She retrieved them and held them out. "I collected your mail with mine. Looks like a week's worth."

On top sat an envelope made of thick white paper embossed with gold initials. Before she touched it, Eaven knew it was from her mother. She held her breath. A simple call would have done. A letter most likely involved a formal explanation on why it wouldn't work for her mother to have her there.

"What's up?"

Eaven blew out a puff of air. "Nothing. I'll open it tonight. Just collect my mail for now and I'll send you a forwarding address later."

"I'll miss you terribly." Gail rubbed her knee, stiff with arthritis. "You gave this old girl some glorious memories on the lake."

"They were wonderful." She wrapped her friend in a long hug, maybe their last.

Gail limped to her car and drove away, waving as she left.

"Goodbye," Eaven called from her car window. She took one more breath of the familiar scent of pine, listened to the silence, and started the engine. At the end of her drive, she stopped, emptiness overwhelming her. Her heart cried out, *Daddy, I need you.* Warm moisture poured down her cheeks at the ache she'd never forgotten, at the unquenchable hole that had ripped through her confidence. He'd deserted her when she needed him most, how foolish to long for him to hold her and make it better. "No, no, no," she soothed. Drying her eyes, she vowed it wouldn't happen again.

She had a full tank of gas, two hundred ten dollars in cash and six-hundred available on her debit card. The money from Fishburn, and a pittance from an art gallery in Bandon that carried her photos, would keep her from starving, but not for long. She bit her lower lip trying to keep the truth at bay. She was homeless and broke. With no idea where she was going.

Just go.

She nodded. Right. Time for a new beginning. She would figure it out as she went.

Once her tires reached the smooth pavement, the going seemed easier. She turned on her favorite radio station and pretended she was just taking another trip down the coast to drop off her photographs. After driving south for an hour, however, the obstacles that lay ahead multiplied. Her breathing grew shallower in her tightened chest. She pulled into a roadside rest, opened the door, and leaned her head out, dreading she might be sick. Nothing happened and her system calmed.

She sat back and gazed at the trees, her courage depleted. Though she'd put up a good front, the facts demanded an answer. "God, where am I going to go?" No brilliant answer popped into her mind. She shook her head. "What's new?" Sitting a bit longer, she decided to focus on today, not the rest of her life, not even tomorrow. Just south of her, at the northern tip of Oregon, lay Astoria. That would be her first small goal. After dinner, she could find a roadside rest, sleep in her car, and be on her way the following day. Having a plan, even this tiny one, helped lift her spirits.

In the door pocket next to her, the white envelope peeked out. Might as well. She ripped open the thick linen paper with its gold embossing. Lillian would frown that she hadn't used a silver letter opener. Too bad, she didn't have one just now. Her hands tensed while she read her mother's perfect handwriting. It started with, *Dear Eaven.* There was no way Lillian would forgo good etiquette, whether she considered Eaven dear or not.

Thank you for contacting me. I'm sure you don't remember, but my 75th birthday is approaching on December 13. I've enclosed an invitation. It is my wish that you plan your visit in time to join the family for the celebration. I wouldn't have planned this myself, but your Aunt Caroline just informed me of the surprise party she organized.

An invitation was included. Though barbed, her mother had said yes. Eaven dropped the letter to her lap. Her shoulders relaxed. She had a place to go.

A tug of war between bitterness and gratitude ensued. Maybe God had answered. This time. She wanted to shout, *Why didn't You hear when I screamed for the life of my baby?* That anger, however, had worn thin with unending rehearsals. *Let it go, girl.* She lifted her eyes to the clouds that mottled the sky. "I don't know why now but thank You."

She moved to the sun-bleached picnic table and continued to read.

I realize our last conversation was strained, and I regret any actions on my part that may have led to discomfort in our relationship. Please RSVP at your earliest convenience.

Yours truly, Lillian.

Seventy-five. Had it really been that long? Her father had passed ten years ago. Lillian had been alone. No, not alone. She had Cassandra, her darling Scarlett O'Hara clone of a daughter. Still, guilt bit at Eaven's mind. She dismissed it. Lillian chose to be overbearing, yet many people tolerated her behavior, even enjoyed the woman.

She leaned her elbows on the rough table, remembering her mother as the perfect hostess, a blond beauty whose vanity forbade her children to address her as *mother.* Home in Charleston had rarely been a happy place. Failure was not a trait the Alexanders embraced, and she had failed. Again.

With a shrug, she opened the rear passenger door, careful not to let the bundles tumble out. She tugged her inlaid wooden writing box from under a pile of clothes and retrieved stationary and a pen. A small sense of pride welled at the formal heritage that had been hers, a heritage that, for the last two decades, she had rejected.

Inhaling, she drew back her shoulders and matched her mother's southern style. *Dear Lillian, I am pleased to accept your kind invitation. If it is convenient, I may arrive early.*

She paused, wondering how early would be acceptable. The birthday party was nearly two months away. There was no way she and Lillian could coexist until December. She quickly recalculated her budget. It would get her to Charleston, even give her enough to stay in cheap motels every other day. She could sleep in her car on the off days. The money from Fishburn and Marin's gallery in Bandon would allow her to take more time, maybe reduce her time at Lillian's. When Michael's money came, she'd have some cash to sustain her a bit longer. Hopefully.

Visions of Charleston's streets wandered through her mind. Upscale, a tourist destination, it would be an ideal place for an antique store, especially with the kind of treasures she planned to sell. Her interest piqued, her spine straightening. If she stayed with Lillian until she landed a job, she'd be covered until she found her own place. Then she could start planning her store. Surprised the idea was so appealing, a warm glow grew in her chest. This might work.

CHAPTER 5

Astoria, Oregon, Current Day

Eaven let the road gently rock her as she followed the highway cut through thick forests. Cresting a mount, she stared through the windshield at the panorama. Watered by lush autumn rain, the bright green grass served as a backdrop for burnt orange and yellow leaves. Her soul resonated with the rhythm of this country. With its vistas and fresh-washed air, this had been her refuge, had expunged past mistakes and betrayals, the same mistakes she would face again in Charleston.

She needed more time, a space to heal from Michael's betrayal, to find her bearing before facing home. Her fingers gripped the leather steering wheel with determination as a new plan formed. Before she headed east, she would fill up her soul, travel all the way down the Oregon coast and sock away memories to sustain her for the months, or years, ahead.

It could be a working trip. On her way, she could hunt for exceptional but reasonably priced antique pieces for her store, things that would provide substance to her dream. A grin stretched muscles she hadn't used in weeks. With all its shops, Astoria was the perfect destination for her first stop. And the Seafarer's Hideaway would be an excellent restaurant to celebrate her future.

The late afternoon sky was the brightest blue she could remember. She turned onto the Astoria-Megler Bridge to cross the Columbia River. Hanging low in the west, the sun colored the clouds salmon and lemon. Rainbow sunlight sparkled on the waves, whipped by the wind that raced down the gorge. "Wow." She split her glances between the sunset and the narrow lane on the bridge. Brisk air whipped through the car when she rolled down the window. It tousled her ponytail into streamers that tickled her face and blew away the lingering depression.

Once over the bridge, she turned east onto Marine Drive and headed for their favorite restaurant in Astoria. No, *her* favorite restaurant. It was time to think in terms of one. The thought tried to dampen her enthusiasm, yet the promise of fresh fish drew her forward.

Inside the Seafarer's Hideaway, a dark-haired server flaunting thick eye makeup and a nose ring, tapped her black fingernails on the menu. "Just one?"

Wishing the woman's voice hadn't carried across the whole restaurant, Eaven smoothed a loose strand of hair behind her ear and nodded. "Yes. By the window, please." The room was large with one side boasting an 18th century English bar, nearly black with age. Tonight, its tarnished brass foot rail supported Nike shoes rather than leather boots. Ahead, a wall of windows faced the Columbia River. Tables for two sat between the bar and the larger picnic tables on the far side of the room. The server led her to a small table near the window and handed her a menu.

Eaven chose a seat with her back to the room filled with laughing friends and families. She studied what she could see of the dull gray waves below. Last year, Michael sat across from her here. Had he known then he was leaving? Her chest tightened. Of course, he had.

Night was falling hard, taking her emotions with it. Some celebration of her new life. How could she have thought this would be fun? When her server returned, she ordered without using the menu. "I'll have the fish and chips with extra coleslaw and two of your dill pickle spears." The server jotted down the order and rushed to the next table.

"You sound like a local." A man with sleek black hair and green eyes peered from his stool at her end of the bar. A small scar began at the right corner of his mouth and arched downward an inch, creating a hint of a scowl. Pirate came to mind. Three martini glasses sat in front of him, two empty and one filled to the brim.

She tensed at the intrusion. "I'm not local, but it's our favorite destination when we're—when I'm in Astoria." Unwilling to get enmeshed in conversation with a strange man, she pulled a pen and notepad from her purse to start planning out the details for opening her shop. A bank would require a professional reference for the business financing she would need. It wouldn't hurt to ask Christie's for one. The investigation never named her as a thief, and her work had always been exceptional. She tapped the table with the pen.

The man stood and held out his hand, exposing a gold watch encrusted with diamonds. "I'm Greg Sault. And you are?" Beneath his open-neck shirt, a gold coin hung from a gold rope chain. Her father would have remarked he was either from new money or compensating for an inferiority complex.

Years of etiquette training forced her to shake his hand. "Eaven Dal...Eaven Alexander," she answered. Instead of aversion, she'd noticed her maiden name cloaked her in a sense of...self.

"Don't think I've heard that name before. Eaven, like Steven, but not."

She frowned at his attempt at humor. "But not." Her head craned up, noting he must be at least six-foot two, much taller than Michael.

"What brings you to Astoria?" He took his seat but continued to lean her way, his striking emerald eyes trying to catch hers.

The martinis must have clouded his judgment. He couldn't be over thirty-five, too young to be trying his luck with her. She blew out air, striving for patience. "I'm on my way to see my family in South Carolina." She started to write something on her notepad. Anything. One more interruption, and she would—

"I'm from here. Left during high school, after they murdered my dad." His face had clouded.

A shudder, like the tiniest of earthquakes, passed through her shoulders, a foreboding she hadn't experienced in years. "Someone killed your father?"

Greg nodded. "While en route to his arraignment. I promised myself I'd never come back, yet here I am, three weeks and counting." He gulped his drink. "My grandmother died. It's just me now."

She knew that feeling. "I'm sorry for your losses."

"Thanks. Now I have to sort out their stuff. Four generations, and I bet nothing's ever been thrown out. I don't know where to start."

Interruption or not, her heart went out to him. "It's a big job. An estate sales company could help. I did that kind of thing in Europe, sorting and appraising antiques for families."

He frowned, looking even more like a pirate. "It's the last thing I want to deal with. I might need your services."

She hadn't thought about working along the way. There might be items worth buying for resale, but did she want to take the time, stay a couple days in charming Astoria, and make some money? You bet. "I could sort through and tell you what it's worth, but I'll need to charge an hourly fee to cover my expenses."

Nodding, he said, "That won't be a problem." He wrote his number on a napkin and handed it to her. "Call me tomorrow."

She took the napkin and smiled inside. That was easy. "I'll make an honest offer on anything I might want."

Her server brought her iced tea and fish. "Here you go, ma'am." Greg turned back to the bar.

"Thank you," Eaven said, hating the *ma'am* comment that reminded her too much of the south. Yes, ma'am. No, ma'am. Beneath that polite exterior, those women had steel souls that she'd never enjoyed contending with. She lifted a bite of crisp coleslaw to her lips, the tangy scent of vinegar dressing making her mouth water.

A loud bang shook the building. Startled, she dropped the coleslaw to her plate. "Sheez."

A stocky man with a black beard had thrown open the entry door. Heads jerked in his direction. Behind him, a taller man in a suit offered a mild smile at the nose-ringed server. "Sorry about the racket, Brandy."

Brandy shrugged. "No problem, Mr. Mercer."

Greg spun around and glared. "Clayton Mercer and Billy Angler." The words escaped his lips with a low hiss.

Clayton Mercer, his ruddy face indifferent to the scene around him, sat at the bar with his companion, two seats away from Greg. "Dan, two rum and Cokes."

"Yes, sir." The bartender quickly set up the drinks.

The other diners had returned to their meals, except for Greg. Glowering, he grabbed his credit card from the counter and abruptly rose to leave.

Sensing a problem, Eaven edged back in her seat. What in the world was going on?

"Thank you, Mr. Sault," the bartender said and picked up the check.

Clayton turned, his bushy eyebrows narrowing above pale blue eyes. "Greg Sault? Wondered if you'd be back someday."

Eaven dabbed her mouth with her napkin. So, they knew each other and not in a good way.

Greg scowled and strode toward the exit, but Angler shoved him into the table next to Eaven.

She grabbed it just as Greg yanked Angler off the barstool and onto the hardwood floor.

He straddled the bearded man, hands around his throat and issued a quiet threat. "I'll tell you this once. The Mercers killed my father and they're going to pay. Try anything with me and you're a dead man." He jumped to his feet and headed out the front door, slamming it against the wall.

Angler's face turned beet red. He rolled to his side and ran his fingers through his thick black hair.

Clayton frowned. "Get up. Seems we've got another Sault causing problems. Call Pinnick to handle him."

Something, maybe her habit for rooting for the underdog, urged Eaven to warn Greg. She dropped her fork on the plate. So much for enjoying a hot meal. Outside, he was sliding into a silver BMW. The little she knew about him didn't give much insight. However, if the Mercers had the connections to kill his father, she wouldn't want them to get their hands on anyone else. "Wait." She strode across the dark parking lot to the car window.

"What?" he shouted.

She slowed, not certain what kind of violence he was capable of, and now wondering what his father might have done to provoke his death. She kept her distance. "Clayton called someone to come after you."

He smirked. "Let him. I've got friends too."

She shook her head. "And what, start another brawl?"

"Self-defense." He fumed. "The Mercer's have come at us for decades. Angler was the family's bodyguard when my dad was murdered." He started his car. "Sorry for the scene we caused. Call me. I'll make it worth your while."

Her pulse was still racing when she re-entered the restaurant lobby.

Clayton turned on his stool as she walked by. "I apologize for that dispute with your friend, Ms..."

"No need, he's not my friend, but your friend should be ashamed. This is a public place. With kids." She slammed into her seat, finished her lukewarm dinner, then handed the server her credit card.

On her way out, Clayton stood and said, "Just a word of warning. Greg Sault comes from a rough family. Brings trouble to those around him."

"I assure you, I can handle myself."

He assessed her lean frame with a patronizing smile. "Just know, you can call if you need help." He winked. "I'm legit. Own a sport fishing fleet. Here's my card." His pale blue eyes lingered, trying to catch hers.

Oh, brother. She glanced at the card and decided not to make a scene. "Thanks." She took it and left. Outside, she peered back through the window where Clayton talked with Brandy. Greg hadn't actually said the man was a murderer. Yeah, just his family.

Shadows dominated the parking lot. Though full of himself, Clayton was right. She was alone in this town and knew nothing about Greg. Still, he hadn't acted dangerous until he'd been shoved. If she'd been a man, she might have done the same thing.

Feeling unsettled, she decided not to stay in her car tonight. Instead, she called to reserve a cheap motel room. As her car passed the restaurant, she glanced at the window. Clayton stood just inside, his face as expressionless as a snake, his eyes following her. He gave her a little salute.

She pressed the lock button, comforted to hear the clicks on all her doors. Turning onto the highway, she mused over reasons why he needed a bodyguard. Apparently, a dark element lurked under Astoria's serene surface.

CHAPTER 6

Portland, Oregon, June 1891

"You're working stock, nothing else." Marie Sault's younger sister, Francine, smirked at her. "It won't matter how much you flutter your pretty green eyes."

Marie refused to let Francine see her words had hit the aching doubt she kept masked. Yes, she was from poor French stock, fitted with an oft-mended dress that had been her mother's. Today, her hair and face were clean, a rarity. Red, calloused hands from washing stranger's clothes spoke of her natural lot in life.

Still, despite her meager beginnings, she lifted her chin, grabbed her small worn trunk carved with her initials, and hauled it to the wagon. Since she could walk, she'd helped her family but had never lived away from home. Now that she was almost sixteen, Papa had arranged her first real job.

Overly thin from too little food to go around, Papa glared down his narrow nose. "You'll have a room, enough to eat, and a small allowance in Captain Mercer's home. Look at your brothers and sister and your maman." He pointed at her little family gathered to see her off. "Send every bit of money he gives you. We're counting on you."

Feeling very small, she drew back at the burden of responsibility and the gravity in Papa's voice. "Oui, Papa." When he'd first spoken of her new position, he'd said she was chosen because she was pretty, something he'd never said before. It had seemed a fun adventure to ride the train from Portland to Astoria and work in a grand home. Until today.

Now, at the moment of departure, questions flooded her mind, anxious questions with no answers. What kind of man was Captain Edward Mercer? She looked at her brothers, barefoot in the heat, hair ragged, cut with Papa's dull knife. And at her maman and Francine, both small like her, but strong from taking in washing. When would she ever see them again? She swallowed and kissed maman's wet cheek. "I'll send every cent to you. Please, don't worry."

She climbed aboard the wagon with the other travelers heading to the train and waved until they rounded the first corner. As maman had warned, some of the men stared, causing heat to flood her cheeks. She turned her head away and pulled her small trunk closer to her ample breasts, trying her best to keep her spine straight. Tears smarted but she blinked them away. Just wait, Francine. I will be a lady someday, with a big house and beautiful gowns. Just you wait.

CHAPTER 7

Astoria, Oregon, Current Day

Clayton Mercer inched the curtain back from his office window. A silver BMW, though common, had driven by again. Could be someone from his father Frank's old crew, or was he being paranoid? Regardless, there was little security in this house, technically still Frank's until the estate cleared probate.

He dropped the curtain. Frank's death had left his drug empire void of leadership, a void attracting the foreign drug trade. That slimy element needed to be stopped before it had a chance to take hold and ruin the town's tourism, the lifeblood of Clayton's fishing business. What he needed was information, more manpower to stop the cartels from overrunning his town, sullying its reputation.

A black leather bag sat on the bar, the last of Frank's drug money, freshly removed from its careless hiding spot in a kitchen cupboard. Clayton turned to Angler. "Take this cash to the dock."

Angler frowned. "The docks aren't safe right now."

Clayton looked at Rex, the new recruit taking in the scene. Known for his brutality, Frank's men would never have defied him. Clayton chose to be a man of reason in his business, one who understood the value of strategy and refinement. Though it had cost more, had taken more time, he'd used his sense of justice, had weighed the facts, before he'd had Angler systematically rid the docks of Frank's rats.

Without raising his voice, he held Angler's eyes and repeated, "I said take it to the dock." Angler flinched but grabbed the bag with a logger's strong hands and left. Clayton would teach him the value of refinement later. He glanced at Rex. "Whiskey?"

Rex read the label and grinned. "Never catch me refusing a quality drink."

After he poured two glasses, he handed one to Rex, a thin but capable man, a charmer with a knack for gathering information, a vital tactic for gaining control of the situation in town.

"Thanks." Rex unbuttoned his jacket, loosened his striped tie, and took a seat.

Clayton dropped into the other leather chair in his spacious office and pointed at a large oil painting of a luxury steamer. "That vessel belonged to my great-grandfather, Captain Edward Mercer. No one knew, or cared, that below the decks he transported opium from Victoria to Portland. That steamer lays rotting under the sea, the Captain under six feet of dirt."

"Death comes to us all."

"Unexpectedly to many." Next to the steamer hung two smaller pieces painted with the same quality. "After the Captain died, his son Jake, my grandfather, bought those two smaller steamers and a tugboat for a more prosperous undertaking." He swirled the amber liquid. "Though good old grandpa Jake continued the opium trade, he added smuggling Chinese to the mix, aiding British Columbia in unloading their Asian addicts and prostitutes onto U.S. soil. Later, he ceased to discriminate between nationalities."

Rex's mouth sobered.

Clayton stared at the wooden hulls and imagined the human cargo stuffed between the false double decks. "The ships passed to Frank, who installed diesel engines to speed his turnover. I've often wondered if the Captain would have any qualms with the misery his son and grandson smuggled."

Rex smirked. "Rich heritage."

Clayton's hand jerked, spilling his drink. Heat burned his cheeks as he strode to the bar and grabbed a rag. When he turned, he spoke carefully. "Get this straight. I make my own heritage."

Rex's eyes opened wide. "Sorry, sir, didn't mean anything."

As Clayton worked to slow his breathing, he cursed himself for his lack of control. He grabbed a clean glass and poured more whiskey. "I have no stomach for slavery, or the lowlifes Frank dealt with. He attributed his success to *Mercer luck*, but with the secrets he held on people, he didn't need to maintain a front. It's been hard to turn the Mercer image around, but with a concerted effort, I'm succeeding."

He sat again. "Frank had his men swear allegiance to me. I let him think I would continue his empire." He laughed. "Made it easy to disinfect the cesspool my family created in the shadows of Astoria and beyond." He scrutinized Rex's twitching eyes. Not a perfect candidate, but a good shot and observant. "My gig is prosperous, but I need more manpower. I think you're the man for the job. If you're with me, you'll share *my* Mercer luck. In?"

"You bet." Rex leaned back and crossed his leg. "I'm a lucky guy myself. Reliable too. Do what I'm told."

That remained to be seen. Clayton raised his glass. "Here's to success. I'll be in touch." Rex threw back the remainder of his drink and left.

Clayton locked the door behind him, then mopped the spilled whiskey from the floor. He forced his teeth to stop grinding. Yes, his business was successful, but even with the investment capital he'd been given, he'd been cash-poor since purchasing the fast, luxury fishing boats for the new Mercer venture. He'd counted on Frank's estate, but it was taking forever to settle.

After washing the crystal tumblers, he polished them with a dry towel before setting each one back in line on the shelf. Rex would do. The stream of undesirables coming into town had to stop, and Greg Sault was at the top of the list. And the woman? Brandy said she came into the restaurant after Sault, that the name on her debit card was Eaven Alexander. So, how did she fit in?

He called Branson, another associate. "We've got two suspicious characters from out of town. Watch them."

CHAPTER 8

Eaven rolled over and glanced at the time, surprised it was after nine. It had been years since she'd slept this late. On Lake Quinault, the promise of crisp mornings had bounced her out of bed with each new sunrise. Her new life came flooding in, causing her to clutch the faded motel comforter over her heart and stare at the popcorn ceiling through watery eyes. A weight like an anchor pressed on her chest.

Enough. She untangled her feet from the sheet and rolled out of bed. The sting of an icy washcloth jolted away the tendrils of self-pity. Losing Michael didn't mean the end of life. She faced the mirror. She just couldn't imagine a future. Yet.

Plopping in the frayed gold chair, she squirmed to get comfortable while the blatant disparity between her former life and the one she'd lived with Michael confronted her. Extravagant versus rustic. She brushed dog hair off the chair arm. Extravagant had its perks.

She stretched and checked her phone, happy to read Greg's answer. He had hired her to manage his grandmother's estate, agreeing to an hourly salary plus expenses for two nights. He'd left the address to his cottage but unfortunately, he couldn't meet her until nine tomorrow morning. Though disappointed for the delay, she grinned. Her first marketing effort had paid off. A tiny flame of excitement grew in the pit of her stomach. If she kept this up, one job at a time, she wouldn't remain homeless for long. Most importantly, she wouldn't have to depend on her mother, or anyone else for support.

Until tomorrow, her time was her own to start filling her heart with new, happy memories, maybe find the first item for her new business. She heaved her suitcase onto the bed. No sense jostling through it for the next two days.

Just as she set the last of her clothes into a dresser drawer, the phone buzzed. *Michael.* She wanted to hang up but hadn't even answered yet. "What?"

"Good morning to you too."

"What do you want, Michael?"

"Where are you?"

"That is none of your business."

"Look, Eaven, we don't need to play games. You didn't sign your paperwork right."

"Oh, am I interrupting your wedding plans?"

She heard his loud exhale. "Not the divorce papers, your financial paperwork. You used your maiden name. Clarence Fishburn can't release your funds until you sign it correctly."

"Oh." Her face burned. "I'm in Astoria. I could drive back. Or better, I can find a place here where he can send them."

"Fishburn closed the office and left for New York this morning. I took the papers and told him I'd get them to you. Didn't imagine you got too far. I'll be in Portland tomorrow and can bring them by on the way."

She huffed, hating to accept any kindness from him, but gave him the name of the motel. "Call me when you arrive."

Someone shouted in the background. He covered the phone and shouted something back. The honeymoon seemed to be getting off to a rocky start. "Be there around five."

As she put the phone down, her heart screamed, *No.* She didn't want to see him again. Didn't want him invading her new world. She plopped on the bed, then changed her mind and jumped to her feet. She wouldn't let him rob her of another day of happiness. Astoria was full of antique shops and had a two hundred-year history—not as old as Europe's, but old enough to stimulate her interests. She trudged downstairs, said hello to Kari, the motel clerk, and found a Chamber of Commerce brochure.

"Crazy time of year to be sightseeing." Kari said.

Eaven stopped turning the pages. "My job doesn't start until tomorrow. Thought I'd find some shops and things to occupy my mind, so I don't go crazy in that tiny room."

Kari was a big girl with a friendly way about her. She raised a mischievous eyebrow. "Ah. So, you're stuck here like in one of those movies where the woman gets locked in an old roadside motel." Her eyes widened with mock terror. "You know, where every door she opens leads to another ghoul, each one worse than the last."

She chuckled. "You've watched too many horror films."

Kari laughed. "Impossible." She glanced around. "That's why I prefer working the night shift—the only thing that makes it bearable working here." She took the magazine, flipped through it, and pointed. "Go here. My dad works at the Maritime Museum. He'll talk your ear off, but he knows everything about our town. I promise, Astoria's history will hold your interest." She tore out a coupon. "It's also dirt cheap during the off-season."

"I was hoping to find some antique stores."

"Oh, you'll find plenty of those too."

"Thanks for the recommendation. What's your father's name?"

"Lawson. You can't miss him. Big, smiley guy."

"He's lucky to have you as a daughter."

A shadow briefly touched Kari's expression. "Yeah."

Kari's answer seemed to suggest either she doubted her father felt that way, or she felt she hadn't measured up. Eaven empathized, wondering if women were born doubting their worth, or if experience pounded the confidence out of them. Her thoughts deepening, she chewed the side of her cheek. More important was how could it be reclaimed? What magic concoction could strip away that anxiety and doubt? She'd like to bottle and sell that potion.

CHAPTER 9

After slipping a flannel shirt over her long-sleeved thermal, Eaven pulled on an old rain slicker and black rain boots. On the way out the door, she grabbed her umbrella. Despite all her layering, the low October temperatures nipped her face when she opened the motel door. She started off through the industrial area toward the Maritime Museum at the opposite end of town with a loose plan. Greg said the trouble between his and Clayton Mercer's families went way back, a fact that generated a list of questions that begged to be answered. Maybe Mr. Lawson could enlighten her.

Walking briskly, head bent into the breeze, she glanced toward the water between the long metal buildings and stopped abruptly. Partially obscured by shadows, she spotted an angry Clayton Mercer on the dock with the man Greg had called Billy Angler. She watched Clayton's red face as he poked his finger into Angler's chest. Another man, less than five feet tall, stuck his hands in his pockets and stared at the ground. Clayton grabbed a duffle bag from Angler and strode to his black Porsche. The other men stalked away and disappeared behind a line of boats.

Clayton unlocked his car, threw the bag into the trunk, and was about to slide into the seat when his head snapped toward her. The distance between them dissolved, and she found herself staring into his pale eyes.

She gasped and hastened ahead, glad for the cover of the next building, deriding herself for spying into other people's business. Her mind reasoned against the apprehension she felt. He'd said he owned fishing boats, probably moored here. Completely logical, yet that didn't ease the suspicion gnawing at her. He'd put a lot of attention on that duffle bag.

A frigid gust hit, and she pulled her scarf higher over her chin. Michael would have dismissed her concerns as foolish, but she was through with hearing someone else's voice in her head. Her instincts were usually right on.

Something smelled fishy and she would bet it wasn't the fish on Astoria's docks. Still, it wasn't any of her business. She had all the trouble she needed.

Hustling forward, she followed the Riverwalk east past docks and warehouses. Seagulls sat on rotted pier posts that peeked above the Columbia River flowing along Astoria's north shore. She scuffed along the ancient train rails embedded in the wooden planks and imagined the busy days in the early 1900's. That bustling heyday gone, only the back entrances of the wood and metal structures lined the walk, some abandoned, rusted and weathered—like I feel. "Oh stop." Great. She was already starting to talk to herself.

"Thanks, Jim. I'll get it from here." An athletic-looking woman with black braids, wearing tight jeans and cowboy boots, cinched a strap around a used freezer in the back of a white pickup truck.

The salesman in the store's back entrance offered his services, but the woman had it under control. "Good-looking knot," he said.

She gave the strap one last tug against the freezer. "Tied up more than one heifer tighter than a tick with it. Can't let this gal jump off my truck."

He laughed. "Don't think there's a chance of that, Sheila. Business good?"

"Couldn't be better for this time of year. That's why I need more freezer space."

He lingered with an enamored grin. "Hope you stay."

"No way I'm going back to Texas—survived my last tornado."

"Good to hear. Your smoked salmon has me hooked."

"Come summer, watch out."

Eaven slowed to listen, admiring the woman's self-determination.

Sheila jumped from the truck bed. "I thank God every morning that I can gaze at this river, do what I love in a place that feeds my soul and doesn't dry out my youthful complexion." Her grin widened. "Folks are coming out of the woodwork to make me feel at home."

Eaven winced at the gap between their situations and hurried past. Some people were like that, able to attract friends—real friends. She'd had two in her life, Paisley from high school and Gail. Was Michael right when he'd accused her of acting aloof? It had never been her intention.

A homeless man pushed his shopping cart along the pier that supported popular restaurants above the river's surface. A sign taped to a Mason jar said, *Anything helps.* Another man wearing a tattered Army jacket sat on a bench and stared at the water. His gaze turned her way, then back to the river as though she didn't exist. Maybe in his world, she didn't.

She considered her worn, drab clothes and grimaced. Could anyone tell her from the itinerants on the street? Her stride slowed. Everything she owned fit in her car—bigger than the shopping carts these guys used to push their meager belongings around, but not by much. An ache tightened her chest. Her forty-six years of living had been reduced to a few boxes.

Anxious wails pierced the air and interrupted her morbid thoughts. Her head jerked toward the commotion. On the pier ahead, obscured by old buildings, it sounded like sea lions roaring. Caged? Hurt? She raced to the location of the racket and grabbed the rail to lean over. In the near darkness between the pier posts that held a brewery aloft, the mammals scurried in and out of the gentle waves onto the rocks, their barking loud and persistent. Her shoulders relaxed. Glad she'd come prepared, she dug her travel camera from her bag and snapped some shots.

A thought hovered, then came into focus. She stopped clicking. These animals didn't need a *place* to call home. Most of the abused creatures she had photographed would have been better off without homes. Cages, no matter how well designed, kept animals confined. Kept birds from flying.

She stilled. Is that what Lake Quinault had been? A glorious cage?

A fissure opened in the hard crust around her heart and made way for gratitude. Inadvertently, Michael's betrayal had provided an opportunity, had freed her to create a new story, a healthier one.

She observed the veteran on the bench, the chattering young couple walking their dogs, the barking sea lions below her. Astoria made room for them all. This is what she appreciated about the Pacific Northwest. This is what she would never find in her mother's high cotton world in Charleston.

In her mind, she captured the images of the soldier, the couple, the panting dogs. Then, she lifted her camera and snapped several shots.

She sucked in frigid air. The last shot captured the small man who'd been with Clayton twenty minutes before. When he caught her watching him, his face filled with surprise and he ducked behind a building. Was he following her? More likely, it was a coincidence. Astoria wasn't that a big of a town. Still, that same sense of *something not quite right* called for her attention.

She scanned the area, then hastened her steps. The last of the brisk three-mile walk to the Maritime Museum left her shivering, and not just from the cold. She'd looked back several times. The little man was following at a distance. Enough. Ready to confront him, she turned, but he stepped around another building. She stood with her hands on her hips and waited but he didn't reappear. And it was freezing.

Inside the museum, a short line formed to buy tickets. After glancing over her shoulder again, she lowered the knitted scarf to her neck and allowed the air to warm her tingling cheeks. A cheerful face greeted her. She noticed the man was missing an arm. Had he been injured in a war? Accident?

"Welcome. Name's Lawson. What can we do for you?"

Eaven smiled, glad for a friendly face. "I'd like to know more about Astoria."

"This is the best place you could start," he winked.

"Kari highly recommended the museum."

His smile faded as he inspected her. "Where did you meet my daughter?"

Protective. "I'm on my way to South Carolina, so I'm staying a few nights at the motel where she works. She's been very helpful."

His face relaxed. "I see. Do you have a particular interest?"

Her answer must have reassured him, but of what, she had no clue. "Do you have information on Astoria's founding families?"

A smile filled his face, hiking his cheeks so high they made his eyes squint. "My family has been here for generations. You interested in maritime history?"

"Yes, though not just maritime. I hope to pick up a few antiques while in town."

"We got it all. Don't miss the videos of our Coast Guard rescues. You'll get a sense of what our waters can dish out." He pointed. "Just start over there. If you have any questions, I'm your answer man."

"Thanks." She started to pass by an area that focused on the early canneries, but her curiosity stopped her. The photos before 1900 showed most of the solemn-faced workers to be Chinese. The captions indicated they were contracted to the canneries by their own countrymen for low wages.

One 1908 map showed the red-light district along the river, the buildings designated by *F.B.* for Chinese *female boarding* houses. She counted dozens between Astor and Bond Streets. A notation said they were built on pier posts over a swamp filled with fish parts and sewage. She wrinkled her nose at the imagined scent.

Farther on, an account of the 1922 fire said it purged the forty blocks of piers that supported the Chinese Quarter and downtown businesses. Fill dirt was hauled in and businesses were rebuilt on solid ground. The Chinese were run out of town. Many women were trafficked to Portland and other areas by riverboats, below deck. Helpless. Unheard. She steeled herself against her imagination, only comforted by the fact they were long gone from this world.

The fierce roar of waves lured her to another room where speakers recreated the threat posed by the *Graveyard of the Pacific*, the disastrous bar at the mouth of the Columbia. She sat on a bench, glad to be off her feet. A video showed river bar pilots risking their lives to deliver ships safely through the clash of river and ocean. Leaning forward, she watched as the tiny figure of a bar pilot struggled to stay upright in a small boat that heaved with the waves. Arms extended, he judged the exact moment to grab a rope ladder that dangled from the side of the huge ship. The man and ladder were whipped by raging winds while he struggled to climb. She shivered, remembering some treacherous waters she had fought while sailing.

"You wouldn't get me doing that," a tourist said. "They must have a death wish."

Eaven shrugged. Or hearts of courage. She stood and touched the wooden rim of a nearby boat used by the river pilots until 1965. It was barely more than a large canoe. Maybe they did tempt death.

Mr. Lawson trudged toward her. His side to side swing mimicked a rocking boat. "See you found my favorite section."

She nodded. "I can see the need for river bar pilots, but how on earth did they figure out that shallow channel?"

He grinned. "I think Lady Luck played a part. We owe a lot to the most famous, or infamous, of the river pilots, Captain George Flavel."

"Why infamous?"

"Depends on who you talk to. He was also a shrewd businessman. Arranged a monopoly over river bar piloting, then charged a premium for his services."

"So, he settled in Astoria?"

He nodded and led her to a photograph of a thin, wavy-haired man. "One of our first families. He built a fancy house on Duane Street. It's a museum now. Kept real nice by the State."

"Thanks. I saw an ad for it. Do you have any information on the Mercers or Saults here?"

His smile fled. He pointed across the room to a photograph of another sea captain. "Just the Mercers. The Saults were…let's just say they never amounted to much." He leaned forward. "The Mercers were the black eye of our town. We're still feeling their effects. Excuse me." He left to help other visitors.

Standing two feet from the painting, she studied the image. With his nearly black eyes glaring under thin eyebrows and his narrow mouth drawn tight, Captain Edward Mercer's portrait captured the perfect image of a pirate captain. The haughty expression had been passed to Clayton.

As she read, Captain Mercer's story explained the hardness in his face. As a boy, he was Shanghaied and forced to work on the *Ann Marie* until it sank while trying to enter the Columbia River in 1860.

Lawson strolled her way and she pointed. "How did Edward Mercer become a captain?"

"Gambling. Won a small steamer in a card game soon after he was stranded here. Made some money ferrying people and freight from Astoria to Portland. Below deck, he carried opium, which was unsavory but legal at the time."

Similar predators had ruined her brother's life. "So, he got rich by destroying people's lives."

Lawson pressed his lips together and nodded.

Next to Edward's picture hung his son's, Jake Mercer. She couldn't get over his strong resemblance to Clayton, the same snobbish lift of his round chin, hinting of the same arrogance. "His son any better?"

"Nope." With a disgusted frown, Lawson explained, "After Captain Mercer's death, opium became illegal for white folks. Jake's fortunes skyrocketed by transporting drugs from Victoria to Portland. No one ever turned him in. He was a dangerous man who gathered information on important people."

She studied Jake's empty eyes. Lawson's account painted a colorful history, if you liked dark colors.

"Here's Jake's son, Frank, the worst of the bunch. Died this year. I worked for him until my arm got caught in his rotten equipment. Never gave me a cent of compensation, threatened me if I tried. His men were just as mean, picking fights, hurting girls." The muscles of his jaw tightened.

"Kari?"

His face reddened. "I got her out of that. Just in time."

Eaven studied Frank's round, sullen face. Her hair stood on end. Clayton had stared at her with the same lack of expression through the restaurant window last night. "What do the Mercers do now?"

Lawson hesitated. His gaze flitted around the museum and back. "Clayton's the only one left. Got himself a business degree and came back." He scratched his head. "Supports community projects and runs a high-end sport-fishing operation. Acts like he's cut from a different cloth than the rest of the Mercers."

From her interactions with Clayton, she doubted that. The Mercer history had provided valuable insight into the family who'd ostensibly murdered Greg's father. It helped her understand the emotional makeup of the man she was about to work for. Kari had been right, this museum was the perfect place to acquaint herself with Astoria's undercurrents.

CHAPTER 10

Astoria, Oregon, 1891

Captain Edward Mercer finished a column in his ledger and shoved his pen into the silver holder that sat on the leather inlay of his desk. His gaze followed the delightful form of his French housemaid, Marie, as she dusted the books in his office. How could he possibly work with such a distraction? She'd been in his home for nearly a year and every month he'd found himself more drawn to her. He pushed back his heavy armchair, causing it to scrape against the wood floor when he rose.

Marie turned at the screech, dropped her eyes demurely, then returned to her dusting. Her arms reached high overhead, causing her dress to rise above her ankles. He swallowed. What delicate ankles. She moved to the elaborate red velvet chaise to fluff the pillows.

Enough. Despite her presence, he'd finished his accounting, having pinned the drain in his finances on his wife and son. Justine had feigned ignorance, but she would hear about this at dinner. He left the office and closed the door to lock out the image that had settled in his soul. Marie. Beautiful Marie. So innocent.

At dinner, he held the list of expenditures and read them one by one, his glower drilling into his wife and son's eyes after each amount. "I am cutting off your credit. You'll each receive an allowance and no more." He let them rail and whine until he'd had enough and raised his hand for silence. Justine bowed her head, but being of a strong will, he had no doubt she was already working a way around his wishes.

Having delivered his ultimatum, knowing that the expenditures meant little to him, he searched for the reason for his underlying dissatisfaction. He gazed at Justine, a handsome woman with hazel eyes and rich brown hair. At least it had been. In the candlelight, her eyes looked more tired than usual, her jowls more pronounced. Gray, frizzy hairs refused to be tamed by her hair ribbon. No warmth exuded from her once full lips. Passionate lips as he recalled. He finished his potato soup, set his spoon in the bowl, and wiped his mouth with the damask napkin.

Their son Jake, nineteen and of no use to anyone, sat to his right. A constant pout clung to the boy's mouth and flaccid, ruddy cheeks. Too much coddling by his mother and too much time on his hands had all but ruined him. Edward determined to remedy that. The room felt suffused with sourness and dissatisfaction. His chest threatened to explode. In a room fit for a king, he, Captain Edward Mercer, had none better than these two dismal humans to dine with.

Marie entered with dessert, bringing the sparkle of health and vitality with her. When she sat the porcelain plate of layered cake in front of him, her arm grazed his hand. His breathing stopped while he savored the sensation of youth and passion. His hand burned with it. He glanced at her kind eyes, and she smiled.

"That will be all, Marie," Justine snapped.

Surprised, Marie's small mouth opened, her pink lips parted. She turned and scuttled from the room, taking her essence with her.

Edward tore his hungry eyes away from her retreating form and encountered Justine's glare. He would not be reprimanded in his own home, at his table. He stared her down with a scathing expression. Defeated, she wiped her lips and looked away.

Jake's face blanched. He slammed his silver spoon on the linen tablecloth. "Excuse me, my stomach has soured." He rose, kissed his mother's cheek, and strode from the room.

The sight of Jake's rounded, retreating shoulders filled Edward with disappointment. He had hoped for a worthy son to inherit his estate. While he ate his cake, his attention lingering on the kitchen door, willing Marie to return. When she brought coffee and poured it, her hand shook. He sought her emerald eyes and smiled. "No need to fear, my dear." She smiled, and he thought the world had stopped. Years, decades, had passed since he'd felt so alive.

Justine rose. "My stomach, too, has turned." A vehement expression pinched her once-fine features.

"Then go," he said.

Justine left the room, her spine straight as a pillar. Marie glanced from his wife back to him. "Monsieur, have I upset madam?"

Edward took her hand, delicate and white. He'd dreamed of this softness. He lifted it to his lips and kissed it, heard the slight intake of her breath. Her eyes widened in surprise, but she did not pull away. "You've done nothing wrong. In fact, your sweet presence makes my days bearable."

"*Oui*, monsieur?"

He nodded, turned her hand over and kissed her wrist. Their eyes met, and she blushed. "Do you see how my family scowls at me? They certainly want the money I make, but am I loved? No."

"No?" The color darkened in her cheeks.

Moving his lips farther up her arm, he kissed the soft skin again. The delicate scent of rose water engulfed him. "Could you love a man such as I, Marie? A lonely man who thirsts for the love of a good woman?"

In her heart-shaped face, Marie's compassionate eyes revealed her answer. Certainly, she had listened to the harping of his wife and son. She laid her other hand against his cheek. "*Oui*, monsieur. I could love such an honorable man."

He stood, catching her tiny waist, and held her. His mouth met the willingness of hers. When he drew back, her face glowed with the new sensations of love. He glanced at the door, then back at her. "We must be together. Meet me in my office tonight. I will come to you at eleven."

CHAPTER 11

Astoria, Oregon, Current Day

Eaven left the Maritime Museum, her mind on the town's history and its provocative characters. Outside, the winds had stilled, allowing soft sunshine to penetrate through the high clouds. She hugged the rail overlooking the water. In contrast to the terrifying waves in the videos, the Columbia rolled amiably. A variety of birds soared, adding their own magic. She would love to spend hours photographing the area, but she needed to get down to business and scour the antique shops.

As she trekked back along the Riverwalk, she dropped a dollar in the homeless man's empty Mason jar and caught his downcast eyes just long enough to give him a smile.

He ducked his head but not before she witnessed a shy grin in return. "Bless you, ma'am."

"Blessings on you too." Her heart warmed at the simple human exchange that had little to do with a dollar. When she reached the Vintage Hardware store, it felt like she'd reaped a hundredfold for her small gift. She drooled over furnishings, brass lamp hardware, and nautical lanterns. On one aisle, she found a Jenny Lind wood and brass stagecoach trunk. If only she had a place to ship it.

Her phone rang. *Lillian.* It had been ten years since she'd received a call, and that was about her father's death. It rang three times before Eaven stepped outside the shop and composed herself. "Hello, Lillian."

"Hello, Eaven," she said in her slow southern drawl. "Ah'm callin' to ascertain that my invitation reached you,"

"About your birthday?"

"Umm, uh, yes." Her mother stuttered, something Eaven had never encountered. "When Ah sent the invitation, Ah wasn't certain if you were at the same address or island hopping like some gypsy," she continued, in her prickly tone.

Eaven gritted her teeth against a harsh reply. "Michael and I lived at the same address for the last eighteen years." Inside, she screamed, *and if you had kept in touch, you would have known that, would know he deserted me.*

"Well, did you bother to RSVP?"

Determined not to explode and give Lillian a larger target, Eaven silently vented. "I sent it yesterday. It hasn't had time to reach Charleston."

"And?"

"And what?"

Lillian sighed. "Ah see you still have no control over your emotions. You asked to come for a visit. This is a courtesy call to see when you and Michael plan to arrive, so Ah can have a room ready. My home will be quite inundated with out of town guests for my birthday."

"Michael isn't coming." Eaven bit her lip, not ready to explain.

Her mother paused. "Well, since he won't be accompanying you, Ah think the Rose Room will be open."

Eaven shut her eyes against the images that assaulted her memory. Of all her mother's seven bedrooms in her Italianate home on the bay, she had offered the small room facing the alley, decorated with pink ruffles from ceiling to floor. "Thank you, Lillian. You're very generous. Are you certain?"

"Yes, yes," Lillian said in her dismissive way. "No sense going on. Now then, when are you planning to be here?"

"I don't have an exact date, but would sometime mid-November be too soon?"

"Oh. That's well before my party."

"If that's too long..."

"Ah'm sure Ah can manage. Please inform me when you have an exact date. Good day."

Eaven stared at the phone feeling...angry? Yes. Didn't most mothers cherish their daughters? Care about what was happening in their lives? More than anything, she was disappointed in herself for continuing to expect more from Lillian.

She tucked her phone away and returned to the aisle she'd been perusing. Her eyes lit on an intricately-cast silver fish tail poking from a stash of old door knockers heaped in a wooden box. She lifted it out, delighted at the mermaid baby rattle. She tinkled the bells that hung from the body of a four-inch mermaid blowing on a conch horn. It had no price tag. She quenched the smile about to give away her interest and nonchalantly dug through the rest of the box until she'd found three other pieces. Depositing them on the counter, she smiled at the salesman. "These were in a box. Can you give me a price on them?"

The salesman took them from her and examined each. "These three are knock-offs. Five bucks each. But this..." he turned the mermaid around. "Don't know how she got in that box." He shrugged. "I've got a new salesclerk who's been reorganizing merchandise I've had in the back." He continued to study the object. "Completely forgot about her. A woman brought her in ten, fifteen years ago. Said her relative worked for an old sea captain who'd given it to her. She's a cute little thing. Silver. How about thirty dollars?"

Eaven's heart fluttered. Thirty dollars was a small sum for such a find, but the money would be better used for groceries. She bit her bottom lip. "I'll take her. Thank you." Inside, she screamed with delight. She couldn't wait to research its provenance, know its story. Sunlight blinked off the silver like it did off Charleston Bay. It suddenly felt settled. Certain. She would open her shop in Charleston with a mermaid motif. It was perfect for her antique store. This was her touchstone.

Ready for dinner, she stepped inside a tiny hole-in-the-wall restaurant. The smell of hamburgers and fries engulfed her, making a healthy choice nearly impossible. She compromised by ordering a small salad and sweet potato fries, then took out the mermaid to study. "What shall we name you?" After searching on her phone for mermaid names, she finally grinned. "Nirvelli, water child," she whispered. If any description fit herself, that was it. But was it a strong enough name for branding her store?

A text buzzed her phone. *Michael.* She read his message. *Something's come up. Can't leave Zoe alone. Be there with your papers Monday morning.*

Sheez. Why couldn't Crystal take care of her? She pushed her plate away. Greg's job would be done by Sunday afternoon and he'd only agreed to cover Friday and Saturday nights. She could either stay in her car on Sunday night to wait for Michael, or splurge to extend her stay at the motel. She held up the rattle. "What do you think, Nirvelli?" No answers there, either.

While the server was running her card, Eaven flicked through the day's photos. She stopped at the image of the guy who'd been following her. He had hard, black eyes and it was clear he was looking right at her. But why? She took her credit card and stepped outside, wrapping her scarf securely around her face. Even then, her nose stung with the cold.

On the long trek back to her motel, she shielded her eyes from the low, brilliant rays of the setting sun. With a blink, the evening's long shadows disappeared completely. She dug her hands into her pockets as she headed toward the industrial wharf section of town to her motel. Fog rolled in. Intuitively, she increased her gait. Unfamiliar noises murmured from the water and whined from the paint-peeled buildings she passed.

A quick, uneven shuffle from behind joined the mix.

Footsteps? A chill shimmied her shoulders. She glanced behind. Fog obscured her view. There it was again. The plod of unsteady steps. She could have sworn the little man had favored one leg. She stopped and listened.

It stopped.

Heart thumping, she tried to shake the sensation of a wharf rat being stalked by an alley cat and increased her gait.

The shuffle sped up. No—two sets of steps.

Her pulse raced as every fiber of her being shouted, *danger*. She was definitely being followed. She wanted to run but had nearly reached the end of the buildings and would be out in the open, easy prey. Breathing hard, she bolted between two storage buildings and flattened against the rusty metal, waiting to see who passed. Far away, a buoy bell clanged. The water lapped. The steps grew louder. They slowed as they drew near.

The sound stopped all together.

She slid down the metal warehouse. Its rusted metal scratched her hands and caught at the threads of her jacket. She crouched behind a stack of wooden pallets.

A small light swept the sides of the two long sheds on either side of her. It bounced off the crowded pathway stacked with pallets, just inches from the toes of her boots.

She held her breath, unable to see the face of the person holding it.

"Did you see where she went?"

"Naw, skittered off. Probably back at her room by now. I let her see me just enough to put the fear of hades in her. Put on my nastiest face. Tell Clayton by morning that little gal will be long gone."

She listened while the steps shuffled away. Water dripped steadily from a roof. A cardboard flap fluttered in the breeze. So, Clayton was having her followed, wanted her to leave. She shot to her feet. That wasn't happening until she decided to go. She had half a mind to become the pursuer and see who those men were. The smarter half of her mind won out. This was an unfamiliar town, not Lake Quinault.

Ready to defend herself, she moved back toward the Riverwalk and peeked around the corner where the steps had gone. If they were lurking, waiting for her, darkness blurred their presence.

To the west, the black, empty lot between her and her motel offered no cover. *Courage, girl*—Dad's words. He'd been such a large part of her life. The best and worst parts. She took a breath, slipped from between the buildings, and raced. Her boots slapped the damp pavement for anyone to hear. She dashed across the dark, open space and didn't stop until she reached her motel door.

Once inside her room, she turned on the lights and bolted the door. She shrugged off her wet clothes and pulled on her flannel pajamas. Thoroughly shaken, she wrapped the thin comforter over her shoulders and dropped into the lumpy chair, tucking her feet under her. She wanted to feel protective arms around her. She wanted to call someone, tell someone how scared she'd been, but who would she call? No one knew what had become of her. What if she'd been attacked tonight? She swallowed against the fear. What had she done to end up alone like this?

Wrong question.

She closed her eyes and nodded in agreement. It was the wrong question. As Paisley's mom used to say, revisiting past mistakes was as worthless as walking over hot coals. Both burned but were a useless pastime. Mrs. B was right.

Eaven adjusted in her seat to sit straighter. She wasn't a child anymore, not a daughter or a wife. She was a capable woman, able to manage her own emotions, be her own counselor and confidant. Feeling calmer, she threw off the comforter and finished getting ready for bed.

Determined to calm her mind before sleep, she plopped against the headboard and flipped through a magazine. A tempting ad for the Flavel Museum caught her attention. The tickets were inexpensive, and it would be fascinating to study its architecture before she left town. She turned off the light and fluffed the pillows. Soon, dreamy images of Queen Anne mansions battled with those of a gnarled seaman staring brazenly at her with his beady eyes.

CHAPTER 12

Eaven navigated through an older part of town to Greg's grandmother's cottage on Lexington Street. Mud puddles from the early morning rain dotted the driveway as it wound its way to an old house tucked behind the newer residences. Moss covered the shake roof. The wood windowsills were split and weathered. Greg's grandmother must have lacked the strength and resources to keep it up. Several easy ideas came to mind that would make the place charming. She bit her bottom lip. It was not hers to fix. She stepped over a puddle and rang the doorbell. It took Greg longer than she expected to answer. She checked her watch.

He opened the door wearing loose sweatpants that hung beneath his belly button. He ran his hand through his tousled hair. Clearly, he hadn't been in bed long. "Wha' time is it?"

She tugged her attention away from his well-defined torso. "Nine o'clock. Maybe I should come back later." She turned to leave, unwilling to waste anymore of her time or energy where it wasn't valued.

"No, wait. Just give me a minute. Come on in."

She exhaled her frustration, looking everywhere but at his broad shoulders and narrow waist. So, he was a hunk. Michael had been too. She had tossed all night, pushing away images of him and Crystal making love on *her* furniture. She shouldn't have left any of it. A lock of Greg's hair hung over his eye, looking extremely cute. And she shouldn't let her mind wander into treacherous territory. She followed him inside and bit her cheek hard.

He disappeared into a back room, leaving her to assess the living area. Large cushions from an old, flowered sofa lay on the floor. On a low walnut coffee table sat an empty wine bottle and two wine glasses. She lifted one with a red smear on the edge.

He stumbled back, wearing a gray hoodie pulled over the sweatpants. Glancing around the room, he grimaced. "Sorry about the mess."

"Looks like a heck of a party," she said without mirth. The late night with a woman had left him groggy, certainly not ready to do business. Resentment followed the disappointment of a day that was sure to be wasted.

Without comment, he pulled back the sagging curtains from the kitchen's sliding glass door. What sunlight filtered through the tree canopies did its best to brighten the tiny area. "Coffee?"

"Sure." She took off her coat and sat at the kitchen table, glad the surface appeared clean.

"I ran into a friend from high school, Jenny Gellens." He offered the scant explanation while he opened the drawer and took out a bag of ground coffee.

She watched a dozen plastic pill bottles roll to the back of the drawer. A large stack of bills shifted. Uh oh. Instincts on alert, she searched for other signs of drug use. She followed his movements, leaning to peek inside the cupboard when he opened it. Only mugs. "Thought you didn't have friends here."

He laughed but it sounded hollow. "Just one. She's having some problems."

And I'm sure you solved them. Snarky, aren't we. She frowned at her miserable attitude and tried for a reset, remembering she had a job and a safe place to sleep because of him. After the coffee was brewed, he sat the two hot mugs on the walnut table. "Thank you," she said, and rose to find coasters in a drawer.

He grabbed her wrist. "What are you doing?"

Instantly inflamed again, she pulled her wrist away. "Relax, I won't steal your stash."

Eyes flashing, he stammered. "What do you mean?"

"Look Greg, it's obvious you've been drinking. Which I couldn't care less about. But you're probably using as well. That I care a whole lot about. My brother was an addict. Overdosed. It's not something I choose to be around." She started for the door.

"Wait, Eaven. It's not what you think." He caught her shoulder and turned her toward him then quickly let go at the look she gave him. "Yeah,

I had a few drinks but I'm not a user. Not anymore. Those were my grandmother's medications from ages ago. The bottles are empty."

His vision appeared steady. It could be true. She sat again. "How long did you use?"

"High school—kid stuff. Mostly weed. Some pain killers." He dropped the discussion and lifted his cup. "Come on, let's talk over here." He strode ahead of her to put the cushions back in place.

Seated on the sofa, she picked a strawberry blond hair off the table and dropped it to the floor. Stacks of cash, late-night visitors, she should be horse-whipped for staying. Perhaps it was the similarity between Greg and her brother's stories that caused the familiar conflict. She hoped he was telling the truth. She looked around the room. "How did your grandmother die?"

He frowned. "She died in a nursing home."

"Your grandmother died alone?"

He stared at the floor. "I know. For years, I wasn't in any shape to come back. Then Alzheimer's set in. She wouldn't have recognized me anyway. I sent money for her bills, paid the taxes. Every check piled on more guilt, but I guess it wasn't enough to bring me back."

She resisted adding more criticism. "So, her house has been empty?"

"Yeah. When I returned, it was in grim condition. I faced my demons and moved in. Started cleaning it up."

She observed the mess around her. "So, I see."

He glanced at her, one eyebrow raised. "You should have seen it before." He handed her a photograph. "Found this piece of history while I was cleaning. Thought with your background, you'd appreciate it. It's a picture of my great-great-grandmother, Marie Sault."

Flattered that he'd thought of her, she studied the image. The dark-haired beauty exuded life. Though printed in sepia tones, it was easy to imagine the color in her eyes. A crucifix hung around her neck. "She's lovely. Your family is Catholic?"

"She was. Her son, Sebastien, abandoned his faith, but my grandfather brought our family back to its religious heritage. For all the good that did us."

"I take it you don't believe?"

"My dad pushed me to be an altar boy. Maybe I thought if I did the right things, God would remove the curse against the Saults. I found out He doesn't work that way and haven't stepped foot in a church since I was fourteen."

She thought of her own disillusionment, the moments when God had the perfect chance to swoop down and part the seas, giving her a story of victory instead of—

His phone buzzed. He checked the caller and answered it solemnly. "Hey Brett." He listened for a moment, his expression darkening. He glanced at Eaven and excused himself to head to the bedroom. The door remained ajar, and she heard the conversation clearly. He nearly shouted, "Yeah, Jenny was here, as a *friend*! How could you let her get into that?"

Wanting a clearer picture of who she was working for, Eaven moved closer and peeked through the doorway as he sat on the bed. Glowering, he listened then said, "You have that wrong. She hates him and is willing to get closer to help us." He rubbed the back of his neck. Frustration grew in his voice. "I promise you, he's going down with my foot on his throat." He nodded at something that was said. "Okay. Gotta go."

Eaven cringed at the hate in his voice. She stepped back to the kitchen for more coffee before he reappeared.

When he returned, he had dressed in tight faded jeans and a black leather jacket, a diamond stud in one ear. "I need to take off." His words sounded terse, dismissive.

She planted her feet and crossed her arms. "You're involved in something. Tell me the truth or I'm out of here."

He hesitated, but when she started to leave, he moved in front of the door. "A local drug runner got Jenny hooked on black market prescription drugs. She's agreed to turn him in but hasn't actually seen the guy dealing. I'm working another angle to bring him down."

Truth? Maybe. If so, she could support that.

Dropping the appeal, he straightened. "I hired you to sort this mess, not be my chaperone."

Her mouth opened but had no retort. "You're right. Sorry. I'll appraise the pieces as I go."

"Good." He stepped closer. "Sorry to provoke painful memories of your brother." For a moment, they connected, concern showing in his eyes. "Thank you for staying." He turned abruptly and sped out the driveway.

Leaning against the wall, she crossed her arms and suddenly felt very alone in the abandoned old house. She splashed her cold coffee into the sink. Time to work.

Decades of collectibles cluttered every surface in view. Grandma Sault did not appear the kind of person who threw out much of anything. She began with the tall secretary desk in the living room. The cubbies and drawers were stuffed with old bills and receipts that she placed in a bag for Greg to manage. In the first of two bedrooms, she pulled out boxes and suitcases from the closet and under the bed, piling them onto the faded blue bedspread. The clothes were obsolete. In a dresser, she found a few delicate beaded bags and checked the clasps. They might sell well online or to a collectibles store. She'd make Greg an offer.

After hours of sorting, she stretched her back and assessed her work. Neither the bedroom nor kitchen revealed anything of value. At the bottom of the stairs, she opened the door to the basement and peeked into the underground room packed with decades of trash and grime. She crept down and used her phone as a flashlight. The dank repelled her, but she couldn't resist hauling up a small old suitcase. Upstairs, a brush with a soft rag revealed two initials crudely carved on the top. *M. S.* "Marie Sault?"

Thrilled with the find, she opened it on the kitchen table. Near the top, lay two faded letters. She eased a delicate missive out of the stiff envelope. It was addressed to *Mrs. Philippe Sault, Portland, Oregon*. A black 1891 cancellation mark covered the two-cent stamp. Her thumbs softly rubbed the old fibers. The thin sheet of stationary showed smudges that revealed where fingertips had blurred the ink.

November 4th, 1891

Dear Maman,

As she read, her pulse sped. She opened the second letter and was equally incensed. Greg had to see these. She tucked them into her purse and decided to call it a day. Since he hadn't returned, she locked the door from the inside and stepped on the stoop to pull it closed.

Ping! A bullet! The glass window next to her cracked, fissures instantly spreading like a spider web. She dropped next to the house and covered her head, but not before she caught a glimpse of a beat-up station wagon with wood panels speeding away. She scrambled to take a picture, but it was out of sight.

She called Greg but had to leave a message. "Someone just shot at me and broke the front window of the cottage. Should I call the police, or do you want to? Call me ASAP."

He called immediately. "Are you okay?"

"Yes. Just shaken. And furious. This is not some kid's prank."

"I'll bet Clayton's behind it."

Clayton? His man followed her yesterday, probably stalked her last night.

"Get out of there."

"Wait. I found some letters I think might be important to you."

"Bring them tomorrow. Gotta go."

CHAPTER 13

The shock from the shooting the night before had Eaven on edge, her body screaming for exercise. She'd asked Greg to meet her at the Street 14 Café today to show him the letter and find out what he or the police had discovered. Stuffing a hand towel and extra clothes into her backpack, she put on running shoes and a waterproof jacket and opened the door.

"Eek!" She jumped back.

A black crow lay there—dead, feet up, twine wrapped around its neck like a noose. Heat radiated up her neck. Frowning, she searched the motel landing and parking lot. No one. This was getting bizarre. Irked at Clayton for the juvenile prank, she called the front desk to handle the disposal.

After another sweep of the motel grounds, she sprinted downtown, determined to rid her body of the excessive stress that had been building. Rain pelted her face but didn't faze her. When she reached the cafe, she ducked into the alcove and blotted off the rain, then changed in the bathroom. Her favorite white blouse, slim gray jeans, and leather ankle boots gave her a lift after weeks of sweatpants, tennis shoes, and depression. Using the small mirror, she touched up her makeup.

Feeling like a professional, she took a window seat in a quiet corner and ordered. The barista brought her latte with a concentric heart design in the foam. The tiny kindness warmed her. She smiled. "Thank you."

Greg passed the window with a tall man in a raincoat and a brimmed hat that obscured his face. The man continued down the street while Greg joined her. "Hey." The frown he'd come in with changed to a nuance of a smile as he appraised her face. "You're glowing."

If anything was glowing, it was his eyes. She forced her gaze away. "Got a run in."

He sat. "Are those the letters?"

"Yes. There's a darker history than I realized between the Mercers and Saults. Shall I read?"

He nodded, his face sober.

"November 4, 1891

Dear Maman,

It has been so long since I've heard from you. Can Papa walk yet? Will they let him go back to work after the accident? Though I eat well and my room is warm, I have had little extra to send to you. That has changed, and I am enclosing ten dollars.

There is a sorrowful thing I must say. Though the Captain is a hard man with so many people, he has become very kind to me, giving me little gifts and making sure I have enough covers to keep warm. Oh, mama, how can I say this without heavy shame. Captain Mercer's child grows inside me.

Madame Mercer and their son, Jake, must know. They give me the evil eye at every opportunity. Edward told them I was taken advantage of by one of the boys in town. They would throw me out, but he insists they act charitably. I am ordered to stay in my room when my work is done. I cannot go anywhere without enduring whispers and sneers. Please, speak to Papa and let me come home. I cannot bear it here.

Your loving daughter,

Marie

"He was a monster." Greg's hands clenched into fists.

She dropped the letter to the table. "That poor girl. How old was she when she was placed with the Mercers?"

"About sixteen, I think."

"Sixteen. With no one to protect her. Listen to her father's response." She lifted a yellowed envelop similar to the other one and read.

"November 30, 1891

Marie Suzette,

How can you dare add grief on top of our grief? No, I cannot return to work after the accident. Your mother takes in washings seven days a week. Her hands are raw, and she cries at night. We counted on your placement in a good home to save us. But what do you do? You bring shame to our family and take the food out of your brothers' mouths.

I am stricken that you accuse Captain Mercer of this crime. I pray to God you have not soiled his good reputation among his family or the townspeople. Tell the truth or keep quiet.

I cannot take you back here, nor would I. If the child is born healthy, take him at once to the sisters to raise, or find a family. Then pray you are still welcome in the Captain's fine home. Send what money you can. The winter has come early, and life is especially hard this year.

Philippe Sault"

Greg's fist hit the table, causing her cup to rattle and heads to turn from the other tables. "She was a child herself, with a baby on the way. How could a father reject his daughter like that?"

Eaven swallowed, remembering her own situation at seventeen. "I don't know."

He rested his elbows on the table and leaned forward. "I'd always heard the Captain was Sebastien's father, but his descendants adamantly denied it, said Marie slept around."

"This letter says something different."

"Well, now *I* know the truth, even if no one else believes it."

"Yes, but shouldn't they know what we've found? Should Clayton be allowed to continue smearing your name? Run you out of town? The truth needs to come to light. I could write an article and include her letters for all the world to see." The same passion that had compelled Eaven to photograph and defend abused animals swelled on behalf of the Saults. She wanted to even the score, to see the truth rubbed in Clayton's proud face.

He shook his head. "I can understand your desire to place blame where it belongs, but it's too dangerous for you to cross Clayton. Trust me to deal with him."

"That sounds ominous."

His lips contorted into a thin sneer. "In high school, I was blamed for vandalizing one of Frank Mercer's ships and stealing cargo. I barely escaped a harsh sentence."

"Who did the vandalizing?"

"I don't know, but Frank paid my best friend to say I did it. The Mercers caused trouble for every generation of Saults. It stops now."

She shook her head at the drama that surrounded him and must certainly have added to his temper. "You said your father was killed. Is your mother still living?"

"No. Gran raised me until I left."

Silence hung between them for a moment. She broke it. "I want to know if there are more letters. Will you stay at the cottage tomorrow and help me search the basement?"

He studied her face. "Why?"

She couldn't explain the emotions, so said simply, "I'm curious."

"You know what curiosity did to the cat."

She held his eyes. "I don't scare easily."

CHAPTER 14

Astoria, Oregon, November 1898

Marie's protective instincts sent her running toward a commotion from the carriage house. Sebastien! How could she possibly finish her work and keep him safe? As she scrambled over the brick path, she caught sight of him through the window. Eight-year-old George, the meanest of the boys, clutched Sebastien by the shirt and hoisted him to his feet.

"Let me go," Sebastien cried, fists flailing at George.

"Who's gonna make me? Your daddy?" At this, the other boys howled.

Frantic, Marie stumbled through the barn door.

George slapped Sebastien. "I think we'll put you down the well."

Blood trickled from Sebastien's nose and dripped on his clean white shirt. He kicked George in the shin, then clenched his small fist and hit him directly on the nose. He turned on the other boys, ready to whack the next one. "Mama!" he screamed when he saw her.

She ran to him and rounded on the boys. "Get out of here you brutes before I spank you all." It wouldn't be the first time they'd had a thrashing from her.

She knelt and wiped her son's nose with her cleaning rag. "I told you not to play out here by yourself. Where is Monsieur MacDonald?"

Sebastien pushed her hand away and wiped his own nose. "He drove Madam Mercer to the doctor. Then George came and..." His eyes watered, and he fell on Marie's shoulder and sobbed.

"*Mon petit bonhomme*, my little man. You were very brave to stand against them."

"They said things about you and a Chinaman." He searched her eyes. "Is my father a Chinaman?"

"No. Your father was a brave sailor who died in a horrible storm." She stood and led him toward the back door of the mansion.

He resisted. "Madame said I couldn't go in."

Marie eyed him calmly. "You above anyone are welcome in this house. Come, let us taste a bit of lemon meringue."

At that, he grinned, the worry gone from his face.

She glanced back at the empty carriage house. She had long disapproved of Madame Mercer's frequent spending trips. Mr. MacDonald carried so many loads of shopping bags to her quarters, it seemed Madame was determined to spend all of Edward's money. Recently however, the lady appeared frail, requiring many trips to the doctor, her outings producing fewer shopping bags.

Marie pulled last night's dessert from the ice box and cut a thin slice of lemon meringue. Sebastien's face danced in anticipation. She kissed his forehead and set the plate in front of him on the small kitchen table.

Leaving him licking his fork, she rushed through the large hall to Edward's study. She stopped before the huge door, caught her breath, and tucked a stray black curl under her cap before tapping lightly.

"Enter." The Captain's voice boomed against the wooden door.

She stepped inside and curtsied. He was alone at his huge desk, its legs gripped with horrid carved snakes. She approached with the bloody rag in her hand. "This bullying needs to end, Edward. Sebastien—"

His dark eyes grew wide at the rag. "What has happened?" He rushed around his desk and grabbed her shoulders.

Relieved to feel his strength and support, tears tickled her cheeks. She swiped at them. He despised hysterical women. "Madam forbid Sebastien to come into the house, fully aware those brutes would attack him again."

He started toward the door. "Is he all right? I'll whip them soundly!"

"A bloody nose, but he is fine now. I left him in the kitchen." She lifted her chin. "He fought them. Punched the biggest boy's nose."

Edward stopped mid-stride. A smile lifted the corners of his mouth. "Did he now?" He held open his arms. "He's a good boy, Marie."

She rushed into his protective embrace. When he kissed her, all felt right with the world. "He takes after you, his courageous father. If only we could be a family, no one would dare hurt the son of Captain Edward Mercer."

He moved her aside. "Hmm."

She bowed her head. Surely, he loved her. If not, she couldn't face what she'd become, or combat the rumors that swirled around her and her son. At least no one had concluded Edward might be Sebastien's father, except perhaps Madame Mercer and Jake, his son. It would explain their vehemence toward him. So far, Edward had successfully shielded her from Madame's attempts to drive her from the mansion.

He stepped to his desk and opened a drawer. "Take this and buy something special for the boy. And for yourself as well, my love." He handed her a stack of five Morgan silver dollars, then pulled her close. "Let Sebastien sleep at the MacDonalds tonight." His expression said he wanted only her.

She smiled. "I'm certain they would love to have him." Her stomach knotted, conflicted with guilt and relief that he still cared. If she lost favor with him, where would they go? She clutched the coins, planning to hide them with the rest, just in case. For now, she and Sebastien were safe.

CHAPTER 15

Astoria, Oregon, Current Day

After she dragged her suitcase to the lobby on Sunday morning, Eaven dropped into a chair until time to meet Greg at the cottage. Despite the frigid temperatures, she planned to sleep in her car tonight, then meet Michael on Monday.

While waiting, she picked up the local newspaper. On the front page, an article with a photograph of the Mercer Mansion piqued her interest. The building that once belonged to Captain Edward Mercer would soon come on the market for the first time since it was built over a century ago. She studied the lines of the house. Good lines.

Kari Lawson sauntered by. "Did you like the Maritime Museum?"

Eaven smiled at the rosy-cheeked girl who resembled her father. "I did. Your father is as knowledgeable as you said." She paused. "He seemed personally put off by the Mercers for some reason."

Kari's eyes shifted. "He's too protective. I had some problems awhile back." She nodded to the paper, changing the subject. "That's a travesty."

"What is?"

"The Mercer Mansion, rotting away. They don't deserve it." With a smirk, she sat on the chair next to Eaven. "I think they're cowards. If there's a ghost there, it's the family's own fault." She leaned closer. "I have friends who shimmied under the porch into the basement. They said it smells like bleach and it's full of rats."

"Rats?" Eaven writhed inside. Their scratching in the ceilings above her head while exploring old buildings in England had unnerved her. Kari laughed and strolled back to her desk.

The newspaper's black and white photo wasn't flattering. White paint had flaked off the horizontal siding, leaving a resemblance to birch bark. A

77

wide covered porch sagged with decades of abandonment. Too bad. Though the windows were boarded, and its cornices blackened with mold, she could tell it had been a striking home at one time. Why did Captain Mercer's descendants, with all their money, let it deteriorate?

Her phone rang. She checked the caller and straightened her shoulders. "Hello, Lillian."

"Ah apologize for interrupting your day, but you haven't informed me of the exact date you are arriving."

Eaven bit her cheek. Already Lillian was pushing. Staying at her home in Charleston would stop the bleed from her finances, but at what price? "I should be there around November fifteenth."

"What do you mean? Don't you have your plane ticket yet?"

"I'm driving."

"Driving? Whatever for? Charleston is clear across the United States, girl."

To avoid the tirade of I-told-you-so's that would ensue when her divorce was announced, Eaven said, "Because I like to drive."

Lillian remained quiet, the way she did when calculating how to get the upper hand with her disappointing eldest daughter. "You're driving by yourself to South Carolina? How uniquely you."

Eaven found herself clicking her fingernail, waiting. Her mother was capable of a far sharper barb.

"Ah guess ah will see you on the fifteenth then. Goodbye, Eaven. Keep in touch, dear."

She stared at the phone, unused to her mother dropping a subject without twisting the knife. And she had never called Eaven *dear* in the earnest sense. Something was up. She didn't trust Lillian one iota.

Time to go. Unsure of what kind of food Greg would provide for lunch, she grabbed a bagel from the breakfast bar, packed her bags in her car, and drove to the cottage. She knocked tentatively, not knowing what state he'd be in. Or if he'd be dressed. The image of his bare torso invaded her mind. She shook it away, surprised the wayward thought would even come to mind in the middle of all the pain she still battled.

He opened, unsmiling. "Morning."

She released her breath. He was fully dressed in faded jeans and a gray wool sweater, his gold coin hanging around his neck. When she passed him, she caught his eyes. "You look tired."

"Long night." His dangerous good looks and green eyes were magnetic.

She pulled her eyes away. "Let's get started in the basement."

He led the way. "I moved an old dresser that hid an alcove down here and found some boxes."

"You're kidding?"

"Nope."

They edged down the narrow steps into the dank basement and carried the boxes to the living room to sort.

After disappearing into his room to take a call, he returned pulling on his leather jacket. He surveyed the cluttered room. "Looks like you're in your element. I need to leave for a bit. You good?"

She nodded, surprised at the disappointment she felt when the door closed after him. Okay, what was that about? Sure, he was attractive, but romance was not on her radar. With the distrust she felt, she doubted it ever would be. Just chemistry.

For the next two hours, she opened boxes, stacking her finds in neat piles on the sofa and floor and marking prices on the furnishings.

Someone knocked lightly on the front door. Hesitant, Eaven rose and edged back the kitchen curtain. A small woman stood on the porch. When Eaven opened the door, the woman's eyes grew wide and she looked like she was about to bolt. "Wait. Can I help you?"

The woman, eyes casting around, took a quick step forward, jammed a letter toward her and scurried away.

Eaven studied the scrawl on the envelope. *Deliver to Greg Sault.* She shut and locked the door and set the letter on the kitchen table before going back to work. After another hour, the few things she was interested in lay on the coffee table. She stretched her neck from side to side. At least it was done. That left only one more room to sort.

Feeling like a trespasser, she hesitated before entering Greg's bedroom. It was furnished with twin beds and a pedestal desk and had faded blue curtains. This must have been the room he'd shared with his father. His things were flung in piles across the floor. He was definitely not a neatnik.

As usual, she checked the desk for hidden springs that might reveal a secret compartment but found nothing. No surprise, the furnishings were modest like the family who had lived here. Stationary, pens and stamps filled the center drawer. She opened the four side drawers on the left pedestal and removed everything to the desktop.

The bottom drawer of the right pedestal stuck. She reached under it and found a black travel bag hindering the drawer. After tugging hard, the bag finally pulled free. Stacks of hundred-dollar bills were stuffed inside. She sat back on the floor and stared at the money. If not dealing, why would Greg have so much cash? He said he'd sold his grandmother's car, but this amounted to tens of thousands of dollars.

If he was doing drugs, what did that mean for her? Was she in legal danger? Her mind raced over their interactions. She had never seen any drugs around him. Also, she could prove the extent of her involvement with the itemized list she had been making. What about physical danger? It could become a problem if competing dealers thought she was involved. "Oh!" Is that what the shot had been about? Her mouth went dry. She should just leave, get in her car and drive away from this mess.

No. She was through leaving when things got tough, through letting other people's agendas dictate her life. She wanted this job. After inhaling long and slow, she exhaled her runaway imagination. Greg said he wasn't dealing. She would accept that until she knew better.

She stuffed the bag of cash back under the drawer and headed for the closet. Wow. No wonder his clothes were strewn about. Old suitcases and boxes were stuffed tightly from the floor to the ceiling. One by one she pulled them out and took them to the living room, still hoping to find more of Marie's letters.

She started with the suitcases, but it wasn't until she was halfway through a ripped cardboard box that she hit gold—a letter addressed from Marie to Mrs. Phillipe Sault, Portland, Oregon. While she scanned the letter, she grew more hopeful for Marie. Tenaciously, she dug into the remaining boxes, hoping to find more letters. She was sitting on the floor of Greg's room, surrounded by piles of empty boxes when she heard him come home.

"Hello?" he called.

"In here." She rose and stretched her back in every direction she could coax it.

When he peeked his head into the room, his jaw dropped. "And you accused me of being messy."

"It's an organized mess." She smiled. "I found something fascinating. And I need caffeine."

In the kitchen, he made a pot of coffee. "What's up?"

She grinned. "Marie wrote this letter seven years after the last one we read. Want to hear what's happened during that time?"

He smirked. "I'm almost afraid to."

After sipping her coffee, she read,

"February 12, 1899

Dear Maman,

These years have taught me the depth of cruelty in mankind. My only joy is Sebastian, nearly seven years old. He is a remarkable child with black hair and green eyes like me, but he's much smarter. Our groom, Mr. MacDonald, and his wife keep him out of the way while I clean and help cook. He sleeps soundly at night and always wakes happy.

Yet, there is much venom toward him in the house from everyone except Edward. Mrs. Mercer was especially given to raving spells aimed at him. The doctor prescribed bed rest and laudanum to calm her, but illness consumed her. She died last month. I am telling you this because Edward has been very generous to me. I believe he will ask to marry me once the year of mourning is complete.

Although I have not heard from you, and Papa forbid me to send letters with the money, I have enclosed more to help with your expenses. Please forgive me. Perhaps, someday there may be a reason to love me again."

Your loving daughter,

Marie"

"She said he planned to marry her. What if he did?" Greg had a hard time containing his excitement.

Eaven shook her head. "We have no record of that. Mercer could have promised her the moon and she'd have believed him."

"She was too young to resist his seduction." His words held sorrow and resignation.

Eaven recognized the empathy in his face. "You were about the same age when you lost your footing and got into trouble. I'm glad you escaped that world."

His eyes twitched sideways. "More coffee?"

"No, thank you." She moved to the slider and skimmed the gray skies before she turned to face him. "Though it's a sad story, do you realize how lucky you are to have these letters that document your family's history?"

His eyes rolled toward the ceiling. "I don't see lucky. Grandma Sault said Marie's father died young, and the boys were forced to work on ships at an early age. The family lost track of them after that."

"How horrible. Would you like me to do some research? I might be able to find out what happened."

He glanced at his watch. "I'll think about it. Are you about finished in here?"

"Not quite. I was going to ask for another day, but I'd need another night's lodging."

"No problem." He headed to his bedroom and came back with a roll of hundred-dollar bills. "Here's three hundred dollars to cover your expenses so far. I'll pay the rest when you're done. Great job."

Relief calmed her mind. No sleeping in her car, at least not tonight. "Thanks."

He picked up the envelop. "What's this?"

"A woman came by and left it for you."

As he read the enclosed letter, his lips grew tight and he drew in a jagged breath. "I need you to leave."

"But I still have time—"

"Now." His friendly demeanor vanished, revealing the edgy side she'd seen in the bar fight.

"You don't have to be rude about it." She gathered her things, frustration building at having to deal with another erratic man. Without a backward glance, she shut the door harder than necessary. The letter must be bad news. Regardless, he'd offered no apology.

After renting a room for the night, she lugged her suitcase up the stairs, and flopped onto the ratty chair. Three o'clock. She huffed at the wasted time. She could have been done in another hour. Her eyes fell on the ad for the Flavel House Museum. "Why not?" She needed something fun, stimulating, with no moody men.

CHAPTER 16

Eaven hiked up the wet streets breathing hard. She'd always wanted to see the Flavel Museum, but Michael was never interested. Her chest tightened as she recalled her penchant for ignoring her own desires, or at least, placing them at the back of the line. From this distance, it became clear that it hadn't been love, it was bargaining. She had expected a return for her selflessness, maybe his willingness to do what she wanted the next time.

She paused on the sidewalk, welcoming the understanding. Fear had driven her, not love. Fear that like her father, Michael would abandon her. Her gaze drifted to the top of the mountain dotted with houses. All that maneuvering had gained her nothing. Worse, she'd abandoned her self-respect bit by bit until she'd all but disappeared.

Well, she was here now, doing what she wanted. Yet, it felt hollow doing it alone. Her lips tightened. Michael's scent, and how she'd melded into his chest when his strong arms surrounded her, flooded her memory. Unable to stop the tide, she pulled her umbrella lower and let the bittersweet memories come, let the tears fall. How long would these bouts continue? How long until being alone didn't equate being lonely? *God, help me get over him.* She wiped her cheeks, hoping these feelings were temporary, an adjustment that would right itself in time.

Looking forward to a distraction, she walked another half block until she was gazing from under her umbrella at the lovely Flavel House. Her interest in historical architecture instantly rekindled. Patterned shingles, cut like scalloped lace, lodged under the steeply pitched roof. A sign to purchase tickets led her to the Flavel Carriage House at the back of the property.

"Good morning," said a spry, elderly lady.

Eaven smiled. "Hello. I'd like a ticket please." She studied the ceiling structure in the small gift shop and noted a side room where horse stalls had been converted to house early automobiles.

Two bickering women entered the building. A plump lady with a flushed face wore a colorful orange tunic. Multiple rings adorned her fingers. The second woman was tall and fine-boned. Even the toes of her boots were angular. They headed to the bookshelf, their chatter filling the quiet gift shop. The heavyset woman said, "Joe told me Gina brought Clayton Mercer's dog in yesterday. Pretty roughed up."

Eaven's attention piqued. Clayton hurt his dog? She added that to the list of things she detested about the man and moved closer to listen.

"Really, Carol, that woman has no business caring for a dog. Another broken leg?"

"Nothing that shows, but Joe said Roscoe whimpers when he tries to lie down. Gina said they had gotten tangled in a bicycle accident, showed an ugly bruise to prove it."

"I don't believe her. Is Joe going to report it?"

Fear filled Carol's face. "We don't need trouble and neither does Clayton. People look for any reason to tie him to his father. Do you know how much he has donated to the animal shelter?"

"But he has no control over Gina. Do you want the dog to end up dead?"

Carol's head drew back. "It didn't seem like she planned to return this time."

The tall woman smirked. "Of course, she'll return. You saw the diamond necklace he gave her last Christmas."

Eaven's breathing accelerated, wondering what she could do keep the dog from Gina's *care* if she returned. A half-dozen ways she'd learned from PETA flew through her mind, but she had to find him first. She forced a smile. "Excuse me, did I understand you know a vet?"

Carol's face broke into a friendly smile. "Well, yes, my husband. His office is just a few blocks from here on Franklin Street."

"Wonderful. What's his name?"

She laughed. "Joseph Franklin. So, he called the office, 'Franklin on Franklin Veterinary Hospital.'" She handed Eaven a card. "People tend to remember that."

The tall woman smirked. "Hard to forget."

Carol frowned at her friend's attitude and turned her attention to selecting a book. Her voice lifted with excitement. "Here it is. Evelyn said this one had the best stories about Astoria's haunted houses. Perfect for my Halloween party."

Her friend peeked at the title. "Ooo. I might die of fright."

"I can only hope," Carol said sarcastically. She paid for the book and they left, still bickering.

Eaven stared after them, her mind stuck on the image of a small dog cowering in a cage. What if Gina came back? Eaven slid the vet's card into her purse, determined to do whatever she could to protect him.

"You can view the museum any time," the clerk said.

"Thanks."

When Eaven stepped inside the Queen Ann-style mansion, old sensations and hints of emotion from the past immediately swirled around her. Her rational mind still contended with the impressions that had begun as a teen, especially when in old houses. Confused at what it might mean, she'd kept it between herself, Paisley and Mrs. Benson. Until London. When her colleagues witnessed the phenomenon, they cynically dubbed her the *house whisperer.* What had been an oddity became an embarrassment. She straightened her shoulders. Those people were long gone from her life.

An elderly docent greeted her. "Welcome. Captain Flavel's daughters, Nellie and Katie entertained company for hours at a piano much like that one. Nellie's niece removed the original before she donated the house to the state as a historic site. The girls—"

"Very interesting. Thank you," Eaven interrupted.

His lips smacked shut and he frumped away.

It wasn't that she didn't appreciate his comments, but she wanted to experience her own impressions. Leaning through the door, she studied the music room where a square grand piano occupied center stage. Such graceful specimens were rare. Few people knew how to tune them anymore and most had been destroyed for firewood.

She stood quietly and let her eyes drift around the room. Music floated just out of the reach of time, accompanied by a high, sweet voice. A sense of what life had been like for the two young women filled the room with joy.

But also, a sense of burden. What was that about? She read the account of the two sisters who never married but were said to have led rich, fulfilling lives. The choice to remain single would have been odd for that time.

She huffed. Today, it wasn't a matter of choice for a growing sea of women. Her own life proved that. She massaged her finger where her ring had been. Could she be happy alone for the rest of her life? Would she have the choice? Such somber thoughts. Where was a good crystal ball when she needed it?

Wide stairs beckoned her feet and spirit upward. Her fingertips swept over the smooth wooden handrail while she climbed to the second story. A photo in the hall showed that Captain Flavel's lookout tower was accessed from the third story. How would it feel to stand in a sea captain's private lookout? If she still worked for an auction house or historical architectural firm, getting permission to access the non-public rooms would be easy. She bit her lower lip and slipped to the far side of the hallway where she tested the door. Locked. An old, simple lock.

Though she'd never become a true locksport, she had spent hours amusing herself with a set of lock picks her father had given her in middle school. She dug out her key ring that held only one. The *rake pick* had often been her friend in London, where missing keys could halt the investigation of old furniture.

You don't have permission.

Ignoring her better sense, and feeling like an older version of Nancy Drew, she leaned her ear in the direction of the stairs. The docent was quiet. No other visitors moved about that she could hear. She held the cold brass knob and deftly worked the pick. In an instant, the handle turned. Behind the door, a narrow set of stairs led upward to the third story.

With each step, the old boards tested solid in the dark passageway. She stifled a sneeze from the musty air that swirled as she brushed by. Quietly, she reached the attic room door and entered. At the far end of the poorly lit space, more stairs led the last few steps to the tower room. She squeezed between boxes and old furniture laden with cobwebs.

A spider dangled in front of her face. "Eek!" She covered her mouth and jumped away from its striped body. After calming her breathing, she listened for movement below. Nothing. Once inside the tower room, she moved soundlessly to the window and her heart fluttered. The full-flowing Columbia River spread before her. Captain Flavel had stood here and overlooked his docks and the Occidental Inn, where sea captains had lodged during Astoria's glory days.

A car's brakes screeched somewhere around the mansion. The front door slammed three stories below. Eaven jumped. Footsteps tromped down the main hall, too fast to be taking in much of the ambiance. Had someone seen her through the window? Her face flushed. This was not one of her better ideas.

She rushed out and caught her shin on the corner of an old bench. Gritting her teeth, she massaged her leg, then limped down the narrow servants' stairs to the second-floor landing. She opened the hall door a crack, then whipped through and quickly closed it behind her.

Someone continued to tread loudly up the main stairway. Eaven bent over the rail. Her pulse quickened. Clayton Mercer. His appearance at the marina was logical, but what was he doing here? The same unsettling feeling caused her stomach to churn. She gripped the banister, resisting the urge to flee.

His face unreadable, he continued to climb and stopped on the top stair. He rested his polished shoe on the landing. "You get around."

"Taking in the town."

He scanned slowly from her feet to her face. "Lots to see."

She lifted her chin and glared.

"Why'd you come here, Ms. Alexander?"

He knows my name. Though her heart thumped, she kept her voice cool. "I'm interested in old things."

"Antiques?"

Lucky guess? She didn't think so. "Yes, actually. I'm helping someone with an estate sale."

He kept his focus trained on her face. "Hmm. If that's so, have a mansion full of antiques I need to sell. I could give you a personal tour." His eyes dropped to her lips.

She started past him down the stairs. "No thank you."

He touched her arm and a jolt shot through it. "I heard you ended up with Greg Sault. I'll say it again, not a good choice."

After stepping around his reach, she turned. "I'm not *with* him and it's certainly none of your business."

"If you are, that makes you my business."

"Your issues with him don't concern me. Besides, I'm leaving on Tuesday."

He called after her. "If you change your mind, I'd pay a hefty commission. In your situation, I'm sure you could use the money."

The hair on the back of her neck prickled. How does he know? "I think you should stay out of other people's lives, Mr. Mercer."

"You may regard me as intrusive, but I'm trying to rid this town of gutter rats like Sault."

Before she could think, she matched fire for fire. "What about Gina and her penchant for abusing dogs? Maybe you should start at home."

His jaw dropped.

She turned and forced herself not to run down the stairs. After closing the front door, she let out her breath and quickened her strides toward town. She glanced back and saw him emerge from the museum, slam into his black Boxster, and attack the steep hill.

He knew she would be there. She quickly checked in all directions then continued downhill. Though she saw no one, she felt someone's eyes on her back.

CHAPTER 17

Clayton barged into his home office and dropped into his leather chair. Eaven's comment about Gina was a low blow. It was hard enough dealing with her bipolar personality without everyone's criticism. Her illness had become more of a liability than he wanted to live with. His thumb tapped a hard rhythm on the chair arm. Change had been overdue. Then Eaven had come into his life. Serendipity? She was electric when riled, one of the few women he'd been attracted to in a long time. He huffed and shook his head. Always the difficult ones.

Feeling antsy, he headed to the bar and dropped ice cubes in a glass. While he poured the bourbon, questions nagged him about the suspicious silver BMW that frequently passed his house. Bransen had reported that Sault drove one, but so did another character who'd recently come to town. Both about the time someone started stealing from him. So far, there was no evidence Sault was messing with his business, but his intuition told him differently.

He sipped his drink. Eaven said she wasn't with Sault, but they certainly spent a lot of time together behind closed doors. Why lie? Was she really working on his grandmother's pitiful estate for the cash she needed? Or was it attraction? Could be. She'd just been jilted, and Sault was good-looking. Did she wander innocently into Astoria, or did they have a plan before she came here? His questions needed answers. To succeed in life, he had learned to stay two moves ahead of his opponents.

He walked to the kitchen and paused. The Mercer inheritance, muddled in probate, dangled like bait for interested parties. Was that it? Was Sault in town to sneak into the old Mercer mansion like his father had, looking for some proof of his ancestry? Those rumors got Greg's father killed at Frank's orders. Clayton never believed them, though Grandpa Jake had drunkenly ranted that the Captain hid something that threatened his fortune. What if it was true and not the ravings of a drunk? It could still be in there. What if someone bought one of the antiques and found it? He rubbed his chin. He needed to keep Eaven out of there.

Unless... If she was as good as her credentials said, she could go over every stick of furniture before it went out the door. If she found anything, he'd have his man watching. If not in the furnishings, however, he'd have a fine time finding it in the building. Might just have to torch the whole place. After it sold.

He sat his drink on the counter, haunted by a different story he knew wasn't a rumor, one that Frank revealed just before his stroke. A sick family secret that concerned the mother of a dark-haired little boy. If that were ever unearthed, it would undo all his efforts to rewrite the darkest Mercer legacy.

CHAPTER 18

Clayton's reminder of her destitute situation had stirred Eaven's fear from its dark cave to the surface. The resultant broken sleep left her thoughts groggy, her mind off-kilter. Alone in her dingy motel room, she sank into the lumpy chair and stared at the window where little morning light seeped inside.

Bone-weary, she longed to reawaken in the life she had counted on—her home, her husband, and good friends. But it was gone. Crystal had taken her place. Every beautiful scene she had shared with Michael entered her memory entwined with loss. Her fingers reached up and pressed against her temples as if she could squeeze out the pain.

Coach's voice from high school yelled from the past. *Run! Move it! Faster!* No matter how tired she and Paisley had been, he'd been unrelenting. *Get mad,* he would shout. And they would. And they'd win. He had believed her to be a track and field contender for the state championships. She still remembered the shock and disappointment when she'd quit.

She checked her phone again. Nine-thirty and not a word from Michael. Her plan was to meet him before going back to the cottage. He was a thoughtless, self-centered, loser. After their only meeting, her mother had described him in similar words, but Eaven couldn't believe she had been that blind for eighteen years. He *must* have changed.

Half an hour later, he finally called.

She answered her phone. "It's about time."

"Hey. I umm, I can't make it until Wednesday."

"That's two more days! I planned to be on the road tomorrow. What am I supposed to do without...?" She swallowed the rest of her sentence. He didn't need to know her finances were in shambles. He'd always resented her coming from old money, though she had never seen a cent of it.

"Look, Crystal's car broke down in Raymond. Zoe and I are almost there now."

Zoe and Crystal. "I should have just come back," she snapped.

"No, you should have just signed your married name."

"But I'm not married anymore, am I? Tell Fishburn to FAX me the copies."

"His office is closed. It will be faster all around if you just wait for me to bring them to Astoria."

"So, I put my life on hold while you rescue Crystal? How old did you say she was?"

He hung up.

Paying for two more nights would eat a hole in the salary she had earned. She could stay in her car, but as she listened to the wind and rain beat against the thin windowpane, it seemed an insane idea. She tromped downstairs. "Kari, sorry to keep doing this, but is there a chance I can stay two more nights?"

"You bet, and I can give you a discount."

Kari's perkiness helped ease her disappointment.

"Eaven."

She turned to see Greg striding determinedly across the lobby. "May I speak with you?"

Sure, now he wants to talk. "It couldn't wait until I got to the cottage?"

"I couldn't handle being in the cottage today."

She hid her disappointment at losing another day's work. "Why not?"

He frowned. "I need to talk privately. Can we sit over here?" He led the way to a pair of olive and gold chairs on the far side of the empty lobby. After they sat, he said, "I'm sorry. I was rude." Deep lines furrowed his forehead. He pulled out his wallet and removed the neatly folded letter. "This is the letter I got yesterday. My dad wrote this right before he was shot. It's all I have left."

Anger dissipated and her heart hurt seeing this tall, capable man retreat into his boyhood sorrows. "I'm so sorry."

"Before he died, I visited Dad at the jail. He told me he'd answered Frank's late-night summons to the docks, even though it didn't feel right. When he neared the Mercer Shipping office, he tripped on a body and called for help. Seconds later, Frank turned on the light outside his office at the same time a squad car arrived. Frank said the man was Timothy Foyle, that my dad and Foyle hated each other. My dad tried to explain he'd just gotten there, but they arrested him. Two weeks later, Dad was being transferred when he was shot. No one saw where the bullet came from."

"Surely not in this day and age?"

Giving her an incredulous expression, he said, "Where have you been living?" He dropped to his seat. "The letter was written while Dad was in jail. He says there's a document in the Mercer Mansion that proves Captain Mercer was Sebastien's father."

"How would he know about that?"

"Charlie Thornton was a guard when dad was arrested but was also a friend. He told dad he'd lived his whole life in this town and had heard the Mercers' account that Marie was a loose woman—that God Himself judged her with a fiery death. His dad used that story to keep him and his sisters on the straight and narrow. Every parent in town did.

Charlie had worked for the Mercers years before dad's arrest and overheard Jake ranting about needing to find a document the Captain wrote. He'd also heard a drunken confession of what Jake had done to Marie. At that moment, he knew Marie had been innocent. Dad wrote it all down. Charlie was supposed to give the letter to me, but he never sent it."

Eaven shook her head. "You waited all this time for your father's last letter?"

"Yeah. Charlie knew the Mercers would come after him if they found out. Instead, he left an apology and instructions with his sister to send it after he died. His sister didn't have my address, so she kept it. As soon as she heard I was staying at the cottage, she brought it by."

"It sounds like your father went through a lot of trouble to get you that information."

He carefully folded the letter and put it back in his wallet. "Finding that document will be the only thing he and I will ever accomplish together."

"After all the grief the Mercers have caused your family, I think they need to do some compensating." She rummaged through the stack of old newspapers on the lobby table and showed him the photo of the Mercer Mansion. "Before they sell this place, we need to find that document."

"I'll bet anything it's a marriage certificate. Wouldn't that burn Clayton. If you're serious, I'll pay you to find it."

That thought perked her interest, but she couldn't imagine a wealthy man like Captain Mercer committing what amounted to social suicide in that day. "I could check the records. Marriage certificates need to be filed with the county clerk."

"I think your other talents would be more helpful." His smile became seductive, a disingenuous expression that put her on alert.

She crossed her arms. "What do you mean?"

"You have an interesting reputation in the world of antiquities." His mouth twitched. "*House whisperer*. With your gift, I think you could help me find the document." He raised an eyebrow. "That caused you some problems, I gather?"

She blew out a puff of air. "A bit. A pair of Meissen pugs disappeared in an estate I was cataloging." At Greg's blank expression, she explained, "They are extremely valuable models of pug dogs produced at the Meissen factory in Germany. I'd visited the factory with my parents when we lived there. It's what initiated my love of antiques."

"Were you the only one in the estate when they disappeared?"

"No. I had an assistant, Casey Cane, who as much as accused me, though why he turned on me is still a mystery." She swallowed. "I felt desperate. I can sometimes feel sensations in old buildings and have been guided to find things. I felt led up a curved staircase. To my left, a shallow alcove was built into the stone wall. On a hunch, I pressed my hands onto it and pushed. The wall moved."

"You're kidding?"

"No. After I caught my breath, I shoved the wall inward. Behind it was a small room with one high window. The Meissen pugs sat on a black lacquered table. I was so excited, I gathered them and rushed to the office where the officials sat and tried to explain how I found them."

"But they didn't believe you."

"No. I'd never heard the term, *house whisperer*. I think someone made it up on the spot. It wasn't complimentary. I was put on probation though was never actually accused. But it didn't matter. I met Michael on holiday and never looked back."

He tapped the tips of his fingers together. "I think it's a gift that could come in handy." A grin spread across his handsome face as though delighted about the very thing that ruined her career.

She lifted her chin. "You think the house will just tell me where something is hidden? It doesn't work that way."

"It did once. Look, Eaven, if they married, that makes me heir to half the Mercer fortune—half of everything that belongs to Clayton."

She examined the photo of the old house. Its mystery and the possible freedom it held for Greg intrigued her. Her mind raced at the idea of rifling through the old mansion for the hidden document. Maybe her skills could be useful.

His phone rang. "Excuse me." He stepped away and said, "Hey, man." As he listened, a scornful grin marred his face. "That will hurt. I'll meet you in ten."

She stood. "Before you leave, let's settle on my compensation. I want to get started."

He nodded. "Text me an amount." He rushed out the door to his car and sped away in the direction of town.

She relaxed into the chair. Now, this was a job she could get excited about. She didn't want to take advantage of him, but she was also done with living on the edge. She texted, *My base fee is one thousand dollars a week plus expenses, meaning decent lodging and a food allowance. I can only promise two weeks. And under the circumstances, I can't guarantee I'll find what you are looking for.*

Within minutes, he texted back, *Agreed. I've arranged a room at the River's Glory Bed and Breakfast. I believe it qualifies as "decent" lodging. Thank you.*

Elation fluttered like a school of minnows in her stomach. That would be seed money for her store. She grinned and sucked in her bottom lip. She'd loved to see Clayton's smug face when she found Marie's marriage certificate. Where in that old house could it be? Curiosity burned like a day-old sunburn.

CHAPTER 19

After she said goodbye to Kari, Eaven loaded her bags and drove to the River's Glory Bed and Breakfast, a gorgeous old Victorian home perched on the hillside. Parked at the curb, she pounded happily on the steering wheel.

The owner met her at the door and introduced herself as Claire. Though an attractive older woman, her brows and mouth pinched while showing Eaven to her room. "I trust you'll be comfortable." She held out the key. "This room is single occupancy, only." Before Eaven could think to respond, Claire was down the stairs.

"Thanks for the reminder," Eaven spoke to the closed door. She unpacked and took a moment to gaze out the picture window at the wide river. Sunlight sparkled off the tips of the waves as if in welcome, causing her heart to feel it would swell out of her chest. Her life was beginning. It was really happening. Feeling sheepish for all the complaining, her eyes lifted. "Thank You."

After tucking the last of her clothes in a drawer, she put her attention on the thing at hand. They needed a plan. She texted Greg. *Can you meet me here?*

Close to two o'clock, she glided down the elegant steps that reminded her of her parent's home. Growing up in high society had been challenging, but sometimes it was...glorious. Smiling, she entered the parlor through the open French doors. Light gold walls with pristine white molding amplified the sunshine in the room.

Greg rose from one of the winged-back chairs and shook her hand. He smiled into her eyes. "I see you like your new digs."

She met his gaze briefly. He'd warmed since receiving his father's letter. "It's lovely, thank you."

"Claire left a plate of cookies on the buffet and said we could use this room for our meetings."

"Great." Next to the cookies stood a crystal water pitcher and glasses, and an electric coffee pot with cream and sugar on a tray. "The coffee smells divine." She poured them each a cup and sat in the matching chair next to his.

He sat forward. "I've been thinking about the plan. You can pose as a potential buyer for the mansion and examine possible hiding places in the furnishings. If anything looks promising, offer to buy it. I'll cover it."

Hmm. "Suppose the Captain did hide the document in a piece of furniture, how do you know it wasn't already sold or taken by another family member?"

"Jake locked the house after the Captain's death and refused to let anyone in. People began to believe it was haunted and he let them."

"Clayton doesn't seem to have a problem with it."

"He's the last Mercer, grounded in greed. I doubt he believes in the spirit world."

"Okay, but the document could be anywhere, not just in the furnishings. And your idea of me posing as a buyer is too easy to disprove. It would work better if I can spend more time and thoroughly examine anything of interest. The newspaper said the house is to be sold without the furnishings. I could offer my services to Clayton." Even as she spoke, she recalled her last words to him. He would never agree to hire her.

Greg was already shaking his head. "No. I don't want you anywhere near him."

She studied the concern in his face. "What's he going to do, kill me and lock my body in the refrigerator? It will be crawling with realtors and their clients as soon as they open the doors. Trust me, I've seen scenarios like this."

He pursed his lips. "No. We'll do it my way."

What? "I'm the expert here."

"And I'm your employer."

Yes, he was. And the whole reason she was saving money was so one day she'd be her own boss. She checked her watch. "Okay, but first I'm headed to the Clapsop County Offices to check for a marriage certificate. It's not likely I'll find anything, but I want to check it off my list."

"Yeah, I've got stuff to do too."

She hesitated as heat washed over her face. Trying not to feel like a little beggar, she reminded herself this was business. "Sometime soon, I'll need a three hundred-dollar advance for expenses."

"Sure." He pulled a roll of cash from his leather jacket and handed her three large bills.

She tried not to speculate as he stashed the money back into his pocket. "Thank you."

He nodded and left.

She put most of the money in her room safe and sat down. Pretending to be a buyer was awkward. She'd never been good at acting and felt certain the realtor would see right through her, but that was what Greg wanted. Before leaving for the county offices, she called the real estate office.

A man answered. "Jensen Realty, Tad Jensen here. May I help you?"

"Hello. I'm calling regarding the Mercer Mansion. When is the soonest I can arrange an appointment to see inside?"

He cleared his throat. "Is this a serious inquiry or just curiosity?"

Snagged already. She took an offensive position as her mother had on occasion. "I am Eaven Alexander of the Charleston Alexanders. Is there someone else I can deal with?"

He faltered. "No. I'm sorry. It's just that half the town is turning out to see what's inside. I'll be glad to help you."

She continued in an icy voice. "Well, I'm not from this town and I'm certainly not a curiosity seeker. Is the property available for inspection or not?"

"Yes, of course. That is, we'll begin showing it when it clears probate, probably in about three weeks."

Oh. She couldn't hang around here for three weeks. "I'm only in town for a short while. Are you certain there is no way I can see inside sooner?"

"Not without Mr. Mercer's approval."

"I know Mr. Mercer. I'll give him a call. Thank you."

Sheez, what was she thinking? She stood and paced. Clayton was her adversary, but he held the keys to any forward movement. She bit her bottom lip and wished she hadn't reacted so badly, even if he'd deserved it. She hated eating crow.

Worse, she hated pretending, burying her feelings to get what she needed. Really? She winced. Maybe she did have a lot of practice. This time, however, the price of the charade was worth watching him get his due. She took out his business card and dialed the number.

He answered. "Well, Eaven Alexander."

Her breath caught. It sounded like he knew she'd be calling. "Hello, Mr. Mercer. I wanted to apologize for my rudeness. I've been under a lot of pressure lately."

"Yes, divorce is hard on a woman your age."

She gripped the phone, ready to launch through it. "Be that as it may, I shouldn't have directed my anger at you when you were trying to...protect me." She closed her eyes and seethed at the taste of crow.

"Yes, it was. Thank you for recognizing your error in judgment. Goodbye."

"Wait, please. It turns out, I have some time on my hands here. I don't know how you knew, but I do need the work. Would you consider hiring me to appraise your antiques? I have quite an extensive background." She waited.

"Yes, I know. Let's have dinner tonight and discuss it. I'll text you the address."

Swallowing the protest that swelled in her throat, she said, "Sure." She sat still in her room. The serene control and lack of empathy she'd witnessed in his face chilled her. *Psychopath* came to mind. Gathering her purse, she headed to the county office. Tension crept up the back of her neck at the task she'd just taken on. She was about to oppose Clayton Mercer. Not just oppose, deceive. She'd better be very good at it.

At seven o'clock, Eaven drove to the Bridge Bistro. Inside the door, she paused. Nice. Not the usual bar and grill she and Michael had been able to afford. She hadn't expected Clayton to spring for something so upscale.

"Hello, Eaven." Clayton stood in the foyer and took the raincoat from her shoulders.

"Your table is ready, Mr. Mercer." The waiter led them upstairs to a table that overlooked the restaurant below and the Columbia beyond. He pulled out their chairs.

"Thank you, Donald." Clayton's manner was gracious, elegant.

She tried to smile naturally. "Thank you for your invitation. What a lovely spot."

His gaze moved from her hair to her eyes. "Lovely. Would you like a drink?"

His smile transformed his stocky features from formidable to almost handsome in a rugged sort of way. She could tell he knew it and played along. "Yes, please. A glass of Viognier."

"I'll join you." After selecting a bottle, he gave the order to their server and started the conversation. "So, tell me why you like old things."

While they enjoyed an appetizer of crab-avocado crostini, she shared the highlights of her passion for antiques then turned the conversation to see what she could learn. "What made you decide on a sport fishing business?"

A shadow crossed his face. "You can't be in town too long before the sordid facts of the Mercer family enter the conversation. They were all abusive, drug-smuggling addicts. Not anything I'm interested in. I left it all and attended college out of state."

She hadn't expected a full disclosure. "But you came back?"

He sighed. "After university, I could have moved elsewhere, but why let my father's behavior drive me from my home? I know the area, the river. Love being out on it."

"I feel the same way." She smiled, glad she'd found a common thread to discuss this evening.

His face grew serious. "Before we continue, I would like to clarify the facts about Gina. I met her on an extended business trip and brought her to Astoria. Unfortunately, I didn't realize until I'd already fallen in love that she suffers from bi-polar disease. We have been together for four years and it's gotten worse every year. Obviously, you heard about my dog." His wide jaw clenched. "She left me. Sadly, I hope it's for good. I need a new start." He wiped his mouth with his napkin.

Dang. She hated when someone she didn't like poked her empathy button. "It's a difficult situation. I'm sorry for acting so callously."

"It's forgotten." The server brought their dinner, wild salmon with a cream caper sauce.

She had planned to order something less expensive, but Clayton insisted she would love the sherry *beurre* sauce. She did.

"Another sore subject is Greg Sault. I'm sure I know the story he's been telling you, but are you open to hearing the other side?"

Am I? Even if he lied, it would be valuable to understand him better. She nodded.

He described a similar story to Greg's but denied Marie's claims that Captain Mercer was the father of her child. "Even at the time, it was common knowledge she was a wild girl. The Captain was a wealthy man. For generations, we've had to fight for our family's reputation and battle the Saults' attempts to extort money from us. They've been unrelenting. I thought it ended when Greg left, but obviously not so." He studied her. "With the estate in probate, it seems the obvious reason he's back."

She did her best to hold a poker face. "His grandmother passed away and he asked me to appraise her furnishings."

He glanced up from his plate and held her eyes. "She passed away two years ago."

Her chest tightened. "He didn't mention when. Thank you for telling me."

"He also blames my family for his father's death. Did he mention that when his father was shot, the police had an eyewitness? They fingered the son of the man Russell Sault murdered, but he disappeared before they could book him."

Greg had left that out too. "No. It appears he has tarnished the truth a bit."

"A bit. Glad you understand." He sighed. "You would have been better off leaving town."

It was time to put him in the hot seat. "So, if you don't like a visitor, you have them shot at?"

His forehead wrinkled. "Shot?"

Not wanting to owe him another apology, she said, "I know you've been having me followed, so I assumed you'd also ordered your little friend to fire at me in front of Greg's cottage."

Unruffled, he said, "Yes, my man did follow you, to see what your intentions were, but, no, I don't have women shot at."

Either he was a great liar, which she supposed he was capable of, or someone else had wanted to scare her. Or worse. "Thank you for clarifying that. I hated to think you'd scare a woman away from a legitimate job."

"Working for Greg might not be as legitimate as you suppose, but I understand your desperate situation."

Her jaw clenched. She didn't comment, unable to decide if he lacked tact or enjoyed provoking her.

"I've decided to let you manage the sale of my furnishings. However, because of my funds being tied up in probate, I won't pay your commission until I receive the cash. Tad will take you through the house. I would show you around myself, but I have only been there once." He shrugged. "And I don't happen to like old things."

"Not everyone does." Though delighted she was in, her stomach churned at the conflict she'd stepped into. She kept cool and smiled when he refilled her glass. "I'm confident I can find buyers and secure a good price on your antiques."

He leaned back, eyes prodding. "You've been out of the business for twenty years. Who would you still know?"

Her mouth opened, surprised, after his apparent digging, that he called her ability into question.

Eyes steady, he watched for her reactions. They were enacting a cat and mouse game, and she had the sinking feeling she was not the cat. It seemed he deliberately kept her off balance. He was calculating. Intelligent.

She held his gaze. "I'm good at doing research."

"I'll bet you're good at whatever you put your mind to. Let's meet again after you have a chance to examine my property." He paid the bill and helped her into her coat. "It's been a pleasure getting to know you. Good night, Eaven." He lightly touched her shoulder and opened her car door.

"Good night." She shut the door and waited for the engine to warm in the parking lot. The night had been a challenge, but she'd learned a lot. He was highly educated and well-traveled, yet modest when he discussed the projects he'd initiated to lift the town's economy. She didn't want to believe it, but maybe some of the positive things people said about him were true.

And maybe Greg was still chasing the ghosts of Mercers long gone. For now, she would watch, take her time to see through the cloak of mystery that surrounded both men. In the past, she'd been quick to make uninformed judgments of character. With devastating results.

CHAPTER 20

Clayton drove up the hill, enjoying the lingering essence of his dinner with Eaven. Surprise had brightened her eyes and softened her features when she'd tasted the wine and the dishes he'd suggested. His chest filled, knowing she'd been impressed.

It had been fascinating to watch her lie. Pretend interest. Get him talking about himself to find some weak spot. She also omitted she'd checked the county records for all the Mercer marriage certificates. Greg had really sold his story. Clayton grinned. So, had he.

His phone rang insistently. "What?"

"Tony was hijacked. They stole all forty grand and the Oxy!"

"You said you'd be ready for them," he screamed. He stretched a kink from his neck. That meant he had no product to sell his customers. Delays in payment would strain his standing with his supplier. With the White Jade Cartel, the first offense involved the loss of a digit, their choice. But he could be tough too. "Contact Jin. Tell him we need more. Now."

Angler stumbled over his words. "I just spoke to him. Says he's out of product, but I think he has a buyer who's paying premium prices."

"That slime!"

"What do you want me to do?"

"Follow Jin. See who he meets. Take pictures."

"Will do. It has to be someone with a lot of cash."

"Yeah, maybe my cash." He slammed his fist on the steering wheel and cursed. He hadn't dismantled Frank's organization just to let others grab the gold. New dealers were swarming from Mexico and China, passing through Astoria from Canada to Portland. But this was a small town. It wouldn't take him long to find out who they were. He drove home and was pulling under his carport when his phone rang again.

"Got the product?" Rex asked.

He scratched his neck. "There's been a delay."

"What! I have people crawling out of their skin."

Outside his carport, he studied the night sky. Not perfect weather, but not a storm. He'd have to do this the hard way, take Bransen and motor to Victoria. "I'll be back in twenty-four hours."

"What about our clients?"

"Tell them to smoke pot and take a couple days off work." He hung up. Not the way to do business. He opened his satchel and took out the last of his cash, screaming internally against the rage that never left him. His fists clenched. Jin will wish he'd never crossed a Mercer. So will his new buyer.

CHAPTER 21

Claire ran the River's Glory efficiently, but Eaven felt she lacked the warmth she'd experienced at other bed and breakfasts. From what she gathered, Claire's late husband had helped run the inn until he'd gotten sick. She didn't mention what took him, but Eaven recognized the ravages of sorrow when the innkeeper wasn't smiling at her customers. Or when baking alone. Regardless, the woman was brilliant in the kitchen.

Eaven ran her fingers over the crisp linen at the beautifully set table while chewing a bit of lemony pastry. Her heart filled with gratitude about more than the dessert. The knowledge she'd gained about antiques and architecture might help Greg in a significant way, one she'd never considered. And it was providing seed money for her dream. She smiled at the thought of her own store in Charleston—a desire that continued to surprise her. But first, she needed to find the document. And if it didn't exist? That wasn't her responsibility, but she'd search as thoroughly as was possible.

She stopped chewing, hating to admit that Clayton intimidated her. He'd also shed a different light on Greg. Was he trouble? He disappeared a lot and never mentioned what he was doing in Astoria. She'd only seen him with one other person, a man in a long raincoat, whose face was obscured by his hat. Also, that wad of hundred-dollar bills stuck in the back of her mind. Did she trust him? No need. This was a short-term job. She didn't need to trust him or anyone else.

Later that morning, she treaded down the stairs on the lush carpet and met Greg in the glowing parlor. Two weeks in this place would cost him a small fortune, but he didn't act concerned. She smiled and closed the French doors to deliver her first report in private. "I searched through all available county records. No trace of a marriage certificate for Edward Mercer except with Justine Reynolds. Here's a copy of that. No marriage record at all for Marie Sault."

He shrugged. "It doesn't mean it doesn't exist. We'll find it."

His confidence seemed premature. "I don't think Captain Mercer was the kind of man to do the right thing by Marie. Do you? *Really*?"

"You're the one who convinced me to pursue this. Are you trying to talk yourself out of a job?"

She shied away from his huffiness. "Not at all. It's just that men in that day didn't do that kind of thing, and I don't have much history to go on to validate Marie's story over the Mercers.'"

He glared. "You're siding with them?"

She shook her head. "No. I'm sorry it came out that way. I think if I had more information about your family and the Mercers, it would help me see the whole picture."

"The letter proves the affair. I don't know how the rest can help." When she continued to wait for an answer, he exhaled and sat back. "After the deaths of Marie and the Captain, Jake vilified Sebastien. The kid was only seven when he was orphaned and moved into the cottage with Marie's mother, Michelle Sault. She did what she could, but the kid grew up in a mean world. Fought a lot." He gave a humorless half-grin. "Gran said he won most of the time. Despite the Mercers, he did all right. Married a local girl and had a son, Jeffrey Sault."

"And the Mercer's attacked him too?"

"You could say that. The Ku Klux Klan moved into Astoria near the time of Jeffrey's birth. A lot of other Oregon cities caved to the Klan's agenda, but the Astorians were mostly immigrants with different religions. They unraveled the Klan's power, but that didn't stop their influence. Jake Mercer had been a reigning Klansman—one of the most violent and bigoted. Folks didn't want to get on the bad side of him and the *good old boys.*

"It was after Jeffrey married into an affluent Catholic family that Jake and Frank Mercer started new attacks, rehashed stories about the Saults' supposedly sordid past. They were ostracized from *polite* society. His wife, Rebecca grew weak from the strain and died during a miscarriage with their second child."

Eaven shook her head. "Bully begat bully, begat bully."

His eyes pierced hers from under his narrowed eyebrows. "There's only one bully left, and he won't live forever."

Watching his growing agitation, she moved to calmer waters. "Your family suffered a lot of pain through the years."

"And then they murdered my dad. But at least he made sure I knew there was proof about the Captain and Marie."

His story lent weight to the Sault side of things. She gauged his temper and decided she'd better come clean. "I had dinner with Clayton—"

He jumped up, veins bulging in his neck. "What?"

"Calm down. I had to. Besides, it worked. He's making arrangements for me to evaluate and sell the furnishings in the mansion."

Greg ran his long fingers through his black hair. "Don't get close to him, Eaven."

She swallowed. "Clayton won't hurt me." The words didn't sound as confident to her ears as she'd supposed. He'd been a complete gentleman last night.

His eyes held hers. The muscles in his jaw tightened. "Maybe I should call this off. You don't know the kind of hurt the Mercers are capable of."

"Absolutely not. This is my job and I plan to finish it. In fact, I need to leave for the Heritage Museum soon to do some research."

He shook his head, his face burdened with a frown. "When is your appointment at the mansion?"

"Tomorrow at eleven."

They stood and he held her eyes. "Promise you'll be careful." He touched her shoulder and left.

His touch carried a message of concern, warmth. Her hand covered the spot, then brushed it off. The longing to be cared about had been her undoing.

So far, Clayton's allegations against Greg didn't add up. Marie's letters provided a solid story. She felt her determination mounting to learn the truth. Yes, Clayton was a handful, and the Mercers had a reputation, but she refused to let his bluster daunt her efforts. Really, what could he do?

CHAPTER 22

Clayton stumbled at another night sound and crashed into something on the dock. "What the..." He sighed and righted the bucket he had kicked over. Unworldly shadows flitted around the docks in the black of night. He imagined the ghosts of Chinese cannery workers hopping silently like ninjas from post to rotting post—the only remnants left of the pier that had fallen into the water during the 1922 fire. Despite his disdain for the esoteric, a chill ran up his spine.

After fumbling with his keys, he shoved the correct one into the deadbolt and opened the dented metal door to his office. It creaked and launched a rustle of river rats in all directions. Something intangible remained and sent crawling fingers along his spine. He stepped inside and switched on the light. Instantly, the old spirits scampered back to their shadows.

When he closed the thick red velvet drapes, dust whirled to the wooden floor and spiders crawled into hiding. The once opulent space created to impress Captain Mercer's passengers had disintegrated under Jake and Frank's management who obviously didn't believe human trafficking needed smart digs for success. The scent of opium mixed with decades of waterfront mold lingered inside the small room.

Despite the challenges, a sense of satisfaction grew in his gut as he gazed around the old marine office. Warped mahogany cabinets lined two of the walls. The Captain had them handmade from imported wood. Now it was all his. His to burn. Unlike his ancestors, he would purge the old and create his own legacy—a fortune and reputation that would soon live above the shadow world.

But it wasn't perfected yet. His new enterprise kept hitting roadblocks. Surprise Coast Guard inspections of the marina had increased. Eyes seemed to be everywhere. Tonight, with seconds to spare, he had slipped between the buildings to avoid a patrol. It would have been hard to explain the amount of cash he carried. He dropped his satchel on the grime-coated desk.

After he counted out enough cash to buy replacement product in Victoria, he felt under the desk for the soft spot cut into the threadbare Persian carpet. A hard push caused a thirty by thirty-inch section of carpeted floor to spring open like a hungry mouth ready to devour him. Instead, he shoved the bag of extra cash into the cavern. It rattled against the steps and landed with a soft thump at the bottom. He closed the lid to the low-ceilinged smugglers' hideout and applauded grandpa Jake for creating this space for his *passengers*.

Tonight, fentanyl, not trafficking, occupied his mind. An uneasy feeling twisted in the pit of his stomach. An employee's recent overdose had sent a ripple through his network. The Shady 80's they were moving somehow carried triple the fentanyl potency. He grimaced. Nine junkies he serviced between Astoria and Portland overdosed within a two-week period. He refused to pity any druggie, but he couldn't afford the attention.

He plopped onto the swivel chair with his phone and thumbed through the photos his man sent of Jin's meeting with the mystery buyer. Tall and thin, wearing a long coat, only the man's jaw and neck showed from under his hat. Ragged gray hair hung around his large ear. Slack, lifeless skin made him look strung out. The filthy scum walked away with his product. He swore and called Angler. "Got the photos. Did you follow the mystery man?"

Angler paused. "Thought you wanted me following Jin."

He growled. "We *know* where Jin hangs." He wrung the phone with his fist until it trembled. "I need to know who the stranger is and who he's working for. Follow Jin and see if he contacts the guy again." He slammed the phone onto the desk.

Did Jin's brother know about the betrayal? If Jin had the cartel's blessing, Clayton would have to watch his back after he retaliated. And he would retaliate. Exploring possibilities, he drummed the desk with his thumbs. His attention drifted to the eight-inch rusted shark hook that hung on the wall.

His hands stilled and his teeth clenched at what he had to do. If he wanted to protect his operation, he couldn't afford another betrayal. He dialed Angler. "Changed my mind. Bring our pal Jin to my boat now. Time to chum the water."

CHAPTER 23

Astoria, Oregon, October 1899

"Let me see that bruise." Edward Mercer sat the seven-year-old boy on his lap in the dining room. Light from the glistening chandelier reflected off the highly polished Chippendale table. He loved beautiful things, his son highest among his treasures.

Sebastien swiped at the tear. "I'm sorry I cried."

Edward pretended a serious frown. "We'll let it pass this time." He stroked the boy's fine hair, black like his. His or any number of other men. The nasty rumors hovered persistently and sought to slide a barb into his soul. Marie was a beautiful woman. He had seen how men desired her. His jaw tightened, concerned that her tender affections toward him had cooled these last months.

The child's clear emerald eyes gazed at him. Marie's eyes. "Okay young man, go and visit Mr. MacDonald. Tell him I said to let you feed Breezy."

"Yes, sir." Sebastien squirmed off the Captain's lap.

Marie opened the back-porch door, and Edward watched Sebastien speed out to the carriage house to visit the caretaker, Guy MacDonald. The handsome MacDonald was a charmer with the ladies, Marie included. Edward had often seen her blush under his teasing. Distaste rose in his throat over the festering thorn: Did he have one son or two?

Edward studied the hard set of Marie's mouth, the worried lines that wrinkled the perfect skin on her forehead. He cleared his throat. "Same boys?"

She nodded. "Without a father, he has become a target for bullies. I fear for him." A tear trickled down her cheek. "Edward, I cannot bear to see him degraded. I've written to my sister in San Francisco to see if Sebastien and I can begin a new life there. I will keep the story that Sebastien's father died at sea."

He shook his head. "No. I need you here."

She pulled her shoulders back. "Justine has been dead almost a year and you've made it clear there is no future for me." Her face held a defiant pout, her spunk heightening her allure.

"There will be no talk of leaving." He rubbed the ache in his arm. In truth, he loved the boy, knew in his heart Sebastien was his son. But marry Marie? She was stunning but just a maid from poor French emigrants. The leading families of Astoria might not ridicule him for siring a bastard if they found out, but they would destroy him for marrying a common housemaid, no matter how attractive. He ignored her downcast expression. "Go out and let me think."

He knew, almost to the penny, the extent of the fortune he'd amassed. All would pass to his heirs. Jake was already a bully and a spendthrift. Sebastien was bright and full of courage, even at his young age. But claiming him and his mother would come at a price to his ego. A very high price.

He pressed on the ache in his chest, a reminder that he needed to make decisions sooner rather than later to safeguard the Mercer fortune.

CHAPTER 24

Astoria, Oregon, Current Day

Clayton sat in the Boxster and warmed the engine. The trip up and back to Victoria had been savage. The seas had been tranquil enough, but once they heaved Jin's body overboard, his screams broke the quiet as the fins increased. Bransen had cut the line to save his fishing pole.

He pulled on his driving gloves. Heck of a trip. People shouldn't force him to act against his even-tempered nature. The duffle bag of opioid tablets stuffed under the passenger's seat had cost extra time and money. All because of Jin's greed—and that skeletal man with the big ears. He scrolled through his phone and sent photos that carried a clear message to Jin's gang. And his people as well. A two-for-one object lesson. There would be no more mishaps.

Rex met him at his office to pick up the product. "Heard lots of threats from our customers about getting their supplies elsewhere. Hope this doesn't happen again."

"It won't. What have Eaven and Sault been up to while I was gone?"

Rex shrugged. "Eaven's movements seem benign. Other than the River's Glory, she spent a few hours in a museum. Sault's been more elusive—good at ditching our guys."

Clayton set the duffle in front of Rex and peered hard into his eyes. "It's your job to keep on top of him."

Rex hefted the bag and quickly dropped his eyes. "Yes, sir."

Clayton drove home. It was done. He fell into his chair, brutally aware this was not how he saw himself. But sometimes a man had to act in unfortunate ways.

CHAPTER 25

"Claire, that was a fabulous breakfast, again." Mr. Ewing folded his napkin neatly on the table.

Eaven agreed, amused with the quirky English novelist, the only other guest. His shabby gray hair and rumpled clothing, not to mention his accent, conjured a character from a book she'd read. She added, "It's a good thing I don't live here, or I would be rolling down these hills in no time."

Satisfaction relaxed Claire's face for a moment. "I'm glad you enjoyed it." She cleared the table with delicate, heavily wrinkled hands, only managing a few dishes per trip to the kitchen. Eaven recognized the strain and would have offered to help, but Claire guarded her domain.

Instead, Eaven turned to Mr. Ewing. "What brings you to Astoria?"

"Tying up loose ends on a story. Think there might be a murder." He wiggled his silver eyebrows and grinned. "How did you come to be here?"

Not feeling at liberty to explain her work with Greg, she said, "Exploring the town. Meeting people."

He nodded. "Ah, an adventurer. Where do you hail from?"

"I just drove down from Washington." And I'm homeless. Instantly, her mood plummeted.

"I see. The lone traveler." Keen gray eyes shown from his gaunt face. He studied her, a question on his partially open lips, then seemed to change his mind. He excused himself. "Enjoy your exploration."

Were her wounds that transparent?

He started out of the room, then turned back. "If I may offer a comment? I can see the strength that emanates from you, but I also sense the sadness. At my age, I've found that joy is always just around the corner, ready to pounce on you when you least expect it." He cocked his eyebrow then entered his room on the main floor.

Her heart warmed at his kindness. He was right. She returned to her room to get ready for another meeting with Greg and glanced in the full-length floor mirror. Jeans, shirt, tennis shoes—the same things she'd worn for years. It was lake gear. Sporty. She frowned. Crystal wore flowing gauze skirts and had tattoos. Exotic. Feminine. Could she really blame Michael for being attracted? "Absolutely."

She perched on a chair and exchanged her tennis shoes for the leather designer boots she'd purchased in London years before. Then she pulled on a fitted green sweater that complimented the rich chocolate of her hair. She smiled. The look still worked.

After gathering her research notes from the Heritage Museum and adding the small stack of photos from the cottage, she went downstairs to meet Greg.

His eyes swept over her. "Nice sweater—good color." He abruptly dropped his eyes to her notes and sat. "What did you find?"

The appreciation he'd expressed took her aback. It also buoyed her confidence, something that had been lacking in recent years. "Thanks." She opened a large envelope and pulled out copies of old black and white photographs from 1879. "I compared these with others in the Heritage Museum. See? They were taken by a professional photographer at the completion of the Captain's mansion. Marie must have taken them to the cottage."

He flipped through the photographs. "Why so many of the fireplaces?"

"I don't know, but I'll check them for hidden compartments along with the furnishings."

He opened his mouth to reply but his phone rang. "Excuse me." He stepped a few feet away into the wide hall. As he listened, he grew still. "He took pictures? Send them." He waited, then clicked open the message with his thumb. His hand shook as he scrolled.

She thought he might drop the phone. What on earth?

He leaned heavily against the door jam and spoke to his caller. "Did Jin's brother see these?" He scowled while he listened, gripping his forehead with his free hand. "If they won't play with us anymore, we'll have to get to him another way." When he returned, his face was pale, his eyes shifted in every direction but hers. "I need to go. Have everything you need?"

She nodded, watching a series of hard emotions distort his features. "What's wrong?"

He stood in front of her, reached to take her hands, then stopped and curled his hands into fists. "An associate was brutally murdered. The killer sent out pictures, Mercer-style. Be very careful while you search for the document. Make it obvious you're doing exactly what Clayton has asked. Make sure you take a notebook. And a camera."

She threw a warning look. "I'm a professional."

He took a deep breath and nodded. "Okay."

After he left, she remained in the parlor, its calm beauty at odds with the tremors in her hands while she put away the photos. Yes, she was a professional, and had faced irate beneficiaries before, but Greg was accusing Clayton of murder. She recalled him being hard, but rational, committed to getting out from under his family's dark shadow, not someone who would brutally murder another man. Greg must be overreacting.

CHAPTER 26

Eaven had succeeded in gaining access, now what would she find in the old mansion? As she approached the Jensen Real Estate office, her breathing accelerated with excitement. This was how she'd felt in Europe just before entering every new estate, only this one held more than treasures, it might rewrite the Sault family's story.

And Clayton's. Her hand pressed against the tense muscles of her stomach. A local man had been murdered. Greg called the victim an associate. In what business?

A young man waved at her through the office window as she approached. She waved back and entered. Just how close would she be watched today, and by whom? "I'm Eaven Alexander. I have an appointment to see the Mercer Mansion."

"Oh." His smile faded. "I'm Tad Jensen." He closed his computer. "My father left instructions to show you around the mansion. Said you're checking out the furnishings."

"Yes. I'll be doing a detailed evaluation."

He huffed. "That doesn't really fall under my job description."

Hmm. Then maybe spying on her didn't either. "I'm sure Mr. Mercer can straighten this out."

His eyes widened. "No. I'll take you—it's really not a problem."

"Good."

His shoulders slouched. "I'm getting showings scheduled, but I know most of them are curiosity seekers with no intention of buying."

"Real estate is a hard business. Hope it's worth your effort."

"Me too." He glanced at her leather boots. "It's good you wore solid shoes. I have a flashlight we can use. We're afraid to use the original electricity from the 1890's. Might start a fire."

"That bad?"

He shrugged. "It was quite a showplace, has a lot of value as a historical landmark. It also sits on prime view property." He offered her a sales packet from a large stack. "Just in case you know someone."

Printed on the front page was a sepia photo of the mansion when new, and another of it in its current condition. Her finger traced the plumb lines behind the sagging porch. "It looks as though it was built with great care."

"The Captain used only the best materials, workers, and decorators, although most folks thought it over the top. I toured it with my dad when Clayton opened it for the first time. There's a lot of grandiose furniture, but it sat in there for years. Doubt there's much value."

"Well, let's go see." She followed Tad up the street and stopped her car outside the Mercer Mansion. The decaying structure seemed to loom over her. Hovering black clouds over the city added to the surrealism.

On the side, rounded windows covered in grime spoke of the building's lost beauty. A thick, dead branch leaned precariously over the north dormer window that rose from the third story.

Above her, something flitted from the front dormer. There it was again. Her pulse quickened. Behind one of the diamond paned windows, a face turned away. She blinked, uncertain of what she'd seen.

As Tad approached, she wrenched her eyes away from the window. "Is someone already inside?"

His attention darted to the attic windows and back"

"Ghosts?" she asked.

"I don't believe in them, but strange things have been reported over the years. Ready?" They navigated the broken concrete steps that led up from the street through a sloping bank of weeds and ended on a cracked walkway. The rotting wood stairs creaked with their weight. Tad stepped onto the moss-colonized wood porch. "This whole thing should probably be removed and rebuilt. The house has good bones if someone is into restoration."

She pulled at a peel of moldy paint. "And if they have a million bucks."

On the north side of the porch, rusted iron trellises leaned away, pulled earthward by dead climbing roses that had perished along with the Captain. The wide entry door, a faded, stained piece of oak, was the only thing on the front porch that still stood plumb.

He pointed to the rusted screw holes around the sills. "Clayton had all the plywood removed from the windows last week to prepare it for sale. It didn't take long for the criminal element to figure it out. We installed this heavier lock after a neighbor saw someone on the porch and called the police. Whoever it was fled before the squad car arrived." He unlocked the dead bolt and pushed open the door.

She stepped inside and let the sensations drift toward her. Anxiety. Desperation. Another emotion, more violent, also pervaded the room. The filmy windows that flanked the front door cast a dim light inside the foyer. As she advanced, even that light was consumed by the thick darkness oozing from the near-black interior. Two tapered columns with acanthus capitals stood guard at the entrance to the main rooms. They supported a heavy cornice artistically incised with vines and vipers. "All pine, stained to look like mahogany."

"Yep," Tad said. "That's done a lot here. Had plenty of pine in the local forests. It lowered the cost of importing." He passed through one of the three doors off the entry. "This is the sitting room." Thick velvet drapes covered the long windows. He secured them to wall hooks with old rope tassels. Still, minimal light streamed in. "The original carpet must have been an expensive asset."

Her nose crinkled at the acrid smell of mold. "Not anymore." She ran her fingers over the settees that clustered near the fireplace—ornate Louis XV style. "Now here's an asset." Despite their original Aubusson upholstered cushions shredded by rats, and carved legs thick with dust, she assigned them a high value.

Chairs, paintings, and statues stuffed every shadowy corner of the room. Several pieces could house hidden compartments. Almost drooling, she made notes on her wireless tablet and took a few photographs. After briefly examining several pieces, she moved to a chest-on-chest dresser and ran her fingers down the edge to feel for a latch.

"Searching for a spring?"

She swung around and studied his face. He'd been hovering, watching which pieces interested her, no doubt on Clayton's orders. A shiver passed over her like a light web. She shook it off. "Furnishings with hidden compartments are more valuable."

He shrugged. "I don't see the value in this junk, but I thought this was cool." He directed her attention to the white and black marble fireplace. Its arched crown nearly reached the high ceiling. Ancient smoke had plumed from the firebox and blanketed the mantel with a dark film. Bronze inlays of vipers wriggling up slender trees adorned the mantel leg.

She stroked the cold metal. "My studies on snake symbolism uncovered many meanings, from fertility and rebirth, to sinister and vindictive. However, snakes can also represent guardians, protectors that would hold and defend their ground." From what she had learned, Captain Mercer would have fought to the death to keep what was his.

After she surveyed the room, she said, "I'll need a lot more time here, a week at least."

"That's up to Clayton."

"From what I've seen so far, he'll agree."

"The library is the most impressive room. This way."

They stepped into a grand library through a massive ten-foot entrance, its pocket door resting in the wall. Above the wainscoting, old wallpaper hung in shreds, revealing water stains. She noticed that the junctions between the ceiling and walls remained surprisingly plumb.

On the far wall stood three matching French Country breakfront library bookcases. Really? She stepped toward them and gasped at the rare inlay she had only seen once in a French castle. Though camouflaged with decades of cobwebs and dust, these alone would fetch a small fortune. The shelves were packed with books. She dusted a couple of them. Very old books. "Why didn't the Captain's son just sell these after he died?"

"Hard to say. Rumor has it, Jake despised everything that belonged to his father. Said he wanted everyone to see it rot before their eyes. Each generation acted a bit more *off* than the last. I mean, not Clayton." The uneasy pinch of his face told her he wasn't so sure.

The floor groaned overhead. Tad scanned the ceiling. "Some say the Captain's ghost resides here."

Her attention shifted upward. It felt more feminine.

He cleared his throat. "Of course, that's stupid."

"Of course." Still, a small shiver tingled her spine.

He pointed his beam at the marble fireplace. "Look over here." Unlike the white and black marble of the sitting room, the library's fireplace was even more spectacular. Green and white marble crawled in a beautiful pattern up the legs and carved columns that flanked the overmantel. Bronze accent snakes slithered with the marble swirls. A full-size snake coiled on the high mantle shelf.

"This is magnificent." Fangs jutted from the open mouth of the serpent. "It looks so real." As she reached toward the viper, its reflective eyes distracted her attention. "Ouch!" Her hand jerked back, pricked by a bronze fang. Sensing movement above, she raised her face. "Oh!" She jumped away from two smoky images peering down at her.

Tad flashed his light above them where a gilded mirror tilted downward. He laughed at her. "It's just our reflection."

She held her hand over her thumping heart, surprised she felt so jumpy. Another creak jerked her head upward. She fought the foreboding that repelled her from going upstairs, but gave in. It was too dark to see anyway. "This preliminary tour was helpful to see what I'm dealing with, but it's silly to try and examine anything in detail without proper lighting."

"But the system's so old..."

"I don't care if you have to bring a generator, the house needs to be lit properly for me to do my job, or for any serious buyer to consider it."

He glared. "I don't have a generator."

"Then borrow one, and several extension cords and lamps. I will reschedule when you have it ready." She moved back to the foyer, doing her best to ignore the creaks that followed over her head.

Happy to reach the cloudy light of outdoors, she took a quick look at the third story window. A curtain moved, but no face. Certain it was someone playing a prank, she determined to come back and check every corner of the upstairs. "You said there were rumors about a ghost. Did anyone ever mention a woman?"

He shook his head. "Besides Justine Mercer, Marie Sault was the only woman who ever lived here." He pointed to the third-story window. "Up there, in the servant's quarters."

CHAPTER 27

Astoria, Oregon, October 1899

Exhausted from a long day of housecleaning, Marie settled Sebastien into his small bed then slipped into her room next to his. The light from the candle seemed dim tonight, barely casting shadows. With aching arms, she pulled her apron overhead and let it fall onto the floor. More washing. Always more.

It had been two weeks since Edward promised her a secure future with him. A tear leaked down her cheek. What did he mean? He'd frowned when she brought it up today. She flopped onto the springy metal bed and laid her head on the pillow. A mouse gnawed on something in the wall. This was not the life of a lady. Her sister's stinging words failed to discourage her. She must believe. Soon, she would be Mrs. Edward Mercer. Soon, she could lay down the burden of shame she'd borne for seven years, the guilt that hounded her more each day for coveting another woman's husband, possibly driving Justine to her death.

CHAPTER 28

Astoria, Oregon, Current Day

Eaven cataloged notes and photos of items from the mansion, many that would be perfect to sell in her new store. Excitement pulsed through her creative veins, ready to burst if she didn't share her finds with Greg soon. He'd agreed to meet her downtown but not until dinner. She'd just have to wait.

Claire brought tea out to the deck where she was working. "Please, join me." Eaven smiled, hoping to find a way to connect to the distant innkeeper, whose eyes spoke of loss, an emotion that begged for comfort even while it isolated.

Claire hesitated. "No, thank you. I can see you're working."

Closing her computer, Eaven said, "Please. It will be nice to have a conversation with another woman."

Claire perched on a flowered cushion. "Just for a minute. Is your room comfortable?"

"Wonderfully so. You wouldn't believe the rat trap where I stayed when I came to town."

"Quite a difference, I imagine. Nice of Mr. Sault to arrange for you to stay here." Her eyes shifted.

Curious. Eaven grinned inside at the perceptions that must have been lurking in the conservative mind of the elderly innkeeper. "Yes. It's part of my employment package."

"What kind of work are you doing for him?"

"Family research. I had to leave my home when my husband asked for a divorce. Thankfully, I found temporary work until I can get my life together."

Compassion seemed to take the edge off Claire's features. "That happens too often, I'm afraid."

"I'm hoping to save enough to start my own business by helping him with his grandmother's estate."

Her face softened into a smile while she poured a cup of tea for herself. "He's lucky to have someone to help. When my husband died, it all fell to me."

"How long ago was that?"

"Eight years." She sighed deeply. "I'm just getting back on my feet, emotionally and financially. I had to mortgage the inn to pay for his care."

"I'm sorry for your loss."

Her eyes misted. "I'm afraid I'll be too old to make the payments much longer. I need more help every year."

"I can't imagine how hard it is to manage everything, but you do a wonderful job. While I'm here, I'll be happy to help."

Her chin lifted. "Absolutely not, you're my guest."

Eaven smiled. "I'd also like to be a friend. They're in short supply in my life right now."

Claire swallowed. "In mine too. For some reason, I'm feeling it more than usual lately. Probably the holidays approaching. Say, you are booked for two weeks, but perhaps you'll consider staying in Astoria longer."

Her eyes looked so hungry that Eaven wanted to promise her anything. "We'll see. My mother is expecting me to visit in November."

"Lucky woman. Let me know how I can help while you are here."

"I will. You too."

Claire rose and patted Eaven's shoulder when she passed to go back inside. "You know, I watch that unstoppable river every day and feel how it mimics my life, caught in the surge and pulled along. Then I meet you, truly down and out, doing your best to direct your own path against the current. It gives me hope that it might be possible."

Tears smarted behind Eaven's eyes. Somehow her messy life was encouraging someone else. She rose and gave Claire a long hug. "Maybe if we link arms, we can at least keep each other from going under."

Eaven gathered her notes in a hurry, trying to decide what to tell Greg first. She entered The Pastaria on Commercial Street and spied him at a table. The smells of garlic and pesto had her salivating.

Greg's face relaxed when he saw her. He stood and cupped her hand in his, the surprising warmth in his touch caused her fingertips to tingle. He tilted his head. "It went well?"

The attentiveness in his eyes added to the heady emotions already swimming in her head. She took her seat. "I wish you could see the antiques. They're worth hundreds of thousands of dollars. The house is coated with grime, but the interior is still in surprisingly decent shape. It needs extreme sanitizing..."

He sat across from her in the cozy alcove and smiled. "Slow down."

She exhaled and let her mind relax. "Right. I need to eat." A warm fire burned next to them. Servers bustled by while cheerful conversations filtered to their table. She ordered Mediterranean sole and handed the server the menu.

Scooting closer to Greg, she scrolled through the images on her camera. "You can see that the downstairs rooms are packed with antiques, hundreds of places the certificate could have been hidden. And that's just the furnishings. The fireplaces and built-ins could easily house secret panels. It could take weeks to go through everything. We need to narrow our search."

A diamond ring flashed on his finger as he rubbed the thickening stubble on his jaw, making him look even more roguish. "Marie lived there for years, she must have had some idea of where the Captain kept it."

Eaven wasn't as certain. "If she did, it would make my job easier. I never imagined the extent of this collection. With the boards off the windows, it could become a prime target. I can't believe it hasn't been vandalized."

"I can. Frank didn't allow anyone to mess with him or his property. Anyone would be just as foolish to steal from Clayton. He's no one to cross."

The trepidation she experienced around Clayton returned. She would do the job he expected and stay on his good side while also working for Greg. She swallowed. "Tad Jensen will call when he's found a way to light the interior." She took a bite of bread. "Oh. Someone is there. Upstairs. A woman."

Greg leaned forward, eyes questioning. "You saw a woman?"

"I think so. More of an impression. Do you know something?"

He frowned. "No. Marie lived upstairs until she died in the carriage house early Christmas morning."

"What was she doing there?"

He shrugged. "Sebastien loved horses and spent time with the groom, a Mr. MacDonald, I think. Maybe she'd gone to look for him."

"How old was she?"

"Twenty-three. Grandma Sault said her death wasn't an accident."

The fire next to them crackled sharply. A chill shimmied her shoulders. "I hate to admit it did feel haunted."

Eyes softening, he reached across the table and squeezed her hand. "I'll keep you safe." When her jaw dropped in surprise, he laughed. "See, that pulled your attention away from the ghost."

"Ghosts have never been my problem." She clasped her hands on her lap, her fingers rubbing where he'd touched. The guy had more charisma than was good for him. Or her. "You'd do better to use that charm on someone your age."

His lush emerald eyes hung onto hers. "I've never considered age an issue."

"My age, or age in general?" Her phone buzzed, interrupting the question. *Michael.* Maybe he had finally arrived. She itched to take the call, but her meeting wasn't over. When it continued to buzz, she glanced at Greg. "I need to take this." She raised the phone to her ear. "Hello."

Michael cleared his throat. "Hi, Eaven. How are you doing?" He sounded concerned. What if he had changed his mind? "I'm fine, working a temporary job."

"Really? That's great. Hey, I didn't want to upset you, but I can't make it to Astoria for a few more days. Will you be okay?"

She glanced at Greg, at the people around her, and choked down her anger. "That's unfortunate."

"There's a delay on my job. Nothing I can do about it." He paused.

She huffed loudly. "Did you want something else?"

"Yeah, I, uh. Well, I wonder if you've changed your mind about the furniture. Are you sure you don't want any of it?"

Her spine straightened but she lowered her voice. "I have no home to put it in, remember?"

"I'll take that as a no." His voice grew sharper. "Crystal hates this style and wants new stuff before my birthday party. I'll just sell this and be done with it. Bye."

"Wait, what?" she said in unison with the click on his end. His party. Their friends. Crystal. Her fingers trembled when she slipped her phone into her purse.

"The ex?" Greg asked.

She nodded, not trusting her voice.

His lips pressed together. "I know it's tough."

"Thank you."

They finished their meal and he paid cash again. He had mentioned being an investor. His car, clothes, and confidence exuded success. Only when he discussed his family did she catch a glimpse of his vulnerability. He glanced at his watch, its diamonds reflecting tiny sparkles on his water glass. "Need to go. Let me walk you out." Next to her car, he scanned the darkening street.

She unlocked her door. "I could use some help emptying the storage shed at the cottage tomorrow. I'm hoping to find something more that would narrow the search inside the mansion."

He nodded. "Did the realtor say why Clayton put the place on the market?"

"It seems he wants the money, fast."

He smirked and headed toward his car. "Good."

She rolled her eyes at the continuing feud. When she started her car, her phone rang. *Clayton.* Hmm, just after dinner with Greg. Instantly, she checked to see if someone was watching her. She didn't see anyone, but that meant nothing. She took comfort in the fact that he knew she was helping Greg with his grandmother's estate as well as working for him. "Hello, Clayton."

"Good evening. Jensen said you seemed impressed at the mansion."

"It is impressive. I have preliminary photos and some notes, but Tad is bringing in lighting so I can examine the pieces more closely."

"Let's meet tomorrow and go over what you have. Then I'll see if it's worth a return visit. I'll text you the address."

Her mouth opened to protest, but he disconnected. She didn't like the idea but needed his approval if she wanted to continue. Even more important, she needed time to find something that would help Greg, hopefully something written in the Captain's own hand.

CHAPTER 29

Astoria, Oregon, October 1899

Edward's gaze swept over his impressive dining room. White marble floors reflected the morning sunshine onto the pristine walls, the gilded frames of fine oil paintings, and the ornate wall sconces. He sighed at the beauty, wishing he could linger. Instead, he dragged his attention to the problem at hand.

If Marie lost hope that her situation could change, she would leave and take his son. Standing behind the armchair, he gripped its carved back. She was beautiful, pleasing, and had given him Sebastien. He had toyed with the idea of marrying her. After all, a man with his wealth should be able to do whatever he chose without caring what society thought. Yet he did care. There would be no end to the ridicule he would suffer. He could already imagine the whispers as he passed people on the street. He felt his face flush at the thought.

Unless. Could he give Marie what she wanted but keep it private until his death? He rubbed his chest. After what his physician said, she might not have long to wait. He strode to his office, pulled out pen and paper and wrote a greeting to Judge Eric Gleeson, a man who, for a price, would help with Edward's proposal. Make it legal but keep it confidential.

He hesitated. What if Marie used it against him? Embarrassed him? Another thought, a brilliant thought, made him smile. He licked his bottom lip and continued to write the note.

Jake Mercer knocked before he entered his father's disgustingly opulent library in the equally gaudy house. He felt nothing but contempt at the man's attempt to hold his place in the upper crust of society. Glancing around, he shuddered at the failed attempt.

"Enter," the Captain said, his voice more graveled as he approached his sixtieth birthday.

Jake reassured himself that the man could not live forever. The brass doorknob, twice the size needed to open any door, even an eight-foot-high door that dwarfed those entering, felt cold in his hand. "I have the signed bills of lading from the *Justine*." It was still hard to say the name of the ship christened after his mother. She had once confided she would die of a broken heart from marrying the wrong man. He believed any man would have been better than his father, Edward Mercer.

Without raising his head, the Captain pointed to the far corner of his ornately carved desk. "Set it there."

Jake stepped forward and extended his arm to drop the report, easily reading the Captain's words.

Dear Eric,

It has been nearly a year since Justine's demise. We have discussed my intentions regarding Marie and Sebastien. I believe it is time...

Jake stifled a gasp.

The Captain set his pen aside and glared. "What else?"

He stood speechless. Grandfather Reynolds had shown him the Captain's will that named him the sole heir. But this? Sweat broke out on his upper lip. Surely his father would not be that foolish to marry his harlot, the cause of his mother's early death. His mind jumbled at the ramifications.

"If there is nothing else, I'm busy."

His father's detestable smugness, as if Jake were just another servant, caused his gut to burn. "What do you think you're doing?"

The Captain turned the paper upside down. "Nothing that concerns you."

Fury emboldened him. He pulled back his thick shoulders. "I beg to differ. Thus far, you've covered your sins and avoided ridicule, but I won't stand to have that harlot and her bastard strapped to my reputation."

"*Your* reputation?" His father scraped back his chair, knocking it over. He grabbed his walking cane and raised it to strike. Jake lifted his arm to block the stick swinging down at him, but the tip struck and smashed the massive glass globe that hung above them. Chards of white glass rained onto the desk.

His father, taller than him by six inches, whipped around the desk and grabbed Jake by the hair. He slapped him hard and screamed. "*Your* reputation? What a joke. You're a useless oaf. A dead weight!" His father's dark eyes glared while his face convulsed with rage. He shoved Jake against the door. "Get out."

Jake pinched his split lip to stop the blood flow. His eyes smarted, but he refused to let the Captain see the tears welling. He opened the door and fled. "I swear, I'll see him rot and everything he loves."

CHAPTER 30

Astoria, Oregon, Current Day

After a full morning clearing the crammed space, Eaven stood and surveyed the garage. Greg had begged off early, acting tense and short of patience, so different from the man he was last night, making her glad to see him go. Behind her, mounds of black trash sacks squatted at the edge of the driveway. If she had any grandiose expectations of her new career, this was not it. Yet, the stacks of letters and a few interesting collectibles she'd found had kept her going. She'd also set aside a box that had been mailed from San Francisco to check out later.

There were more boxes in the rafters, but she was done for the day. She swung the warped doors closed and padlocked them, more out of habit rather than protecting anything valuable. Stretching her aching back, she kicked a nearby sack of molded clothes, reminding herself she was doing this because she needed the money. It all hinged on that. Once she built her own business, she could pay someone else to do the dirty work.

Greg had expected her to finish today, but she needed to meet Clayton. Keeping him cooperative was also part of her job. Maintaining the fine line that existed between their competing interests was becoming harder, but not impossible. She would deliver exactly what she'd promised to Clayton—a fair evaluation—and do her best to find Greg's document.

Though she felt more than provoked at Clayton's spying and prying into her business, she was determined to remain professional. At least, that was the plan. He wanted a report. Good. She had organized an initial summary of his possessions, but only in the first two rooms. It would be obvious she needed more time. Much more. She pulled off her grimy gloves and tossed them into the trash. The commissions she'd make on his antiques would compensate for having to put up with him.

She used Greg's shower and changed into navy slacks and a gold sweater she'd brought for her meeting. With Astoria bathed in sunshine today, her yellow windbreaker would keep her warm enough. And the color brightened her mood.

The navigation app led to the address Clayton had texted. It took her miles east of town, onto deserted roads. She stopped, took a drink of water, and re-checked the address. Certain she hadn't made a mistake, she continued tentatively, eyes darting in all directions to see if anyone followed her. When she turned onto a rutted dirt road, rocks scraped the bottom of her car. She slammed on the brakes. Was this his idea of a joke?

"Enough." She crept forward, looking for a place to turn around. The road turned and a decrepit house came into view. Behind it, Clayton stood on an old pier next to a sleek blue and white sport-fishing boat. Expecting to be heading to a restaurant, not an isolated rendezvous, her simmering anger threatened to blast in his direction. She parked and gripped her keys.

He smiled and hoisted a picnic basket. "I brought sandwiches and beer. Iced tea if you'd rather. I thought you might enjoy an excursion on the Columbia."

Heart hammering, she studied his smiling face. The picnic basket. No one else appeared. Aside from the remote setting, nothing felt sinister. Though Clayton was full of himself, the evidence she'd seen so far made Greg's accusations against him appear overblown. "Why didn't you moor in the marina?"

"Limited time. I wanted to show you the river upstream, so I motored here yesterday."

Not something she'd do, but he knew this area. She scanned his calm face. He'd given her no indication of ill-will. Dismissing her dramatic imagination, she grabbed her files and walked toward the streamlined yacht christened the *Hot Toddy*. "My uncle had a Hatteras. She's a beauty."

He grinned, "Yes she is, all forty-five feet of her. Powerful too. Let's get you onboard."

After they got underway, her apprehension eased. Sunlight and blue sky reflected off the smooth water through the wide windshield in the helm. He perched on the elevated captain's chair and motored out of the cove. They headed east. "Drinks are in the fridge downstairs. Look around."

She stepped into the cabin below. *Hot Toddy*, indeed. Clean modern lines ran throughout the ship, from its leather upholstery to sleek teak cabinets. Her fingers stroked the soft cream leather. It would have cost a fortune, and he owned three. She turned to come back up but jumped back and inhaled sharply. An eight-inch rusty shark hook dangled beside the stairs, totally out of sync with its surroundings. *It's a fishing boat,* she chided herself. When she came back up, she was speechless.

"Like it?"

She swallowed. "It's like a four-star hotel." Feeling warm, she unzipped her windbreaker and scanned the view of Washington's rugged shoreline rising from the river. A few homes huddled under trees along the shore. She breathed the fresh air and asked Clayton questions about his boat, wanting to gain a better understanding of the man she worked for.

After an hour, he slowed. "I'm going to pull into one of these side channels for lunch. Less current. You can show me what you've discovered."

This also was not part of the plan she'd envisioned for today. The area grew more isolated as they moved away from the main channel. Feeling uneasy, she chose not to overreact but scrutinized the area. "You're going to like what I have to show you."

His face remained relaxed as he watched his navigation equipment for the bottom. They lowered the anchor. He smiled. "Why don't you set lunch out on the deck?"

"Sure." The picnic basket held turkey pesto sandwiches, gourmet carrot cake, and a package that read, *Sheila's Smoked Salmon, with love from Astoria, Oregon.* Sheila—the woman buying the freezer on the Riverwalk. Eaven chuckled at her marketing skills, expelling some of the tension, and set plates on the table.

"Thanks," he said and opened the drinks.

"No. Thank you. This is a treat." She bit into the fresh sandwich.

"I have to treat my employees well if I plan to keep them around."

Her head drew back. She hadn't considered herself his employee, but supposed it was true in a sense. She took a drink of iced tea. "So, how many employees do you have?"

"A few." A thin scowl communicated that was a subject to avoid.

She rubbed her hand over the teak table. "Your boat is in perfect condition. Do you take fishermen out yourself?"

He leaned back against the cushion. "Yes, I'm on the water a lot. But unlike my family, I've forged a different path, bringing people pleasure instead of pain."

"That's an admirable goal."

"It's a work in progress. How about you? As you mentioned, I did some background checking."

She hadn't expected him to be so forthright. "Since you brought it up, I have to say, I resent that and don't understand why you'd go through the trouble. I'm nobody."

His head cocked sideways. "Because you lived a quiet life with a man who jilted you? I think you have no idea what you're capable of. As to why, I feel protective of my town, Greg Sault is a bad egg and you are with him. That simple."

"I'm helping with his grandmother's estate. I'm not *with* him."

He smirked. "But you are. Breakfasts, lunches, dinners, time alone at his cottage. Is it just business, as you say, or a quick romance?"

Fire invaded her cheeks. Cool down. She swallowed and faced him. "I was broke when I arrived here. He asked me to help him at his grandmother's cottage. It's grunt work, but I need the money."

"He buys you dinners, provides posh digs, then has you sorting through his garbage." He smirked and swigged the remainder of his beer. "Women. Give you a little money and you become...appreciative. Gina was like that. Makes me wonder what else you're willing to do."

Her jaw dropped. "How dare you." She threw her sandwich in the basket. "If that's what you think, take me back. Now."

"No sense getting worked up. That's Greg's style. What I expect from you is purely business."

Her mind and emotions whirled off-balance. "I need to use the head." She stepped below and locked the door. He'd had people watching her at the cottage today. She splashed cold water on her face. What did he imagine Greg was doing in town that threatened him? Looking for the document as his father had? Did he suspect she was helping by searching the mansion? If so, why did he let her continue? She leaned against the sink. If she had to guess, he was keeping her close in case she found it while using her expertise to make money from his antiques. Two for one.

Calming her breathing, she climbed the stairs, determined to maintain her story. "Clayton, the work I do for other clients is none of your business, but I will tell you I am not romantically involved with Greg."

He watched her with a patronizing smile. "What did you find in the mansion?"

She blinked, unsure if he was asking about the antiques or Greg's document. He was toying with her, but she had a hunch about how to stop that. "There's a small fortune in your antiques."

His stupid smile disappeared. "How much?"

"Two or three hundred thousand dollars. And I haven't seen the upstairs yet."

"That's good news." He pursed his lips. "I apologize if my comments offended you. I was referring to my experience with Gina. That was a catastrophe." He opened another beer and guzzled half of it.

"I heard she attacked your dog, and it wasn't the first time."

A red flush started in his neck and reached his face. "It was unfortunate."

"Unfortunate? Only someone who is mentally unhinged would be that cruel." The accusation was out of her mouth before she could stop it.

He stood, nostrils flaring. "Shut up! You don't know what you're talking about." He threw his bottle at the shore with such force, it hit a tree trunk and smashed into pieces.

She kept her eyes on him and edged toward the water. "You're right. I don't." Her heart pounded. How far would this escalate?

Face flushed, he grabbed the picnic basket off the table and threw it toward the back of the boat. "We're finished. Pull the anchor." They motored to the main channel of the Columbia and headed west toward Astoria. Neither spoke.

With a jerk, he opened the throttle. The powerful boat flew over the water. The bow rose and slammed, chattering her teeth. Wind hit her face, pulling tears from her eyes. She swiped at them. "Please, slow down."

He turned, eyes narrowed. "I'm the captain, Ms. Alexander." He glanced back at the picnic basket bouncing in the aft cockpit. "Get that before it blows out."

She stumbled, barely keeping her footing, and reached for the basket. At that moment, he jerked to their left in a tight move.

She launched into the river.

Hitting hard, her body flipped several times before she landed on her back, stunned. She struggled to stay afloat while the boat continued forward at a fast clip.

Catching her breath, she treaded water and scanned the river. No boats in sight. The shore was a quarter mile away. The water was cold but not freezing. It was doable. She held her breath and sunk under the surface to shed her shoes and jacket. Floating on her back, she tried to relax then turned over. A sliver of land stretched into the channel. She began a steady crawl to the nearest point.

After several minutes, she lifted her head to check her progress. A pang of panic hit. The brisk current had carried her well past that point and farther into the main channel.

She chose another target down river and started to swim for it. Her sodden sweater clung like a silken weight to her back and arms and sucked her under. She fought, focusing on each stroke. Fifteen minutes? Twenty? Exhaustion set in. Her muscles began to shake.

"Hey there!"

Shouts? She stopped swimming and turned in a circle. A fishing boat had spotted her and sped closer. The motor slowed. Three men worked to pull her onboard their trawler.

"Good thing we saw your yellow sweater, missy. Here's a blanket." A grizzled fisherman helped wrap it around her while the captain headed back to Astoria. "How'd you get way out here?"

"A snake dropped me in the river." She trembled, more with anger than fear. "Do you have a phone I can use?" He dug into his denim jacket and handed his over. She pressed *911*. "I want to report an attempted murder."

"Whose"

"Mine."

CHAPTER 31

Clayton's forearms strained. Sweat dripped into his eyes as he polished and re-polished the rails of his boat for the next excursion. Eaven had survived. And reported him. Lucky for her she wasn't in reach right now. His spur of the moment plan to get rid of her hadn't worked. Maybe later. Lucky for him, he'd gone back to look, and that Pinnick had been the officer to answer her 911 call.

He threw the rag into the pile with the rest. The worst part was having to call and apologize. Which he had. Her expertise was still useful. She'd agreed to continue working for him—without much persuasion, he noticed. She wanted in that mansion, possibly for the fool's errand Greg had her on, but she was smart. He'd bet it was mostly for the money she could make selling his furnishings. He had her hooked, as long as he wanted.

He looked up, startled to see Brett Gellens approaching. "What are you doing here?" He glanced around the marina and quickly motioned Brett onto his boat.

Brett followed him to the cabin below. "I needed to say this personally. Stay away from Jenny. I don't care if she offers you a fortune for drugs, she is off limits. Am I clear?"

Standing well above the esteemed doctor, Clayton poked Brett's chest. "First, no one tells me what to do. You may think your reputation puts you out of my reach, but how would the community react if they found out your wife was a junky instead of a high-spirited social drinker?"

Brett lifted his weak chin. "Don't believe for a moment you've risen that high. To everyone here, you're still the son of Frank Mercer, the drug dealer. Proof or no proof, when they see you zipping around in your little black Porsche, they know the money came off the backs of the women he trafficked."

Clayton grabbed Brett by the throat, nearly lifting him out of his loafers. "Shut your trap."

Brett's hands struggled to loosen Clayton's grip. His face reddened, eyes bulging.

Clayton smiled. "Done?"

Brett nodded.

"Get off my boat and stay out of my business," he growled and shoved him toward the teak stairs. He followed him topside and watched the coward scurry away from the marina. Brett was a mouse, following a maze to a trap. He'd served his purpose, along with his wife.

CHAPTER 32

Still shaky from yesterday's swim, Eaven's backpack dropped from her hand when someone knocked on her door.

"Ms. Alexander? It's Mr. Ewing."

When she opened the door of her suite, his concerned eyes met hers. "I heard what happened. How are you feeling?"

"Like a fool for taking a lone cruise with Clayton Mercer. And I feel silly for accusing him of attempted murder without proof. He was smart to come back, though he took his time."

"He's slippery."

"Like slime." Doubt clouded the facts, yet one thing had solidified on the drive home yesterday. An indelible image pierced her mind of a woman and a dog, *both* battered by Clayton, *not* hurt in a biking accident. She hoped Gina stayed away this time.

"Well, just glad you're safe." Mr. Ewing nodded and treaded down the steps.

She was safe, but Clayton's dog wasn't, and she wasn't waiting another moment to see the little guy. Unable to suppress the urgency, she buckled her backpack and jogged the few blocks to the Franklin on Franklin Veterinary Hospital. Facing the receptionist, she smiled more brightly than she felt. "Hello."

The older woman took forever to drag her eyes from the computer. "Yes?"

"Good morning, my name is Eaven Alexander. I used to volunteer at my vet's office in Washington, walking dogs, that sort of thing. Thought I might be of help here."

The woman frowned. "I don't know...do you have a written recommendation?"

Eaven bit her bottom lip. "No, but you could call Dr. Carr if you need."

"Stay here. I'll get Dr. Franklin."

Within two minutes, a short, balding man wearing black-rimmed glasses appeared. "I'm Joseph Franklin, pleased to meet you. Lenora says you'd like to help. We can always use a hand around here. Many of our animals have to stay with us for quite a while, and though we try to give them the exercise we know will aid their recovery, well you can imagine the limited amount of time in a day."

Eaven took a breath for him. Despite his motor mouth, his good nature filled the room. "I love animals and am glad to help." She checked her watch. "I have time today, if you'd like me to get started."

Dr. Franklin glanced at Lenora. "Why don't you get Ms... I'm sorry, what did you say your name was? I remember faces and animals very well, but sometimes names evade me and..."

"Eaven Alexander," she said.

"Right. Lenora, get Ms. Alexander a jacket so her clothes don't get soiled." He shook her hand and disappeared behind a door.

Lenora didn't look too pleased. "This way." They moved through a door to the treatment area. "We keep the dogs in this wing." When she opened the door, one dog barked. Another slept. The room smelled sterile.

"These guys look perfectly healthy," Eaven commented.

"They are. Just moved from males to *its*." She smirked. "Doing our part to keep every dog a wanted dog."

Eaven searched the other cages. Near the back, a large red cocker spaniel sat completely still, but its eyes watched her. When she approached the cage, the spaniel cowered. "Who's this fellow?"

"That's Roscoe." Lenora squatted and cooed to the wavy-haired spaniel. "Come on, fella. Come to Lenora." He whined and ducked his head.

"What happened to him?"

Frowning, Lenora said, "Internal injuries. He's really bruised, but nothing shows on the X-rays."

"Abuse?"

Lips tight, the woman nodded. "Some people shouldn't be allowed to own animals."

It had to be Clayton's dog. Eaven was glad to see the woman had a soft spot toward her charges. "How long has he been here?"

"Two weeks."

"That's a long time."

Lenora stuck her fingers through the cage and wiggled them for the dog to come over. "We're keeping him under observation." She glanced up with a knowing look. "As long as we can."

Eaven squatted next to her. "A walk might cheer him."

"I thought so too, but I can't bear to make him cry while forcing him out of his cage."

Her heart broke as she watched him lower his muzzle and avoid eye contact. "Let me try. Do you have any treats?"

The phone rang, and Lenora pointed. "I need to answer that. The treats are there."

"Thanks." Eaven grabbed a handful and squatted by the open cage. "Come here, boy." She laid a treat near his nose. He didn't even sniff. She tried for several more minutes without success. What had he suffered at his master's hands? What had Gina? Remembering the ferocity in Clayton's face, and the danger she'd put herself in, she shivered at her foolishness. Something was seriously off with him.

She sat full on the floor and leaned toward the cage, eyes misty as she watched Roscoe's quivering body. "Here, boy. You're safe with me."

You're safe with me.

A tremor passed through her, a current pulling her toward the memory, the incident that had devastated her young life. Struggling against the flow, she wrapped her arms around her body, closed her eyes, and recited her counselor's words in her mind. *Feel the ocean spray on your face, the cool wind blowing off the water.* For several minutes, she rocked, not resisting the fear, the loss, letting the mantra do its work. *Breathe in. Breathe out. Breathe in. Breathe...*

A soft tongue licked her arm. She opened her eyes and blinked. Roscoe stood next to her, sadness filling his warm spaniel eyes. Her throat thickened. "Hey boy." She wiped her cheeks and gently scratched the side of his head. He tried to sit but whined and stood again.

She touched her cheek to his muzzle, two kindred spirits working their way back to wholeness, possibly even trust someday. Roscoe licked her chin as she continued to scratch his neck. Tilting her head, she asked, "Want to go for a walk?" His ears lifted, and his tail gave one wag. Across the room, a lead hung on a hook below a flyer for an upcoming dog food drive. After attaching it, she started toward the door and he followed, moving cautiously. She smiled at his growing trust. Maybe to heal, you just needed the right person.

He followed her out the side door and they strolled back and forth slowly while she spoke soothing words. When she sat on a bench, he cuddled close to her leg, setting his chin on her knee. She leaned forward and kissed the silky fur on his forehead. "Oh, little buddy, I can't let you go back to Clayton."

Weighted with concern after leaving Roscoe, Eaven unlocked her door at the inn and dumped her backpack on the bed. Back to work. Clayton still wanted her help and had eaten crow to ask for it. A grin expanded in her chest the more she thought how tough that had been for him. She should work on researching comparable prices for his furnishings before Greg arrived today. The corner of her mouth twitched. After the dunking he gave her, burning him by finding a marriage certificate would bring infinite satisfaction. With that happy thought, she shelved Clayton's project in favor of Greg's.

"Is that you Eaven?" Claire called up the stairs.

She turned. "Yes."

"I just made poppyseed muffins." She tilted her head and smiled. "With sliced almonds on top?"

"You got me." Eaven joined Claire in the dining room.

"You seem down, dear."

Between bites of muffin, Eaven told her about Roscoe. "The worst thing was leaving him there alone in his cage."

Claire nodded, her crinkled eyelids drooping. "No one can imagine the ache that grips your soul when you leave, knowing how much they're hurting."

"Your husband?"

Tears welled in Claire's eyes for the first time. "He smoked, you know. The cancer started as a small lump in his throat. Within a year, it was everywhere. Even with all the chemo." Her brows knotted. "He never complained, suffered in silence. Then they opened his chest to take a better look. Just like they'd known, he was full of cancer.

"I brought him home and had to close the inn to care for him, couldn't have served anyone anyway. I grieved every time I had to leave him alone in his suffering." Tears flowed down her cheeks. "I don't know how he did it, but he gathered enough pain pills to take all at once. I came in and he wasn't breathing."

Eaven knelt before her and let Claire sob on her shoulder. She stroked the older woman's soft white hair. "And you were left alone."

Claire shuddered and sat back while Eaven continued to hold her hand. "Completely alone. Our son blamed me. The life insurance policy was void because of the suicide. I was left with this inn to run." She sniffed. "Thank God, I had it."

"My grief pales after listening to yours."

Claire patted her hand. "Thank you. Not many want to listen to such a story."

She understood. "No, they don't." She watched Claire return to the kitchen where the breakfast dishes still waited to be washed. This was too big a job for one woman. Working on a hunch, she climbed the stairs to her room and made a call. She left a message, telling herself it wasn't really meddling, then grabbed her things for her meeting with Greg.

In the parlor, she studied the photographs she'd taken at the Mercer Mansion, most focused on the furnishings for places that might hide the document. A million other possibilities included hidden panels and trap doors. Really, there was nothing solid to give to him.

He arrived, concern emanating from his eyes. "Better today?"

"Much," she said, ready to move on. They sat on the two wingback chairs and she launched into her report. As she described the beauty of the furnishings, the rarity of the pieces, her mood rose.

He gazed with a bemused smile. "Sounds like fun. Maybe you should be paying me?"

"Maybe not. Anyway, no secret compartments. Yet." She unrolled a layout of the mansion she'd found at the Heritage Museum. During the next hour, she pointed to the rooms and explained what she'd seen. "Bottom line, it was a good first survey." Her stomach grumbled and she glanced at the grandfather clock. "Would you like to get some dinner?"

Their eyes met, his face considerably more relaxed than he'd been. "Thanks, but I have plans tonight." He squeezed her hand where it rested on the chair's arm. The corner of his mouth turned up. "But before I go, I need to ask a favor. A big one."

Removing her hand from under his, she steeled herself against a gaze that hinted of flirtation. "What favor?"

"Just before I left high school, Jenny dumped me for Brett Gellens. Later, she married him." His fingers rubbed across the black stubble on his chin. "She invited me to their house for a fundraiser to hang out with old friends. When she asked if I was seeing anyone, it caught me off guard. I said yes, and she asked me to bring her. There really isn't anyone. Would you come with me?"

Eaven's cheeks warmed. "I don't know, Greg. It's not true, and there must be at least a ten-year age difference between us."

He raised an eyebrow. "With a woman as beautiful as you, what man would count?"

She glanced sideways, amazed at how easily he could turn the charm on or off. "Slick line."

Light pink flushed his cheeks. "Please. It comes with no romantic strings attached."

She raised her hand. "Trust me, there's no chance of that." She sat back and shook her head. "I'm so raw from my divorce, I'm not in the party mood."

"It's not like that. Very formal and for a good cause." His eyes sought hers, a playful smile on his lips. "Come on. I owe you a night out."

She frowned. "When is it?"

He pressed his lips together. "Tomorrow night. Sorry about the late notice."

She drew a hard breath. October twentieth, Michael's birthday, one of *the* annual events on the lake. A sharp pain surged through her head as she fought to rebuff the memories from her mind.

Greg faced her, his verdant eyes hopeful, his face too handsome for anybody's good.

She had two choices, spend the night alone with tormenting thoughts of Michael and Crystal, or in Greg's company, in a house full of good cheer. No contest. Besides, she was curious to meet Jenny. And find out more about what Greg was doing in Astoria.

Thinking about what was needed, she caught herself clicking her fingernail and stopped. "I've been living in the outback for eighteen years. If I can do a Cinderella gig and find a dress, I'll go."

His face lit up. "Deal. I'll be here at seven." He stood to leave and smiled down at her. "You could come in rags and outshine everyone there."

She smirked. "You're good." After he left, she took an aspirin for her headache and rushed out to find a dress on the spur of the moment.

As she shopped downtown, the memory of her father's words nudged her to smile. *Eaven Kensington Alexander, you are far too impetuous for an ambassador's daughter.* Then he'd winked. *But you'll have more adventure than the lot of us.*

Life was certainly proving to be that adventure.

CHAPTER 33

Clayton moved from the dirty aquarium to his desk and called Tom Jensen. "I gave Eaven the go-ahead to come back. Tell your boy he's at her disposal. I want those antiques sold ASAP."

Jensen drawled. "Tad said she spent a lot of time looking for hidden compartments."

He pursed his lips. "Have him keep track of anything she's especially interested in and let me know. And have him make sure she doesn't take anything from the house."

"Will do." Jensen hung up.

So, it was confirmed. Eaven was helping Greg. Jake had searched the house before he locked it up and burned all the Captain's papers. Still, if Eaven found something, Clayton would be waiting to destroy it.

His thumbs drummed the desktop. His sources said Greg met with a tall man who resembled the drug buyer captured with Jin in the photos. Clayton's mind skirted along alternate tracks. What if Greg was behind the thefts and his real reason for coming here was to take over Clayton's business? His hands balled into fists. What if...? No. Yes. What if Eaven was only a distraction? If this whole *get into the mansion* thing was a ruse?

Musing how to manage the new scenario, he rose and resumed cleaning the fish tank. Algae obscured the glass. Geisha, his pet Oscar swam toward him. He hand-fed her a favorite treat, and gently stroked her beautiful black and orange back with his finger. He drew back and frowned. Neither he nor his Bristlenose Plecostomus could alleviate the cloudy mess Geisha created. What good was owning an aquarium if he had to squint through the filth?

Stalking Geisha with the net, he followed her graceful movements. With a flick, he scooped her out of the water and carried the frantic fish out the kitchen door. An orange and white neighborhood cat sat on the fence in the unusually warm sunshine. Clayton flung the fish onto the grass. "Goodbye, Geisha."

Inside, he mashed eggs and mayonnaise to make a deviled egg sandwich. It was past time to clean up another messy situation. He dialed Jennifer Gellens. "Hello, Jenny. Heard you invited Greg Sault to the fundraiser. You had me believe there were no other invitations available."

"I... uh...Greg is an old friend I haven't seen for years. I was able to make room for him."

He frowned. Jenny had just trashed one of the crucial steps in his strategy to edge into Astoria's upper crust. He needed to hit back. "And you included his girlfriend. I didn't think you liked to share."

"He means nothing to me."

"Really? Then you wouldn't care that he's supplying her needs, financial and otherwise."

"Look, Clayton. I broke up with him in high school. Haven't given him a thought since." Her voice sounded heated.

"My gut says you're lying."

"Sure it's not something you drank?"

His frown deepened. If she still carried a torch, how long would it take for her to switch allegiances from him to Greg? Best to keep her tethered. "You need anything?"

She hesitated. "No. I'm cleaning up."

He snorted.

"Wouldn't hurt you to clean up your act either. I heard Gina finally left you. Smart woman. Goodbye, Clayton."

He slammed the phone on the table. "Goodbye, *Geisha*." While thinking of something especially fitting for her, his fist clenched the sandwich, spurting gooey yellow egg between his fingers. He flung the mess into the sink and turned on the garbage disposal. New plan.

Greg Sault was complicating his life. Once the last Sault was dead, no one would care who'd done what to whom. He dried his hands, folded the towel in thirds, and hung it in the middle of the rack. He sent a text. *Set a trap for Mr. Sault. Time to make him disappear.*

CHAPTER 34

At seven o'clock on Saturday evening, Eaven answered her phone. "I'm downstairs," Greg said.

Glad for a happy distraction from the trauma of the last few months, she examined her reflection in the antique floor mirror. Her fairy godmother must have been on call. Fresh hair color and a cut took years away. Chocolate tendrils streaked with caramel strands hung loosely from the chignon pinned to the top of her head. Feeling younger than she had in ages, she twirled, enjoying the way the vermilion off-the-shoulder dress floated. The heels she'd found were a little small but otherwise perfect.

Pulling on her wrap, she caught her smile in the mirror. Paisley used to say it could *slay on demand*. It had seemed that way for a time. After she'd been selected for state tryouts, young men had competed to ask her out. She'd felt exuberant in her untried womanhood, like a butterfly with still sticky wings. The glory was brief and shattering. Her wings lost, she retreated to Europe where no one knew her, then with Michael to Lake Quinault.

Her mood plummeted. Tonight, Michael and his new family would be hosting *her* friends in *her* home. Crystal's beguiling smile and Zoe's angelic face would certainly worm them into good favor. They would dance and laugh and eat, their thoughts on the lively music, not on what had become of her.

Betrayal knifed between her shoulder blades, twisting up her neck and forcing her to grab the rail. She breathed and stretched, moving through the pain, refusing to let them steal another moment of her life. With shoulders back, she met Greg at the bottom of the stairs.

His eyes widened. "You're white as a sheet."

She fanned her face and ordered her tears to stay put.

He rubbed her hand. "What's wrong?"

She tilted her face up and met his concerned eyes. "Michael has a daughter, and a lover. I never knew...not for years. Just give me a moment." She grabbed the crystal pitcher in the parlor and poured a glass of water. After wiping away the smudged mascara and reapplying her lipstick in the oval mirror, she said, "There, good as new."

His lips pressed tightly. "Are you certain you want to go?"

She nodded. "I have to get out or my imagination will overrun me tonight. Do you mind being a distraction?"

"Not at all. *I'm* counting on you for moral support. The Gellens are big in community affairs—on all the charitable boards you could name. Brett will be gloating that he got the girl."

"Jenny?"

"Yeah."

Had he returned to Astoria to win Jennifer back? From what Eaven had seen at the cottage, he was well on his way.

He took her hand. "Ready?"

Despite their confident guise, they both seemed to have breached walls that needed shoring up tonight.

The BMW glided smoothly up the sloping hill and stopped across from a grand house. Light beamed from the bay windows, illuminating the arriving women in their evening gowns and furs, the men in black tuxes. It brought back images of embassy balls and Christmas parties in Charleston where the blue bloods counted it a privilege to receive Lillian's invitations. Where her father had beamed when he introduced her as his daughter. Lillian's approval had been ever evasive.

She felt under-dressed and let out a quiet sigh. Years of social failings under the watchful eyes of two of Charleston's top socialites came rushing back. Her childhood had all the ingredients for an ideal life, yet somehow, she'd side-stepped it. She bit her bottom lip to stop the replay button. None of that mattered. Every day, her determination grew to write her own future, one that fulfilled the dreams she'd only been vaguely aware of, that had been encased in a misty fog.

Greg straightened his shoulders and tugged at his black sleeves as they strolled toward the house.

She smiled to lift her mood, but also his. "You look dashing. Thank you for inviting me."

He chuckled, a refreshing sound that calmed her nerves. "It doesn't usually take this long to get a woman to go on a date with me."

She narrowed her eyes. "*Not* a date. Just playing my part."

He wiggled his eyebrows and gave her a roguish grin. "We'll see."

A thin, curly-haired butler met them at the door. His eyes twinkled at her. "May I?" He took her wrap, revealing her dress.

Greg's mouth opened as his eyes swept over her. "Wow."

It did her wounded pride good. She repaid him with a wide, flirtatious smile. They entered the ballroom laughing. Heads turned, but she didn't recognize anyone.

He chuckled and whispered in her ear. "Right now, I'm the most envied man in this room." He took her hand and caught her eyes.

"Stop." She pulled free and gazed around. The room sparkled with crystal and candlelight. She spied two striking fireplaces. One flickered at each end of the long room, keeping the night chill out of the gathering. Happy butterflies fluttered in her stomach. It was beautiful.

A petite, buxom woman with strawberry blond hair headed their way. An odd mix of boisterous smile and tense features on her overdone face made her appear...loopy? Too much Champagne?

"Greg, so glad you could come." She kissed him on the cheek, near his mouth. "And this is the...*friend* you are showing around?"

Eaven flinched. It made her sound like he found her at an escort agency. She'd met this type before—her sister, Cassandra, was the queen of underhand.

"This is Eaven Alexander." He turned to Eaven, "May I introduce Jennifer Gellens."

She waited to see if Jennifer would extend her hand. She didn't. "Thank you for your kind invitation," she said.

Jennifer gave a quick nod, then turned her flirty blue eyes on Greg. "People are dying to see you now that you're back in town." Leaning close to him, she whispered, "We need more time at the cottage." She threaded her arm through his and pulled him across the room with a sly backward glance.

Eaven sucked in her lips to keep from chuckling at the high school antics. It appeared that Jennifer was more than just an old friend, but was she what brought Greg back to Astoria? He glanced back sheepishly but let Jennifer lead him away. Eaven smirked and shook her head. This would be an interesting night.

The butler stopped and offered a glass of Champagne. She took a drink and regarded the retreating couple. Jennifer leaned heavily on Greg, whispering in his ear. He held her at bay, darting quick nods at the other guests as one pair of eyebrows after another rose. Eaven smiled at his discomfort. His choice.

She strolled toward the nearest fireplace. Its white wooden mantel joined the magnificent crown molding at the ceiling. Flocked wallpaper covered the walls, too gaudy for her taste, but she'd seen worse.

A tall, rugged man with thick gray hair approached her. "Nice to see you again." He grinned. "I'm Tom Jensen. Met you in my real estate office."

She smiled. "Yes, hello. Your son has been extremely helpful." She offered her hand.

He shook it. "I understand you've been exploring our city."

Her smile faltered. Had he been talking to Clayton? She was about to ask how he knew that when a smaller man with sandy blond hair interrupted their conversation. Tom's mouth twitched, and he excused himself.

"Ms. Alexander, I don't believe we've met. I'm Brett Gellens. My wife has run off with your escort." His smile was affable. Forcibly so.

Though annoyed at his dismissive behavior toward Tom Jensen, she extended her hand to her host. "Thank you for your invitation."

He squeezed it gently. "Glad to have you. Jenny didn't mention where you're from."

She cleared her throat. "I'm moving from the Olympic Peninsula back to Charleston, South Carolina."

His forehead furrowed. "That's quite a switch. What kept you busy in that remote part of the country?"

She shrugged. "Sailing, photography."

"Fascinating," he said, without a hint of interest.

Greg and Jennifer joined them. He unwound her hand from his arm and pulled Eaven next to him, his devilish eyes measuring her response. "Eaven's photographs have quite a following."

A thrill shot through her from the touch of his fingers on her waist. He was teasing, knowing she couldn't react in front of the very people she'd agreed to help him impress. Regardless, he was a pleasant tease. She gave him a sweet smile. "You're exaggerating."

He grinned at the unspoken messages sparking between them. "She won the Natural History Museum Wildlife Photographer of the Year award."

That seemed to impress Brett. "Really? What did you photograph?"

"I captured a rare albino fox in the English countryside when I lived in London."

"London? Right." Jennifer slurred as if the idea was incredulous.

Greg frowned. "Not everyone stays where they grew up."

"And not everyone runs away."

The polite smile fled Brett's face. "Bill and Alice just arrived. Let's greet them." He steered Jennifer away by the elbow. Instead of greeting anyone, however, they headed upstairs.

Eaven's shoulders relaxed, glad they'd gone. Well, she'd met Jenny—Jennifer. Her unfortunate husband had his hands full. She turned and caught the look of pain on Greg's face. "That was a low blow," she said, laying her hand on his arm. "Is there anything I can say to take the sting out of it?"

He stared after Jennifer and shook his head. "No, I had it coming. We were almost engaged. Of course, she was a league above me, so I doubt she would have gone through with it."

"You underestimate your charm, Greg Sault," she said, allowing her gaze to connect to his magnetic eyes. A light flickered in them. She pulled away from the force, too aware it could be dangerous.

Hand still on her waist, he pulled her to his side. "Eaven Alexander, you're a rare date."

"Not a date." She moved out of his caress and back to reality.

He shrugged. "Okay, not. I'll introduce you to some of the nicer people I know." While they milled around and chatted, she listened to the most beautiful music she'd ever heard. Though not from a composer she recognized, the compositions lifted her spirits with their glorious strains. Greg swung her around for another introduction. "Eaven, I think you've already met Ralph Ewing."

"Oh!" She was surprised to see Mr. Ewing from the River's Glory. She offered her hand automatically, impressed at the difference a tuxedo made. With his thin gray hair combed back, he appeared almost regal. "Hello Mr. Ewing."

"Please, call me Ralph." He took both hands and gazed at her face and hair. "I was right. I told Greg you were a gem, a diamond fit for a crown." He bowed over her hand and kissed it. "What a delight you are to this old eccentric's eyes."

She blushed, laughing at his good nature. "How do you know Greg?"

"Met him in a bar." He smiled, losing his mock formality. "I came to town to do research for a maritime mystery I'm writing. Greg was good enough to add some historical color to the dry events and to arrange an invitation for me tonight. I think he promised the hostess I'd make a large donation." He seemed about to say more when a loud cackle pulled everyone's attention toward the grand stairs.

"Alice!" Jennifer's laugh filled the room as she descended the last step. Face fully animated, she greeted her friend with wide open eyes and a huge smile.

Alice glanced at the stunned faces around Jennifer and blanched. "You look fabulous, Jenny. Come here. I've so much to tell you." She took her hands and pulled her into a hallway.

Eaven winced, embarrassed for the loaded hostess, then glanced at Greg's reddened face. Thankfully, the butler announced dinner, breaking the tension. She followed Greg and the other guests into the connecting dining room. Dazzling service for twenty people garnished the glittering table. Crystal candlesticks glowed at perfect intervals. She hadn't seen such elegance since she'd left Charleston. She smiled, every sense heightened. Why had she abhorred it so?

Seated between Greg and Ralph, she immediately fell prey to Ralph's quest for information. "Greg says you're only staying in Astoria a short while."

"A couple of weeks," she said. "I plan to spend the holidays in Charleston with my family." She took a sip of wine and gathered her thoughts. The idea that Ralph had just met Greg and was staying at the same inn felt too coincidental. "How did you pick Astoria for a setting?"

Ralph's eyes flitted to Greg's before he quipped, "A dart on the map." He gave her a mild smile and turned to the guest on his other side. Greg had also turned his attention away.

That went nowhere. She glanced around the room buzzing with conversation while two waiters served the first course, a radish and fennel salad. She savored the pomegranate-honey dressing. The guests nodded approval, uttering lavish praise. Across the table from Eaven, Jennifer glowed.

Ralph turned and resumed his questioning. "What does your family do in the land of gentility?" He skewered a bite without taking his attention off her face.

"My father was an ambassador."

"Where was that?"

"Many places. Every two or so years when I was younger, we moved to a different post. Brussels, Germany, England."

"Ah. My stomping grounds covered West Sussex. Mostly on or under a horse."

She laughed. It had been years since she'd spoken with anyone from the U.K. "Dad was posted in London."

"During what years?"

"My first two years of middle school."

Greg leaned forward and spoke across her. "More research?"

Ralph laughed. "One never knows what fascinating bits can materialize during innocuous conversations." His attention fully on her, their conversation covered a variety of topics. He asked. "Did living in London influence your decision to choose Oxford for college?"

She glanced across the table to find Jennifer and Alice watching her, snickering behind their napkins. Her neck heated but she ignored them. "Yes. I'd found England irresistible as a kid, and Oxford offered the courses I wanted. After college I worked at Christie's Auction House."

"What a fraud." Jennifer's voice rose above the rest of the conversation, which immediately hushed. All eyes flew to her, then to Eaven.

Greg scowled, looking as though he might jump over the table and strangle her. Ralph too.

Brett grabbed her hand. "Jenny, that's enough."

Her voice rose, eyes wild. "Come on, Greg. You really think she lived in London and worked at Christie's? She's wearing Alice's dress from the Goodwill, for pity's sake."

A collective gasp hissed around the room. All eyes turned toward Eaven. Smirks filled the women's faces as they studied her dress, stripped her naked.

Not again. Eaven glanced at the open door, then changed her mind. Body trembling, she lurched from her chair, knocking over her water glass. She threw her linen napkin onto her plate but kept her voice steady. "You're right, Mrs. Gellens. When Greg invited me to spend an evening with his friends, I had nothing to wear. By the way, thank you for the dress, Alice."

She peered fiercely into Jennifer's eyes. "My husband left me two months ago. I came through Astoria with only what would fit in my car. I had hoped to forget my troubles for a night in the company of good people. That, unfortunately, is not the case." She cast a gaze around the table. "Please, enjoy yourselves and your gracious hostess."

Jennifer's face turned cherry red under her fake tan. Her husband scowled at her. Heads wagged all around the table.

More than finished, Eaven pushed back her chair and headed for the front door. In her wake, arguments erupted, possibly in her defense, but she couldn't care less. She thought she'd left all this behind in Charleston.

"Eaven." Greg rushed after her. "I'm so sorry."

Breathing heavily, she barely controlled her voice. "I've had my fill of small people."

He blew out a puff of angry air. "This was worse because of Jenny's addic...because she's jealous of you. I'm sorry that made you a target."

"Greg, wait up." Brett headed their way.

Greg glared at him. "Really? You gave her more?"

Brett paused and said quietly, "This is a fundraiser with *very* important people. I did what I had to." He lifted his chin. "You didn't help matters by bringing her." He tossed his head in Eaven's direction. "You know how jealous Jenny can be with her...problem."

Greg's lips thinned. "So, be a man. Do something about it."

Brett frowned and leaned near Greg's ear. "Two a.m. at Clayton's. It's in his office. That's all I know."

Though Brett's comments infuriated her, the conversation revealed they were involved in something and Clayton was the target. Right now, however, she didn't care to know more. She stormed down the sidewalk.

"Eaven, stop. It's too far to walk." Greg reached out to catch her arm.

She pulled it away and would have kept going, but her feet were already cramping from the heels. "Take me home. I'm done being used."

CHAPTER 35

"Interesting evening," Ralph said. In the early morning hours following the fundraiser debacle, he leaned back against the seat in Greg's BMW.

Greg clenched the steering wheel. He had dropped Eaven at the inn. Her downcast expression seared his mind and pricked his conscience. No one should have to hurt like that. He had wanted to hold her, draw out the pain, but she raced up the steps, out of reach. He huffed, hating how he'd used her. "I'd like to hit something. Hard."

"Like Jennifer Gellens? She's a real piece of work."

"Never used to be that malicious."

Ralph shook his head slowly. "And how about Eaven? That brave woman. If I'd brought my piece, I would have put Jennifer out of *my* misery. She's harsh."

"Besides her gorgeous face, her laugh is the only thing I remember from high school."

"Gorgeous? Can't see you with her, bud."

He sighed, appreciating his friend's concern. "Beneath the drugs, she's still soft as silk."

"Pain meds?"

"Started that way. Though why she felt her body needed enhancing is beyond me. Gets it done free by her husband. It's all the rage."

Ralph huffed. "So is taking heroin when your OxyContin runs out."

He raked his hair. "Brett's a wuss. Who'd let their wife get hooked?"

"Plenty of guys. And Clayton is only too happy to help."

"I've waited all my life to turn the tables on him. Tonight, we can capsize his enterprise, squash his smug face in the muck and watch him drown. He'll get another blow when he finds out Jenny's turned on him."

"There he is," Ralph whispered.

Clayton walked from the side door of his house to the carport. A few seconds later, he drove out and turned at the first corner.

Greg opened his car door. "Let's do this." He zipped his black jacket and they slipped through the dark night to the side entrance Clayton had used. Greg jimmied the lock and opened the door. "After you." They moved quietly through the house, picking their way around furniture on route to Clayton's office. "Look for the shipment schedule first. I doubt we'll find a big stash here."

Ralph growled and grabbed his leg. "With this knee, I'd settle for any version of Oxy."

"No way. Tonight, I need you focused. Once we find the schedule, we'll have access to his whole business. Can't wait to see his face when he discovers a Sault undid him." If Clayton gave him any trouble, Greg would be happy to settle the score on behalf of his father. This time, however, no Sault would see the inside of a cell.

Ralph rifled through drawers while Greg chose the file cabinet. Frustrated, he quietly closed the last drawer. He wanted to slam it. "Safe?"

"Must be." Ralph searched around. Moving a club chair out of the corner, he pointed at a floor safe. "You breaking or me?"

"You better. I'm all thumbs tonight."

"That gal got you rattled. Shake it off," Ralph said.

He wasn't certain which woman undid him the most. Right now, he felt powerless to help either. *Powerless*, the theme of his family for over a hundred years. Not anymore.

Ralph unbuttoned his long raincoat and sat on the floor. Listening intently, he turned the lock with his thin fingers.

Greg paced. He checked his watch and wiped his sweaty palms on his jeans. The Mercers and their associates were murderers. His own father was proof of that. "You close?"

Lights flashed through the window. A car engine stopped in the drive. Ralph jumped. "Back awfully soon."

"Too soon. It's a set-up." A pang twisted in his chest as it often had living in this town as a Sault. Someone had betrayed him. He rushed to the window and tipped down a slat in the blind. "There's four of them. Let's go."

The house door crashed open.

Heart pounding, he flung up the office window and kicked out the screen with his boot. He dove out and rolled onto the front lawn, his shoulder hitting hard.

Behind him, Ralph worked to get his long legs over the sill.

"Come on!" Greg ran, pulling out his gun with a shaky hand.

Ralph's foot caught on the blind, rattling it against the window. "I'm stuck."

Voices grew louder. Doors slammed. Knowing what Mercer's guys would do to Ralph, Greg turned back to help.

Ralph yanked the cord, sending the blind crashing to the floor. With a hard kick, his foot broke free, and he slid outside.

"Let's go!" Panic gripped Greg as he bolted toward his car. He turned and saw Ralph limping hard to keep up as they raced down the street. Reaching the car, he flung open the door and slipped inside. A glance back showed lights blazing from all the house windows.

Ralph crossed the last few yards as if in slow motion. Finally, he opened the door and jumped in.

From inside the house, Clayton's roar broke the dead silence of the quiet neighborhood, sending a shudder through Greg's being. He let off the emergency brake, put the car in neutral, and let it roll down the other side of the hill and out of sight.

"Close," Ralph gasped. "Who do you think set us up?"

His mind settled on one person. "I need to have a chat with Brett."

Ralph's head jerked toward him. "You don't think he'd turn on you?"

He shrugged. "Jealousy is a nasty motivator. Jenny came to me. She's determined to quit using, something he's failed to convince her to do."

They drove without speaking until they arrived at the Gellens' mini mansion. Greg pounded on the front door. When it opened, he shoved Brett against the wall. "You told Clayton we were hitting his house."

Brett raised his hands in submission. "Hold on, Greg. Let's talk."

"Yeah, let's. Clayton and his guys knew we were coming. How do you suppose they found out?"

Brett edged toward the living room, keeping the sofa between them. "I have no idea. Do you think I want Clayton to know I'm helping you take over? He'd tell the whole town about Jenny's addiction. My practice would collapse. All the community projects I've worked for would be tainted."

"Yeah, your precious reputation. Always the do-gooder, but we know different, don't we?"

"Look, during high school you already had a reputation for trouble. So what if I added to your extensive list?"

"What you added was robbery, not graffiti," he shouted. "I would have gone to jail if Jenny hadn't sworn we were together. You're slime, Brett. What excuse are you using for Jenny's addiction?"

Brett rubbed his temples. "It's not my fault. Scrutiny on prescription abuse was intense. I had to cut her off. Her pain was horrifying."

Greg shook his head. "So, you introduced her to a drug dealer?"

Brett raised his chin. "*She* found Clayton. I can't stop her from buying. You know how headstrong she is."

Remembering the way she'd pushed every boundary, he almost pitied the guy. "What's your plan for her?"

Brett placed his hands on the back of the couch. "I had a program arranged, but she wouldn't go." He sighed. "After last night, she finally agreed. Embarrassment is a powerful motivator."

Greg glared. "She should be more afraid of the garbage Clayton is passing out. If I hadn't decided to come back, she could have ended up in a morgue."

Brett's eyes narrowed. "You need to destroy him. If not for Jenny, then for what he's done to your family. With him gone, you can make sure people get what they need, and no one gets hurt."

"You're certain you didn't tell anyone about tonight?"

"No one. Jenny crashed right after the party broke up."

Greg's fist clenched and unclenched, releasing pent up tension. He could think of no reason to doubt Brett. He glanced around the glamorous house filled with pricey furnishings and headed for the door. "Keep your mouth shut and maybe you'll stay alive to enjoy your wealth." He turned to Ralph. "Let's go."

Brett started to follow. "What's your plan?"

Jenny came into the living room, hair tangled, and makeup smeared. She gave him a languid smile. "Hi, Greg."

He glared at her then at Brett. Disgust rushed through his body. He yanked open the door and slammed it in the face of the town's upper crust.

173

CHAPTER 36

The day after brilliantly tossing Jennifer's scorn back in her face, Eaven celebrated by sleeping in, luxuriating in the silky sheets and feather pillows. She stretched and yawned, feeling an immense sense of satisfaction that she'd found the right words at the right time, not two hours too late, as had usually happened between herself and Cassandra. Paisley would be cheering. Surprisingly, her performance blotted out most, no all, of the humiliation. Awed, she wondered when she had stopped caring what people thought.

In that happy mood, she decided to take a long bath before heading downtown to help Dr. Franklin with his dog food drive. She loved his idea of feeding hungry dogs but wished it were next weekend when she'd have more time. This week, curiosity to finish Marie's story grabbed for her attention. Her thoughts kept returning to the box from San Francisco she'd found in Greg's shed. After punching in his number, she left a message asking if he could bring the box by later.

She breathed in deeply, also surprised how unaffected she felt about Michael's party. In fact, she felt more relaxed than she had in a long while. He said he would show up today, but she wasn't holding her breath.

Soaking in the hot water, she rested her feet on the edge of the claw foot tub and studied her red toenails, polished especially for Jennifer's party. Greg's interactions with the Gellens had elevated her suspicions that he was into something dangerous. Should she dig into it further? She sponged hot water onto her neck. No. She had enough problems of her own to sort out. He was her employer. Period. Whatever else he was doing in Astoria had nothing to do with her. In the meantime, her passion had morphed from just finding the document, to unearthing Marie's story.

Greg returned her call as she was drying off. "I was relieved to hear from you. How are you doing?"

She pulled on a sumptuous robe Claire had provided. "Fine. Really fine. You?"

He exhaled loudly on the other end of the line. "I'm good. Still cringing at Jenny's behavior. I was afraid you'd leave town."

"I'm not letting a glitzy drug addict direct my life." Or whatever shady activities you're involved in.

"Good. Your response was brilliant."

"That's what I've been thinking. So, can you bring over the box I set just inside the shed? I'm hoping to find more letters or anything else that would help narrow my search."

"Sure, but why that box?"

"It looked like someone had taken extra care with it. It will go faster if you go through it with me."

"Okay. I have plans for the evening, but I'll meet you at four. And Eaven, thank you for pushing this forward. You're an amazing woman." He clicked off.

Yes, I am. She calculated the time. The dog food drive should finish early enough for her to meet him. She pulled on jeans and a sweater while her thoughts returned to Marie's fiery death, an intentional murder according to Greg. Clayton Mercer and his ancestors were scum, preying on the weak. It would feel luscious to see him lose. Really luscious. She had just finished blowing her hair dry when a knock sounded on the door.

In the hall, Claire smiled and handed her a huge bouquet of yellow roses. "These were just delivered."

"Thank you." She took the flowers and read the message. *For your beauty and courage. I think I would have ducked and run. Thank you for staying, Greg.*

He was trying too hard, but at least they weren't red. She buried her nose in their fragrance and grinned. The sweet-spice scent was reminiscent of her grandmother's roses that had surrounded her gazebo. Soft ocean air had carried their scent across the gardens she'd planted in Charleston.

"From Greg?" Claire asked.

She nodded.

"He's certainly a charmer."

"Yes, he is." It seemed forever since a man had spoken to her like that—or sent her flowers. She let out a soft sigh. He was charming, and she couldn't deny his attentions were flattering, but she sensed he'd do anything to reach his goal. Or goals. The question of his other activities, despite her resolve to ignore them, continued to gnaw at her mind.

At one o'clock sharp, Eaven kissed Roscoe's head and left him in his cage, then joined several other volunteers at Dr. Franklin's office.

Carol Franklin got everyone's attention. "What a wonderful turnout. Especially for a Sunday. Thank you for caring. Though many of our neighbors have recovered from our economic downturn, many have not. When we started seeing an increase in abandoned animals due to their family's inability to buy dog food, we just had to help our four-legged friends."

"How many dogs are we talking about?" Eaven asked.

"We have almost fifty families who responded to our ad for free dog food." Carol lifted a canvas bag from a stack on the table and showed everyone the adorable puppy on the front. "We'll go door to door and hand these out, then send a monthly schedule when we'll be back to exchange an empty bag for the full one."

An older man scowled. "How long do you think this needs to continue?"

People frowned and wagged their heads as though used to his temperament.

Carol's mouth opened, but Dr. Franklin stepped up next to her. "We hope just a year, but if it takes longer, we'll continue to do what we can. Take as many bags as you feel you have time to hand out. I think it's best to go by twos."

Carol pointed. "I've circled different areas on these maps, so we don't overlap. We also have bottled iced tea for you."

Eaven glanced around, not recognizing anyone. Most people had paired up and were heading out the door. She swallowed, beginning to feel self-conscious. Someone tapped her shoulder and she turned.

"Hi. I'm Sheila Lanza. Wanna team up?" The woman smiled and tilted her head. "Hey, didn't I see you on the Riverwalk last week?"

Glad for a friendly face, Eaven nodded. "You were buying a freezer for your smoked salmon business."

Sheila brightened. "Surprised you remember. I have to get used to people pausing their own lives long enough to care about a stranger." She laughed. "Now, all that's missing is the love of my life."

Eaven offered a quick smile. Her own mission involved *not* missing hers.

Sheila handed her a small package. "This is a sample of my smoked salmon. I've been shamelessly handing them out all over town."

"I've already tasted it. Great marketing idea." She tucked it into her purse.

They gathered their bags and a map while Sheila chatted. "Astoria's like living in a resort, but it's a real community. Like today. I've never seen this kind of compassion."

Having watched the thirty or so enthusiastic faces, Eaven ached for Lake Quinault, the only place she'd ever fit in. Or maybe not. She swallowed, realizing, for the most part, it had been an illusion, one she'd labored to maintain. Deciding in that moment to choose friends more carefully, friends who actually liked her, she turned to Sheila, a woman who seemed as genuine as Gail. "Can we take your car? Mine is packed."

"Sure. My truck is right around the corner."

They walked toward the truck but stopped for a car to pass. Greg slowed and lowered the window. Eaven tilted her head suspiciously. "Are you following me, Mr. Sault?"

A gorgeous smile lit his face. "Just monitoring my employee's time." His attention diverted to Sheila. "Hi."

Eaven smirked. He was incorrigible. "Sheila, meet Greg Sault. Greg, this is my new friend, Sheila Lanza."

"Good to meet you, Sheila." A horn honked behind him. He winked at Eaven. "See you later."

As he drove away, Sheila remarked, "What a hunk. What kind of work are you doin' for him?"

"Family research. Just temporary. I'll be leaving soon."

"I don't know if I'd be leaving. That was some gleam in his eye."

Eaven shrugged. Handsome and charming were not as seductive as they used to be. Still, her heart had leapt when their eyes connected. What was up with him lately?

They set the bottles of iced tea in the console of Sheila's truck and studied the map for the area they would be covering. "I chose my own neighborhood to get to know my neighbors better," she said. She started her diesel engine and let out the clutch to climb the hill. The truck's cab had seen better days, as had the jiggling rear-view mirror on Eaven's side. Sheila glanced over while she swept dust off the dashboard. "She's not so pretty anymore. My daddy bought her brand new, his face glowing like a cherub when he drove her off the lot."

"Where was that?"

"West Texas."

"You're a long way from home. Do you talk with him much?"

Sheila shrugged. "He's gone to heaven now." She pulled to the curb for their first stop.

"My father's gone too." Eaven stepped out and grabbed a handful of bags.

Sheila's face took on a wistful expression. "I was a daddy's girl. You?"

"Yeah." At one point. "What about your mother?"

"Gone before daddy. I still have an uncle, but don't count him kin anymore. After daddy died, he swept in and took over my ranch, basically booted me out."

"So, you moved here? Out of the blue?"

Sheila exhaled. "I tried resettling closer, but he tracked me down, hounded me to sign over my share of the property—even threatened me. I wouldn't do it."

Eaven faced her. "You didn't get legal help or call the police?"

Sheila huffed. "Didn't have the cash to fight him, besides, my uncle is the police in our little Podunk town. I think I would have disappeared. But I'm bidin' my time, countin' on all the greasy corn dogs lining his arteries and the whiskey killin' his liver. He wasn't lookin' so good last time I saw him. When he keels over, I'm waltzing back into town and taking what's mine." She grinned again, satisfaction accentuating her feminine features.

As they walked to the truck for more bags, Eaven sighed. "I can't believe how similar our situations are. I was basically run out of my place too." They opened the bottles of iced tea.

Sheila raised her bottle and tapped Eaven's. "To girl power."

"To starting from scratch."

"Yep. I trust the Lord, but while I'm here, my last name is *Lanza*."

"You think your uncle is still looking for you?"

"Oh, yeah. But he'll never think to look in Astoria. Ready to go?"

They knocked on doors until their bags were gone. Eaven anxiously checked the time when Sheila dropped her near the vet's office. "Thanks for the ride."

"It's so great to meet you. Sure you can't settle here?" Sheila asked.

Eaven wasn't sure. It was a great town with opportunities for sailing, hiking, and biking—all the things she loved, but some force was drawing her home to Charleston. "I need to go back for my mother's birthday. After that, I have some ideas, but who knows?"

"I hope we can get together before you leave." Sheila gave her a quick hug and returned to her truck.

Eaven watched her leave, wishing all friendships were as easy to form. She chewed her cheek. Why had Gail been the only one at the lake to really take to her?

Michael.

The answer was instantaneous. And clear. Her hand flew to her throat. She recalled little comments, slights. He had undermined her with their friends out of his petty envy. And guilt. Her lips tightened. She peered in the direction Sheila's truck had gone. Without him talking her down, people seemed to like her just fine.

She jogged to her car, concerned she would miss the window of time Greg had available. When she opened the door, she noticed her tire was low. A closer check revealed a thick nail protruding from the rubber—still hissing air! She jerked up and scanned the street. Whoever had slashed her tire had been there only moments ago.

CHAPTER 37

Late that afternoon, Eaven trudged up the steps to the inn, weary to the bone, a one-eighty-degree change from this morning. The tow truck took over an hour to arrive and change the tire, and the operator had charged her a small fortune, drawing her account down even further. To top it off, she couldn't get through to Greg to warn him she'd be late.

Waiting inside, he emerged from the parlor. A light whiff of aftershave undulated toward her senses. His mouth tense, he said, "Do you know how long I've been waiting? Where have you been?"

"I'm sorry, I tried to call…" Angry tears threatened.

"I was on my phone." His eyes scanned her face and his voice softened. "What happened?"

She wanted to accuse Clayton for the damage but had no proof. "Flat tire." She avoided the questions in his eyes. "I need to freshen up. Do you still have time to do this?"

He touched her cheek with his knuckle, his eyes smiling into hers. "Relax. I was worried and changed my meeting to a phone call. We have all night."

Those eyes undid her every time. He should be required to wear contacts. In her room, she tossed her purse on the bed. What she needed was a nap and a shower. Instead, she changed into loose-fitting pants and a warm hoodie, pulling wool socks over her frigid ankles. It had been a long wait for the tow truck. She wanted to attribute that to Clayton too but assured herself he couldn't possibly wield that much influence. Padding down the stairs, knowing Greg was waiting, her mood lifted. She scolded herself but fluffed her hair before entering the parlor.

He was sitting on the sofa and patted the seat next to him. "I want to know what's going on. You weren't even this peeved at Jennifer."

Though upset, and wrestling against the need to be comforted, she sat at the other end. He'd been different since the fundraiser. Attentive. Protective. At this moment, it was difficult to recall the misgivings she had about him. Maybe Sheila had been right about the gleam in his eye, but what did it matter? She'd be leaving soon, and she'd never been one to play at love.

While she explained about the tire, his expression hardened. "That's Clayton's style—cowardly intimidation."

She tucked her feet underneath her and rubbed her hands together. "I don't get why. He's hired me to help him. It must be someone else." Their eyes met and she lost her train of thought.

He scooted closer and rubbed her fingers. "You're ice cold."

Warmth invaded her from his touch and worked its way up to her neck. She withdrew her hand. "I'll warm up soon."

He laughed. "I can only hope." He chewed his cheek while continuing to assess her. "I hate that I don't have the resources to protect you."

"I don't need protection. It's just a stupid, juvenile prank." He was too close. They needed to get to work. The cardboard box sat on the coffee table. She leaned forward and noticed a folded poster next to it. "What's this?"

He grinned and opened it. "A chart showing my family tree."

She studied it. The names of Edward Mercer and Marie Sault were written above Sebastien's name, a declaration of his heritage. Blood red lines slashed through Jake, Frank, and Clayton Mercer's names on the other side. She pointed. "What's that about?"

He laughed. "Couldn't help myself."

A line led from Sebastien's name to Greg's. She glanced at him. "Nice work. Let's see if we can document it." She pointed to the postal stamp on the box. "I wanted to ask you about this when I found it. It was delivered to Jeffrey Sault in 1943 from Christine Edwards in San Francisco. Do you know who that is?"

He shrugged. "Doesn't sound familiar." He searched the dates on his family tree and pointed. "Looks like it arrived just after Marie's mother, Michelle, died." He touched the name on the chart. "My great-great-great-grandmother."

"Well, whoever sent it made a job of packaging it. Looks like it was never opened." She cut through the brittle tape and gaped. "Oooh." She gently lifted a vintage French wallpaper hat box out of its undeserving cardboard container. The lovely rose-colored floral design was most likely a Paul Dumas creation, but she would have to verify that. She turned the 1920's hat box around. It presented in good condition, except for a small amount of fraying on the bottom. Packed inside were several bundles of letters and cards. "This looks promising."

He'd been watching her with a grin. "It does." They opened the envelopes, most filled with Christmas and birthday wishes, and most addressed to someone named Francine. Sweet, but not important to their search.

Near the bottom, she nudged a letter from its yellowed envelope and scanned it. Her head jerked up. "It's from Marie. Listen to this!"

"October 10, 1899

My dearest sister, Francine...

Greg stopped her. "Marie's sister." He eagerly wrote her name on the family tree.

She continued reading.

"I am sorry for not writing sooner. Maman said I could bring Sebastien to live in Portland with her, but Edward opposed our leaving. I was very distressed, but it might be in our interest to stay. He has promised to provide a legitimate future for us. I finally have hope that soon I will be the lady of a grand house!

Your loving sister,

Marie"

"See, he's promised to marry her!" Greg put his arm around Eaven's back and hugged her shoulder toward him.

She pulled away, eyes questioning.

He gave her a lopsided grin. "Just happy."

"Uh huh." Sheez, he was cute, and a fun flirt, but she removed his arm and re-read the letter. "Marie should have taken Sebastien and fled."

He lifted an amused eyebrow and returned to business. "Her intention to legitimize her son was too strong. If there was a chance, I can see why she stayed."

She shuffled through the rest of the box. "Most of this is memorabilia." Another letter peeked from beneath a handkerchief. She glanced at the envelope. "It's written to Francine, about three weeks later." She cleared her throat and read it aloud.

"November 1, 1899

Francine,

You cannot know the depth of despair these days bring. I cannot bring myself to share my disgrace with maman, so you will have to bear my confession. Although Edward made a great fuss with a sweet ceremony and has assured me that Justice Gleeson has made everything legal, he won't publicly acknowledge us, and he won't give me the document to prove it. Instead, he has devised a most detestable game, creating clues to its location. Francine, he only gives me the clues in exchange for my favors."

"That monster," Greg hissed.

The page shook as she continued to read.

"Thus far, I have four clues hidden in my quarters. I ponder over them at night and they muddle my mind during my chores by day. His first clue is, 'The prize you seek will warm your heart and hand.' The second is, 'Your love has cost me a fortune to hide, yet I have no regrets.' What do these mean? I am not as clever as Edward. How will I ever secure Sebastien's future?

Pray for us,

Marie"

Eaven tossed the letter to the table and jumped up, striding the length of the narrow room. "That poor child. That despicable man."

A low growl escaped Greg's throat. He pressed his temples with the heels of his hands as though trying to pinch out the image.

Her heart went out to him. He was attractive, strong, and capable, yet even those qualities were no shield for the miseries that followed his life. She put her hand on his shoulder. "They're both gone. I'm sure she has found peace, and I'm equally certain that man is tormented."

He placed his hand over hers with a gentle caress and tilted his head. "You believe that story?"

She shrugged. "I guess it still lurks. But I do believe in justice. And that sounds just to me."

After moments of quiet, an idea sent her back to the sofa. She snatched the letter. "Greg!" Her voice rose an octave. "This says she hid the clues in her rooms! Maybe they're still there."

His eyes widened. "Why wouldn't they be?"

She clicked her nail while thinking. "If the Captain is having her search through the house, that must indicate—"

"—that the marriage certificate truly existed. If she never found it, it must still be there!" A broad smile filled his face.

She nodded. "That would be my guess. So, how does the clue fit in? *The prize you seek will warm your heart and hand.* My first guess has always been a fireplace."

"But there's also, *Your love has cost me a fortune to hide, yet I have no regrets.* I wonder if he might have been blackmailed to keep his relationship with her a secret. There were rumors regarding Marie having an illegitimate child. Captain Mercer was a proud man who wouldn't want his reputation sullied."

"That's a good possibility, but blackmail wouldn't direct her to a spot in the house. What if it's something completely different. Since the Captain didn't know Marie until long after the house was completed, perhaps he had something built afterward to hide the letter that cost him a fortune. Before I go tomorrow, I'll research the archives for changes in the house that he might have made. If I don't find anything, I'll search the mansion for newer structural elements that look expensive. And if I can sneak away from Tad, I'll see if I can find a hiding place for Marie's clues on the third-story."

He laughed. "Anything else while you're at it?"

"Talk to the dead?" she grinned.

He took her hand, his gaze dropping from her eyes to her lips. He didn't kiss her, but his voice grew throaty. "Be careful. I don't want any more blood spilled, especially not yours. That house's owners have a cruel reputation."

CHAPTER 38

Finished with her run, Eaven pulled off her shoes and threw them at the closet. She'd decided to force Michael to make her a priority by leaving messages on his phone every fifteen minutes. He hadn't returned any. Big surprise.

Sensing her time and favor were limited with Clayton, she'd listed some of his items online yesterday, hoping for an interested buyer. Today, she determined to look for a few less valuable, yet irresistible, pieces that might bring a quick sale and buy her more time in the mansion.

She left another stinging message for Michael to get her papers to her and drove to her appointment with Tad Jensen. This time when she entered the Mercer Mansion, bright lights exposed the blanket of cobwebs, including the lively occupants suspended in them. She shivered at the piles of dead flies and moths beneath the sticky webs of the insatiable household arachnids.

"Better?" Tad asked, obviously proud of his resourcefulness in supplying a generator and the small quantity of mis-matched lights that hung throughout the mansion.

"Much." She ducked under a particularly low, messy spider web and wondered how close she had come on her first venture to the large striped spider splayed across the silky threads.

He laughed. "Won't hurt you. Just a common American house spider. It's related to the black widow, but not poisonous." He tapped the web, sending the creature scurrying to the corner.

"Don't, please," she said, wanting to know exactly where that spiky guy was hanging. She glanced around, thankful for the light, but now saw long-legged insects everywhere. Her shoulders shimmied.

"Okay. Where do you want to start?"

She planned to examine the fireplaces, reasonably certain she could uncover any clever hiding place the Captain had devised. It was a smart place to start, especially if she couldn't get away from Tad to get upstairs. He'd already suggested that the third story held nothing of value to Clayton. Also, if she found the document hidden in a fireplace, she wouldn't need the clues. "I want to start from the front again."

He frowned. "Mr. Mercer says you have the run of the place, but honestly, it's wasting my time baby-sitting you."

So, he was told to watch her. Could he have punctured her tire? Still tense about the incident, she appraised him. He was young and seemed intent on building his career, not a likely hoodlum. "When did you last talk to him?"

"He called yesterday to check your appointment time. Said to tell you again he hoped there were no hard feelings about the accident." He shook his head. "If you'd stayed seated, you wouldn't have risked falling out of the boat."

Tad had no idea the risk *he* was taking by lecturing her. Heat radiated to her face, but she clamped her mouth shut. The truth would be twisted no matter what she said. If she found the marriage certificate, Clayton wouldn't know what hit him.

Stepping into the sitting room, she spied the richly carved fireplace mantel that topped the fire box. Was it the original, or did the Captain purchase it later, expressly to hide Sebastien's letter? She ran her finger over the cold marble mantel, not recognizing the style. It looked to have been made to order, utilizing a mix of designs from different periods. "Awfully dusty. Do you have a cloth?"

He frowned. "I'll get one."

As soon as he was out the front door, she pressed and pulled on every point of the marble mantel. She knocked and listened for any hollow place. Bending, she shined her flashlight up the flue and wiggled the fire brick.

"You'll get an eyeful of soot that way."

She jumped back, not expecting him to return so quickly. "Just checking."

"For bats?" He smirked and handed her the rag.

She chuckled to mask her tension. "Never know." Taking the old white T-shirt, she rubbed hard along the sides, wondering what she would do if a hidden door popped open in front of him. She gently swiped over the top, catching a network of webs and dust. "Yuck."

He sighed. "Nothing's been cleaned for over a century." He fidgeted with his phone then stepped toward the front door, probably seeking better cell service.

When his back was turned, she quickly twisted, pulled, and pushed the carved snake on the right-hand marble pilaster. She knelt to examine the brass grate, then checked the snake on the left. The marble was also solid.

Todd returned to her side, grinning.

"Girl friend?"

His grin broadened.

She smiled, her thumb rubbing against the mantel. "The marble is in excellent condition. Odd design though."

"Yeah. He used snakes everywhere. Crazy old guy."

She spent two hours in the sitting room, photographing, measuring, and making notes of the pieces most likely to sell quickly. And while Tad texted, she searched for spots that might hide the document. Nothing presented itself. The rug might hide a trap door that led under the house, but that area would be cool, not warm, as stated in the clue. After running out of places to look, she said, "I'm headed to the library."

They moved into the brightly lit room loaded with gilded lamps, Bombay chests, and carved French chairs. Where to start? After working through a host of mini treasures, she moved to the twin bookshelves and sighed. Hundreds of old books called for her attention, but instead, she pushed, prodded, and knocked on the wood.

Tad sat on one of the larger chairs. "What's that for?"

"Testing for soundness," she said in as serious a tone as she could manage. Nothing indicated they contained a secret compartment, so she turned to the fireplace. White and green marble covered the whole façade, including the flutes on the pilasters. "Superb." It reminded her of a beautiful piece she had seen at auction. That one was early nineteenth century and sold for over one hundred twenty thousand dollars. Would Clayton be interested in selling it? He could easily replace it with something attractive but less expensive.

With a pop and crackle, the lights blinked out.

"Great. I think the generator blew," Tad said.

"Sheez. What else? I'd planned to work for at least three more hours."

"Better go," he said. "Looks like we've got another torrent outside."

She barged out the door onto the front porch and pulled her hood over her head. "Call me the moment this is fixed." Fighting sheets of rain, she jumped into her car and called Greg. "Another delay, but there's an interesting fireplace that gave me an idea. I'm heading back to the Heritage Museum to find information on the mansion's construction." Later, she planned to find comparisons for the pieces she'd chosen and get them listed. At least the day wouldn't be completely wasted.

"Meet me for dinner at the Fort George Brewery?" he asked. "I'm paying."

She smiled, realizing that even though she needed to avert his flirtations on occasion, she was enjoying this version of Greg over the abrupt, grumpy one. Sure."

A few minutes later, Michael called. "I made it to town. Where are you?"

Her stomach knotted. She glanced in the car mirror at her disheveled hair and wet face. She had wanted to look beautiful the next time he saw her. To be confident and pulled together. To...to what? Lure the cheater back? He can't be trusted, never could. Her shoulders slumped from the mass of emotion she carried. "Meet me at the Heritage Museum. I'll be just inside the door." The drive took all of three minutes. The rain felt like liquid ice pelting her face when she ran up the museum steps.

Michael arrived soon after. Battling the wind, he pulled the heavy museum door closed behind him. In the lobby, his gaze swept over her dripping form. He pulled back his jacket hood. "Hi." Water dripped off his blond curls onto his shoulders. He was unshaven, his eyes looked dark and tired.

Pressure swelled in her chest. Her instincts compelled her to wrap her arms around him and make it better, whatever it was. With great effort, she barred the reaction.

"Crystal's car broke down a few blocks from here, so the timing worked out. Finally." He shrugged apologetically.

Crystal had been in Astoria? "What was she doing here?"

He chewed his cheek. "She needed some space."

Eaven peered into his eyes. "What's going on, Michael?"

He rubbed the back of his neck. "Your name came up at my party, and I guess it torqued her. She took off that night and ended up here where her car broke down."

A hot flash surged through Eaven's system. Michael's party had been on Saturday. Her tire was punctured on Sunday. Crystal?

"I needed to get these papers to you anyway. Guess I'll shop for a car while I'm here—kill two birds with one stone."

Dead birds—the crow? Chills fingered up her spine.

"It's too bad, really. She has this classic woody station wagon, but it's dead."

Eaven sucked in air. Sheez, the shooting. An old woody had sped away from the cottage after someone shot at her. And last week, Crystal's car had broken down in Raymond—a town between Lake Quinault and Astoria. That was three strikes. Crystal must have followed her here, but why? The bullet hit at least four feet from where she'd stood, most likely to scare her, get her to leave town, out of Michael's reach.

Should she tell him of his sweetheart's bent for psychopathic drama? Rub the stupidity of his choice in his face? Pale and drawn, it looked as if he was learning the hard way.

"Here." He held out a plastic bag with the papers inside. "Didn't want them getting wet after all the trouble." His tired voice begged for comfort.

Was he sorry? She reached for the bag. For a moment, they both held it. "Thank you." What else did she want to say? Was there some magic word that might draw him back? Is that what she wanted? Certainly, a part of her did. An eighteen-year marriage was a lot to give up.

He gave a tight-lipped nod. Without another word, without touching her hand or showing any acknowledgment of the intimacy they'd shared, he turned and pushed out the door.

She gasped. This might be the last time she ever saw him. The man she loved with her whole heart was walking away. Before she could think what to say or do, his taillights disappeared around the corner. Gone.

The plastic bag shook in her hand. *Till death do us part.* Death *had* parted them. Death of the dream, of growing old with the man who knew her as well as she knew him. That was what cut so deeply. He did know her, had to know what this was doing to her, but there had been nothing, *NOTHING*, in his face.

She fled to the tiled bathroom and sank onto a wooden chair. The tears that had been building finally released. *Oh God, make this pain end.* Mrs. B had tried to drill into her and Paisley that God was the only one who would never leave her. Still, she'd always counted on flesh and blood.

Energy spent, she grabbed the sink and dragged her body from the seat. "Okay, baby. Okay." She splashed icy water on her swollen eyes and face. It was over. Officially time to move on.

In the lobby, she lowered her gaze from the quizzical expression of the female volunteer and showed her research pass. For the next two hours, she focused her mind and immersed herself in historic files, maps, and photographs of Astoria and Astorians. At some point during the afternoon, thoughts of Michael eased into the background.

The brilliant archivist who worked here had every detail of Astoria either memorized or at her fingertips. Gladdened to be working around a professional, Eaven sniffed the stack of photographs in her hand and a smile broke through. *Old.*

The research work she'd done earlier, combined with the lively setting of the Fort George Brewery helped to lift Eaven's spirits. "Good pizza. Thanks." She lifted a string of cheese to her mouth. The bite stuck in her tight throat. She lifted her glass of microbrew beer named after a quest, thinking the name fitting her pursuits in Astoria. Gulping it, she hoped it would either numb her heart or energize her mind. She didn't care which.

Greg raised his glass. "They make some good brews here."

She glanced from the glossy wood table out the picture windows. "I imagine they also enjoy a fabulous view of the Columbia, when it's not raining." She tried for a light chuckle.

"Live here long enough, you get used to it." Bluesy music had his foot tapping and his body swaying. He removed his leather coat and hung it on the back of his chair. A black T-shirt stretched across his muscled chest. "Want to dance?"

Still feeling punched, she shook her head. "I can't."

He raised his eyebrows. "Sure, you can. A little fun will do you good."

One other couple danced and laughed in an open space near a corner of the large room. Greg's smile melted the last of her resistance. She smiled. "Maybe so." His hand, warm and sure, encased hers as he steered them through the tables. When he pulled her close and led her in a slow swing, her pulse throbbed with conflicting emotions, yet she relaxed into it. The rhythm was easy to follow. *He* was easy to follow.

He wrapped her next to his side and held her for a beat. Their eyes met. His mouth sobered. Then, he grinned and unwrapped her.

After a triple twirl, she laughed at the dizzy sensation. "This song is fabulous."

The song ended, and he pulled her close, lips touching her cheek just in front of her ear. "*You* are fabulous."

She gently pushed away. It was fun, but it was just a dance. "It's getting late. Let's get to business."

He replied with a teasing smile. "As you wish." Entwining their fingers, he led her back to their table.

She pulled her hand free when she sat and reached for a folder. "I made copies of some interesting items from the museum."

"He leaned toward her. "What do you have?"

She pushed the papers between them. "From Marie's letters, we know it wasn't until 1899 that the Captain agreed to her demands and created his abominable game. I narrowed my search and looked for a record that he'd had something expensive built around that time."

"Did you discover anything?"

"Only this, but it might be important. A report was filed by a J. T. Hupert against Captain Mercer for refusal to pay for repairs on a marble fireplace. Hupert had carved and installed it, but it doesn't say which fireplace or in which room."

"How many are there?"

"Three downstairs." She clicked her fingernail. "I have to get back into that house. Maybe if I had someone with me, they could distract Tad while I look around."

"Jenny?"

"What?"

"I'm sure Jenny would do it. Look, she was loaded at the fundraiser. Doesn't even remember saying the things she said. She was mortified when I saw her."

She stiffened. "And that means I want to be around her?"

He huffed. "Look, we don't have much time or many options. She is actually a sweet person who wants to help."

Uh-huh. She would probably smile while twisting a knife in Eaven's gut. Her eyes fell to the wood tabletop. Her brother had also done uncharacteristic things while under the influence. Also, it wasn't like they needed to interact much. "Okay, ask her."

He nodded. "Good."

She tossed a copy of a police report from December of 1899 onto the table and pointed. "This confirms that the house was closed after the investigation into the Captain's death."

He skimmed it. "They left out the fact that they never found the murderer. A part of Astoria's darker history."

She stopped herself from saying the Captain deserved it. "I imagine the trauma added to Jake's decision to close the house. How old was he?"

"Nineteen."

"That's young to lose a father."

"Seventeen is even younger."

"I'm sorry, Greg." She glanced out the window. The clouds had lifted. The relatively smooth surface of the Columbia River masked the turmoil underneath. Greg was like that. She could hear it in his voice while uncovering the misery of Marie's fate. More than ever, she wanted to even the score for him. And for Marie.

CHAPTER 39

Astoria, Oregon, December 1899

The game was disgusting, yet Marie put on a gay smile and gave a coquettish glance at the Captain. "What is my clue today?" He had returned from work, more tired than normal. Perhaps he would just hand it to her.

"Come here, my love." Face twisted with the evil of his sixty wicked years, he held out his long fingers.

How had she ever thought him handsome? Inside, rage screamed, but she was held hostage. She let the devil embrace her in his office, then pulled back. "Show me."

He pulled a folded note from his silk vest pocket and waved it. When she reached for it, he held it behind his back. "First, come with me." He led her to his room and unbuttoned her dress. He finished quickly and left the note on the night table.

Tears trickled over her cheeks while she made his bed. She hated him, hated herself, but it was too late for her redemption. All she could hope for was to redeem her son's fortune.

Heat inflamed her face as she read the note. What kind of clue was this? Hardly worth her soul. She'd thought her beauty would gain her privilege. Instead of a lady, she'd become a harlot.

CHAPTER 40

Astoria, Oregon, Current Day

Greg left the brewery and drove back to the cottage. The rain and blackness outside the kitchen window emphasized the emptiness around him. He pulled out a scuffed kitchen chair and dropped into it. As a child, he had sat next to this table in a highchair, then in a booster seat, and finally, feeling proud of himself, in a regular wooden chair like dad. His mother, having died so young, held no place in his memory, no lingering sweetness.

He fiddled with the gold coin around his neck. It had belonged to Marie. Gran gave it to him during high school. At the time, he didn't think it that important. Thought of hocking it. Of course, he had been a regular pothead back then.

Tonight, Eaven had started to soften, had almost let him in. She wasn't just beautiful, she was smart. It wouldn't take her long to see through him. He dialed the number he had memorized since being back.

"Hi, Greg." Jenny's voice, void of its previous melodic quality, rasped through the connection.

"Are you good? The treatment going well?"

She scoffed. "Great. I decided to do this at home. A little at a time."

"What? Brett said he had it all set up."

"Yeah, he set me up alright. Don't knock it. It's working. My doctor's providing support."

He pinched the bridge of his nose, knowing how impossible it would be for her to stay clean by herself. "Sorry, Jen, I know it's hard."

"Today is better. Did you want something?"

"Yes. I need a favor"

"What?"

He gritted his teeth. "Would you go with Eaven to the Mercer Mansion? She..." He paused, still not knowing how far he could trust an addict. "She wants to check out the antiques and needs someone to distract the realtor, so he doesn't suspect how interested she is."

"What's *your* interest? Seems a bit of a coincidence, new girlfriend into antiques, the Mercer Mansion finally opened. Your father's nonsense is a dead end, Greg."

His pulse jumped. Was he that transparent? "I have my own reasons for being here. Eaven has hers."

Jenny said nothing at first, though he could hear her breathing. "This is Clayton you're dealing with. He has eyes and ears everywhere."

"Let me worry about Clayton. Will you help?"

"Eaven must loathe me. I would."

"I told her you weren't yourself. She's willing to let it go."

"Not likely. Who's the realtor?"

"Tad Jensen."

She laughed. "I know that kid. He's hot for me. Guess I could distract him."

Greg chuckled. "Thanks, Jen. The appointment is tomorrow at eleven. Meet her there?"

"Sure. I'd like to see the old place myself. Be careful, Greg. The Saults have never succeeded in the big leagues." She hung up.

Be careful? Big league? Her voice carried an edge. He wondered how much she knew. And what he didn't.

CHAPTER 41

Eaven watched Tad's face when Jennifer exited her red Audi in front of the Mercer Mansion. Already the young man was agog at the busty blond. Jennifer met her on the sidewalk. "Please accept my apology. I was...not myself."

Though Eaven felt icy, she nodded. "That's what Greg said."

"I doubt you'd know what it's like."

"No. I've never done drugs." Images of her strung-out brother, writhing on his bed, still made her cringe.

"Did Greg tell you I'm *better*?"

"Yes." A pang of pity stung Eaven's heart as she watched Jennifer hide her trembling hands. "You have a good doctor?"

She nodded. "The best. Not my husband."

"Good luck to you. Thanks for helping."

Her gaze sweeping over the mansion, Jennifer asked, "What does Greg hope to gain? Stake his claim on the Mercer fortune?" She watched Eaven's eyes.

Shrugging, Eaven said, "Couldn't tell you. I'm just here to evaluate the furnishings, find buyers, and make my commission."

Jennifer smirked. "Uh huh."

They reached Tad, who offered a series of embarrassing compliments to Jennifer as they entered the mansion.

Inside, Eaven breathed easier. The brightly lit rooms would aid her search tremendously. What would *cost a fortune* in here? Just about everything. She revised her question. What would *cost a fortune and warm Marie's hand and heart*? Was it really a fireplace? Marie's collection of fireplace photos showed she must have had the same idea. The two Eaven had already examined proved fruitless.

While Jennifer chatted and Tad pointed out some extraordinary antiques, Eaven took her time to complete her notes and get better shots of the furnishings while surreptitiously looking for hiding spots.

At a signal from Eaven, Jennifer strayed into the library and called to Tad to show her something. His grin widened. "I'll be right back."

Eaven quickly searched more rooms for the third fireplace and was headed toward the back of the house, when Tad reappeared sooner than she expected, Jennifer behind him.

His eyes narrowed. "Where are you going?" His accusatory tone reminded her he was Clayton's watchdog.

She thought quickly. "I haven't seen a dining room."

"Follow me." He led them to the door of the kitchen.

She stood at the doorway and crinkled her nose at the mess. "What happened here?" A marred wooden table stood in the middle of the room, but one could hardly see it. Paper and weeds had been smuggled into the room and chewed by rodents. Nests and tunnels pushed against the black and chrome potbelly stove and wooden ice chest. "Rats?"

"We haven't cleaned this yet, remember?"

"You're kidding," Jennifer said. "How will you sell this dump?" Something scurried under the papers and she squealed and jumped back.

"Look, Clayton said show it to Eaven, so I am."

Eaven pointed across the kitchen. "Where does that lead?"

"That's the servant's staircase."

She peered through the partially opened door. Steps led upward.

He motioned to the door at her right. "The formal dining room is through there." His voice lowered significantly, almost to a whisper. "That's where the Captain was killed."

She laughed. "If you keep that up, you'll never sell this place."

"I didn't mean to be dramatic. It's just..." He stepped ahead of her without finishing. "There's an odd feel in there and the extension cords didn't reach that far."

She huffed. "I brought my flashlight this time." When she stepped into the dining room, her jaw dropped. An antique Chippendale table occupied the center of the long room, flanked by twelve chairs. Probably eighteenth century. "This will bring Clayton a handsome sum." If she found a buyer, her commission would soar.

After snapping several photos, she studied the carpet beneath the table. Unfortunately, the rodents had done a job on one corner. The other corner appeared darker than the rest. She bent and touched the blackened area. A razor-sharp pang shot up her finger. Pain. Panic. Her hand yanked back.

"The Captain was beaten to death. Right there," Tad pointed.

She jumped up. "You could have told me."

"How'd I know you would touch his blood."

"Nobody cleaned it?"

"Like I said, Jake locked this place and left."

She stepped back while sensations assaulted her ears, cries of anguish. *Get away! Stop! Help!* She swallowed. Nothing this specific had ever come to her before. It felt like a presence still lingered. "Beaten you say?"

In the filtered light, he nodded. "With that." He pointed to a brass andiron laying on its side.

"May I?" she asked.

He shrugged. "Not a crime scene anymore, don't see why not."

She squatted and reached to set it upright. Heat seared her hand and she dropped it. "Sheez!"

"What is it?" Jennifer moved closer.

Eaven cradled her hand, ice-cold, not even warm. "A brass cannonball andiron." Her voice trembled at the rage she'd felt when she touched it. She stood, resisting the urge to lean against the chair or touch another thing in this room. Concerned she was acting strange, she assessed the andiron. "I've never seen anything like it. It must have been handmade. Look how the snake curves up the standards and around the ball finial."

Tad flashed his light around the room. "More snakes here."

Her gaze moved to the illuminated fireplace. This was it! Marie's photos showed before and after shots of the mantel. The carved wood had been replaced by marble. With a nod, she pleaded for Jennifer to distract Tad.

The woman shrugged and cooed at the boy only half her age. "Can we go back where the light is, Tad?"

"Will you be all right here?" he asked.

"Yes. Go ahead." When they left, she searched the marble for any hidden chambers. She reached high into the flue, feeling and wiggling fire brick until she exhausted the most common possibilities. The clues had to point to someplace else. Out of ideas and frustrated, she chewed her bottom lip. The document could be anywhere. She needed to find the clues Marie hid upstairs in her room. Something creaked overhead.

She rubbed the chills from her arms. Across the kitchen, the door to the servant's stairwell stood ajar. Again, it sounded like soft footfalls overhead. Tempted to escape outside, she forced her mind to stay calm. Afterall, she'd told Greg she didn't scare easily. Usually.

Taking a breath, she sprinted across the trash, barely keeping herself from falling into the many embedded rat nests, their squeaks sending out warning. She leapt into the servant's stairwell, grabbed the rail, and gazed up. The stairs disappeared into near blackness. Was she ready for this? Memories of her time spent crawling through low-ceilinged subterranean tunnels below an Irish castle returned. She pictured the burial cave with mounds of bones and dozens of skinless skulls. Their hollow eyes and wide grins had followed her every move. Yet she survived.

She pressed her hand against her chest. This was only an old house, stop imagining things. Residual emotions did not equate to ghosts. Exhaling, she climbed lightly up the steps. A narrow door opened onto the second floor. Bits of sunlight filtered through the open curtain at the end of the hall. She listened but heard no sound. No breathing.

Moving forward, she checked the first bedroom on her left. The closed curtains kept out most of the light. Still, she could make out a bed, dressers, and a wash basin. A trunk stood at the foot of the bed and on one side of the room, a small fireplace occupied a place under a large painting of a ship at sea. This must have been the Captain's suite.

A noise from the ceiling above made her jump. Steps. She wanted to run down the main stairs where Tad and Jennifer were, but this might be her only chance.

Returning to the service stairway, she pointed her flashlight upward and quietly climbed the stairs. A door at the top led to the third-story servant's quarters. She stopped before the closed door and listened, then grabbed the cold brass knob and slowly turned it. A loud click caused her to grit her teeth.

She pushed the narrow door open a crack. It squeaked as it rubbed against the door jam. When she peeked through, it was totally dark. She flashed her light down the hallway that ran the length of the house. The sounds had stopped.

Moving carefully, she leaned through the first open door. A child's room. A rocking horse with faded pink reins stared at her from the corner. A small brass bed huddled against the low ceiling where the roof pitched.

Something dropped in the next room.

Eaven tensed, forced her body to move silently to the next room. She tipped her head forward enough to see into it. On one side stood a narrow armoire with no door. No one occupied the room. Holding her breath, she took a tentative step inside. On the far wall, a dark mauve curtain covered the window. She drew it back and glanced through the diamond-pane glass that faced the front street.

A woman had watched her from this room! She whirled around, dropping the curtain.

Something moved under the bed.

Gasping, she dashed past it out the door.

Once outside, with nothing chasing her, she stopped, pulse pounding in her ears.

She stayed outside the door but knelt low enough to shine the light under the brass rail of the bed that showed beneath a pink coverlet. Two yellow eyes gleamed at her.

"A cat." She felt foolish. Still, her pulse pounded. Crossing back to the window, she opened the curtain and caught it on the hook. A shiver passed through her. This curtain had been open when she stared up from the sidewalk. The cat must have knocked it down.

Stealing herself against her imagination, she used the sunlight to study the room. The dresser drawers had been turned out, their contents strewn across the floor. A pillow had been ripped open, its feathers limp with dust. Someone had searched this room. Had Jake searched here for the document?

Where would Marie hide her clues? A small trunk lay upside down, its fabric lining shredded. Eaven bent to turn it over. A pile of clothing lay under it, women's dresses, and a stash of small boy's clothing. Expensive clothing. Not something a maid could afford. Marie must have spent some of the money she received from the Captain. Had she been planning to leave? Had she grown tired of looking for the clues and the Captain's games?

Desperate, she willed the clues to be here. Marie's letter said she had hidden them in her quarters. Maybe that included the whole third story.

"Ms. Alexander?" Tad's voice called from below. "Are you up there?"

"Dang," she hissed. She ran into the hall and checked the one remaining door on the opposite side of the hallway. It was locked.

"I have another appointment," Tad shouted again.

"Coming." Before heading down the stairs, she peeked into Sebastien's room again. Something was off, but she couldn't identify it.

"Ms. Alexander, time's up."

She strolled down the main stairway as though she'd just been perusing the house. At the bottom, she faced a very flustered Tad. Jenny must have left.

"What were you doing?" he demanded.

"What do you think? Checking out the ghost."

His mouth opened, eyes wide.

She shook her head at his drama. "It's a cat." She marched to her car and unlocked the door. Turning back, she spied the diamond-paned window on the third story.

The curtain was closed.

Her voice faltered when she tried to talk to Tad. "There are valuable pieces upstairs as well. I'll need more time to see the whole house—and a lot more light. Call me when it's ready."

In the privacy of her car, she called Greg, holding the phone with both hands. When he answered she launched in. "It's a good bet the clues are in Marie's quarters, but it's too dark to see anything clearly. See if you can find some extra-long extension cords. I don't want any more excuses from Tad."

"Clayton too cheap to supply his own?"

She could imagine Greg's dark smirk as he spoke. "In the meantime, we need to finish searching the loft in the shed. I think Marie made plans to leave. There must be something more that can shed light on her intentions. Maybe she had already found the document. Can we meet tomorrow morning?"

He hesitated. "Let's make it noon-ish."

"Okay, I'll bring my gloves. That loft must be full of black widows and who knows what else."

"Like ghosts?" he teased.

"I don't know what to think." Darkness had seeped into her bones. What had happened in the mansion?

CHAPTER 42

Eaven needed something to offset the darker aspects of her job. The discovery of a sunny, new cafe, this one on the end of a pier overlooking the river, elevated her mood. She added it to the reasons she'd been collecting to like Astoria. It was two days until Halloween and decorations draped the windows—spiders, ghosts, and witches. Every employee donned a costume that seemed unique to their character, a large girl as a pumpkin, a tall man as Frankenstein.

Ignoring the last of her coffee that had now gone cold, she tagged and sorted the photos she'd taken at the mansion yesterday. Without good lighting, the shot of the dining table was dim, but she was still able to identify it and added the last of the pieces to her website. So far, no one had sent any inquiries, but it wouldn't take long.

Watching the abundant water flowing by the window, she smiled at the growing size of her potential commission. Maybe she'd have enough to rent a storefront sooner than she planned. She closed her computer to head for her other job.

While driving to Greg's cottage, she chewed her cheek. The mansion gave her the jitters. There were obvious reasons, but there was something else, more sinister, that she couldn't put her finger on. Also, Greg's playful flirtations confused her. Sometimes, he felt like a common hood, at others, he was smooth and classy. Yes, she felt the attraction, but so what? The sooner she finished, the sooner she could get on with her life. Whatever that was. The investment papers were signed, and Fishburn had deposited her money. There was nothing to keep her here.

She knocked on the weathered door of the cottage.

He opened it immediately. "Afternoon." His thigh and knee peeked through the rips in his designer jeans.

"Stylin," she smirked.

"That's me." He tweaked her chin between his thumb and finger. At her startled expression, he grinned. "You were looking way too serious."

She pushed aside her conflicting emotions. "You're probably right." A sigh escaped.

"What?"

She shrugged. "Even with all the down and dirty history I know about the Mercers, I'm missing Astoria already. And I have plans in Charleston. I don't see how I could have latched onto a new place this fast."

"I'd like to think it had something to do with me."

She felt her face blush. "Yes, well, there have been times…"

He took her hand and gazed into her eyes. "You don't have to go anywhere."

"Yes, I do." She pulled her hand free. "Let's get to the shed."

He chuckled. "You're too strong for your own good."

"No, for my own good, I'm strong."

"Right." He unlocked the shed and they each swung a door open wide. She flicked on the light switch. Using a ladder, he offered to brave the spiders and bring down the boxes and packages that had been shoved under the low eaves. She took the last box and sat it on the dirt floor.

"That's it." He climbed down and raised a cheeky eyebrow. "Do I get a gold star? A kiss?"

She shook her head. "Enough, Mr. Sault. Let's go through these out here. No sense bringing all this dust into the house."

"Agreed. I'll get us something to sit on." Soon, he returned, carrying only one kitchen chair. He rubbed his jaw. "I need to leave, got a call from my associate." His mood had turned hard again.

Her's too. She grabbed the chair and turned her back on him. In a couple of minutes, his engine started, and he drove away. Getting him to help was like trying to nail Jell-O to the wall. She shut the doors against the cold wind and went to work. After searching through four of the boxes, she grinned and leaned back in the chair. She had what she'd been looking for. Thrilled, she set it and the letter aside to go through the rest, then took her findings into the house.

Sometime later, Greg returned, his face grim. He peeked toward the street before locking the door then flung his jacket on a chair. "Want a beer?"

She shook her head, hoping he hadn't been doing something stupid, then quickly reminded herself his actions were none of her business. "These are the rest of your grandma's keepsakes."

"And?"

"And I found something that might tell us where Marie hid her clues."

"Where?" The tone of his voice barely elevated. He plopped on the flowered sofa.

She lifted a blue satin belt. "Watch this." She unclipped the two metal clasps and let one side slide down the belt. The satin fell open, revealing a pocket. "The perfect hiding place, say for small scraps of paper with clues written on them."

"Let me see." He studied the careful stitching that caused the lined fabric to close when stretched, or open when the tension relaxed. "Simple, but ingenious. But what makes you think it was used for clues?"

"*Might* have been used for clues. Listen." She held a faded letter, eyes searching it. "Here. This was with it, from Marie's mother."

"*...Continue to save the gold and silver coins Captain Mercer gives you. I have someone willing to buy my house in a few months, so we can purchase something for the three of us. Then, you can raise your son properly.*

Since you've seen Jake searching your rooms, I am sending you this pattern for a pocket belt to keep the coins safe. The belts can be made in many sizes. I know you dislike blue and I would make another, but my fingers are gnarled and painful. I have enclosed a wide strip of woven tapestry and another of pink satin. You are clever enough to copy my design. This was how we stowed our valuables when we crossed the ocean from France. Be smarter than you have been, my daughter. I will arrive before Christmas.

With much love, Maman"

Eaven gripped the letter. "Apparently, the Captain was very generous to her."

Greg's lips thinned. "Yeah, he didn't want her to leave, so he gave her money, ostensibly for Sebastien."

"He was a low life, even more reason to uncover the truth. If we can prove Sebastien was his son, then that makes you an heir to whatever is left of his fortune."

"From the suffering they caused my family, they owe me big time."

"Yes, but it might take a lot of money to defend your position."

"Well, there's only two of us left. Maybe that will change."

The hair stood on her forearm. "Let's focus on finding the marriage certificate." She fingered the soft satin of the blue belt. "It's likely Marie made more of these—oh!" She stood so fast, the letter dropped to the floor. "I've seen it."

"The other belt?"

"Yes! It's pink and hangs like reins around the neck of a rocking horse in Sebastien's old room."

Standing, he grabbed her hands and finally grinned. "Way to go, Eaven Kensington Alexander."

She laughed. "You remember that train of a name?"

"I remember everything about you, from the first time we met."

She looked up, captured by the admiration of his gaze. Heat fanned between them. He reached his hand toward her cheek.

Loud pounding on the front door startled them. "Police. Open up."

Greg's mouth transformed to a snarl. He pushed her away. "Get in the kitchen and don't come out." He pulled a gun from the drawer closest to him and tucked it behind his back in his waistband.

She held her breath and watched him replace the chain on the door before opening it a crack.

"Yeah?"

"You new in town?"

"Yeah, so what?"

Eaven bit her lip. Why would he act so cocky with the police?

"We received a complaint about cars coming and going up this driveway at all times of night. This is a nice neighborhood. Want to keep it that way."

"Will do." Greg shut the door in the officer's face. He came back and shoved the gun into the kitchen drawer.

"Do you have a license for that?"

"I do."

"I assume Jennifer is coming and going. Who else?" She hated how close she'd come to letting him pull her in.

"Jenny's been here once. No one's coming and going. The cops must have gotten the address wrong. More likely, Clayton sent them."

She rubbed her temple. Michael lied to her for nine years without her having a clue. Police. Guns. Sudden meetings. "Greg, what are you really doing in Astoria? Are you dealing?"

His face reddened. His fists clenched and unclenched.

She took a step back, wondering if he would hit a woman.

Instead, he hissed, "I shared my soul with you. More than with anyone. You better go."

"That's just what I was thinking." She grabbed her purse and stomped out the door, anxious to get away from his combustible anger. Three blocks away, her phone kept buzzing until she finally pulled over. "Hello?"

"Hi, Eaven. This is Brett Gellens. Do you have a minute?"

What part did he play in this pot of stinking fish? "Yes."

"Just wanted to apologize to you again."

"For what?"

"For my wife, of course. But also for Greg. I know he's been gone awhile, but he was born an Astorian. I don't want you leaving with the idea that this is what our town is about. We're a proud and supportive community. I've been trying to get the Mercer's out of our town for over twenty years. It was my hope that Greg might help, but it turned out he only came back to muscle in on Clayton's territory."

"Mr. Gellens, I think you are mistaken."

"Really? He told me he came back to get rid of Clayton, then plans to double what Clayton's been smuggling through here. Who do you think that Ralph character is? I found out he's a killer. Greg's no better. You should leave town."

Her thoughts swirled into a jumble. All she could manage was, "Goodbye." She pressed her forehead on the top of her steering wheel. What was true? She couldn't bring herself to believe Brett's assessment of Greg and Ralph, no doubt based on jealousy, but she was fed up with all the drama.

Driving away, she considered her options. She could quit. However, unlike the men in her life, she kept her word. Greg and Clayton were difficult, but so were some of the clients she worked for in England. If she finished the jobs for them, the money would provide breathing room until she found something else. Clayton had said to focus on the main level rooms, which she had. Though the upstairs bedrooms held more antiques, she made the decision to call it good. That left her work for Greg.

She clicked her nail until it broke. As soon as she could arrange it, she would go back to the mansion, get the pink ribbon from the rocking horse's neck, see what she could find to get Greg his proof. If not, his two weeks were up, and he owed her the money regardless of the outcome. Then she was done.

What she wouldn't do was get dragged into another drug scam, if that's what this was. One scammer scamming another. Everyone lying, crying, whining. She had stuck it out with her brother until his last overdose. Never again.

CHAPTER 43

Needing to clear her head after Brett's call, Eaven ignored her work and went for a run that ended at Dr. Franklin's office. "Hey boy," she said, scratching Roscoe's chest. He nuzzled his nose under her chin and leaned into her.

"That big boy's in love," Lenora said, a genuine smile brightening her face.

"Me too." Eaven rubbed her cheek on his silky head. "My husband took our dog in the divorce."

Lenora's smile faltered. "Roscoe's almost ready to go back home. Clayton called to check on his progress."

"You can't turn him back over to that man. He's the problem, not Gina."

"No one witnessed the abuse. We can't prove anything. All we can do is keep him here as long as possible."

She surrounded Roscoe with both arms and whispered next to his ear. "We'll see about that."

Mulling over how to keep Roscoe away from Clayton, she ran back to the River's Glory to start repacking. She pushed bags and boxes into the car and frowned. Where had all the room gone? Her only purchases were the dress and heels from the thrift store, which she immediately trashed after Jennifer's dinner.

She put her hands on her hips and breathed deeply. It would feel good to be moving to new destinations, seeing fresh, new things. Charleston tugged at her. The happiness and certainty lasted about an hour, until the most unexpected name appeared on her phone. *Cassandra.*

Eaven let her sister's message go to voicemail to give herself time to respond. Cassandra could always think faster on her feet. That's how she intimidated. No one wanted to get on the bad side of her sharp tongue. When Eaven retrieved the message, it was no less than she expected.

"This is Cassandra. Lillian informed me that you pushed your way into staying at her house for her party. I'm afraid that won't do. We have guests coming from around the world to celebrate, and I've promised the rooms. I can send you a list of local hotels for your visit. Please do not pressure Lillian with your needs. She is too frail and I, at least, want her to see her seventy-sixth birthday."

Eaven deleted the message. "Won't this be fun." The prices in Charleston that time of year would deplete her savings. Who else could she stay with? Paisley's sweet, dark face came to mind. Eaven leaned against her car. Were they still friends after all this time? There had been no disagreements, but no time for goodbyes either. She used her browser to locate *Paisley Benson*. Only Mrs. Benson's information appeared. Paisley's father had never been in the picture. Eaven hit the call button.

"Benson residence."

She recognized the genteel voice of Paisley's mother at once.

"Mrs. Benson, I don't know if you remember me. I was a friend of Paisley's..."

"Eaven! Are you home?"

The lilt in her voice caused Eaven's throat to thicken. This woman had been closer to her than Lillian ever attempted to be. "No, but I will be there in mid-November. I was hoping to see you and Paisley when I get to town."

"Oh."

The pause caused a pang of fear to pass through Eaven. "She's all right, isn't she? Is she still in Charleston?"

"Yes, on both accounts. It's just that...she's married."

Eaven could imagine what her beautiful friend must have looked like walking down the aisle. It saddened her that she'd missed it. "How wonderful."

"Uh-huh. Will you be staying with Lillian when you visit?"

She hoped that was an invitation. She had spent most of her weekends at the Benson's home as a teen. "No. Cassandra called and said she's given away all the rooms for Lillian's birthday party."

"Some things never change. My guest room is empty. I can't tell you how glad I'd be to have you here."

Relief spread over Eaven's body like warm honey. "Mrs. Benson, that means so much to me."

"When is the party?"

"December thirteenth. I'm driving, so I don't know the exact date I'll arrive. Will that be any trouble?"

"Not at all. Sounds like you're coming alone. Is everything alright?"

Eaven tensed. Her own mother should really be the first to know, but... "No, it's not. My husband left me..." That's all she could say before tears stung. It was just like years ago when Mrs. Benson was the only safe person she could run to. "My life is such a mess."

"Oh, baby, I know it hurts. You come home and we'll make it all sugar. Right?"

Eaven blinked back the tears and smiled at her words. "Right. I can't wait to see Paisley. Please tell her I'll see her soon."

"Uh-huh. Bye-bye now."

After disconnecting, Eaven sensed something was wrong. Julia Benson had always bragged about her cherished daughter. Today not a word, except that Paisley was married and still lived in Charleston. She would have to wait to find out more when she arrived.

Tilting her face toward the sky, gratitude filled her heart. She had a room with no pink ruffles! Suddenly she couldn't wait to get far away from Greg Sault and Clayton Mercer. Her phone buzzed. Well speak of the devil. She answered. "Hello Clayton."

"You haven't answered my texts. Still mad at the dunking?"

She wouldn't give him the satisfaction of reacting to his barb. "What's a little water? What can I do for you?"

"You've been in my mansion, what, three times? I want my appraisals, and not just for a few things you think you can sell quickly. It wouldn't be healthy for your new business if people find bad reviews on your website."

She wanted to tell him he could sink his property in the nearest sewer but knew what bad ratings could do to a new business. "I finished posting everything online this morning and emailed your appraisals. You should have checked your email before calling." She disconnected, unwilling to waste another second of her time dealing with his control issues.

CHAPTER 44

Greg crouched behind a line of rusting barrels on the dank pier and tried not to breathe the familiar fumes of Ralph's cigarette. No sense tempting himself. Though free from many of his vices, he seemed to have no power to help anyone else clean up their lives. He'd believed Jenny was in rehab until yesterday when Brett called to say she got more heroin from Clayton. He'd rushed to her house and confronted her, but it was useless. When he left, she was flying high, multi-tasking to the max and feeling no pain.

Someone had to take control. Brett's words had spurred him on. *You must stop Clayton, for Jenny's sake.* That was exactly what he planned to do. One bag of dope at a time. Ruin the man. Turn him over to the Chinese cartel, then take what was his.

"Here comes the boat." Ralph snubbed out the cigarette. They pulled face masks over their heads and peeked around the barrels.

He squinted to see who carried the goods. From the stocky frame, he recognized Billy Angler.

Angler tied the boat in the slip and sat for a while, smoking, and checking the area around him. After fifteen minutes, he locked the cabin door, picked up some fishing gear and a duffle bag and trudged up the dock to the pier.

Taking the safety off his weapon, Greg stepped into Angler's path and held the gun to his temple. A voice changing device disguised his voice while the heavy jacket he wore added thirty pounds. "I'll be taking that off your hands. Drop it."

Angler dropped the bag and half-raised his hands. "Don't want any trouble," he said. But at the same moment, he backhanded the gun away from his head and punched Greg in the face. The gun flew out of Greg's hand as he landed on the rough wood. Angler raised his foot, ready to kick in Greg's face.

Ralph sneaked behind him, club in hand, and brought it down on Angler's skull, toppling the man. He gave Greg a hand up and pulled the mask down to check his face. "You'll need to lay low until that heals a bit."

Greg felt blood on his jaw. "Right. Let's beat it." He grabbed the duffle. They hustled down the pier, stuffed the cash and drugs into their hiding place, and took off in separate directions.

Only then did Greg wonder if they had left a dead man on the pier.

CHAPTER 45

After lighting a cigar, Clayton raised the whiskey glass to his lips. Frank had started at ten every morning, like clockwork. Clayton hesitated before taking a drink. He had never wanted to imitate any part of his father's life—a drunk, a man who delivered blows to his crewmen without the slightest provocation, humiliated those around him. No one crossed the bully. Not even his wife.

After draining his glass, he slammed it on the table. Though Frank had boasted of the Mercer luck, his luck had run out at ninety-two. Without a bit of interference, it might have kept going. Clayton savored the sweet burn on his tongue and relived his father's glorious end. He couldn't have planned it any better. He'd arranged to care for his father at home after he was paralyzed from a stroke. For a week, he strategized the best revenge for Frank's abuse. He took his time, and when the scheme came to him, it was pure genius.

The memory still thrilled him.

He'd waited for the nurse to leave, then locked the door and watched through the blinds until she was gone, feeding on the surge of energy. Behind the cupboard door, a surprise waited. His fingers tingled when he grabbed the jar and crept across Frank's room. He bent over the helpless man. "I have a date for you." He held the small glass jar to the light in front of his father's face, watching for his reaction.

His eyes twitched.

Clayton's pulse leapt. "Found this little gal in the pantry. I think she's hungry." He tapped on the glass. The large black widow jerked its spikey legs aggressively.

Frank's eyes, once so cold and callous, widened. His feeble tongue stammered unintelligibly.

Clayton laughed and mimicked Frank's wild eyes and gurgles. "Not so scary anymore, are we Dad?"

Frank's mouth quivered shut. His breath came in fast bursts.

Clayton dangled the jar so Frank could get a good look at the red hourglass. "Red looks good on her, just like it did on Mom." He loosened the jar lid. He knew the minute the fangs struck.

Frank managed one loud grunt.

"Don't want to go too far on a first date." Using the cardboard from a notepad, Clayton ushered the spider back into the jar. She had proved quite a little asset.

He left to wash his trembling hands and pour a drink. Even after pacing and throwing back his whiskey, he still felt jumpy. When he returned, he dabbed at Frank's tearing eye. "Red and puffy. Looks like she got you good." He patted Frank's muscled forearm. "You should heat up soon, get a little crampy. Well, a lot crampy." He wiped the sweat off Frank's forehead with a towel. "It's going to be a long night."

He turned off the light and went to watch TV, waiting for the muscle spasms to kick in. Nearing midnight, he came back and flipped on the light. "Wow, Frank."

The heavyset body spasmed. His father's breath came in short gasps. His eye was the size of a lemon. Frank's other eye found him. His mouth snarled, tongue flicking. Grunts came more loudly.

Clayton sat and watched. He lit a cigar and blew smoke at Frank as he lay there. Impotent. Powerless to do anymore harm. He inhaled the surge of power transferring from Frank's fading life to his. It was heady, like cocaine. "You never knew, but I helped Mom escape. Arranged a fake boating accident." He checked for a response.

Frank's watery eye stared.

"Got her a fake I.D." He puffed on his cigar, recalling what a sweet woman she'd been, a good mother. Before the abuse, she had been beautiful. He smiled, glad he'd been able to give her a second chance. Maybe the one good thing he'd ever done. Because of the danger for either of them, he had not seen or contacted his mother in twenty-six years. He smirked at Frank. "All this time you thought your punching bag drowned."

Frank's eyeball darted furiously under his blinking lid.

"I see that got to you. Bet she found a good man. Heh, the devil would have been better than you."

Frank tried to talk but more spasms rippled his swollen neck.

"The bite won't kill you, but you'll suffer hard in your remaining hours." As the tremors increased, Clayton wasn't sure how much more he wanted to watch.

Frank's mouth worked in tandem with his grunts.

"Got something to say?" He mocked the man's awkward movements and leaned closer.

Frank tried again, this time managing to convey three words. "I. Found. Her."

Clayton sat in his office, hands trembling from the memory. Those were the last words Frank ever spoke.

The door burst open and Angler stumbled in, the back of his head bloody. With no cash. No product.

Clayton swore. He rose and kicked over a chair, sending it scudding into his desk. He would have to call the Chinese and cancel his order. His hand twitched as he thought of how Jin's brother would relish a reason for revenge. A growl grew in the pit of his stomach. Though Angler said he didn't recognize his assailants, this had to be Sault's doing. And the man he'd been seen with, Ralph Ewing. *Not* a writer.

Another Sault would prove inadequate to come up against a Mercer. Though they'd stolen the goods, they would soon be persuaded to repent, and Eaven would provide just the right incentive. She'd betrayed him, running interference for Greg as a cover for his true intentions.

He sat back and lit a cigar, enjoying the twist his mind was taking. His mother had been found. Eaven never would be. He started to punch a number into his phone, then stopped.

A large spider crawled across the floor and crept up the leg of his desk to the curtain where a fly struggled in a web. With precise movements, it encased the fly, round and round, binding its wings and legs, until it could no longer move, completely at the spider's mercy.

He smiled. Tomorrow was Halloween, a night celebrated with spiders of all shapes and sizes. What better night to squeeze the life out of his enemies?

CHAPTER 46

Eaven threw her phone on the bed. She'd tried all day yesterday, but Tad was not returning her calls. "What, he's taking Halloween week off?" She hadn't heard from Greg either, not since the police pounded on his door two days ago. Not since she accused him of dealing. The pain in his face struck at her conscience. She bit her bottom lip, knowing she'd been too fast to rush to judgment. Regardless, they still had a contract.

Lightning flashed outside the window and she counted the seconds until the—*BOOM*!

"Geez," she squealed when the whole house shook.

Watching the torrent outside, she worried the bed and breakfast might slide down the hill. She dreaded facing the storm but needed to finish her job. She tried to call Tad again. Straight to voicemail. Her determination grew. Maybe she needed to let herself into the mansion.

She dug her warmest socks out of the drawer and layered a heavy wool sweater over a turtleneck. Lightning flashed again, making her doubt the wisdom of what she was about to do. Slipping on her rain boots, raincoat, and wool hat, she grabbed her flashlight and left the room before she could talk herself out of it.

Rain pelted the windshield making it hard to see the road. After parking on the street above the mansion, she tucked her ponytail under the tight-fitting wool cap and recalled what her dad used to say while waiting for her summon her courage, *now or not*. It took a good deal of strength to push open the car door against the wind. No use taking her umbrella, the wind would shred it.

Trudging forward, she moved quickly. No one else was crazy enough to brave a typhoon like this, which, she reasoned, made it a perfect day for breaking and entering. She dashed under the porch at the back of the mansion and jiggled the locked door. No surprise. The double-hung window next to it, however, looked promising. Someone had left plywood tacked over the broken glass. She tested it. Flimsy.

After a quick glance around convinced her she wouldn't be seen, she grabbed the edges and tugged. Several nails pulled easily from the rotten window frame. Another effort and the whole board released. She lowered it and peeked in. The kitchen. Rats. Her skin crawled with the reminder of the nests inside. Reaching through the window, she undid the door lock and stepped inside, her flashlight searching for red, beady eyes.

Wind gusted through the open window and rattled the shredded paper and debris. Lightning and thunder hit almost simultaneously, shaking the house, and rattling the windows. Squeals enlivened the shadows. She leapt across the kitchen in three long strides and lost her balance when she reached the dining room. The door handle saved her from doing a face plant. She stopped to catch her breath.

The house howled as though a huge monster chomped at its roof. Sneaking down the hall, she paused at the Captain's office, a room that Tad insisted held nothing of interest. She'd make her own decision today. Once through the overly large doors, she halted and used her flashlight to orient herself. A dark, ornate desk held the place of honor in the ample room. Fallen to its side, a matching chair lay behind it. To her left, sat a red upholstered chaise. A lingering sense of despair drifted toward her. Marie's?

She raised her flashlight toward the ceiling above the desk. Her breath caught in her throat. She stepped closer and studied the chandelier. Its five foliate-S-scrolled candle arms were masked with dust. Her mouth opened in surprise. In this forgotten mansion hung an unmistakable George IV chandelier. Exquisitely crafted in a unique Louis XIV revival style, she would bet anything it was stamped for its creator, *Thomas Messenger and Sons*.

Obviously, no one knew what a valuable piece this was, or they would not have left it. The thought of selling it on commission made her heart flutter. But owning it would be... She bit the inside of her cheek, frustrated at her financial limitations.

Get to work. Only a brief time remained to get what she needed.

At the bottom of the main stairway, she jumped at the banging of limbs against the roof and sides of the house. If anyone upstairs wished her harm today, she would have no warning. Each step creaked, sending amplified echoes to her ears. She worked to convince herself it was only her imagination, but her nerves wouldn't listen.

On the second-floor landing, she flashed light over the long drapes hanging on the window at the far end of the hall, then lowered the light to the floor. No sense announcing her presence to the neighbors.

A small door led from the second story to the servant's stairwell she had used before. Inside the dark passage, she gripped the rail and climbed. Something crawled across the top of her hand. She hopped to the other side of the stair and dropped her flashlight. It banged down the stairs, its light broken by the time it reached the bottom. She fished her phone from her pocket and turned on her flashlight app. Continuing upward, she swept it ahead of her face against any new surprises. The stairwell ended on the third story.

Something ominous seemed to hover around her. A surge of panic urged her to turn around. She refused. Get. It. Done.

In front of Sebastien's room, she swallowed and peered inside. Lightning suddenly lit the room like daylight. The pink reins still draped from the rocking horse. She rushed over and ran the old satin through her fingers. Lumps. The clues? She set her phone on the floor while she knelt in front of it and untied the ribbon.

"What do we have here?" A voice boomed behind her.

She shrieked and dropped the ribbon. Before she could turn around, strong hands stuffed a rag in her mouth and pulled a sack over her head. At the same time, someone else pulled her arms behind her and tied them. They laid her flat on the wood floor and rolled her in a blanket. Her head and elbows hit hard each time they lifted and dropped her.

She wanted to scream, beg them to let her go, but she could only gag at the cloth. The hood covered her face. She squirmed to free her nostrils for air. Around and around, a rope secured her within the cocoon.

God, she cried silently. *Let me live. Send help.*

They finished, panting hard from the effort. "She's still a looker, should bring in a pretty penny."

Clayton's men? Images shot through her mind of the Chinese prostitutes shoved under the decks of the Mercer slave boats. She twisted her wrists against the bindings, but the rope held tight.

Claustrophobia hit as they hoisted her by the shoulders and legs and trudged down the stairs, headfirst. It felt like she was tumbling forward but could not free her hands to break the fall. Black despair swamped her mind, while her heartbeat pounded hard against her chest.

The front door opened, and a rush of wind buffeted the blanket. She heard the trees and shrubs scraping against the house like a mad dog trying to get at the occupants. The men rushed forward. A van door slid open and they tossed her onto the floor. She moaned when her shoulder and hip jammed onto the hard metal. The door slammed.

After revving the engine, the driver made a tight U-turn, throwing her body against the door. She slid forward, head bumping into the front seats as they headed downhill.

Toward the docks!

CHAPTER 47

Frantic from trying to reach Eaven, and afraid she had already left town, Greg pounded on the yellow front door of the River's Glory. He pulled his black hood closer around his face to hide the gash on his chin. Claire finally opened the door. She smiled. "Hello Mr. Sault."

"Hi, Claire. Eaven tried to call me, but I wasn't available. She isn't answering her phone. She's still here, right?"

Her brows furrowed. "She hasn't checked out, but she drove away an hour ago. I didn't think it wise in this weather, but she was warmly bundled. Looked like a lady on a mission."

"Okay, thank you."

He ran back to his car. Maybe she set another appointment with Tad. He drove to the mansion and skidded to a stop on the slick pavement. In this storm, the place looked like a true haunted house. He approached the porch. Odd. The open front door banged with the wind. Pushing inside, he called, "Eaven. Are you here?"

Two sets of muddy footprints covered the wood planks of the main floor. Big footprints. He followed them to the stairs. His adrenaline accelerated as he listened to the roof creak under the pressure of the heavy gusts. He pulled out his gun when he reached the second-story hallway. The door leading to the servant's stairs stood open. He entered it and touched the stair rail. Moisture. Someone had been here recently. Eaven?

Brushing away cobwebs as he climbed in the near darkness, he exited on the third-floor landing. Lightning flashed along the hall, revealing three doors. He rushed to the first room that Eaven had described as Sebastien's and shined the phone light into the room. Tiny red eyes gleamed from under the bed. Rats—Eaven's favorite.

The mouth on the rocking horse pulled back into a hideous smile like a wicked clown in a horror movie. Near its rocker lay the pink satin belt. Eaven's white phone lay partially concealed by a baby blanket. She'd been here.

He pocketed the ribbon and phone and searched Marie's small bedroom but found nothing. Peeking in a door across the hall, he called for Eaven, but the house seemed empty.

Water dripped from his wet hair into his eyes. Eaven was missing and at least two others had been here. This had to be Clayton's doing. Shaken to the core, he fled down the stairway and dashed back outside. As he jumped into his car, his phone rang.

A muffled voice said, "Mr. Sault, seems you're a popular guy. I have two pretty packages for you. I want all the money and product back. Bring it to the dock by the office at seven tonight and maybe you'll get your packages back in good condition."

Greg rubbed his scar and swore under his breath. The caller was cagey about who might be listening. "I don't have your product anymore."

"Get it back or I'll send pictures that will make Jin's photos look like a birthday party. Come alone."

"I'll be there." Clayton had Eaven and Jenny—two innocent bystanders. This was his worst nightmare. Stomach twisting, he hung up and dialed Ralph. "Get the money and drugs we took from Clayton."

"Why?"

Greg recounted the message.

"I can't think how this will go down well."

"Maybe with the stash, they'll let Eaven and Jenny go."

"They won't."

The shocking truth sliced through him. Jin was proof that Clayton had no limits to his barbarity. After he finished with them, they were as good as dead, but he had to try.

Greg checked his watch. Six o'clock.

"You sure about this, bud?" Ralph asked.

He shook his head. "Not at all, but what choice do we have?"

"They could be anywhere. Dead, or on their way to China."

Greg stopped him. "That's not helping." He zipped the duffle bag he had taken from Angler and lugged it from the trunk of his car. Clapping his friend on the shoulder, he said, "Having you here helps. Thanks, man."

The storm's intensity had increased over the last four hours. Not a soul moved around the docks. Above him, a hint of moon highlighted the edges of the swirling clouds below it. Bursts of lightning pulsed through them. "If we can get the drop on them, maybe we can survive the night." He ground his teeth. It looked like Clayton might win again and take everything he held dear. He so wanted his hands around Clayton's throat.

Ralph checked his gun. "Who do you think will come?"

"Angler, Bransen. Maybe Rex. Clayton's a coward, but he'll be close enough to see the whole thing going down."

"You sure? So far we don't have him directly connected to the kidnapping or the drugs."

"That's your job. He'll only show if he has to. I'll resist to make sure he does. Let's go."

Greg crouched in the shadows with Ralph. At seven o'clock he stood, the boisterous Columbia sloshing a few feet to his left.

Ralph set his hand on Greg's arm. "I have a real bad feeling about this. Stay close to the water. Jump out of harm's way if needed."

"Will do." He hoisted the duffle over his left shoulder and edged east on the dock toward the Mercer Enterprises office. His gun handle poked him through an inside pocket of the bag, within easy reach. The temperature had dipped but sweat trickled down his back. He shouldn't have set this up. Shouldn't have involved Eaven or Jenny, but it was all too late.

A light hung by the door of the Mercer office. An old light, the kind with a cage wrapped around a yellow bulb. He willed his sight to find a figure lurking, a movement anywhere.

To his surprise, Brett opened the office door and stepped out. "Greg?"

Greg stopped, senses on high alert. "Why are you here?"

Brett tilted his head. "Clayton told me to come, but why are you—" His eyes grew wide, frantically scanning the area.

POP. A muffled sound split the air from a silencer. Brett's body lurched backward and bounced off the office wall before it flopped on the dock. Greg drew his gun from the bag and rushed forward. He dropped next to the office door, ready to spring in any direction.

"Drop your weapon, Sault." Angler's deep voice came from out of the darkness.

"Not happening. Come out and let's talk," Greg said.

Ralph howled. A thin man in a suit and tie, face covered by a ski mask, pulled Ralph's body downward by his thin hair, a pistol pointed to his temple.

Heart racing, Greg dropped the gun. They were dead men. No way to help Eaven or Jenny. He swallowed a scream. This wasn't supposed to end this way. Not this time.

"Kick the bag away from you." Angler stepped into the yellow light while keeping his gun trained on Greg. He pulled the duffle bag away and unzipped it. "Thanks for my money." He unzipped the side pocket. "And my product." He took out his phone and made a call. "This is Billy Angler. I just witnessed a shooting. I'm on the dock at the Mercer Enterprises office near Front Street. Yeah, I'll be here." He turned to a third partner. "Get Sault's gun. Keep it clean."

After the man retrieved it with gloved hands, Angler nodded. Ralph squirmed frantically but was unable to get free from the masked man who put the gun to his head. *POP.* Ralph's body slammed to the wooden pier.

Greg roared and lunged toward Ralph, unable to help. Angler's gun fired but missed Greg as he rolled. The third man wrestled Greg's arms behind him, foot holding him to the dock.

The other shooter stepped to where Brett lay and fired two more shots into his head. The action made no sense to Greg. "But Brett supplied your customers."

"Little slow on this one, Sault," said a muffled voice from the shadows.

Clayton? Maybe. He listened harder.

"Brett approached *me* about smuggling for *him*. Once I had the goods on him, however, he felt... exposed. He was using you to take me down, but I turned the tables." He laughed. "Guess history repeats itself. Let's see, I think you shot up on your product, went berserk, and killed your colleagues. You came at Angler and he had to shoot you."

Greg's gut tightened. This couldn't be happening. Not again.

"Did you know the Mercers used to smuggle human cargo? A pretty woman still brings a big price."

They're alive. Greg's eyes darted toward the shadows. He had to escape. "You said you'd let Eaven and Jenny go."

"I did. They're taking a river cruise. Guess there was a good reason we never got rid of that old tug. Perfect time to scuttle her. Should take the current anywhere from say, two to three hours to carry the old girl to the bar." He chuckled.

The air left Greg's lungs. How could he get to them? The boat would be torn to shreds in this storm. As if to confirm his fears, lightning flashed. The air jolted with a loud crack. White-capped swells punctuated the dark Columbia waters.

Angler grinned. "If they even make it that far." He nodded at the masked guy. "Kill him."

Greg heard a police siren almost on top of them. He might still have a chance. He leapt to his feet and knocked the masked guy to the ground. He flew to attack Angler, but just as he grabbed his throat, he saw something move in his peripheral vision. A sharp pain shot through his head.

CHAPTER 48

Eaven drifted in and out of awareness. Wind roared, blending with crashing waves. She loved the sea. Loved Michael. The boat lulled for a moment and she smiled. Helloo God. She wanted to say it, but a cloth filled her mouth.

Her body lurched side to side, pounding her aching head against solid wood. Deep cold stung her spine and skin, raising her consciousness. Her eyes fluttered open then widened in alarm. Inches from her nose, splintered boards framed a rough opening. Though her hands were untied, the tight space pinned them to her sides. Her tongue worked frantically against the cloth until she was able to spit it out, leaving fibers stuck to her dry mouth.

"Eaven?" Near her, a weak voice called. "Are you awake?"

The voice sounded familiar. "Who're yooo?" Eaven slurred. She tried again. "Who are you?"

"Jennifer Gellens. Greg's friend, remember?"

"Nasty Jenny," Eaven said. Or did she just think it?

The voice sounded angry, scared. "Yeah. Nasty Jenny."

"Where are we?"

"In the river. I think the boat is sinking."

Eaven's head pitched upward. A large wave splashed over the side and spilled through the hole, drenching her. She shrieked at the stinging water. Now she was cold *and* wet. And infinitely more awake. "Where are you? What happened?" she croaked.

Soft crying placed Jennifer close by. "Under the deck. They drugged us."

More fog cleared. Eaven twisted her neck side to side. She lay on a wooden platform less than eighteen inches below the deck, wedged on both sides by wooden timbers. Directly above her face, the deck had rotted, creating a ragged hole. She thrashed as burning, icy pain seared through her backside. "We have to get off this boat."

"I've wriggled and shoved, but I'm stuck."

Eaven forced her mind to calm. She pressed her palms on the deck above her. No give. What about the hole above her face? If she could move her body toward her head, her hands would be even with the hole.

Though her feet felt numb, she dug the heels of her rain boots into the boards that penned her on either side and pushed with minimal success. Another wave breached the side and the boat tilted. Her teeth chattered. How long did they have?

Her heel caught on a rough spot. Traction! She pushed until her hands reached the hole. Grabbing the rotten board, she wrestled it back and forth. Dull pain from sharp splinters barely registered. Several inches of wood snapped away. Not enough.

Heart pounding, she fought the wood, the rising water. Her head thrashed against the enclosed space. "I can't!" Her head fell back in paralyzing despair.

Move it, Eaven—Coach's voice from track, prodding, unrelenting.

She took a deep breath. Crying, attacking with both hands, she fought a disintegrating plank. It broke! Then another. With a shout of victory, she thrust her head through the deck. A splintered board sliced her cheek. Warmth spilled over her icy face.

She pulled the rest of her torso through the hole and pushed with her feet. With one last effort she scrambled free and fell against the side of the ship, her breath coming in shudders. "I'm out!" She peered around her. They had been shoved below the main deck in the stern of an old tugboat, maybe sixty feet long. High, frothy swells lifted and dipped the ship. "How did we get here?"

"Bransen and another man towed the boat into the river and left us over an hour ago. They said Greg stole Clayton's drugs and money. They're using us as barter."

Tremors overtook Eaven's muscles. Greg had lied, had been bent on revenge all along. He had Clayton where he wanted him. Would he really let that go for two women he held with so little regard? A wave swamped over the side. Frigid wind added its misery to her wet skin.

A bright moon peeked between the monstrous storm clouds, its light exposing the urgency of their situation. The boat sat low in the water. Too low. She held onto the side rail, shocked by the situation. She'd never imagined her life would end by drowning. Another huge swell lifted the bow of the boat. She screamed and held tighter until the boat righted.

Jennifer choked and coughed.

Fighting her instincts to hold tight, Eaven forced her hands to let go. She scurried across the heaving ship and lifted the hatch that closed Jennifer in a wooden coffin. The water level rose in the hull. Jennifer lifted her head, struggling to breathe.

Eaven leaned toward her face and shouted. "Can you push with your feet and scoot closer?"

"No. My foot popped when Branson shoved me in here. I think it's broken."

Fury strengthened Eaven's grip on the hatch while another wave hit. Once it washed over them, she gulped for air and shook the water out of her eyes. She couldn't let them win. "I found a couple of notches that gave my heels a hold. If there's something like that by your good foot, try to push with your heel."

"I found it!" Jennifer moved.

On her knees, Eaven straddled the hatch. "I'll pull you out. Ready?" Her hands barely reached under Jennifer's armpits. "Push hard." Jennifer's petite body inched toward her. Eaven found a better hold and pulled her a foot above the deck. Jennifer grabbed the deck boards while Eaven helped lift her out and onto her side.

Just then, the boat tipped them toward the water. They screamed and grabbed the rotting hatch, hoping it wouldn't break away. The boat righted and they scurried to the rail to grab a more secure hold before it tipped again.

"How do we get to shore?" Jennifer wailed.

Eaven stared through the rain at the blurred lights of Astoria in the distance and didn't answer. She helped Jennifer move to the crew quarters near the center of the boat. They each looped an arm through the bridge ladder as an anchor against the intensifying waves.

Jennifer sobbed. "I thought we'd be dead before you woke. It would have been better for you, but I didn't want to die alone."

"I'd rather not die at all." Eaven pulled her shaking leg against her chest and bowed her head onto her knee to calm her breathing. "They kidnapped me. How did you get here?"

Jennifer sniffed. "I needed my pills. Bransen said to meet him at this boat, but the stuff he gave me made me drowsy." Her jaw shivered uncontrollably. "He said they were going to kill Brett and Greg. They're dead by now. It's over for us."

Jennifer's words brought a new kind of chill to Eaven's mind. These men were thugs, had guns. How could she fight them? Fight these seas? Greg had pitted her against Clayton, used her as a smokescreen, but Clayton got even. She chuckled mirthlessly. "Clayton got *Eaven.*"

Another wave crashed over the side of the boat, sobering her. She sensed the bygone anguish rising from the hull. Her spirit wept. For decades, the Mercers had slipped doped bodies under the deck like sardines. Let them wet themselves. Defecate in their clothes. Vomit with seasickness until they reached freedom to become slaves for the rest of their short lives.

And the Mercer's built their fortunes.

She tried to block the image of humans filling the cleverly disguised compartments. A ship design like this took genius. Creativity. Gifts that could have been used *for* humanity.

Have your gifts made a difference? The inaudible words pierced.

What gifts? She wasn't pure enough for her father, polished enough for her mother, and for Michael, not woman enough. An image of Lake Quinault appeared. There, before Michael's betrayal, she'd been more than enough, had felt admired.

Like breaking glass, the idyllic image shattered, more deeply this time. She struggled against the truth, but the reality descended with certainty. Her chin dropped to her wet chest. Michael was right. She'd hidden in a small pond, flaunting her accomplishments, just like those she judged in Charleston. She yearned for the top, lusting for significance from those around her. Her eyes squeezed shut. She was a fraud, using her talents to impress, using people's admiration to fill the void. An endless task.

Her courage began to sink as surely as the boat she was in. Her life was over, and she'd done nothing but take.

A giant wave roared, heaving the bow high into the air. They held tight to the ladder, feet dangling, screams filling the air. She stared down the stern into a black hole. This was it. She loosened her hold on the ladder.

Do you want to die? The question flew to her from the deep.

"No!" She grabbed the ladder again. The boat leveled. Mad with fear, her mind caught at fragments. Did she even deserve to live after the useless choices she'd made?

Choices or reactions?

Reactions? Yes. Her life flashed in front of her, revealing one reaction after another. That's all she'd been. Never making waves so she'd be...what? What was she trying so hard to be?

Enough.

A lump formed in her throat as the truth solidified. Her need wasn't grandiose. It was just to be enough. But she was enough. Always had been. She wanted to laugh and cry. Her whole being tingled with rising joy. Exhilaration silenced the lies. The boat lurched in the angry waters, but peace settled, thawing the frozen core inside her chest.

She saw beyond the menacing black clouds that severed her from the moonlight, beyond the stars she knew hung above the earth. It took a shipwreck for her to see the truth. She was unquestionably loved by God, already complete in His eyes. Enough.

A flash of memory dropped like a life ring. She'd stood, eyes locked onto her father's confident face as he laid his life in her hands during a raucous regatta gone bad. His wrist broken. With a valiant effort, she defied the seas and maneuvered them to safety in high winds. On her own. The weight of failure lifted. Despite her other failures, she was a good sailor.

Riding the waves on the heaving boat, she squeezed Jennifer's hand and shouted above the clamor. "We aren't dead yet." She scrutinized her surroundings and saw a hint of shoreline. If the cold and waves didn't get her, she might be able to swim it. Jennifer, however, with just a shiny quilted jacket and an injured foot, would never make it.

A roar, louder than before, jerked Eaven's attention forward. Her breath caught in her throat. Ahead, mighty waves rose, one after another, ready to pummel them.

They'd reached the bar.

CHAPTER 49

Greg awoke in a jail cell. Eyes blurry, brain fuzzy like gauze, it felt like the bad trip he took in high school. He touched the dried blood on the side of his head. With the police bearing down on the dock, Angler must have decided to burn him instead of killing him. As soon as he got out of here, he'd make sure Angler got his.

"Sault." A stern-looking guard with a name tag that read *Sergeant Cooper*, swaggered toward the cell. "Following in your father's footsteps? You did him one better. Two murders."

Greg's chest exploded when he remembered. "Ralph."

"Yeah, and Brett Gellens, your girlfriend's husband, from what Billy Angler said."

"He's a liar! He had them shot!" Frantic, he grabbed the bars. "Listen. They put Brett's wife and another woman on a rotten boat to sink in the river. You have to call the Coast Guard."

Cooper shook his head. "You been shooting up too long."

"Come over here and say that!" He wanted to tear the smirk off Cooper's face.

"Shut your mouth."

The guard's venom was meant to pierce Greg's courage. It would have in the past, but this time he was on the right side of the law. "I'm with the DEA, you idiot."

Heads turned, conversations stopped mid-sentence. Cooper gave a kind of half laugh, "Right, and I'm Rudolph."

"I was sent to dismantle Clayton's racket, the mess you've allowed in your own backyard for too long. Check my wallet, there's a phone number on a blank card."

The sergeant's eyes widened, revealing a kink in his confidence.

"Get it now! If you blow this, two women will drown," he screamed at the man's fat, complacent face. "They may already be dead!"

Everyone in the jail got remarkably busy. Phone calls were made. Through glass partitions, he watched as superiors were consulted. Still, it took forever. Enough time for Eaven and Jenny to sink.

He perched on the thin mattress and raked his shaking hands through his hair. He should never have taken this assignment. He'd underestimated Clayton. And overestimated his own competence. It got Ralph killed. And Eaven and Jenny...He closed his eyes. *God, help them.*

CHAPTER 50

The rain stopped, revealing the full horror of their fate. Thinning clouds swirled light and dark, allowing filtered moonlight to illuminate the torrential sea around them. Eaven's heart sank as the mighty currents of the Columbia churned and crashed into the rising tide of the Pacific, pounding in her ears like Niagara Falls. Helpless, she watched while storm force winds and thirty-foot monster waves twisted the creaking planks of the wooden boat. "If we had a light, someone might see us," she shouted to Jennifer above the fray.

"Bransen had one, but what good would that do?"

"It might help. Life vests would be golden too." At least their bodies might be found. Jennifer would be identified, but would anyone even know who Eaven was? Her throat constricted. *Father, I'm not ready to die.*

She untangled her arm from the ladder and crawled into the crew cabin to look for a flashlight. Straining to see in the tiny bit of moonlight, she tossed aside old cushions and heard something land on the floor. The boat rocked to one side and a glint of metal rolled toward her. Yes! She scrambled for it and clicked on the blessed light. Her spirit sent out another *thank You.*

Not finding life vests, she searched for a line to lash themselves to anything that might float but found nothing. The hull groaned beneath her. Water sloshed around the cabin floor and she grasped the wooden frame that had once held a window. Tucking the light into the waist of her jeans, she made her way back to Jennifer. The once proud woman looked like a drowning kitten clinging to the rungs.

"I found it!"

The boat rose again.

Eaven glimpsed the giant wave above her and screamed. When it hit, the boat lurched sharply starboard. Water washed over her body, dragging her legs out from under her. Arms flailing, she caught the wet rung of the ladder, her hands gripping with every bit of strength. Her cramping fingers started to slip.

The boat rocked the other way, letting her scramble to her knees and thread her leg around the ladder. Her breath came in ragged gasps.

Jennifer sobbed. "We're not going to make it. I've lived here all my life, heard the stories of the bar."

"Well, I haven't." With numb fingers, Eaven pulled the flashlight from her waistband. For several minutes, she pointed it toward Astoria, clicking it off and on in an S.O.S. pattern. "If help is near, or looking this way, they might see us."

After several minutes shivering in the cold, her finger grew too numb to move the flashlight switch. Exhausted, she stopped trying and let it fall to her lap. Having done all she could, she braced herself against the precipitous waves and rode out her fate.

Roscoe's large, trusting eyes filled her mind. She had promised to take care of him. Her heart wept at the dog's bleak future. And hers. Though a seasoned sailor, she was coming close to seasickness. The boat shuddered and cracked as though it would be torn apart. Spray hit her face and another huge wave swamped them. By some miracle, they stayed afloat.

The growl around them grew louder, so loud, it filled her very being with dread. She coughed and caught her breath. The sound grew, adding a harsh roar like spitting bullets. Suddenly, a cone of light illuminated the whole angry sea around them.

Her face shot upward. "A helicopter! Oh God, we're going to live!" The tears she'd been holding back flowed with relief.

It circled the boat high overhead then lowered and circled again.

"We're here," she screamed. She shined the flashlight onto the main deck to illuminate their position. In and out of the helicopter's spotlight, she caught sight of a rescue swimmer being lowered. "Jenny, we're saved."

Just then, however, a powerful gust of wind caught the helicopter. The dangling swimmer swirled in a wild circle. The chopper bounced in the wind and tried to steady the cable. When the swimmer was about twenty feet off the surface, he released the cable and hit the water. At the same time, a huge swell crested over the man. He disappeared underwater. For too long.

Eaven searched wildly, clinging to a tenuous hope. Finally, he appeared four yards off their heaving boat, taking long strokes toward them. She willed him to stay afloat. He had to make it.

When the port side was lowest, he caught the edge and hoisted himself up, then climbed the rocking deck toward them. The boat lifted and he grabbed the mast to keep from sliding back into the churning water.

She freed herself from the ladder's rungs and stretched to grab the mast and his vest. Above them, a rescue basket descended. She reached high, clawing for it. It was so close. "Hurry!"

The swimmer grabbed it. "Get in," he shouted.

Everything faded except that basket. She was safe. She was getting off this boat. Heart racing, she lunged toward it. With one leg over the side, she caught sight of Jennifer, curled in a fetal position, her expression blank. Shock. Eaven's trembling fingers released the basket. "Take her first. Her foot's injured."

The swimmer rushed to Jennifer. "Let's move, ma'am. This vessel won't last much longer." He pried her hands from the ladder and tossed her like a fish into the basket, then motioned for it to be raised.

When he turned toward Eaven, his head craned up, eyes wide. "Hold on!"

She grabbed the mast with all her strength. The swimmer grabbed them both.

A colossal wave sucked the ship upward until the bow pointed at the sky. For a moment, they seemed suspended in midair, straining to hold onto the mast, staring up at the stars.

Terror ripped through her gut. They were dead. Great sobs erupted uncontrollably. She'd almost made it out alive.

As though in slow motion, she watched the roaring wave crest over them. It toppled the boat upside down, driving the mast toward the bottom of the wave. She screamed as her feet left the deck.

Water filled her ears. All sound ceased, but the turbulence increased. Upside down, the mast shuddered and twisted out of control. Though being tossed like a tuna in a shark's mouth, somehow the swimmer managed to keep his hold on her.

She inhaled water. Thrashing to get to the surface, her limbs fought the swimmer's strong arms. More icy water burned her lungs until fog clogged her mind.

Almost too late, her face broke above the water. She gasped and choked. The thunderous sounds returned. She'd made it to the surface, but where was the swimmer? In the light of the helicopter, she searched on all sides.

Her head craned up. *God, help me.* A wave, laden with wood and debris from the vessel, crashed over her before she could dive.

CHAPTER 51

"Agent Sault." Sergeant Cooper's demeanor had changed. He led Greg to a chair and handed him a cup of coffee. "Sorry for your loss."

Greg's throat thickened. The truth bit him again. Ralph was dead. "Any word about Jennifer and Eaven?"

Cooper shook his head. "Coast Guard said they'd send a chopper, but it's rough out there. Maybe the full moon will help. Truth is, they have no idea where Mercer's boat is."

He bolted from his chair. "Have you questioned him and Angler?"

The sergeant tugged him into the privacy of his cubicle. "They're with Clayton's lawyer now. Clayton was nowhere near the docks. Angler hasn't changed his story. Said you showed up at his office and started shooting."

"If the women die, their murder is on Clayton's head."

"If we find them. And if there's proof he was involved."

"It's his boat."

"He's a Mercer, reported it stolen."

Greg clenched his teeth. He wanted revenge in the worst way. "Can I go now?"

"Yeah. Your personal items are at the desk. We're keeping your gun as evidence."

Shoving out the front door of the police station, he pocketed his and Eaven's phones and the pink ribbon. He exhaled deeply. The last time he had been here was when visiting his dad. He wanted to run, get away. Instead, he slumped onto the steps and pressed the heels of his hands to his eyes, controlling sobs that wanted to burst free.

Jenny was probably dead. She could have won her battle with drugs. He'd seen pride in her face. Fury raged inside his chest. The Mercer's had played dirtier than anyone else and won again. He'd tried to beat them and got his friends killed.

An officer exited the station after his shift. Greg ducked his head and wiped his cheeks. There was nothing he could do. "Hey, can I get a lift downtown?" He needed a drink. The man nodded and Greg slid into his car. Neither tried for conversation during the short drive.

"Thanks," he said, and jogged across the wet street to the Astoria Brewing Company, its windows plastered with ghouls and ghosts. The local crowd was loud and boisterous, many in costume. He sat on a bar stool and ordered a pint. The server brought his beer and he gulped half the glass. He ground his teeth. He should never have come back to Astoria.

A cheer filled the room. Greg ignored it and chugged the last half of his beer. Another cheer broke through the crowd. He skimmed the room. All heads were turned toward the flat-screen TV as an announcer gave a blow by blow account of a daring rescue only moments before. The image bounced as a camera followed a rescue basket to the waiting arms of a Coast Guardsman who hung halfway out of a helicopter. It held an unmoving figure.

He squinted, mouth open. Eaven? Jenny? His heart started pounding. He wanted to hope. The image broke back to the thrashing sea below. A wooden vessel twisted, caught in the fierce water battle of the bar. The basket lowered again. It hung no more than twenty feet above the vessel when a massive wave pounced. It rolled the boat upside down, crushing the craft and sending the pieces in all directions like tiny splinters.

The viewers hushed. Minutes passed. All remnants of the boat vanished. The searchlight swept across the waves in a frenzy.

He held his breath, mind screaming for a sign of life.

Finally, it pinpointed the swimmer and sent the basket toward him. He shoved a body over the side and climbed in. Up they went.

A unified cheer filled the bar. Friends clanked their drinks. As the rescue replayed, the TV commentator announced, "The first unidentified woman is alive. The condition of the second woman is not known at this time. The victims will be transferred to Columbia Memorial Hospital where they will be assessed and treated for exposure among other things."

Among other things.

A stranger turned to him. "Hey man, can you believe that rescue?"

Choking back emotion, Greg threw a twenty on the counter and raced out the door to check out the West End Mooring Basin on Pier 1. The red glow of the ambulance's emergency lights pulsed in the misty sky. They'd be heading to the hospital soon. He turned and sprinted over the slick pavement down Marine Drive.

Sirens blared, their sound blasting as the ambulance passed him. He increased his speed and turned on 20th Street, crossed Exchange, and sped across the parking lot to the emergency entrance. When he arrived, the ambulance was already empty. He bent over, hands on his knees, breathing hard.

A small crowd had gathered around an EMT. "What is the condition of the women?" a reporter asked.

"I can't comment," the man said, lips tight.

"Are they both alive?"

The EMT glanced at his partner. "No comment."

Greg tried to dash inside but slipped. His forward motion propelled him into the glass door.

"Hold it," shouted another technician. "No one inside."

"I'm with the women," Greg grimaced, holding his shoulder.

"Family?"

"Employer."

The reporter scurried to him. "What were the women doing in that boat at this time of night?"

The two EMT's and the technician exchanged glances. They blocked the reporter and escorted Greg inside. "Since you're not family, we can't let you in, but you can wait in here for questioning."

His whole investigation was trashed. He gritted his teeth and followed the technician down the hall, where he slumped onto a plastic seat.

Doctors and several nurses scurried in and out of two rooms across the hall. He attempted to peek around an aid when the door opened to his right. He caught a glimpse of blond hair above a blanket. Jenny! She was moving. He released a heavy breath.

Most of the frenetic activity happened in the room on the left. "Clear," someone said. Then came the jolt of a defibrillator.

"Again."

Another buzz.

Greg jumped out of the chair and paced. It was all he could do not to tear through the door. He almost decided to do just that when Jenny's door opened.

"Mr. Sault?" a nurse asked.

"Yes." He ran back.

"Mrs. Gellens would like to see you."

Relief hit him hard. He rushed into the room and gathered her hands. "Jen."

She clung, polished nails clawing into his palm. Her body trembled violently. "They were all trying to kill me. I was almost clean. Honest." She grabbed her stomach. "I'm gonna be si..." She pushed at him and dipped her head over the side of the bed. Vomit spewed over the floor and onto his shoes.

"Out of the way," a nurse shouted and yanked him away from the bed.

Tears burned. As he watched Jenny's torment, he remembered his own, the excruciating agony, the fear that accompanied an overdose. He wanted to bash someone.

A heavyset nurse caught his arm. "Can you identify the other woman?"

Fear twisted like a knife in his chest. "Eaven Alexander. Is she...? Did she drown?"

The nurse shook her head. "No. Your friend received a bad bump on her head."

His head tilted back, eyes closed. *Thank God.* "Can I see her?"

After checking the hall, the nurse said, "You can take a peek, but she's still unconscious."

He stepped quietly to her bed and took her hand. Blood soaked through the bandage around her head. Scratches marred her beautiful face. "Eaven." Grief overwhelmed him. Unable to stop the tears any longer, he sank onto a chair and let them flow. He wouldn't let Clayton get away with this.

CHAPTER 52

Eaven woke in a sterile-smelling room. Her throat and lungs burned. Pain radiated through her head. The boat. The helicopter. Relief overwhelmed her. She'd made it. She rubbed her cheek against the pillow, never imagining she would reawaken in this world. Or ever see anyone she cared about again. Who would that be? Who could she call? "Will you bring me a phone?" she asked the nurse.

The nurse scooted a table over with a phone and left while Eaven dialed.

"Benson residence."

Relief hit at the familiar voice. "Mrs. B, it's Eaven. I'm...hurt." A sob stuck in her throat.

"Honey, what's happened to you?" Though three thousand miles away, Mrs. B's concern wrapped her like a baby blanket.

"Someone tried to murder me. I almost drowned." That was all she could explain for now. "I'm alone. I... I just needed to talk to you and Paisley."

"I'm here, honey, but God is with you. You're never alone, remember?"

She wiped her eyes with the palm of her hand and smiled, glad some people never changed. "You never let me forget."

"The truth is the truth, sugar." She paused. "I'm afraid Paisley is unavailable. She doesn't want any contact from me."

"No." Paisley had been the center of Mrs. Benson's life.

"She'll come around, soon as that scoundrel is out of her life. She married a bad man, Eaven."

"Guess we both made bad choices."

"Two months ago, I brought her home from the hospital with a broken jaw and moved all her things in here. They're divorced but why she went back with him is beyond me." She sniffed. "I'm sorry to burden you when you called for comfort."

"Please, no need to apologize. Is there something I can do?"

"You're a good soul. I may have reason to hope. She called. Sounded frightened and confused. Wanted me to come get her from John's Island. Then she called back and said she was fine. I asked if Denny was there and she said no, she'd left him for good. She hung up but I haven't heard anything since. I'm beside myself."

"Maybe I can talk to her when I get to Charleston."

"Yes. I think that would be real good for her. For you both. She was lost when you left."

Eaven shut her eyes and bowed her head. More fallout from running away. "Me too. I'll call when I arrive." She laid the phone on the sheet.

Sheila stepped into the room, her smile as broad as her cowboy hat. "Want a visitor?"

Eaven almost cried. "Yes, please. I must look like a drowned kitten."

Approaching the bed, Sheila stopped smiling and took her hand. "You almost were a drowned kitten. What happened?"

Sighing, Eaven said, "To be announced. The police don't want me talking yet."

"Well, thank God you're alive. I started praying as soon as I heard." Sheila opened her saddle bag-styled purse and set a box of chocolates on the nightstand. "I have salmon packets, but I don't imagine they'd sit well right now."

She nodded in agreement. "Thank you for thinking of me."

"I know what it's like to be alone. To have someone after you. When the news mentioned it was Clayton's boat, I knew immediately that man was behind this." She clasped Eaven's hand. "You're not alone, kiddo. God has your back."

"I don't know why. I've spent most of my life mad at Him, pretending He wasn't there. Sometimes, I think I stepped too far over the line."

"What line? Christ wiped out *all* your missteps, past, present, and future. Right?"

"Maybe."

Sheila raised her eyebrows. "Oh, you callin' God a liar?"

Brought up short, she shifted on the bed. "No, it's just that—"

"—that it's easier to pile on the guilt, believe the lies people tell about Him and walk away?"

"What lies?"

"That He's up there with a big flyswatter waiting to smash you upside the head."

She chuckled. "Guess I was sort of feeling that way."

"Girlfriend, the best day of my life was when I finally saw there was nothing I could do, or not do, to make God love me more, or make Him love me less. I grabbed onto that truth so hard, no one's ever gonna pry it loose."

Sheila's words clashed with ideas Eaven had long believed. She stared at her friend. "Are you sure about that?"

"Absolutely. That's not to say gravity won't get you if you decide to jump off a cliff. Decisions have consequences. But He never stops loving his kids." She grinned. "In Christ, you are as complete as you ever will be." The nurse came in again and Sheila moved aside. "I have to get back to my smoker, but I'll keep in touch. Call me when you're ready and we can meet for lunch. You name the place, I'm all yours."

"Thanks, Sheila. Could you check on Roscoe? Give him a scratch and a treat for me?"

"You bet."

After Sheila left, Eaven's eyes misted. Her new friend understood exactly what she needed. Paisley had been that way, before Eaven had walked out on her. She was about to let the flyswatter hit her upside the head again but stopped. The pattern was so familiar. Too familiar. When had she started beating herself up so badly, second-guessing? Harshly judging everything she did? High school? No, before that. She rubbed her forehead. Certainly, by the time she hit grade school. She'd deferred to others to make decisions for her. Her father most of all. That fear, or voice, had run her life. Had intruded into her thoughts like a drag against her aspirations.

Her chest swelled as she caught a glimpse of the truth. That hadn't been God's voice. She sucked in her lips, stifling a grin, but it broke over her face. She imagined how it would feel to let go of that struggle to be perfect, to make decisions without expecting repercussions. This would take getting used to. Letting out a deep sigh, she thought about Paisley and the guilt she'd born. Yes, she'd left without saying goodbye, but she would make that right. Another reason to return to Charleston ASAP.

She'd just set her food tray on the table for the nurse when Greg rushed into her room.

"How are you?"

She wished she had a full bedpan to throw. His humble demeanor made her even angrier. "You used me! You stole Clayton's drugs and nearly got us killed!"

The nurse's eyebrows raised.

He shook his head. "It's not like that. I..." He waited until the nurse left. "Ralph and I were working undercover with the DEA to expose the drug ring here. Turned out Clayton was in the middle of it."

Oh. Relief washed over her. So did her dismay at her jump to judgment, to assume the worst. The voice in her head had it out for everyone, not just her. It had to go. Greg hadn't been lying about dealing or using. She studied his crushed expression and offered a smile. "You don't know how happy that makes me."

Face sober, he perched on the edge of the bed and set his hand on top of hers. Tears welled.

"What?"

"Clayton's men killed Ralph."

"No." She squeezed his forearm. "I'm so sorry. He was a good man."

"Yeah. He insisted on moving into the River's Glory as a precaution for you."

An ache twisted in her chest. The compassion and wisdom Ralph had offered had been genuine. What a useless loss. "What happened?"

The scar on his mouth accentuated his scowl. "I got a call saying if I didn't bring the drugs and money we took, you and Jenny would be killed. Ralph sensed it wouldn't go well. But what choice did we have?"

"Do they have Clayton in custody?"

He rose and paced. "No. He said he never made the call and wasn't even there."

"But you saw him!"

He shook his head. "No, I saw Angler. He swears he thought it was an ambush and is claiming self-defense. I was knocked unconscious."

She sat forward. "They're getting away with murder?"

"So far."

She bit her cheek. "What about the money and drugs you were carrying?"

He studied the floor. "The police didn't find anything." His face creased with fatigue, he stood near the bed and caressed her hand. "You almost died." His eyes darkened with emotion. He leaned close, let his mouth pause above hers, then kissed her cheek.

The sheets suddenly felt hot around her body. "How is Jennifer?"

"She's coming around, trying to deal with Brett's death."

"Brett?"

He sucked in his bottom lip. "Yeah. Also shot. Turns out he used Clayton to provide the drugs while he supplied the customers. They split the profits."

"Wait. What? How did Brett manage that?"

"Built-in clients. He got his patients hooked on OxyContin after their surgeries, then abruptly stopped their prescriptions. Then he arranged for someone to introduce them to street drugs at a fraction of the cost they'd been paying for their meds."

"They deliberately ruined all those lives." Her teeth clenched, sending a sharp pang to her head. Didn't Jennifer know Brett was involved?"

"She says not. Clayton kept her well supplied, which I think made Brett feel threatened. He offered me the same percentage if I'd take Clayton out. It provided the cover I needed to get into the drug scene."

"So, did having me look for a marriage certificate." She rubbed her temples, hoping her head would stop hurting soon.

"That wasn't a cover. You have to believe I would never put your life in danger on purpose."

She peered into his eyes, beautiful and full of regret. One of the good guys. She could grow to like this man.

He shoved his hand in his pocket. "I found the pink belt. It was still lying next to the rocking horse in Sebastien's room."

"Oh, Greg." She reached for the old fabric and rubbed the soft satin between her fingers. The stories were real, they were closer to learning the truth. "Were the clues in it?"

He closed the door to her room then pulled a chair closer. "I read them. We already saw the first three in Marie's letters, but there's one new one. Number four says, *A beam secures our secret.*"

She frowned. "The whole house is built with beams."

He pulled out a slim notebook and looked over his notes. "Here's what I get. It's hidden in a dark but warm place, a messenger will shine light on it, and an actual beam hides it."

She tilted her head. "Or holds it up. See, it says, *secures.* A beam would have been needed to support the weight of the new fireplace and chimney."

"Maybe it will be more obvious once we're there. Are you ready to search again?"

Dread caused a wave of weakness. "Let's not plan anything yet. I need some time." She gripped her searing forehead. "Do you mind leaving now? My head is pounding."

He scanned her bandaged head and scratched face, unable to disguise a bitter frown. Gently squeezing her hand, he said, "Get some rest." As he turned toward the door, his face turned ferocious.

"Where are you going?"

"To make certain Clayton gets everything he deserves."

After he left, she rested her head on the pillow and considered her reaction to revisiting the mansion. Pure dread. She saw two men outside her door and her whole system tensed. Clayton's guys? She held her breath until they passed. Fear had leeched onto her mind. She fought it. With closed eyes, she prayed. *Father, you saved me from the storm, please keep me safe. I can't let another Mercer get away with murder.*

CHAPTER 53

Christmas Eve 1899, Astoria, Oregon

The leer in Edward's eyes turned Marie's stomach sour. It was Christmas, but he had ordered her to leave Sebastien with her mother. She sighed, wanting to be with them in the new little cottage that had nothing to do with Edward. It had only one room and a basement but was warm and provided a glimpse of the river. If only she could have spent this first Christmas there. She huffed her frustration. That would come later. For now, she needed to put up with Edward's game. When she brought his dessert, he grabbed her hand.

"I have a special treat for you tonight."

She turned her head, unwilling to meet the aging eyes that had once captivated her. The misery he'd caused had etched his face with a continuous scowl. Fixing her attention onto the wall beyond him, she pretended to smile.

He tugged her closer. "Want to know what it is?"

She poured the last of the wine into his glass from the crystal decanter, hoping he would soon tire. "I'm certain I will love whatever you choose to give me."

"Tonight is Christmas Eve. I am giving you a clue *and* a gift. Come. Let me show you."

She followed him to his office where he sat on the red chaise and patted the seat. Forcing herself to move toward him, she asked, "What have you written?"

He grabbed her arm and pulled her onto his lap. His thin, dry tongue penetrated her mouth. She tried not to gag and pulled back coyly. "First, let me see."

"You little tease." He raised an eyebrow. The expression used to be dashing. "Here they are, tied with red ribbons."

While slipping the ribbon off a tiny, rolled scroll, she desperately hoped for a meaningful clue. She read, "*Finding the treasure will brighten your lovely eyes*." She thought hard. "Is it by firelight? The light will brighten my eyes?"

"Aha! I am making this too easy."

She sprang off his lap. "They are not easy at all. I think they go nowhere, and you have abused me." Angry tears streamed, and she batted them away. "Give it to me by tomorrow, or I am leaving this house forever."

The front door slammed. "Father? Where are you, old man?" Jake's slurring voice called from the grand hallway.

Edward grabbed her arm. "You're not going anywhere." He pushed past her and strode out his office doorway. "What is going on?"

Marie wiped away a tear. What was the use fighting him? If she left, Sebastien would have nothing. With her reputation, no one would hire her. She moved to the dining room to clear the dishes. From the table, she listened to the ruckus.

It was only ten o'clock, but already Jake sounded drunk. "It's Christmas Eve. You should open your best wine and celebrate with us."

"No, I should not. You disgust me."

Marie neared the door and saw the two friends, arms draped over each other's wide shoulders.

Jake growled at Edward. "Don't be so stuffy." He turned to his friend. "Kelly, don't you think my father is stuffy?" Stepping forward, his strong hand gripped Edward's sagging shoulder, making him wince. "You know my friend, Kelly? He's Mr. MacDonald's fine son, back in town, all grown up." He dropped his hand but peered into Edward's face. "And I'm all grown up. Stronger than you now." A wicked grin filled his face. "Kelly, let's take my old man down to the river for a Christmas Eve swim."

Marie gasped at the threat. A plate slipped from her fingers, smashing on the marble floor. The fine china! Her hand covered her mouth.

Edward broke away from Jake and peered into the dining room, his face white as a ghost. "Clean that up." He had snarled at her, as though she was nothing but his maid.

She ducked her head and brushed away the tears, feeling foolish she'd ever thought she was more to him.

Jake's countenance darkened. "Still a bully." He shoved Edward against the wall. "Unlike everyone else, I'm not afraid of you anymore, old man."

Scowling, Edward tried to push him away. "Get off me."

Jake scoffed. "Your heart is black as coal." He poked his finger into his father's chest. "Maybe the ghost of Christmas past will visit tonight. I wouldn't count on making it to morning." He smirked and left.

Marie bent to gather the broken china, awaiting a scolding from Edward. Instead, he lumbered toward his office. "Go to your room until I call."

Marie waited in her room, her fists pressed against her temples. It wasn't her fault she dropped the china plate. Or that Jake barged in full of liquor. So why was she ordered to her room like a child awaiting punishment? She recalled the strange look in Jake and Kelly's faces. Edward was the one who should be afraid. She laid her tense hands on her lap. What if they planned him harm? What would become of her?

The bell rang and she dawdled going downstairs. Edward was in his office, a second bottle of wine half empty. His face appeared flushed, his eyes wild and frantic. Folded papers lay on his desk. "Come here."

She swallowed. "What, sir?"

"Here. I've been saving these clues. This one will lead you directly to what you want, although you'll have to do a little work. I'm not just going to give it to you." It was written in Edward's elegant scroll.

She read, "*A precious document safely rolled, but a golden snake has swallowed it whole.*" Poetry? She was certain he had gone insane. "A snake? Where?"

He grabbed her chin. "Look around Marie."

"Stop, you're hurting me!"

"You need to set your sights higher if you're ever going to find it." With a scowl, he let go of her chin and sat the next clue on her lap. "I'd planned to give this to Sebastien later, but time has flown by."

She opened the note and read, "*Though my roots began in dark despair, I have gained much to give my heir.*" She tilted her head. "You are giving him an inheritance?"

"Of course. He is my son." He set a gift in her hand. "Open it. I'll trust you to save it until he is older."

She pulled free of his icy fingers and tore off the paper. "A gold coin." Her shoulders slumped. Hardly a fortune. Over the years of their relationship, he had given her a handful of these.

"Look," he said, pointing. "Do you see this image?" She nodded. "This is a *rare* coin, worth much more than the others."

She slipped the coin into her pocket. "Thank you, Edward."

He shook his head. "You think too small. There are more of these." His eyes gleamed, watching hers.

She ordered her mind to be smart for Sebastien's sake. She gazed up through her lashes and smiled. "How many more?"

He leaned close. "Enough to make him a rich man." His breath reeked of alcohol and garlic. Suddenly, he straightened to listen. Boisterous shouts. Jake was back.

She held her breath, hoping he hadn't returned to carry out his promise.

Eyes wide, Edward stared at his office door.

Loud steps tromped up to Jake's room, then down and out the front door again.

Edward's shoulders lowered and he rubbed his chest. "I fear I may not be long for this earth."

Alarm tightened her chest. Was he referring to his heart condition or Jake's threat. "Please, if you won't be here, show me where to look."

He grabbed her wrist. "After you've earned it." He pulled her onto his lap and kissed her neck.

She removed her mind from his advances and replayed his words. It must be upstairs.

Fiery eyes blazed at her. "You are bored?" He pushed her away and stood unsteadily. "There are more beautiful women who do enjoy my company."

"Edward, I..."

He pulled his hand back to slap her but stumbled, toppling his chair to the side. "You think I don't know you are only after my money?" He left the office and slammed the door.

Her heart pulsed. If he died or changed his mind, she might never... She had to find it tonight. After rereading the new clues, she tucked them inside the tapestry belt around her waist. Think, Marie. A crash sounded overhead. Had he fallen? She rushed up the stairs to his bedroom. He was not anywhere on the second floor. More thuds from above.

On the third floor, she crept past her room and peeked through the open door across the hall. Metal clinked. Inside were assorted boxes and old furnishings. A full-length mirror lay on its side, shattered. A telescope stood in front of a paned window that framed the lights of the city and docks below. In the middle of the small room sat a rolltop desk. Edward sat erect on a leather chair, his back to her. Books lay scattered on the floor where he had likely swept them off in a rage. In front of him lay a slim wooden drawer that held many glittering coins.

She covered her mouth. Sebastien's inheritance. All her searching had been done on the first two stories of the mansion. The only time he visited the third story attic that housed the servants' quarters was to enter this room across the hall from hers, the observatory. The door was always locked.

After replacing the pen, he had been using, he rose. She ducked behind a chest in the hall and hid in the shadows. Something scraped and creaked. Edward's footsteps grew louder as he approached. Trembling, she pressed backward. If he found her here, she would lose the chance to take what was Sebastien's.

He threw the door against its frame and charged down the stairs. Below, his bedroom door slammed.

She crept from her hiding place and turned the door handle, grateful he hadn't locked it. Quietly, she sneaked down the servant's stairwell to the kitchen and worked until she was certain he was asleep. After stealing quietly to her room, she packed her and Sebastien's clothes. If she had the gold, they could leave this town with her mother. It wasn't stealing, it was her son's inheritance. She could start a new life, even without proof of his paternity.

Using a candle to light her way, she sneaked back to the observatory. The floorboards creaked. She stopped frequently and listened. No sounds drifted from the Captain's bed chamber below. The door handle to the observatory turned easily. Only a small squeak escaped when she opened it. She searched his desk drawers and cubbies. None contained the gold. Kneeling, she twisted her head to check under the desk.

"You would steal from *me*?" Edward's roar echoed throughout the room. He grabbed her elbow, fingernails digging into her skin.

Her heart leapt to her throat and she tried to wriggle free from his grip. He'd become a madman tonight.

He yanked her from under the desk and shoved her to the floor, his hand raised to strike her.

She screamed. "Edward, stop. You gave me the clues to follow."

Confusion halted his rage, but only for a moment. He pulled her to her feet. This time he did slap her, stinging her cheek. "You'll leave this house and not take a cent with you."

Instantly angry, her eyes flooded. He'd never hit her before. Once she got away, he never would again. He dragged her by her hair across the room, shouting curses. "Stop," she screamed. She should never have followed him tonight. Should have left years ago. Guilt sent a pang through her. What a fool she'd been.

"Do you think I don't know about the trysts in the carriage house with MacDonald? Well, tonight, he won't be there to keep you warm."

"Edward, I would never..."

"Shut up." His eyes were wild, possessed, not caring that she stumbled and bruised her legs as he dragged her from the observatory. Huffing from the exertion, he pulled her into a cold alcove and shoved her against the wood planks. "Give me your apron."

Her chest tightened. He was dismissing her. How would she feed Sebastien? With trembling fingers, she untied the sash and lifted it over her head. He shoved her into a chair and ripped the apron in shreds like a drunken madman. What was he doing?

"I'll teach you a lesson on thievery. Stick out your hands."

Her mouth went dry. If he tied her, she'd be at his mercy. She rose and tried to skitter around him, but he threw her back in the chair. Grabbing her wrists, he wound the torn strips of apron around them and tied them to the rungs. "They're burning, Edward." Tears tickled her cheeks, but she couldn't brush them away.

"Captain Mercer to you." He stuffed a wad of apron in her mouth and secured it with a rag. Then he tied her feet. "Sit here and contemplate your treachery. Tomorrow you are out on the street."

Heat surged through her body. Despite the snow outside, beads of sweat trickled down her forehead and neck as she squirmed hard against the rags. Useless. She tried to scream for help, but the cloth muffled her voice and made her choke. Breathing hard made it worse, so she stopped fighting. Thirst parched her mouth and throat.

There was no heat here. Soon, chills stole up her feet and legs. What if Edward didn't let her go? Panic played with her mind. Her mother had no idea she was in danger. No one knew where she was. Alone in the dark, with only the sound of her frantic heart pounding, she feared she would go mad by morning.

CHAPTER 54

Astoria, Oregon, Current Day

Though Eaven's headache persisted, she convinced the doctor to release her and returned to the River's Glory. Sitting by the cozy fireplace didn't keep the teacup from shaking in her hand. She told Greg she'd go back to the Mercer mansion and try to make some sense out of the new clue, but her body wasn't having it. She'd called him to come over before she changed her mind completely.

When he arrived, he looked at her and swore. "I'm so sorry for what you went through, Eav."

"I know I'm safe, but I feel like I did that night, sinking under the pounding waves. Gulping water."

He sat on the sofa and covered her hand with his. "But you didn't sink."

She had rebuffed his affection since she met him, but today it was comforting.

"All that matters is that you're here." He kissed the top of her head.

Leaning into him, she closed her eyes and savored how good it felt. "It isn't all that matters. Who would have missed me if I'd died? I have no one."

He wrapped his arm around her shoulders. "You have me as a friend. More if you would let yourself." His eyes searched hers.

She shook her head. "There's too much drama in my life right now."

"I'd like to change that."

She laughed, releasing some of her tension. "Like your life is all sunshine?"

He shrugged. "It will be."

"Look at me, Greg. Do I look like I can handle any more complications?"

He chuckled. "No. But you are still on my payroll and have a job to finish."

Part of her wanted to climb into a hot bath and forget everything, but what he said was true. She stood and set her cup on the buffet, not at all ready to face her demons. "I'll finish this, but Clayton better hope I don't run into him."

"That won't happen, I checked. Sergeant Cooper wants to ask him more questions, but Clayton left town on *business* when the police finished with him. There's a warrant out for Bransen. Neither he nor Angler have been seen. Besides, I imagine Clayton thinks he's scared the curiosity out of you."

That knowledge further buoyed her courage. "If anything, my determination is kicking in. Let's go." She grabbed her coat and pocketed the clues, then got into Greg's car. The day was as dark and stormy as when she was kidnapped. Her knees bounced of their own accord. It was useless to stop her jitters. After he parked by the mansion, she opened the door and craned her head up. "Sheez, half the tree crashed into the roof."

They ran in the rain to the rear porch, where Greg reached through the broken window and unlocked the door. His flashlight illuminated the kitchen trash. They dashed across to the dining room.

"The clues from the pink belt don't seem to tell us much. There may be more if we can find the tapestry belt Marie made. Let's check her room." She turned on her own light and led the way up the main stairway to the second story. More carefully, they took the narrow steps to the servant's quarters on the third level. She stopped short at the door to Sebastien's nursery. The flashlight shook in her hand and bounced over the walls and floor like a strobe light.

He gripped her hand. "I'm here."

She entwined her fingers in his, glad that he was. What that meant, she'd have to figure out later. They carefully searched Sebastien and Marie's rooms but failed to find any other clues. Frustrated, Eaven moved back into the hall, Greg behind her. Creaks and groans sounded like a storm behind the door across the hall. A sharp bang made her jerk. Feeling silly, she said, "Probably just wind through the broken roof."

They opened the door and crept through the attic space, avoiding fragments of broken mirror and old boxes. The room housed a rolltop desk, chair, and telescope. She let out the breath she'd been holding. "An observatory." The broken tree limb had punctured the roof and smashed through the outside wall. Wind howled and rain pelted the walls and floorboards. Branches shuddered, their dead twigs scratching like claws against the wood floor.

Greg reached up and broke off a piece of roof that hung precariously. "It's eerie."

She swallowed. "Yeah." She squinted past the thick branches to the far side of the room, where an inside wall had also been smashed. Alarm increased as she moved closer to the black chamber that lurked behind it. "Something dreadful happened here."

CHAPTER 55

Astoria, Oregon, Christmas Eve 1889

In the early morning frost of Christmas day, Jake Mercer paced under the cover of the back porch. Glorious black smoke billowed out the open window of the carriage house. He squinted in the near dark and swore out loud at what he saw. "No!"

The Captain stumbled from the back door of the burning building, pulling on his thick velvet smoking jacket. Coughing and gagging, his father ran toward the main house but tripped on the steps. He grabbed a tree for balance and spied Jake. "Fire!" He pointed to the carriage house. Raising his hand to protect his face against the heat and flames, he sunk onto the frigid soil and gasped for air. "I got the horse out but the girl's in there!"

Jake's stomach roiled, hating this man. Even on Christmas, he couldn't resist a clandestine meeting with Marie, in the stable, like animals. He had followed his father, intending to humiliate him. Then a better idea occurred.

His father tried to shout above the crashing timbers, licked by flaming tongues, but his voice was hoarse.

Disgust filled Jake at the man's uncanny ability to cheat death, first, from the sinking frigate that brought him to Astoria, and now from the fire. A loud crack made him jump. The nearby tree, its heavy branches nearly consumed, crashed on top of the burning carriage house, adding fuel, and stoking the raging flames.

Turning to leave the failed plot, he thought of locking the old man outside. If the fire wouldn't kill him, maybe the cold would. Jake lingered a moment longer under the porch roof before slipping inside. He stamped his boots on the kitchen floor. At least Marie didn't escape. The bane of his family was dead. He had finally evened the score for his mother. This latest escapade would spread all over town and he relished the humiliation his father would suffer. Yet, he felt robbed. The inferno should have finished the job.

He rubbed the frost away and stared through the window at his father coughing violently, unable to catch his breath, then looked at the street. This early, everyone was still snug in bed. Apparently, no one had called the fire brigade yet. No other structures were threatened. No one would see Jake if he finished the job and dumped his father's debilitated body into the smoking carnage.

Just then, his father managed to rise onto his wool-stockinged feet and amble through the back door. He left a trail of wet footprints across the kitchen into the dining room. At one end of the table, he collapsed onto a chair. "Water." Face purple as a beet, he choked out the word and coughed harder, bending over his knees to breathe.

The white and gray marble fireplace stood near the gasping man. Jake's gaze moved to the brass andirons designed with heavy cannonballs. They beckoned him. No one knew what was happening. Maybe he could still manage.

In a quick motion, he lunged toward the mantel, grabbed one of the serpent-headed andirons, and raised it high over his head.

CHAPTER 56

Astoria, Oregon, Current Day

Inside the observatory, Eaven tugged on the branches that had crashed through the roof. "Can you help me?" Greg grabbed the main limb and pulled it to the side. She tugged back more branches and gasped. "A hidden room."

He pulled at the thick wooden boards to get into it, but they were too strong. "I think I saw a bar I can use."

She stepped closer to the broken wall and peered into the blackness. Her pulse raced with sensations of the panic emanating from it. Burning pain shot through her wrists. She grasped them and jumped back. "Greg!"

He rushed back and pulled her to him. "What happened?"

"I have no idea." She backed away from the room while he wedged off two boards and set them aside.

Cautiously, she edged through the hole, monitoring her impressions, and shined her light in front of her. It landed on a gruesome sight. Her hand flew up to muffle a scream. Surely, she wasn't seeing this.

"What?" He wedged away another piece, ducked his head, and joined her.

The full light from their flashlights revealed the grisly scene.

With wrists and ankle bones tied by shredded rags, a petite skeleton hung from a heavy ladder-back chair. A deflated blue dress still draped over thin bones, the skin and organs long since decomposed. The skull had fallen forward, a rag still holding the jaw open. Around the tiny waist hung a tapestry belt.

"It's Marie." Eaven drew back, wrapping her arms tightly around her waist.

"Everyone thought she'd died in the fire, but Captain Mercer locked her in here to die. Why would he do this?" Greg snarled. His flashlight shone on Marie's hair, still tied in a wilted ribbon. A layer of dust covered everything like a shroud.

"I found packed trunks in her room. Maybe she'd had enough and was about to leave."

"And to keep her from leaving, he killed her."

Rattled, Eaven steeled herself to assess the details. Instead of the angular nose and the emerald eyes that Marie had passed to Greg, only three dark cavities remained in the bony skull. Bare white teeth chomped on the fabric that still gagged her and had kept her from calling for help. How long had she lingered until death released her?

Eaven swallowed rising bile. "I guess I should get the rest of the clues." She held her breath and stepped closer. Her fingers fumbled while she undid the tapestry belt and backed away. She handed it to Greg and followed him out of the room into the observatory. "The man was sick."

He didn't answer, just eased into the cracked leather chair.

She put a hand on his shoulder. "I'm sorry you had to witness another family tragedy."

His head hung until his chin nearly touched his chest. "I don't want to be related to the Mercers."

"He's your ancestor. Period. I don't see an ounce of his despicable character in you."

He blew out a breath. "You're a kind woman, Eaven." He handed her the belt. "Why don't you see what she hid?"

She opened the clasp and pulled out a gold coin, turning it in the light. "This is valuable, much more than the one you wear around your neck." Gently sliding the metal clasp all the way open, she unfolded the stiff tapestry and coaxed out three small scrolls. "Here."

He leaned forward to read the first. "*Finding this treasure will brighten your lovely green eyes. That gives her nothing. A precious document safely rolled, but a golden snake has swallowed it whole.*" He frowned. "What's that about?"

"The snake symbol is one of the Captain's favorite decorating themes. I found them everywhere."

"Show me."

"I will, but there's one more clue."

He read, "*Though my roots began in dark despair, I have gained much to give my heir.* He thinks he's a poet. It sounds like he hid something valuable for Sebastien."

She nodded. "Does to me too. Let's find it, for Marie's sake."

He stood. "She wasted her life to prove Sebastien's heritage."

They left the corpse and stole down the staircase to the main floor. Eaven led the way to the fireplace covered with snake designs. "Here's one example of the snakes."

He touched the prominent viper slithering up the mantel. "Fitting mascot." He bent and peered up the flu with his flashlight.

"I already tried that. None of the common secret compartment features have been used. Besides, our new clue says the document is rolled inside a golden snake. These are black."

The front door opened. Tad's voice.

Eaven and Greg ducked into the next room and listened to the footsteps in the main hall. Another huge gust hit the house, rattling the loose windows.

A woman's voice squeaked. "Darren, I don't want to go in. I could never live here."

"Linda, please," her husband pleaded. "Clayton specially arranged for us to see it. Let's just take a look."

"If you aren't interested, he also arranged for another couple to see it this afternoon," Tad said.

While the man and woman argued, Eaven and Greg slipped out the back door and ran to his car. He sped down the hill, squealing around corners. "How could the Captain do that?"

Eaven scowled. "I don't understand how Marie could demean herself and stay with a bully like that in the first place."

"She believed he held the key to her happiness."

Eaven shook her head. The finger of judgment pointed back at her and she sucked in air. "Like I felt I needed Michael, put all my hope for happiness in him." She stared through the swishing wiper blades. If he hadn't left, would she have stayed, excusing his behavior until something drastic happened to boot her out? Apparently, yes. She'd been insecure enough to do just that, no matter what the cost had been. She squared her shoulders. That would never happen again. If Marie had lived, maybe she would have come to the same conclusion.

At the inn, Greg followed Eaven into the sitting room and accepted a cup of tea without comment. His subdued mood darkened.

So did hers. They'd found Marie but not the document. After witnessing the way the Captain treated her, Eaven strongly doubted there ever was one. "Should we call the police?"

He shook his head. "Hard to explain why we were trespassing. Besides, it's a hundred plus year-old homicide."

"And someone needs to pay for it." She laid the tapestry ribbon on the coffee table. "I'll be right back." She returned with the briefcase she had been using to organize her findings. "The new clues mention brightening her eyes and being supported by a beam." She laid them all out and fingered through her research from the historical museum. After tugging out some papers, she spread them across the table. "I found several receipts for repairs done to the mansion."

"What are you thinking?"

She shuffled more papers. "Here's the bill from the carpenter who installed a new fireplace mantel and was suing for payment." She leaned toward him so he could see the receipt. "This second page of the invoice was for *ceiling repairs*."

He rubbed his chin. "The carpenter would have used wood, maybe even a beam. Could that be it?"

"It could. I thought it meant the ceiling around the fireplace chimney when he had it installed, but maybe not. Like Marie, we've been thinking of the warmth and light of a fireplace. However, these clues begin to hint at something entirely different. A thrill advanced from her toes to her spine. She paused and looked him purposefully in the eye. It could be a lamp."

"I don't know. What about it *hiding in darkness*, or the description of it *costing a fortune to hide*?"

"The lamps the Captain bought did cost a fortune. Their tubes are hollow, so they would be dark inside. And some of them have brass—*golden*—snakes."

He shook his head and grasped clue number three. "How does that fit with the *messenger enlightening the darkness*? Besides there are dozens of lamps in this mansion."

Her hands flew to her cheeks. "No. It can only be one." She took the clue from him and read it aloud. "*In darkness, his fortune awaits your discovery, but my messenger will enlighten it.* When I was in the Captain's office, I noticed an unmistakable chandelier made by Thomas *Messenger* and Sons."

Surprise spread across Greg's face. "Messenger. A company?"

"Yes. The lamp has golden scrolls that end in serpent heads. I'll bet anything we'll find the document in one of them."

He rose. "Then let's go back."

"We'll have to wait. Tad said he had another showing this afternoon. Besides, it's getting dark and honestly, I'm too shaken to go back tonight. I doubt I'll get any sleep with Marie's image in my head."

He raked his fingers through his hair, the corners of his mouth twisted with sadness. "This whole situation is hellish."

She stood and took his hand. He'd risked his life to clean up the mess the Mercers had made of his town, of his family. Instead, he'd lost even more. "I know."

His arms encircled her and pulled her close. She laid her head on his chest, seeing him in a different light than the last time he'd embraced her. He was a good man. Eyes closed, her mind relaxed in the rhythm of his heart and the warmth emanating from his body. His chin rubbed against her hair. Soft lips nuzzled her temple, her ear, then slid smoothly to her lips, nudging them apart.

Tired of fighting everyone, including herself, she let his kiss deepen. Her body responded as one hand slid over her back, the other holding her head while his mouth explored hers.

"Oh, excuse me," Claire said.

Eaven jerked out of his arms, coming to her senses in the nick of time. Though conflicted, her heart knew a romance with him could have no happy ending.

Looking everywhere but at them, Claire set a platter of freshly baked cinnamon buns on the coffee table. "Please help yourself." She hurried away.

He grinned and reached for Eaven. "Now, where were we?"

She moved away. "I'm sorry, Greg, but I'm leaving soon, and I don't need complications."

His gaze fell to the floor, lips tight. "That's what you keep saying, but your actions don't add up. Wish you'd make up your mind." He grabbed his coat and stormed from the room.

"Can we talk later?"

His answer was the slamming of the front door.

Frustrated with herself, she plopped onto a chair. How had she let her emotions overrule her common sense? No sense blaming him, she had instigated it. She knew he had feelings for her. Feelings that might grow into love if she let him. But for how long? A seven-year age difference was too much for Michael. Ten years would soon overcome Greg's desire for her.

The platter sat there. Even with cinnamon wafting upward, it held no appeal. The urge to get on with her life intensified. Surely there was something good ahead of her, something to look forward to, that fit who she was becoming. She had to believe that. She withdrew the metal mermaid from the pocket in her briefcase and gently squeezed it. "Don't worry, *water child*, we'll find our way."

CHAPTER 57

After their rift yesterday, Eaven battled whether to call Greg or wait for him to contact her. He didn't. It was already after noon, with decisions demanding answers. Did he want her to stay or go? When he refused to return her calls, she decided to drive to his house.

He answered the door but did nothing to disguise his sour mood. "Come in."

Another pouting man. She'd made a good decision. "I have things to discuss."

He stepped back for her to enter. Jennifer sat on the sofa, her sweater tight and low.

Eaven tried to contain her surprise, and the fickle disappointment washing over her. "Hi."

Jennifer rose and stood close to Greg. "Hello. You're looking better." Her tone was formal and aloof. With perfect makeup and high boots, Jennifer looked radiant, much different than the fragile, drowned junkie Eaven experienced on the boat.

She offered a tentative smile. "You look better too."

"Thank you for saving me," Jennifer said. I'd be dead right now, stuck in that boat at the bottom of the bar instead of here with Greg."

Eaven shrugged. "The Coast Guard had a bit to do with it too."

Jennifer's big blue eyes gazed up at Greg. "So, did you." Her ringed fingers intertwined with his.

Eaven's heart hammered. They were a couple? Had they been when he kissed her? She swallowed, avoiding his eyes, ready to flee. "I just wanted to...needed to...um. Perhaps I came at the wrong time."

He dropped Jennifer's hand. "Not at all. We do need to talk. Want coffee?"

"Yes, please." She moved toward the old sofa and glanced at a plate of smoked salmon. And wine. What had she stepped into? She'd get the business out of the way and leave.

He returned with her cup. "Decided to try out Sheila's salmon. It's good. Have some." He sat on a chair opposite them. "Jenny and I have been putting our information together to bring a case against Clayton."

"That's partly why I came over," Eaven said. "I have an idea, but what are your plans?"

"Ralph and I tried to eliminate his buying power by stealing his cash and drugs. We figured he'd get in too deep with the cartels and they would take him out, trapping themselves in the process. It was beginning to work. Clayton is hurting. I still think that's the best plan."

"No," Jennifer said. "I don't want you endangering your life again."

Eaven didn't want that either. "Could Jennifer testify that Clayton sold her drugs?"

Jennifer's full lips, obviously enhanced by her late husband, held a pretty pout. "No one would believe me. Besides, I never bought drugs directly from him. He's a very clever man."

Nodding, Eaven said, "I thought of something that might work. Could we put together a list of clients Brett passed to Clayton? Maybe some of them would be willing to testify."

Jennifer shook her head. "None of them ever dealt with Clayton either. I think the chain went from Clayton to Angler to Rex. Bransen and a couple of other guys did a lot of the dirty work."

Eaven studied her, sensing she knew a lot for a drugged-out wife of a plastic surgeon. "You seem to know a lot about Clayton's operation."

"From Brett, just before he died. He said Clayton blackmailed him into getting involved to save our reputations. Obviously, that wasn't true."

Obviously, but what *was* true? "Greg, can't the DEA put pressure on Bransen and Angler?"

He glowered. "They found Bransen's body this morning. Angler still hasn't surfaced."

She jumped from her seat. "What?" Her shin bumped the table, splashing coffee from her cup. "And no one's suspicious that the two men who could point the finger at Clayton are gone?" She mopped the spill with a napkin.

"Suspicion and proof are two different things. Someone will have to take him down another way."

She rubbed her shin. "That sounds ominous."

"Dangerous is more like it. Look what happened to Brett," Jennifer said, spreading salmon on a cracker as though talking about the weather.

Greg leaned back, his gaze settling on Eaven.

She held his eyes momentarily, wishing they were alone so they could talk. While Jennifer was busy munching salmon and crackers, Eaven asked him, "Do you have an idea?"

Tired eyes and down-turned lips spoke of days of worry. "My cover is blown and I'm off the case. Professionals are looking for Clayton and Angler. The only thing left for me is to prove Sebastien's lineage."

Jennifer's eyes widened. "You found something?"

Eaven glanced at Greg, hoping he'd let it drop.

He inhaled deeply and nodded. "Yes. Soon I'll be able to prove Captain Mercer was Sebastien's father."

Jennifer tilted her head. "Then you'll own what, half the Mercer estate?"

"I think we're jumping ahead of ourselves," Eaven interjected, feeling uncomfortable with him sharing what they'd discovered. She didn't trust Jennifer.

"We have a few clues that we hope lead to a document," he said. "I think it's a marriage certificate. If we find it, the Mercer family tree has a whole new limb. I drew it out."

Jennifer smiled. "May I see?"

Eaven winced when Greg unrolled the large sheet of white vellum onto the table. He was too trusting.

He pointed. "Clayton's ancestry follows this line. Mine follows this one. There's one too many of us left in this tragedy."

Jennifer studied the two lines. Her lips parted in surprise as she stared at the tree.

He re-rolled the vellum. "We need to get back inside the mansion and follow our lead."

Jennifer turned to him. "Break in? Clayton is probably having it watched day and night."

A brilliant thought made Eaven grin. "We don't need to break in."

"Then what?" Greg asked.

"We know Clayton has a cash flow problem. And, I know someone who would love to have that Thomas Messenger chandelier."

Jennifer took Greg's hand. "Is that important?"

He sat forward. "It's—"

"It's just a ploy to get us inside," Eaven interrupted.

"And get the marriage certificate." Jennifer kissed him. "Won't Clayton be surprised to know you found it. I need to get going." She strolled to the door and cast a sicky sweet smile at Eaven. "See ya."

When the door closed, Greg wiped the lipstick from his mouth, his cheeks pink. "I'm sorry for behaving like an adolescent yesterday."

"What about today with Jennifer? What's that about?"

He frowned. "Nothing. With all the trauma, she's just clingy. I don't see how it would matter to you anyway."

She sighed. "It's confusing. Sorry for the mixed signals but I can't change what happened. Can we just focus on getting this and get you your inheritance?"

He gave a tight smile. "Sure, what do you have in mind?"

"Let me make some quick calls and see if I can pull this together."

CHAPTER 58

The soonest Eaven could arrange for a moving van was at ten the next day. She anxiously waited at the Mercer mansion for Tad to unlock the door, then led the movers to the Captain's office. "Here it is." She pointed to the exquisite Messenger chandelier hanging above the Captain's heavily carved desk. Years of dust and cobwebs covered both. Excitement tingled from solving the riddle and finding a buyer for the lamp.

Tad glanced at her, a little uncertain. "Clayton will be glad you found a buyer for something."

"Yes, he will. It's fetching a good price too." She forced a relaxed smile, glad Clayton was out of town. So far, the police were keeping quiet about his possible involvement in the murder and her kidnapping. If he were here, she wouldn't be setting foot in this place. "Please move the desk out of the way," she instructed the movers.

They grabbed hold of the edges and jerked it.

"Gently! These may not look like much, but they're extremely valuable." They passed a skeptical glance between them. Eaven couldn't blame them, with so much grime filling the place.

Moving two ladders to either side of the chandelier, they began the arduous job of unscrewing the post from the decorative ceiling rose. After detaching the wires, they slowly lowered the magnificent lamp.

Unable to contain herself, she gently swiped away cobwebs from the sphinxes affixed to the arms. Each of the five brass scrolls ended in a viper head, mouth open, ready to strike. She quickly checked inside each gaping mouth for signs of a paper scroll. Nothing showed.

Once the lamp was settled into a wooden crate in the moving van, she motioned to the drivers. "Follow me to the River's Glory Bed and Breakfast." She heaved a sigh of relief that Clayton never showed.

Claire greeted her outside the basement doors. "Oh my, bring it in here. I love antiques. Here are the things you asked for." She laid a mouth mirror, tweezers, and needle-nosed pliers on the workbench.

Eaven hugged her, feeling giddy. She not only had the opportunity to restore the lamp but had an incredibly good chance of finding the document.

Greg paced at his cottage, waiting for Eaven to signal that the movers had left. No need to make it obvious that a Sault was involved. A rush of anxiety washed over him like the driving rain that washed the hills of Astoria today. This could really be it, the end of generations of searching and grief. The end of the Mercers' lies. He glanced at his watch, hoping he had time before his appointment at the police station. His phone buzzed. *Eaven.* He flew out the door.

When he pulled to the side of the River's Glory, Eaven led him through the basement door on the downhill side of the inn. "You won't believe how gorgeous it is!" Her face glowed.

Drinking in her enthusiasm, he wanted to take her in his arms, but stopped himself. "Let's take a look."

She pulled the moving blanket off the box, exposing the cross piece that held the lamp suspended. "The chandelier was held by an added support *beam.* I also learned the Captain had replaced the light after another lamp broke in his office. This one did indeed *cost a small fortune.* I've cleaned it a little but wait until you see it shine! I've seen these go for over twenty thousand dollars."

"Did you look for the *snake that swallowed it whole?*"

She grinned. "No. I waited for you."

"Thank you." He stepped closer to the lamp. "Where do we start looking?"

"Electric wires are threaded through these hollow tubes. While I was cleaning one of them, I noticed the tube was segmented near the viper's neck?"

He nodded. "Does it twist?"

"It should." She gently twisted the segments opposite each other, without success. "It's been a long time." She tried again, careful not to dent the expensive sculpture. "I think I felt something."

"Here, let me try." He moved in to take over.

"No." She pushed his hands away.

Stunned, he took a step back. "I'm trying to help."

She sighed. "Sorry. I've been trained in this, you haven't. Give me a bit more time." She wiggled until there was a definite movement. "It's coming." With a few more tugs, the segments pulled apart.

He tilted his head to get a better angle. "I see the electric wires."

She handed him a flashlight. "Shine this into the cavity." She maneuvered the pliers with great dexterity, without touching the brass fittings.

He found himself watching an expert, her concentration admirable. "No wonder you gained such a reputation in your field."

She jerked the pliers out of the opening and stretched her neck. "I need quiet to concentrate."

He felt reprimanded but bit his lip and remained silent.

Once more, she used the light and squinted. "Wait, there should only be two wires." She grinned. "But there are three here!" Gently, she tugged each wire independently. One pulled out, dragging a rolled scroll of paper. When it was free of the lamp, she shouted. "We did it!" She did a quick jog in place, then handed him the scroll. "Mr. Sault."

Pulse racing, he hardly dared to hope. His fingers fumbled the rolled note. Moving it closer to a light, he read,

"*My dear Marie. What a pleasant companion you have been, bringing me my greatest joys. I've kept my word. Here are the directions that lead to a codicil, the document you need to claim Sebastien's heritage. He is my son, whom I have loved like no other.*"

Eaven interrupted. "It wasn't a marriage certificate."

"No. It's even better." He continued reading.

"*The codicil to my will is kept in a desk in a secret space off the observatory. To access the room, remove the corner chimney brick, the tenth brick from the floor. Pull the lever and the wall will open.*

If you are in possession of this document, I have most likely passed. I would tell the entire world about my son, but alas, I find I am a coward when it comes to my pride. Always let Sebastien know of my love for him.

Edward"

An ache built in Greg's chest. "I don't get it. He used Marie unforgivably, starved her to death. But here he speaks fondly to her, as if he...loved her."

"Who knows how much time had passed from when he created this note and the time of her death. The sentiments certainly changed. At the beginning, Marie talked of marriage. Toward the end, she planned to escape."

Greg's throat thickened. "He expressed his love for Sebastien."

Eaven put her hand on his arm. "Sebastien was loved by his mother *and* his father."

"That's a far different story than the other Mercers portrayed." He stood and paced, wanting to rub Clayton's face in the Mercers' lies. "That document is in the secret room. I want it."

She glanced at the time. "You have an appointment at the police station. I'll go." She grinned. "As you can see, I have experience with secret compartments."

He squeezed his temples in frustration. The key to unlocking his whole life rested three blocks from where he stood. He peered at Eaven, so determined, so brave, but... "Do you really want to go back there by yourself?"

"Absolutely. Now that we know the story, I want to see justice done."

He rubbed the unshaven stubble on his chin, torn about her decision, wanting to protect her, but there was no telling how long the police would need him. "With Clayton out of town, I guess you'll be safe."

"Exactly." She pushed him out the front door. "I'll be fine."

CHAPTER 59

While Greg met with the police and DEA investigator, Eaven hid from view and watched Tad unlock the mansion to show it to an older gentleman. Outside, she listened until they'd moved to another part of the building. Her chest tightened against her pounding heart as she sneaked in the front door to the dining room. Squatting behind the Chippendale table, she waited until Tad exited and locked the door again.

It grew quiet. Impressions she hadn't felt before filled the dining room. *Anger. Torment.*

The floor creaked overhead. She sucked in a breath and stood motionless, wishing Greg had come with her. The noise stopped. This was her chance if she still wanted it. She stepped over the bloodied carpet and slipped quietly upstairs. Outside Sebastien's bedroom, she paused.

Another creak made her glance behind her. She twirled in a circle, straining to see. Angler was still missing. Could he be hiding here? Why hadn't she thought of that?

After a few minutes of absolute quiet, she stole slowly down the hall and through the observatory door. Passing by the rolltop desk, the gaping hole confronted her. She steeled herself against the sight of Marie's skeleton. This had to be done.

Instead of stepping through the ragged hole near the body, she counted the bricks on the chimney and found the loose one. When she pulled it out and lifted the lever, the wall opened a crack. She pushed on the panel, but it stuck. The fallen tree limb had damaged the frame. Another shove on the panel sent a screech through the room. She jumped back and listened. Pressure pulsed against her temples. Clanging about like this could wake the dead.

She'd do it the other way. After pushing aside the tree branches, she stepped through the broken wall. Rain had flooded through the gash in the roof and drenched the room. The damage to the third story could be expensive if it weren't handled quickly. Probably the other levels also.

From where she stood, she could see out the hole into the neighbors' yards and all the way to the river. She gripped the studs to keep from swaying. It was a long way down.

As she moved past the skeleton, Marie's empty eye sockets seemed to follow her movements like the eyes in a painting. Dread filled the room. *Panic.* She stopped and glanced at the floor where the shredded remnants of a dingy white apron lay. The rest of the ripped garment still held the young mother bound to the chair.

Eaven swallowed. "I'm sorry, Marie. We'll get you out of here soon." An old steamer trunk rested on the wooden floor. Hands trembling, she lifted the unlocked clasp. It was empty except for a short stack of books.

A small writing desk stood next to Marie. The center drawer should have moved out farther than it did. Following a hunch, Eaven reached inside, felt along the underside of the desktop, and found a clasp. She moved it sideways and the drawer released to pull completely out. After examining it, she removed a false bottom and broke into a wide grin. The document!

She lifted the letter and read it.

To whom it may concern,

Attached to this codicil is a copy of my last will and testament and a codicil. Circumstances earlier this evening cause me to believe my life is in danger, the reason for this change...

The letter and the will behind it were written with the same unmistakable handwriting as the clues the Captain had written. She had found more than she or Greg could have hoped for. Elation and gratitude took turns filling her with confidence that she was on the right path. Her skills had helped turn this family's sordid history on its ear and expose the truth.

Footsteps sounded on the main stairs. "Eaven Alexander!"

Clayton! How did he know she was here? The dread she'd felt over Marie's skeleton was nothing like she felt now. He was a murderer. Her eyes dashed around. There was no way to avoid him.

The will trembled in her hands. Would he search her? She folded it quickly and stuffed it in her back pocket.

As he raced up the staircase toward the attic, his shouting increased.

Heart banging against her chest, she parted the branches and stepped out of the secret room back into the observatory. Her breath caught. The desk drawer! Clayton would know she found something. And she knew what he was capable of.

Tremors overtook her whole body as she struggled to step back over the tree limb. Untangling her foot, she shoved in the drawer, then lunged out of the secret room, just as he pounded into the observatory.

"What are you doing in my house?" he said in a low growl. His flushed face sported a two-day old red beard.

Her insides trembled but she kept her voice steady. "I don't know if you played a part in my kidnapping, but this is the truth. I am not *with* Greg Sault. I couldn't care less about anything else he's involved in. I am an antiques expert and your house is filled with irresistible antiques. I apologize for my lack of discretion in sneaking in here. That said, I think you should see something." She edged back toward the hidden room.

Eyes narrowed, he stared mutely.

She stepped to one side and pointed. "Look."

He peeked in and his head jerked back. "What the..."

"It's Marie Sault."

He frowned. "Can't be. Jake said he killed her in the fire."

Her jaw dropped at the callousness in his voice. "No. She was left to die up here."

He stepped forward, a scowl marring his face. "She got what she deserved." His pale blue eyes bore into Eaven's. "Did you find any coins in there?"

Coins? "No. But I wasn't looking for any."

"What were you looking for?" His voice sounded calm. Too calm for the rage that contorted his face.

"Antiques. The...desk and trunk in there may have some value."

Warily, he stepped past her and climbed through the hole. She watched as he pulled out the small desk drawers and tossed them on the floor. When the middle drawer stuck, he jerked it from the desk, breaking it apart, and examined the back. Finding nothing, he headed for the steamer trunk and threw back the lid.

Outside, the wind assaulted the tree, moving the broken branches across the wet floor, scraping and creaking against the wood. Marie's skull fell sideways, the empty sockets turned toward Clayton's back. Red hot emotion surged throughout the room.

Eaven gasped as fear spidered up her neck. Panic built in her chest and she inched away from the hidden room, watching Clayton. Watching Marie. Certain the skeleton had moved on its own.

He slammed the trunk shut. "Jake must have got it wrong." Scowling, he stepped out of the room and glared down at her. "So, you took a ride on my grandpa's ship. And escaped."

She stood her ground, resisting the urge to placate, convince him she wasn't a threat. She *was* a threat. "Yes, I escaped. But Ralph and Brett didn't. That's coming down on you."

"I don't think so." He smiled, his eyes impassive.

She lunged for the door, but he grabbed her elbows and shoved her against the wall, his face close. Alcohol permeated his breath. She turned her face, fighting his hold. Pain shot through her arms.

He rubbed his forehead against hers, eyes cold and calculating. "I think it's time you join Marie in that secret room. This whole mausoleum needs to go up in flames. Tonight."

She couldn't imagine anything worse than being left tied in this attic and burned alive. *Father help me*! This time she knew the cry for help had lifted higher than the rafters as power surged into her limbs.

"Nice of the Captain to leave something to bind you with." Clayton reached down to grab the strips of apron from the floor with one hand. She grabbed his other wrist and twisted it behind his back. Using both hands, she leveraged him to the floor. He fell to his knees to keep it from snapping. "Let go of me!" he grunted. "You'll pay for this."

"No, you'll pay. You have no idea how much you've lost." Pulling his arm higher behind his back, she pushed him onto his face then kicked his backside, sending him flying headfirst through the hole, halfway into the secret room.

Then she ran.

He roared.

A loud crash sounded. A shriek. Afraid to look behind, she slipped and caught herself on the stairs.

Crashing, like the sound of breaking furniture, continued above.

Between Clayton's threats and the vehemence that surrounded Marie's skeleton, Eaven's chest heaved with terror, propelling her forward. She had to get out. Nothing she'd experienced had ever produced such a sense of rage in her spirit. Once outside, she sprinted away.

Greg's BMW screamed up the hill and she ran toward it. He swerved to the curb and stopped long enough for her to jump inside. She slammed the door. "Go!"

"You're shaking."

"That's what fear does," she said, wrapping her arms around herself. "I was looking through the attic observatory when Clayton caught me."

He glared. "Did he hurt you?"

She shook her head. "No. I distracted him with Marie's skeleton."

He tightened the grip on his steering wheel. "Bet that stopped him cold."

Another shiver hit just as they reached the inn. "Let's get inside. You need to see something."

Chapter 60

Eaven held tightly to the hot teacup resting in her lap. She took another swallow to quell the rush of adrenalin coursing through her body, hoping that soon her pulse would go back to normal.

Greg had wrapped a heavy throw over her and tucked it around her legs. He sat next to her on the sofa. "Are you sure you're all right? I've never seen you like this."

She gulped her tea. "I will be."

Tender concern shown from his gorgeous eyes. He put his arm around her shoulder and hugged her close. "You're okay. I won't leave you."

She felt safe in his arms. "Thank you." This would be so easy to get used to. Closing her eyes, she let herself imagine becoming a part of his future. But is that what she wanted? To be part of someone else's life? No. It was time for her to build her own. Learn to trust herself. She stood, shaking off the useless longing and delivered what he'd paid her to find.

"Why are you smiling?" he asked.

She pulled the folded will from her pants pocket. "Because I found this."

His eyes widened. "No."

"Yes." She handed the will to him and resumed her comfy seat, pulling the comforter to her neck.

He read aloud:

"Being of sound mind, I hereby...

...Edward Mercer, signed this 18th day of October, 1899"

"An actual will! He claimed Sebastien!"

She grinned. "And it's witnessed by his solicitor! There's no way this can be disputed."

"For once, we beat the Mercers." A smile lit Greg's face, making him look even younger. "Eaven, stay with me. Let me show how much I appreciate you?" A tempting grin accompanied his searching eyes.

She shook her head. "I'm sorry."

His smile faltered, but the grin remained. "You're one of the few women who has ever resisted me this long."

She laughed at his roguish expression. "It isn't easy, if that helps your ego."

"Not by much."

The front door opened, and Jennifer pushed into the parlor. Rain dripped from her curling tendrils. She raked the two of them with her eyes. A fake smile stretched her tight cheeks. "How cozy."

Eaven blew out her disappointment.

He stood. "Hi, Jen. What's up?"

"I was just about to ask you that. I've been calling, but you're not answering. I thought something might have happened. This was the last place I could think to come." Her eyes teared.

"Hey, everything's okay." He helped her take off her raincoat. "You won't believe what Eaven found!"

Eaven winced, sensing Greg might be jeopardizing his position. Jennifer's addiction and jealousy equaled unpredictability. According to Brett, she'd been cozy with Clayton before the boat ride. A jolt shot through her. How did Clayton know she'd be at his house? Heat traveled up her throat, an accusation on the tip of her tongue. Without proof, however, she bit it back.

Jennifer sniffed back pretend tears. "I'm glad you're all right. Show me what you found."

He handed the will to her then waited, a grin lighting his face.

Her eyes widened. "So, you'll claim half the Mercer fortune. Well done, Mr. Sault." She smiled and leaned over to kiss him. "You beat Clayton." She opened her purse to put the will inside.

"What are you doing?" It was all Eaven could do to not ring Jennifer's slender neck. Instead, she grabbed the woman's wrist and plucked the will from her hand.

Jennifer smiled, doe eyed. "I was just going to put this in my safe for Greg. It's too valuable to leave it just anywhere."

Greg took it from Eaven. "I have a place until I get it to my attorney on Monday."

Jennifer started to argue, but he had already tucked it into his jacket pocket. "Thanks, Jen, but really, it will be fine."

Blinking back a pout, she said, "Greg, I'm starved. Can we get some dinner?"

He glanced at Eaven. "Yes. Let's all go."

Eaven wasn't excited about spending any more time with Jennifer, but she was hungry, and it was worth it to watch Jennifer bite back her anger. "Sure, I'll get a dry coat." She slipped upstairs and put the other document she found into her safe until she could share it privately with Greg.

Outside, Greg held out his upturned palm. "It stopped raining and it's only a block to the restaurant. Want to walk?"

"Sounds good," Eaven said. Jennifer gave a silent nod.

The restaurant was already noisy, and the band hadn't even started. "Table for three?" the host asked.

"Yes. Somewhere away from the stage," Greg answered.

While they moved through the crowd, heads turned, and eyebrows raised. Many seemed to know Jennifer, and not in a good way. Some whispered behind their hands. As the host seated them at a round table against the far wall, Jennifer lifted her arrogant chin and seemed unaffected by the gossip.

In so many ways she reminded Eaven of Cassandra. Other's opinions seemed unable to touch them. Eaven sighed. All her life, she had paid too much attention to what others thought. That was something she'd have to work on.

Steering the conversation away from the work she'd been doing for Greg, she tried to gain more information about Jennifer's relationship with Clayton. Greg focused his inquiries on what she knew about Brett's business. They didn't get much.

Jennifer acted bored, pushed her food around, and generally played the part of a pouting child. Halfway through the meal, she dropped her fork on the table. "I saw a friend I need to talk to." She disappeared into the dark bar that now emanated with the band's driving rhythm.

"I don't think she appreciated you inviting me." Eaven said.

He rubbed the back of his neck. "It's just a rough time. Kicking a habit that strong makes her seem hard. But she'll get through it." He frowned. "I wanted to encourage her, but she's taking it the wrong way. It will get even more sticky now that I'm staying."

She tilted her head. "You're moving back?"

"I have a fortune to collect. A mansion to restore." He took her hand. "Eaven, please reconsider. Let's do it together. See what might happen between us."

She rubbed at the age spots that marred her once porcelain-perfect hands. Ten years ago, she would have said yes. "Thank you. It's good to feel wanted, but I need to *do* something with my life."

"Don't discount what you *did*. You changed my life and righted a century of injustice done against my family. What else do you want to do?"

She caught his eyes and gave a half smile. "That makes opening an antiques store seem superficial."

"Is that your dream?"

"Part of it. Maybe."

"Want a partner? I have a load of antiques."

She took a deep breath. "The other part is proving I can do it on my own. Without depending on someone else. Without being under anyone else's scrutiny."

He shook his head. "I could shoot Michael for ruining your life."

"Maybe he saved it." She smiled at his pout. "Will you trust that it's not about you?"

"Guess I have to." He grew quiet and picked at his meal.

Her mind searched for another subject. "I think I know who died in the fire. After I left your house yesterday, I drove to the Heritage Museum and found an interesting article from the newspaper the day after the fire. A seventeen-year-old girl disappeared on Christmas Eve. Her father accused Edward Mercer, who had enticed her with gifts in the past. Maybe she met him that night?"

"But she could have gone anywhere."

She bit her bottom lip. "I know, but she only lived a block from the mansion."

Greg's jaw tightened "We'll never know." He glanced around. "What's keeping Jenny?"

"You worried she might find a dealer?"

"Unfortunately, yes. Be right back."

While they were gone, the waiter brought the dessert menu. Eaven ordered chocolate lava cake and decaf coffee. She had almost finished when she saw Jennifer talking with a thin man in a suit and tie.

Jennifer returned to the table. "Where's Greg?"

"He left to find you fifteen minutes ago. You didn't see him in the bar?" She worked to control her worries that Clayton or one of his guys could have gotten to him.

"No. I was with a friend."

"Who?" It was wrong to ask, but she didn't care.

"Like I said, a friend." Jennifer ordered a Mexican coffee and finished it quickly. "You do get that you're only an employee to Greg, right?" Her voice was slurring, too much for just one drink.

Eaven shook her head. "Looks like you found a friend who sold you a little something *for the pain.*"

Jennifer backhanded the empty mug across the table. "The only pain around here is you. Why don't you—"

Greg grabbed her arms from behind. "Jen. Stop." He peered at Eaven. "Let's go." He threw cash on the table and they left. Jennifer wobbled, holding onto his arm. They waited outside the restaurant until a taxi showed up. Jennifer got in and slammed the door.

They started walking home, but he stopped when his phone rang. "Sault here." He listened. "No. Eaven was having dinner with me and Jennifer Gellens since seven o'clock. We just walked out of the restaurant." He glanced at Eaven then replied into his phone, "I understand. We'll be available."

"What's going on?" she asked.

"Clayton's dead."

She gasped, unbelieving. She'd just seen him a few hours ago. "What happened?"

"A neighbor found his body sprawled on the ground. He fell three stories from the hidden room." He put his hands on her shoulders. "The neighbor gave the police your description."

"What? Sheez."

"She saw you go in and come out. And Clayton called the police and reported the intrusion. He said you attacked him."

"He was angry and threatened me."

"And what did you do?"

Her mind whirred over their interaction. Yes, she'd pushed him, but he'd rumbled around in the attic. Still alive. She swallowed. "I shoved him onto the floor and ran."

Greg tilted his head, staring hard. "He's a large man."

She met his eyes. "Leverage."

CHAPTER 61

As they rushed back to the inn, Greg scrutinized shadows and passing cars. "We've got to get you out of here. Get your things." He opened the door for Eaven.

"Why?"

"Because Billy Angler hasn't been found."

She bit her bottom lip. "And he has friends?"

"Same ones as Clayton, and now that the kingpin is dead—"

"Angler rises to the top. Do you think he pushed Clayton?"

He raked his fingers through his hair. "It's a possibility."

Recalling the sense of another presence in the mansion, a shudder passed through her. Her body could have been found, sprawled in the wet grass next to Clayton's. Her throat felt dry, constricted. "Maybe Angler was in the house when Clayton threatened me."

"That's what I'm thinking. He and Clayton talked or made plans. They waited until dark to leave, then for some reason, Angler tossed Clayton through the hole in the roof."

She packed her bags quickly and Greg helped carry them to her car. "Wait. Where are we going?"

"You're staying at a friend's condo for a couple of nights for your safety."

"What friend? I don't know anyone here."

"Trust me."

Her stomach roiled. She felt she was being carried by a wave out to sea. "I don't know, I—"

Claire rushed out and took her hands. "I'm sorry you're leaving in such a hurry. I wanted to tell you how much hope your friendship brought back into my life. Please, stay in touch."

A pang twisted in her chest. "I will. You can't know how much I needed to be here."

After they hugged tightly, Claire said. "And thank you for referring Kari to help me. She's going to be perfect."

Warmth filled Eaven that it had worked out. "Take care."

Greg was already in his car, so she followed him to the east side of Astoria. When they pulled into a parking lot, she couldn't believe her eyes. "Sheila?"

"See, trust isn't so bad." Greg laughed. "She volunteered her place."

"Hey girlfriend." Sheila met her with a one-armed hug. "Got my deer rifle with a scope, and my pistol, just in case some idiot decides to mess with you."

Eaven laughed. The rifle was almost as long as Sheila was tall. "I feel safer already."

Greg raised an eyebrow at Sheila. "I'll take that as a warning."

They each grabbed a bag and followed Sheila inside. Eaven hung some clothes in the closet while Greg set her bag on the bed. He touched Sheila's shoulder before she left the room. "Thank you for doing this."

A grin broke over Sheila's face, a killer grin that was every bit as devastating as Greg's. "My pleasure. Always loved sleepovers. You joining us?"

He blushed but recovered quickly and grinned. "Wish I could, but James, my attorney, said he'd take a look at the will tonight." He squeezed Eaven's shoulder. "I can see you're in good hands. See you tomorrow."

Eaven stretched her legs toward the fire and held a glass of wine. "I don't think I've been this relaxed since...well, in a long time."

Sheila curled on a wide chair. "Wish we would have thought of this sooner."

"It's been a whirlwind."

"For me too." A smile twitched at the corners of Sheila's mouth.

"What?"

"Well, I think I might be a prophetess. My uncle dropped dead of a heart attack yesterday. I'm gonna take my ranch back."

"So, you're moving back to Texas?"

She sighed. "It's home. But probably not. I love it here."

"Then you'll sell your ranch?" Eaven watched her friend. Would she willingly let go of her roots?

"I could hire a foreman and run stock. Manage it from here." She sipped her wine. "I lived my whole life with dust and cactus. Look at it here, all this green. And the river." She shook her head slowly. "Everyone I loved there is gone. It's time to start a new chapter."

"A new chapter." Like in a book. That was a nice way to look at life. "I feel I've been running, avoiding pain. But I want to move toward something. Find a purpose that satisfies me."

Sheila tilted her head. "Gal, let me tell you, that sweet spot belongs to God."

"I get that, but here on earth, I need to find something stable I can call mine, that makes me feel significant. Don't you feel that way about your salmon business?"

"Heck. If I depended on my business, my emotions would be all over the place. No, my stability comes from knowing one thing—I am loved by God and safe in the kingdom. So why would I put my trust in anything here?"

Eaven shrugged.

"Wow, you don't get it, do you?"

"I heard this all as a child."

"Yeah but hearing and seeing are different things. What if there was nothing that could hurt you, or steal your peace? What if when your relationships or businesses got knocked down, you could fly over the despair, knowing the *real* you is safe in Christ?"

Her mind wrestled with the idea. "Michael and Crystal cut me to the core. Wiped out my life."

Sheila quieted then said, "It didn't wipe out your life, it wiped out the boat you put your trust in. Our boats are full of holes. This world is passing away, and don't get me started about people. They are only illusions of safety."

Her throat thickened as she considered the people and things she'd trusted. Illusions of safety, all of them. "How had I never seen this before?"

"Because we're so used to thinking what we see is reality. We need to set our eyes on things above, not on things below." Sheila grinned. "I'm pretty preachy, but when I'm hurt or scared, I get dragged back to the tangle of things below. But even then, I know I'm loved."

A humorless chuckle escaped Eaven's throat. "After we talked in the hospital, I realized I had focused my entire life on my failures, on not measuring up."

Sheila tilted her head and smiled. "You missed half the gospel, girlfriend. The good news is you're *already* a new creation, already raised from the dead, alive in the kingdom."

Already a new creation. "I knew at some level I was forgiven, but I think...I think I've been stuck in the grave." She held her friend's eyes. The ramifications began to knock down a lifetime of misconceptions. If she was truly in the kingdom, why was she putting all her focus and worry on what was happening here? "Sheila, this is big."

"Yeah, it is."

"It's going to take some thought. Greg and I have had some good conversations but, wow, I think he'll be awed by this."

"Speaking of." Sheila sat up, her face serious. "I know you and Greg are working together but I can't tell if you're sweet on each other or not."

She grinned. "Not, but he's sure tempting."

"He sure is, but you saw him first, and I'd never sacrifice a friendship for a man."

Eaven's heart clenched at the thought of letting go of the slim possibility, but there was no future with him. "Thank you, but he's not for me."

Sheila's face lit up. "Then watch out, Mr. Sault! Now how to get him to ask me out."

She laughed. "He's been a flirt, but trust me, you're on his radar, and I'll be leaving soon." The thought of leaving made her suddenly tired. "Think I'll turn in. Thanks for the evening."

"Night."

Eaven slipped into bed and sat against the padded headboard. Their conversation lingered. Through Sheila, she'd caught a glimpse of something huge. She chewed her cheek. The journey to see herself from God's perspective was hard, but it was possible. The thought made her smile. Snuggling into the covers, she felt safe, and completely loved, maybe for the first time. It was a good start.

CHAPTER 62

Staying with Sheila had been more fun than Eaven had had in years. The solid sleep and conversation left her at peace, ready to move on today—after she got paid. Knowing she had some breathing room, she hummed and padded to the kitchen.

"Hi, sleepyhead." Greg grinned and tugged on her tangled hair. "Sheila let me in on her way to work."

He might not be her guy, but he was still danged cute. Wishing she'd combed her hair and washed her face, she dodged him and headed for the coffee pot. The smile she gave radiated from her center, a calm and happy place. "Good morning."

"Yes, it is. Especially since they found Angler's body."

"What? Where?" Her smile vanished and tension gripped the sweet spot. She frowned, amazed how easily she could be pulled back into the tangle.

He pulled out a stool for her. "Something was stinking at the Mercer office when I opened the door. I had a contractor investigate it. Turns out there's a smuggler's hideaway below the dock. Looks like Clayton gave Angler a drug-laced drink. He probably planned to come back and dispose of the corpse."

"But he died before he could..." She dropped her blue and white mug on the counter. "If Angler didn't kill Clayton, then who did?" She sat next to Greg, reviewing possible scenarios. None of them explained Clayton tumbling from the secret room. None of the main players were around to push him. "Was it likely he just tripped and fell? Or..." What she was about to say would make her seem like a lunatic. "Could Marie have had anything to do with it? Maybe the corpse scared him?"

Greg's eyes twitched. "In my interview, I told the detective she was tied to a chair, but that's not where they found her."

Uneasiness settled over Eaven. "Do you think Clayton untied her?"

Greg took a slow breath. "Probably. Here's the weird part. This morning, the detective told me they found the skeleton on the ground, next to Clayton's body."

Chills swept over Eaven. When Clayton entered the secret room, it had filled with burning hatred. Could Marie have…? That *was* crazy. "I had to move a skeleton once. A scary experience. Maybe he was trying to remove the corpse and…tripped?"

Greg's eyebrows lifted. "Yeah, got scared and jumped out the window. Good riddance."

His lack of compassion didn't surprise her, but it left her feeling unsettled. "Well, it's over. The Mercers are gone, their attacks in the past. And your family's birthright is restored." She left and came back with an envelope. "This is yours."

"What is it?"

"A check for the purchase of the chandelier."

He reached for the envelope. "From who?"

"An old client. She wired it."

He glanced at the check. "So, what do you get out of this?"

"I deducted a fat commission." Then, she frowned. "However, now that you own the mansion, you may want the chandelier back. What do you think?"

"I'm not sure. Is the building worth keeping?"

"Absolutely, but it will cost a fortune to bring it back. The resale value of the furnishings would help. I made an inventory list." She glanced at him. "Do you mind your ancestral furnishings being sold?"

He grew quiet. "I suppose not. Though I wish I had the money to give me options."

"I need to ask. Where did you get all that money you've been flashing around?"

He grinned. "DEA. All accounted for."

"Including my fees?"

"Out of my own pocket. And well worth it. I'll give you the rest today."

"Thank you." Inside, she was shouting, yes! The seed money for her shop had moved from a hope to a reality.

"You're welcome. Wish I knew what to do about the mansion."

"Marry a rich, blond widow?"

"Not even funny. Turns out Brett leveraged most of his wealth to help finance the drugs. Jenny doesn't have a cent."

After the threat of living out of her car, Eaven wouldn't wish that on anyone. "So, Brett left no life insurance?"

He frowned "Nope."

"I would think she'd be cozying up to a very eligible bachelor."

"She certainly increased her attentions recently. Makes me wonder what value I had before I was rich." He raised an eyebrow and grinned.

Eaven smiled into his eyes then dropped her gaze to his lips.

He laughed. "Thank you. That said it all. So, other options?"

"Demolition. It's a prime view lot." She shrugged, hating to even suggest it.

"Don't kid me." His face had never been more serious.

"I'm glad you don't like the idea, but you asked." She sat next to him. "There's something else I want to talk about."

"Yeah?"

"He answered me."

"Who?"

"The God we've been doubting. I prayed for help on the boat and I lived. Last night, we were together, so I have an alibi. What if I'd said no and stayed in my room? I would be the top suspect. I'm starting to sense His leading from inside my spirit."

He shifted in his seat. "That's great." He changed the subject. "James examined the will. It's valid, and with Clayton out of the way, I own everything—the mansion, Clayton's house, the property on the dock. Everything. After all this time, Marie got what she wanted, proof of Sebastien's heritage and his rightful fortune. And Jake Mercer's linage wiped off the earth." A hateful smirk drew his scar into an arrogant expression, a semblance of Captain Mercer's photo in the museum.

The deadly change in his expression sent a chill down her spine.

His phone rang. "Sault here." Blood drained from his face. "Be right there."

"What?" Eaven asked.

"That was my attorney. Jennifer is at the police station accusing me of killing Clayton. Swears I asked her to help me. James says I better get over there right now."

Eaven jumped to her feet. "She's crazy. We were together the whole evening."

He eyed the floor. "Actually, not."

She frowned. "You were only gone fifteen minutes." At his anxious expression, her stomach knotted. "Greg, where did you go?"

"Nowhere. Just wandered around looking for Jenny. Went outside and circled the block."

The knot moved from her stomach to her chest. "Did you go back to the mansion?"

He searched her face and glared. "No." Without a word, he left. Outside, his tires squealed on the drive.

Feeling like a fist gripped her chest, she thought back over their conversations. Comments about getting rid of Clayton. That he wanted every last Mercer dead. When Ralph Ewing hinted there might be a murder, she assumed he'd been talking about his novel. A non-existent novel. Greg was an agent capable of murder, just like Ralph. She paced, her mind in a whirl.

Had she helped a murderer?

Did Jennifer expose Greg's plans when he lost interest in her? Eaven grabbed her stomach. Who was Greg Sault? Besides charming and convincing, had he been waiting for his chance to kill Clayton? She ran outside to the river's edge, feeling she might be sick. Would she always read people and their motives wrong?

No.

She stilled her imagination and listened. With few exceptions, she had read people well. So, what was true? Sure, Greg had wanted to gloat, to enjoy the anger in Clayton's face when the document was found. That was a long way from being a killer.

Then why would Jennifer lie? What could she hope to gain? Greg said she was meeting with her attorneys. Did the Gellens have a contract with Clayton for money owed them? Would she benefit from his death? That could be a motive for murder, at least for an addict with serious character flaws. All she had to do was pin the blame on the man who jilted her, a man with generations of bad blood with the Mercers.

She ran back inside and called James Patrick. "This is Eaven, what's happened with Greg?"

"That's confidential."

"Would you tell him I believe he's innocent?"

"Just a minute. He says you thought the worst."

"I was just stunned. Tell him, please."

"Will do."

"Also, James. Can you check to see if Brett had a lien on Clayton's property for the money he invested? Or any way Jennifer might benefit if he was dead?"

James was quiet. "Interesting. I'll see what I can find. As soon as we are finished here, Greg is free to go."

Relief washed over her. Greg wouldn't be another Mercer victim. "That's great, but why?"

"With only hearsay from an unreliable witness, a jilted girlfriend, not to mention a drug addict, they are going to let him go on his own recognizance. Plus, he was with you and Jennifer. Just a minute."

She waited, her mind running over reasons Jennifer might do this.

"Greg says thank you. He wants you to go to his cottage and get the will. It's under the bottom right dresser drawer."

That was where she'd discovered all the cash. "I'm on my way," she said, glad to have something to do, to shake off the bit of nagging guilt for yet another rush to judgment.

When Eaven neared the cottage, Jennifer's red Audi was parked on the street. Her throat constricted. The will! She roared the Suburban up the drive and slammed to a halt, rushed through the open door, and stopped. The house had been turned upside down, the kitchen drawers dumped, cushions thrown on the floor. "Jennifer!"

The strawberry-blond woman sauntered halfway out of the bedroom. She brushed the hair off her forehead and took a long drag of her cigarette. "Ms. Alexander. "What are you doing at my boyfriend's house?"

"The man you just accused of murder?"

She smiled. "That one. I just couldn't go through with the plans he made."

"Says you."

Jennifer stepped farther out of the bedroom and swayed. "That's right. Says me." She lifted the will and held the cigarette to it.

"No!" Eaven dashed across the room, but Jennifer stepped back into the bedroom and locked the door. "Don't do this!" She pounded on the wood, twisting the brass handle.

Jennifer cackled, just like she had at her fundraiser. Finally, she opened the door and pushed past her. "Too late."

The depth of Jennifer's destructiveness was unbelievable. Eaven barely controlled her hands from wringing the woman's neck. "You won't get away with it."

Jennifer sauntered toward the front door and turned. "You should see your expression, full of righteous indignation." Her eyes flicked toward the sofa. She briefly hesitated, her smile faltering, then got in her car and sped away.

Eaven ached for Greg at yet another betrayal. She frowned at the mess around her. Thinking Jennifer seemed uneasy when she left, as though she might have forgotten something, Eaven checked the sofa but found nothing. She replaced the cushions and sank down.

Under the coffee table, lay the family chart Greg had created. It had been a hope. Now it was a reality that she hoped couldn't be taken away. She flattened the vellum on the coffee table and smoothed it. Something had caught Jennifer's attention when she'd first seen it. Eaven studied each name. Her mouth fell open, letting her fears slip away. "So that's her angle."

She quickly rolled the vellum and ran to her car, hoping she could get to the county office before it closed.

CHAPTER 63

Eaven clicked her nail while waiting for the document to copy. Her hunch had been right. She jumped into her car and called Greg. "Where are you?"

"We're downtown at Carruther's."

"I'll be right there. I know why Jennifer accused you." She found the stylish restaurant and saw them sitting on tall stools at the marble-topped bar. She rushed to take Greg's hands. "I'm sorry I doubted you even for a second."

He cupped her chin. "I know."

"Can we eat now?" James asked.

They moved to a corner table at the front window. "Now, what is this information?"

She held Greg's eyes. "Jennifer burned the will."

His fingers clawed through his hair. "Patrick, tell me you made a copy."

"Yes. That is, I left instructions with my secretary to copy it before she gave it back to you. She's very competent."

Greg moaned.

"Wait, there's more," Eaven said.

"I don't want to hear it."

"Oh yes you do."

He tilted his head, looking doubtful.

She placed her hands on the table, ready to reveal the bombshell. "Jennifer is Clayton's sister."

Greg's mouth opened wide with disbelief. "How?"

"I checked at the county offices. Jennifer was adopted. There are no records of her birth mother. But there is a death record for a baby girl who died the same day Jennifer was born. The mother was listed as Priscilla *Donnelly*."

"So?"

"So, Jennifer must have looked for her birth mother and come across the same information. When she saw your family tree, she recognized a name. Clayton's mother was Priscilla *Donnelly* Mercer."

Both men's jaws dropped. "Why would Clayton's mother pretend her baby had died?" James asked.

Greg's lips tightened. "Abuse. She didn't want her daughter subjected to her father's rage."

Patrick shook his head, disbelieving. "That makes Jennifer the only surviving Mercer. Looks as though she's trying to claim the Mercer estate."

Greg sat back, rubbing his forehead. "Can she?"

James raised his eyebrows. "Maybe half. I'm sure she'll fight you for it."

Anger twisted Greg's mouth.

Eaven placed her hand on his arm and smiled. "It's really not so bad." They gawked. Her smiled widened. "There's more." She handed Greg the second note she'd found in the writing desk.

Brows furrowed, he took it and read,

"To whom it may concern,

Attached to this letter is my last will and testament and a codicil. The codicil is signed and notarized by my solicitor and bequeaths my name and an inheritance to my son, Sebastien Sault Mercer. However, circumstances earlier this evening cause me to believe my life is in danger, the reason for this addition. Tonight, I have uncovered the worst of betrayals. The boy I raised as Jake Mercer is the offspring of my servant, Guy MacDonald. Sebastien is my only son. Therefore, I bequeath all my earthly goods to Sebastien Sault Mercer.

Edward Mercer, signed this 25th day of December 1899.

Greg sprang from his seat, rattling the water glasses. Other customers turned their heads at the commotion. He sat again and whispered loudly. "Jake, Frank, Clayton, none of the Mercers were even Mercers!" He rubbed the stubble on his cheek. "What does this mean? Will it hold?"

James said, "It absolutely will. We can verify the signature."

She laughed at the joy in Greg's face. His innocent face. She marked this moment. The demanding work, the research, and even the danger, had rewritten history. That was one reason she loved antiques. They carried history forward, long after the owners had died. And sometimes, like today, they provided a witness to lost events. Across the room, she spotted Sheila and waved.

Her friend nodded and made her way toward them, a bag with her business logo slung over her shoulder. "This looks like a celebration."

Greg laughed. "It is."

"Great! I'm celebrating too. They're going to carry my salmon here. It's my third commercial account this week." Her warm Texan accent and broad Italian smile lit her whole face. Her big brown eyes gazed openly at Greg.

He smiled but averted his eyes. "Congratulations. Want to join us?"

"Sure." Sheila took a seat across from him. "Eaven tells me you're moving back to Astoria, so we'll be neighbors. What are you celebrating?"

"I just found out I am the only legitimate heir of Captain Edward Mercer."

"How could that be kept a secret?" Sheila asked.

"Someone killed him before he could make it known."

Sheila's eyes widened. "Who?"

Eaven glanced at Greg. "I have an idea, but we may never know for certain."

CHAPTER 64

Astoria, Oregon, Christmas Day, 1899

As the fire burned the carriage house, and Marie with it, Jake Mercer watched the mighty Captain cower on the dining room carpet.

His father raised his hand to ward off another blow from the andiron in Jake's fierce grip. Tears coursed from the old man's eyes, along with the blood pouring from a gash above his eyebrow. An uncharacteristic squeak, like a mouse caught under a heavy boot, escaped his lips. "Stop. I must get to Marie!"

Jake lifted the weapon higher. "Admit it..." He brought it crashing down. "Sebastien. Is. Not. Your. Son." He stopped momentarily, chest heaving.

The Captain drooped against his precious Chippendale table leg. His hand dropped, helpless. He spoke in a whispered gasp. "*You* are not my son."

Jake stood over his father, stunned. He snarled, as though an animal possessed him. "LIAR. Where is the will?"

"You thought your mother was a saint. You're MacDonald's brat." Captain Mercer's last words faded with the slightest shake of his head.

Enraged, Jake struck a final blow to the Captain's skull. He stood and panted over his kill. His once all-powerful father lay lifeless and small inside his gaudy mansion.

Shouts drifted through the windows. Fear paralyzed Jake's limbs as voices grew louder. He had to think quickly. He dropped the weapon next to the Captain's body. Then he ran to his room on the second story, stripped off his clothes, and pulled on a night shirt. He raised his window and shouted down at the neighbors who had gathered. "What has happened?"

Mr. MacDonald ran by, a flash of copper hair showing from under his plaid cap, carrying a useless pail. "The carriage house is ablaze," he shouted.

"I'll be right there. Just let me dress." Jake stuffed his legs into his pants and slung his shirt over one arm. Rushing out of his room, he ran down the stairs and met the cook who was just arriving through the side entrance.

"How has this happened, sir?" she asked.

Racing by her, he shouted, "I have no idea."

His stomach tensed when he drew near the dining room, knowing what he would find. He must be convincing. He dashed in, saw his father's dead body, and screamed. "Help! Help!" He ran to the back door. "Someone, help. My father's dead!"

He waited by the door until Mr. MacDonald rushed past him. Jake followed but kept his distance on the far side of the grand dining room.

The groom bent over the Captain and felt for a pulse. He turned to Jake. "He's gone, son."

Son? Across the room, Jake sank to his knees, unable to remain upright any longer. He watched MacDonald. Red-haired MacDonald. Jake raised his chunky hands. Light red hair covered his arms. He glared at the large, oafish groom. His mother couldn't have.

The cook ran in. "Who could have done this?"

MacDonald raised his round face. "Prob'ly the same person who set fire to the carriage house." He studied Jake. "Maybe he came here to steal somethin' and the Captain surprised him."

Jake nodded, his mind split between two tragedies. At least MacDonald had supplied a solution for one. "Yes. That must be what happened." Jake rose on unsteady legs and pretended to search the room for something that might be missing.

"You best call the officers," MacDonald said. The man's wide-set blue eyes held his. "Sorry you had to see this. I'll just close his eyes."

Jake dragged himself across the dining room. There lay his handiwork. How long had his father—Captain Mercer—known? Was it his mother's indiscretion that drove him to Marie? Did MacDonald know? Bile rose in his throat. He let it erupt, obscuring the intricate designs of the blood-stained carpet.

MacDonald rose and held his shoulders. "Let's just move over here, sonny."

"Let go!" Jake shook off the man's soiled hands. He hated this house. Hated his father. And most of all, he hated Sebastien Sault, the filthy issue that had taken his place.

He had burned Marie in the carriage house. He would destroy Sebastien as well. There would only be one heir to Edward Mercer's fortune.

CHAPTER 65

Astoria, Oregon, Current Day

Eaven hiked down from the Astoria Column, stopping to pause and gaze out at the panorama. She'd taken an extra day to relax and enjoy the unseasonable sunshine before heading east. High clouds floated above the sparkling river. The bridge eased over the water to Washington. Beyond that was the home she'd left, along with the discarded version of herself. She breathed in the cool air. This version was better. Healthier. Stronger.

Two nights ago, she'd left Greg and Sheila amid their animated conversation, feeling hopeful for them. As she finished lunch at Sheila's condo, Greg arrived and came into the kitchen. "Have an enjoyable time with Sheila?" she asked.

He tugged the blinds open. "Yeah."

"And?"

His mouth twitched. "She's a fun person."

"Uh-huh." She grinned and moved to rinse her plate.

"She's too good a person to be someone's second choice. Guess it was foolish to try and change your mind when you warned me ahead of time."

She nodded. "It wouldn't have lasted."

He shrugged. "Hey, good news. Yesterday, James obtained a court order. The mansion belongs to me. Would you come see it with me? Give me some pointers? I have the key, so we don't have to sneak in."

She grinned, excited about taking her time to look around the mansion. "I'll get my purse." On the drive into town, she asked, "Isn't it still a crime scene?"

"The police ruled Clayton's death an accident."

"They don't think Jennifer did it?"

He shook his head. "Neither of us had enough time to get to the house and back to the restaurant. We're both in the clear. They could go looking for some criminal element, but I think they're just glad he's gone." He laughed. "Her attorney had to deliver the news that she's not a Mercer. I don't envy that guy."

Eaven grinned at the mental image of Jennifer's fury. "Truth hurts."

The front of the mansion still displayed its neglect, made even worse by the huge broken limb poking through the shattered roof. Yet, inside, it seemed lighter, the antiques more beautiful. "Have you been working here?"

His grin widened. "After I got the key, I took a broom to the cobwebs. I hired some boys to take the trash and rats out of the kitchen. We worked until after midnight. I'll clean out the rest later."

She sneezed. "Hope you wore a mask while you were working." They strolled through the rooms, so much lighter with the old drapes removed. The house seemed to welcome them. She tugged the fringe on the library rug. It disintegrated. "It's a shame, but the rugs will have to go."

He nodded and shook one of the settees. "These feel sturdy enough."

"Reupholstering them will be expensive but beautiful. Did you decide to keep the chandelier?"

"Yes, but I want you to keep your commission. You also earned an additional two thousand dollars for the extra weeks you worked. Plus, a bonus."

"You don't have to do that."

"Yeah, I do. You'll just have to get used to being cared about."

She returned his gaze with a smile. It was a good feeling. And the extra money brought her that much closer to her goal. "Thank you."

Her attention was drawn upward. "Let's go upstairs." They climbed to the third floor. Even here, the peace felt tangible. With every curtain removed, beams of sunlight swept over the dusty floor and walls. She followed Greg to the observatory.

"A hundred and twenty years ago, this was my great-great-grandfather's personal lookout. I wonder if Sebastien ever came here with his father and watched the river boats."

Eaven studied the area, her attention drawn to the secret room. "Something has been nagging me. Why a secret room to hide a trunk and tiny writing desk when he has this huge rolltop desk out here?" She unbuttoned the top of his shirt.

He tilted his head. "This is hardly the place."

Ignoring his grin, she lifted the gold coin he wore around his neck. "This has me intrigued. The Captain's clue said, *In darkness, his fortune awaits your discovery.*"

"Hidden gold?"

"That's what I was thinking. Clayton mentioned something." She stepped inside the secret room, it's floor still damp from all the rain. The chair that had held Marie's skeleton remained in the corner. Sensing the peace that floated throughout the space, Eaven's shoulders relaxed.

Above the writing desk hung a depressing illustration of soot-blackened buildings. She leaned closer and read the title. "*The Devil's Acre* by Gustave Dore. I know this place. It was a slum in London."

"How do you know that?"

She pointed. "That's Westminster Abby in the background. Charles Dickens described this place in *Household Words.*" She gasped. "Greg! In the last clue, the Captain wrote, *Though my roots began in dark despair, I have gained much to give my heir.*"

He touched the painting. "You think he could have lived in that slum?"

"Why else would he have it here? Besides, it's odd. During all the shaking from the storm and the tree crashing through the roof, the painting is still perfectly straight." She approached it and pulled, but it was firmly attached. Running her fingers around the edges, she felt a lever. "Bingo!"

The painting pivoted away from the wall revealing a stack of slender drawer fronts. She pulled the top drawer out, set it on the small desk, and lifted a soft blue cloth. "Greg!" The drawer held a dozen or so coins.

"Wow!" He grabbed the other trays and carried them to the rolltop desk. They each took out a coin.

Astounded, Eaven turned hers over in her fingers. "No way."

"What?"

She bit her lip. In the center of a five-point star were the words, *ONE STELLA FOUR HUNDRED CENTS.* "You are a very rich man."

While he stood with his mouth open, she quickly scanned the other coins in the drawers. "Amazing."

"Will there be enough to redo this house?"

She stopped scanning. "The last time I saw one of these at auction, it sold for over five hundred thousand dollars. And that was a couple of decades ago. You'll have plenty, but do you really want to renovate the house? Your great-great-grandparents were both murdered here."

"I'll have to think about it. The Captain's behavior was inexcusable, but I know Sebastien was loved here, by both of them."

She smiled. "Maybe that's what I've been feeling since we arrived. Marie is at rest."

"I'm no house whisperer, but I feel it too." He made two stacks of the wooden drawers. "Let's get these to a safe deposit box."

As they were about to drive away from the mansion, Sheila pulled to the curb and sauntered over, fresh-faced and beautiful. She reached through the window and squeezed Greg's arm, looking shiny and young, maybe at the beginning of love. It was hard to tell if Greg was there yet.

A wave of loneliness passed through Eaven before she caught it. She was at the beginning of a new chapter in her life too. She waved at Sheila. "You look wonderful, lady."

Sheila came to her side, leaned in the car window, and kissed her cheek. "Thank you. This guy's gonna need all the help he can get if he decides to tackle this monstrosity."

Greg laughed. "She offered to help but we have conflicting ideas on decorating."

Sheila smirked at him. "I have errands to do. See you later." She ran back to her truck and drove away.

They drove to his bank and took the coins inside. After depositing the gold in the bank's vault, they sat in the car. Low chuckles escaped Greg's throat. "If you had left two days ago, we might never have found the coins. You amaze me."

"It may sound far-fetched, but I felt guided." A gentle pressure inflated her lungs. "I'm starting to get how much someone up there loves me. Loves us."

He sobered. "Yeah, I'm starting to get that too. So many of my family's prayers have been answered. It just took longer than anyone expected. Why does it always seem that way?"

She recalled her own journey. "To build our trust? Stretch us?"
"See if we'll turn away?" He frowned and shook his head.
"Thankfully, He doesn't hold that against us either."
"You certain?"
She grinned. "It's gospel. From Sheila's lips."

CHAPTER 65

It was time to go. Eaven shoved the suitcases into the back seat as Greg handed them to her.

"Well, Eaven Kensington Alexander, you did it." He scanned the river. "There's so much I want to say. Thank you for what you did for me, for my family. The Mercers would have won again."

"They did."

"Pardon?"

She grinned. "You're a Mercer now. Although I don't expect you'll be taking the name."

"No. But it's a relief to know where I came from and that I belong."

Her gaze followed his to the water. "That's how you made me feel while I've been here. Thanks for building my confidence."

He turned and smiled. "It was always there, you just stepped into it, learned to trust yourself."

She nodded. "Guess so." She was thoughtful while she rearranged her gear. When she'd left Lake Quinault, she'd made the decision to unlearn trust, but trusting wasn't the problem. It was about choosing someone trustworthy.

"Where are you headed today?"

"Bandon. My friend, Marin, owns a gallery there. I have a small check waiting. By the way, would you write a letter of recommendation? I like the idea of helping people unearth the stories behind their family heirlooms."

"Sounds like a good start on the rest of your life."

"If I can make enough money, I want my home back on Lake Quinault."

"Want to throw Michael into the mix and get him back too?"

Suppressing a response about where she'd like to throw Michael, she said, "I'm too raw to think about love." Their eyes locked before she could turn away. She rearranged another bag. "You'll have your hands full."

He glanced away. "Yeah. It'll be a big change from working with the DEA. I gave all my files to my replacement. They fingered most of the cartel members who were loitering in Astoria. Just a matter of time before they take out the other small-time dealers."

"Where there's a user, there's a dealer," she said.

"Sheila's never done drugs. That will be refreshing."

"She's a good one. Don't let her get away."

He shrugged. "Yeah, she is. Probably too good for me."

She set her purse inside while he leaned against her Suburban. "Don't scratch my car, buddy," she laughed.

He traced a long scratch with his finger. "Wouldn't be the first. Someday, you'll be driving a cool car like my baby."

She smirked. "Your baby, and all this other stuff, can disappear overnight. It's a security boat with holes in it."

"What?"

"Ask Sheila."

Just then, Sheila's truck approached, and he grinned. "We got you a going away present."

"No," Eaven protested. "You've already given me so much."

"Sorry, had to." He strode to Sheila's truck and opened the back door.

Eaven caught a flash of red and her heart leapt. "Roscoe!" She ran to the cowering dog and fell to her knees. When he saw her, he jumped into her arms, wiggling his body and gazing at her with his huge brown eyes.

Greg chuckled. "Dr. Franklin called after he heard about Clayton's death. I guess he really belongs to me, but it's obvious he's your dog."

She threw her arms around Greg's neck, then Sheila's. "You can't know how much this means to me." She glanced back at her packed car. "Can I leave a few things with you?"

"You bet," Sheila said. "I'll ship them when you get settled, but are you positive you can't stay awhile?"

"My mother is expecting me. At this rate, I'll be crashing her Thanksgiving dinner." She looked Sheila in the eyes, amazed at how deep their friendship had grown in such a short time.

"Come here." Sheila gave her a long hug. "I'll miss you something fierce, girlfriend."

Eaven pulled away and sniffed. "We'll stay in touch, I promise." She cleared the front seat and Roscoe jumped up as though this was his usual routine.

Greg stood at her window. "Guess this is it." He smiled, but Eaven sensed his sadness. "Looks like you're both ready for a new adventure."

Her throat thickened. "Bye, Greg."

The green of his eyes darkened. He gripped her forearm without saying anything, then let go and stepped to Sheila's side.

As Eaven drove down the gravel drive, she blinked several times. Letting go wasn't getting any easier. Roscoe put his front feet on the console and licked her cheek. She sniffed and scratched his neck. "Okay, buddy. We're off."

On the outskirts of Astoria, her phone buzzed several times. Finally, she pulled over. "Hello."

"Eaven, this is Julia Benson." Paisley's mother sounded frantic.

She held her breath. "What's wrong?"

"Paisley finally called. I heard a struggle, then the phone went dead. I know Denny's got her."

"I'm three thousand miles away, but I'll get there as soon as I can. Don't worry, we'll find her." She hung up. Paisley needed her. Maybe this was the reason she'd felt drawn back to Charleston.

Beyond where she was parked, the gray-green waters of the Columbia shimmered in the sunlight. Had it only been a month? Her past seemed a lifetime ago, as though it had happened to someone else. Throughout her being, sweetness had replaced the bitter places. So much had changed. Her purpose for helping Greg had been to make money, but it had escalated into something far more meaningful.

A bald eagle lifted off its perch and sped over the water, wings skimming the surface, eyes focused on its target. Her heart lifted at the millionth glorious sight. Her chin trembled, but she smiled. There would always be beauty to experience, even without Michael.

Gratitude swelled. God had seen her pain, had restored her life, and given her the means to help Greg restore his. Maybe she could do that for Paisley.

She started the car, planning to get as far down the coast as she could today. She was still alone, still homeless, but excited about the plans she'd made for the future. She breathed in that satisfying sense of pouring everything she had into one clear purpose.

Roscoe put his paw on her forearm and sniffed her ear. She leaned her head into his. "Okay, fella, let's do this."

If you enjoyed "Astoria Rumors," you may also like "Charleston Tides," book two in the Get Eaven Series.

Eaven summoned the courage to go home, but she's going to need a lot more than courage to survive.

Read chapter one to see what new betrayals Eaven faces and how she conspires to *get even*! dl.bookfunnel dot com/np36fue27h

Also by Cheryl Colwell

The Eaven Alexander Series
Astoria Rumors

The Get Eaven Series
Astoria Rumors

The Secrets of the Montebellis Series
The Secrets of the Montebellis
Adriana's
Adriana's Secrets

Standalone
The Proof
The Land Lord

Watch for more at cherylcolwell.com.

www.ingramcontent.com/pod-product-compliance
Lightning Source LLC
Chambersburg PA
CBHW031936110726
47902CB00001B/201